Charlie spoke in her ear. Without shattering the moment, his tone revealed a seriousness and intensity that Patsy had never known. "Patsy, I need something from you. I need you to look me in the face and say. 'You screw up a lot, but I still love you, Charlie—I always will.'"

Patsy stopped dancing and held him away from her to see his face. She stared at him a long time before she answered, searching her soul. She knew without thinking that, whatever she answered, her life—with Charlie or without him—would never be the same. Tears lingered in the corners of her eyes, but never formed. "You screw up a lot," she answered at last, echoing perfectly the intensity of Charlie's speech. "But I still love you, Charlie—I always will."

Patsy felt warm, wonderful . . . and in love.

NOW A MAJOR MOTION PICTURE!

SWEET DREAMS

GEORGE VECSEY,
WITH LEONORE FLEISCHER

ST. MARTIN'S PRESS
NEW YORK

SWEET DREAMS

An original St. Martin's Press edition, published for the first time any-where.

First printing/October 1985

ISBN: 0-312-90340-5
Can. ISBN: 0-312-90341-3

Printed in the United States of America

ST. MARTIN'S PRESS
175 Fifth Ave.
New York, New York 10010

9 8 7 6 5 4 3 2 1

"God knows somebody deserves to have a happy ending, and it might as well be me."

—*Patsy Cline*

Foreword

WHEN WE WERE WORKING on the book, *Coal Miner's Daughter*, Loretta Lynn liked to tell me about her friend, Patsy Cline—how generous she was, how impulsive, how funny.

They became friends, she suggested, because they had the same kind of marriage—two hard-working country men married to strong country women who made it big in Nashville. Both Mooney Lynn and Charlie Dick suffered from being the husbands of country stars.

But there was more to it than that. The two couples loved to party together, to cook and sing and pass the time. Loretta told the story of how Patsy hired a strip-teaser to materialize in her dining room as the special prize in a birthday dinner for Charlie.

Loretta was convinced Patsy had saved Loretta's career by sticking up for her when Loretta first arrived in Nashville. The way Loretta told it, Patsy had discovered that some jealous female country singers were passing around unpleasant rumors about Loretta, but Patsy cut them off at the pass by escorting Loretta to a party where most of the women were gathering.

"Patsy just showed up at my house, told me what I was wearin', and drove me over there," Loretta recalled with a laugh. "Nobody said a word. That was Patsy for you."

Loretta wasn't convinced that I had even heard Patsy

Cline's music. She knew that even though I had spent a lot of time in Kentucky and Tennessee, I was a Yankee from New York, and she wasn't sure that New Yorkers had heard much of Patsy Cline before her death in 1963.

Not hear of Patsy Cline? First of all, I had spent my summers in upstate New York, listening to WWVA, Wheeling, West Virginia, clear as a bell through the mountains late at night. Second, country music is as popular in upstate New York, just a few hours north of Times Square, as it is in Winchester, Virginia, where Patsy Cline grew up, or in Butcher Holler, Kentucky, where Loretta Lynn grew up. Also, Patsy Cline's records were played right in New York City, as a result of her spectacular debut on the *Arthur Godfrey Talent Scout Show* in January of 1957. You could turn the dial and hear "Walking After Midnight," and later "I Fall to Pieces" and "Crazy" and "Sweet Dreams."

Patsy Cline's full, melodic voice and her strong personality made her one of the first country music artists to cross over into pop music. In New York, Los Angeles, and all the big cities, she had the same vibrant appeal that Kay Starr, Patti Page, and Jo Stafford had. Nowadays, the big goal of a country music singer is to "cross over"—to make it on the pop charts, the way Loretta did, the way Johnny Cash, Dolly Parton, Willie Nelson, and a few others did. Patsy Cline was just starting to make it when her plane hit the mountain.

"Lord, I wish you could have met her," Loretta often said, growing wistful at the thought of her departed friend.

It took more than one tissue before Loretta could finish telling me the story about the last time she saw Patsy, a few nights before the fatal crash, and how Patsy had given her a "little, red, sexy shorty nightgown," telling Loretta that "red is the color men like."

Loretta made her friend seem so vital that the "Patsy" chapter was one of the highlights in the book *Coal Miner's Daughter*. And when the book was made into a movie, producer Bernard Schwartz, screenwriter Tom Rickman, and director Michael Apted created a role that actress Beverly D'Angelo turned into a masterpiece. Who will ever forget the scene of Loretta and Patsy singing together in the rain, or the scene where Patsy is recuperating from a car wreck and telling people in the hospital that the thing she would like most is a cold beer?

Some of Patsy's family and friends were not happy with the film portrayal. It is quite natural that loyal supporters would want to maintain an immaculate image of a departed loved one. But other friends in Nashville, who loved Patsy as well, later admitted that, whether or not these incidents actually happened, they essentially captured Patsy's character.

The cameo of Patsy Cline in *Coal Miner's Daughter* stimulated the imagination of Bernard Schwartz, who knew there was a deeper story in Patsy Cline's living hard and dying brutally. He wanted to know what was behind the powerful voice and lusty smile.

Some Hollywood creators go with their imaginations, but Bernard Schwartz wanted details. He and some colleagues set out on a research expedition that would take them several years, interviewing Patsy's family and friends in Nashville and Winchester, and wherever else they may have scattered.

Doing some of the legwork himself, the Hollywood producer accumulated two looseleaf books, both six inches thick, of transcripts from the people who knew Patsy best— her mother, Hilda Hensley; her husband, Charlie Dick; her brother and sister; her former husband, Gerald Cline; and many of Nashville's major figures, particularly Owen Bradley, the man who recorded her biggest hits. These transcripts became known as "Bernie's Bible."

Then came a screenplay by Robert Getchell, direction by Karel Reisz, and performances by Jessica Lange and Ed Harris. In his screenplay, writer Getchell manages to maintain the spirit of a woman who was a generation ahead of her time.

While the movie was being made, a book was planned about Patsy Cline. Without Patsy to speak for herself, twenty-two years after her death, it seemed better to produce a novel than try for a biography.

I am a journalist by trade, a former Appalachian correspondent, and currently a sports columnist for *The New York Times*. My skill is putting together facts and impressions of reality. After reading "Bernie's Bible," I spoke with Patsy's people, and other contacts of mine in country music, and I wrote a manuscript that was as faithful as possible to the details available. Then, co-author Leonore Fleischer used her novelist's skills that had previously produced books like *A Star is Born, Ice Castles,* and *The Rose.*

The long trail has moved from Loretta Lynn's memories of Patsy to this novel about Patsy. Just as in most screenplays, a few sequences have been altered, a few characters created, and more than a few scenes invented from sheer imagination, because only Patsy Cline really knew what had happened in those moments.

What was Patsy's childhood relationship with her father? What drove Patsy to become a singer? What attracted Patsy to Charlie Dick? What were her emotions as two births and one auto wreck stalled her career? What made her marriage so tempestuous? What were her real feelings toward Randy Hughes, her manager? The journalist and biographer can only guess, but the screenwriter and novelist can take a chance.

Ever since Loretta began telling me stories about Patsy, I have wished I could have sat in Tootsie's Orchid Lounge and enjoyed a beer with her and Charlie, preferably on a day when they were getting along, on a day when they were lovers not opponents. But I got to Nashville too late to meet Patsy. All we have are other people's memories, most of them vivid, of a tough, attractive woman with a magnificent voice. I wish I had met Patsy Cline, but we have her records, and now there is a movie and a book—not a biography, but a novel, an intuitive effort to reach the real Patsy Cline.

George Vecsey
Port Washington, New York

March 5, 1963

They'd had to wait overnight for takeoff, sprawling gritty-eyed and weary in plastic chairs in the smoke-smelly lounge of Fairfax Municipal Airport in Kansas City. Outside, gray rain pelted the tarmac, raising what looked like clouds of steam. Frequent low rumbles of thunder menaced them from a distance, and occasional crackling bolts of lightning lit up the runways in eerie blues and greens. Visibility was close to zero, and all air traffic was at a standstill. Kansas City was socked in.

Randy and the boys had managed to pull a few winks of uneasy sleep, but Patsy was wide awake. Bone-tired though she was, still suffering from a bad cold that verged on flu, she couldn't get to sleep. Her neck and shoulder muscles were aching with fatigue, but her eyes would just not close. Instead, she kept staring out of the grimy window at the teeming downpour, even though there was nothing to see through the rain-streaked panes of glass. Unable to rest, she sat watching her memories replaying in her head, giving her no peace.

All her life Patsy Cline had known exactly what she wanted. She wanted to be a star. A big one. And she'd achieved it. She was a star. A big one. Patsy Cline was the biggest female singer in country music, with a string of number one hits and a new one climbing up the charts. But suddenly now, for the first time, she wasn't so sure. Finding herself standing on the cutting edge of something new, she hesitated. She, whose feet had always been so eager to take that next step. She, who had never refused a dare, never stopped to think twice, never chickened out. Now, for the first and only time in her life, Patsy stood like the sinner in the old hymn—with reluctant feet, where the brook and river meet. . . .

A few seats away, Hawkshaw Hawkins, a Grand Ole Opry star, snored loudly and tried to turn over on the uncomfortable little seats. Hawkshaw took up three chairs; a tall man, he needed at least one just for those big feet in their fancy-stitched western boots. Across from him, Cowboy Copas, "the hillbilly waltz king," turned uneasily and muttered in his sleep. But Patsy didn't hear him; her thoughts were very far away, perhaps in the lush green Shenandoah Valley of the Blue Ridge Mountains she loved so well. Perhaps they were somewhere else, those thoughts she couldn't share with anybody.

Next to her was the solidity and warmth of Randy Hughes, his arms wrapped around her body, pressing her to him even while sleeping. His steady breathing was ruffling the hair on her neck, but he might have been across the room for all the notice she took. Even when he tightened his grip on her arm, she paid him no mind, except for pulling away from him ever so slightly. Still, it was enough to wake him up.

For a moment or two he said nothing, content merely to look at the sweet curve of Patsy's cheek and the graceful length of Patsy's neck, where he loved to let his kisses linger. But when she didn't respond to the increased pressure of his body, he craned his neck to get a look at her face.

Patsy was staring through the window as though the answer to the meaning of life was out there coming down with the raindrops. But he knew that those large dark eyes were seeing something entirely different. Patsy got that way sometimes, walking alone down a road that nobody could follow, locked up inside herself and not handing anybody the key.

"Where're *you*?" he asked her gently.

She didn't turn. "Hmm?"

He pulled her more tightly against him and whispered into her ear. "You look like you're a thousand miles away."

Slowly she turned her face from the window, but the dreamy look still lingered in her eyes. "Oh, not that far," she murmured, half to herself.

"Well?" nudged Randy. He hated to be left out of anything, particularly where Patsy was concerned. When she didn't answer, Randy pressed harder. "What were you thinking? Where were you?"

"Oh, just thinking . . . just floating," she replied softly, her melodious alto voice little more than a whisper. Wherever she'd been, she hadn't yet left that place.

He never could stand this distant tone of hers; it shut him out and diminished his importance. Randy Hughes wanted to be at the very heart, the deepest center of Patsy Cline, and at times like these he knew that he wasn't. "Floating where?" he demanded again, his voice less gentle than before.

Now she looked directly at Randy as though seeing him for the first time. Her eyes, which had seen so much in thirty-one short years, sized him up reflectively.

"I was standing by a rainbow," she told him softly, although she knew that he wouldn't understand. "That's it. I was standing by a rainbow in the rain."

Randy opened his mouth to speak, then shut it again. There was something in the tone of Patsy's voice that eluded him. Although he couldn't make head or tail of her words, he realized that they held meaning for Patsy herself. And there was something more, something he couldn't quite reach, something disturbing. . . .

With a mighty yawn, Cowboy Copas stood up and stretched his big body to get the kinks out of it. Then he ambled over to the two of them, scratching at his ribs underneath the plaid flannel shirt.

"She's gone round the bend, this one," remarked Randy,

jerking a thumb at Patsy. The country music star only grunted in reply. Every muscle in his banjo-pickin' body ached, and he was hungry and thirsty.

But that's where I was. Out there, keepin' company in the rain. Just me and the rainbow. No, me and him and the rainbow.

The small airport lounge reserved for noncommercial flights and private planes offered little with regard to washing or eating facilities in that year, 1963. Improvising the best way she could, Patsy hunched over the ladies' room sink, making do with gooey pink soap from a glass dispenser and some rough brown paper towels. Once she had washed, she felt somewhat better.

For breakfast, they had a choice of doughnuts and coffee or frankfurters and Dr. Pepper. It was too early to watch three men wolfing down greasy wienies, piled high with sweet pickle relish, so Patsy took to staring out of the window again while she toyed with her sugary doughnuts and sipped at her paper cup of coffee. What she really needed was a drink to take some of the ache and chill out of her bones. It had been raining for days, but it seemed like weeks.

There appeared to be no letup. The storm had swept eastward across the midwestern plains, bringing thunder and lightning, strong, gusting winds, air turbulence, and a heavy downpour. Here in Kansas City the foul weather had been accompanied by a thick fog that cut visibility to nothing. Even commercial aircraft were being advised to stay on the ground in weather like this, while a small private plane like Randy Hughes's Piper Comanche 250 four-seater wasn't supposed to even venture out of the hangar.

When the four of them had arrived at the airport last night and learned that the weather outlook was as dismal as it was at that miserable moment, Randy had wanted to go back to the Town House Hotel.

"Get us a meal, a hot bath, a good night's sleep," he'd suggested. "Might's well be comfortable, 'cause there's no taking off in weather like this. I've seen the weather advisories, and this damn storm probably won't let up for hours. We're grounded, Patsy, and that's for sure."

Strangely enough, it had been Patsy, who was usually fond of her comforts, who voted him down. She wanted to go home, and the sooner the better.

"I want to see my babies," she'd argued. "I ain't seen them since before we played New Orleans. Randy, honey, I just want to go home and see my babies."

Helpless to deny her anything, Randy Hughes gave in. They would stay at the airport so that they could get off the ground at the earliest possible moment. Even an hour would make a difference to Patsy.

God only knew why. They'd already been traveling for over a week—New Orleans, Birmingham, Nashville, Kansas City—so what difference did an hour or two more make? This last gig had been something out of the ordinary—a benefit performance for the widow and two children of Cactus Jack Call, the Kansas City DJ for KCMK-FM, an important all-country station.

Jack Wesley Call had been killed in a head-on collision with a truck in January, leaving a young wife, Anne, and two small boys. The country music world had responded almost immediately. A benefit was set up at the Kansas City Memorial Building and some of the biggest names in the business had agreed to come and do three shows to raise some money for the bereaved.

The four of them—Randy, Patsy, Hawk, and Cowboy— had flown in from Nashville to do their bit for a good cause. Patsy was at her zenith, and an appearance by her would sell a lot of tickets.

Sick, overtired, Patsy Cline had nevertheless glowed up there on that stage. She'd given the fans everything that was in her, as she always did. There was nothing in the world she liked better than singing; it made her come alive. She gave them what they wanted—"Am I A Fool," "She's Got You," "Heartaches," "Sweet Dreams," and "Faded Love." But the audience wouldn't let her off the stage until she'd done her number-one hits, and of course, she'd obliged. By now "Crazy" and "I Fall to Pieces" had become her signatures. As always, they brought her audience to its feet, cheering and clapping, whistling and stomping.

They'd played and sung three shows, got a great reception, given the country-and-western fans a thrill, helped raise some money, and now they were on their way back to Nashville. So what was the big deal, a few hours more or less?

But Patsy had insisted. She didn't want to leave the airport. There had been such a high color in her face, and her dark eyes had glittered so brightly, that Randy was afraid that her cold had grown worse and that she was sicker than ever, maybe even coming down with a fever, and he felt obliged to give in. But the weather hadn't lifted, and all they had to show for their night in the airport was stiff muscles, aching bones, and sour breath.

Something was up with Patsy, and Randy had no idea what it could be. Their relationship was growing closer and closer, maybe uncomfortably close for Patsy, but he didn't think that was it. Nor was it because Patsy Cline was a star. She'd been a star long enough so that stardom would already have changed her if it was going to, and it hadn't. She might be riding around in a Cadillac these days instead of a pickup, but she could still cuss with the best of them, still belt down the bourbon and put away the beer. Patsy Cline was still the good ole Winchester girl she'd always been. Besides, Randy Hughes was pretty damn well-known himself, first as a music star and now as manager for Patsy, Cowboy, Hawk, and others.

Patsy wasn't any more temperamental than she'd been when Randy had met her. She did have her moods, but they never seemed to interfere with the way she lived her life. That was one of the things he loved most about Patsy, her energy and her determination to get on with it, keep it moving. That was where so much of her strength came from, her confidence in her own God-given abilities.

It wasn't every man who could keep up with Patsy Cline, Randy thought proudly. Generous though she was, she was also pretty damn demanding. But hellfire, it was surely worth it! Patsy Cline gave as good as she got, and he had never sensed fear in her.

Until this week. Because suddenly, Randy Hughes realized just what it was about Patsy that was disturbing him so. She was afraid of something, whether she knew it or not. All that withdrawal, that hesitation . . . it was fear. He'd seen it before, when men were under fire.

But Patsy wasn't under fire. On the contrary, her singing career kept on climbing its way to even higher peaks. With half a dozen hit songs behind her, including some that made it to the very top of the charts, Patsy had accomplished that near-miracle: she had crossed over into pop-chart success. Her star was on the rise, and nothing could stop her from becoming even bigger. The country fans loved her, and even outside of country and western, audiences knew the name of Patsy Cline. That might scare some people, but it didn't frighten Patsy. She'd been waiting for it a long time, ever since she was five years old, and she was ready.

He looked at her now, sitting apart, her dark eyes turned to the window again. As always, the sight of her face brought a clenching to the muscles of his belly. Patsy had the softest, prettiest skin he'd ever touched, and her thick, dark, curly hair seemed to possess a life of its own, it was that glossy and vibrant. Her neck, as white and smooth as a piece of Italian alabaster, rose gracefully from her strong shoulders.

Whenever Patsy smiled, her face changed from pretty to beautiful, as though a window had been opened to let in the sunlight. She had several different smiles, and Randy knew and loved them all. There was a special smile for her two children, filled with pure, uncomplicated love. Then she had a mischievous, almost evil, little smile that crept around her mouth when she was about to do or say something outrageous. She kept in reserve a big, brassy, warm smile for her audiences, her teeth flashing confidence, her eyes sparkling with the joy of singing. She had a shy, little-girl smile when something special pleased or tickled her.

Randy was probably imagining the whole damn thing anyhow. Probably nothing was wrong with Patsy except wanting to be home and see her two kids. For two whole days she'd been lugging around that great big doll with the red hair for Julie, and that expensive teddy bear for little Randy; no wonder she was so impatient! Patsy was never at her best when waiting for things to happen. She always wanted to run right out and see to it that they happened. To *make* them happen.

Once again, Randy Hughes cursed the easy temperament that had let him give in to Patsy last night. He should have put his foot down, made them all go back to the hotel, or at least to the airport motel.

When the hell was it ever gonna stop raining and let him get his Comanche off the ground? He was getting damn near as jumpy as Patsy. This rainstorm was enough to make anybody crazy, especially a pilot. It was dangerous weather, even for a large commercial jet, let alone a small single-engine craft like his. Too damn dangerous to fly. Maybe they oughtn't to wait for a letup. Maybe he should try to rent a van or a station wagon, and drive back home to Virginia. It might be safer, even on slick, wet roads. Randy looked across at Patsy, a question on his face.

But Patsy was further away from him than ever, locked away somewhere in the private hiding places of her memories . . . past the rainbow. There was no rainbow now, only music. And she was young, so young, and it wasn't raining. . . .

One

To EVERYTHING THERE IS a beginning. Later, much later, looking back down the years, you can say, "On such and such a day and hour, that was when it started." Then, it's plain; then, you can see with clarity the very moment when your life took a turning and you turned with it. But, more often than not, you encounter and experience your most important beginnings without recognizing them for what they are. A casual meeting, a train missed, a different door pushed open—who can know what life-altering event awaits you? Who can foresee that an ordinary evening, embarked upon without excitement, might turn into a beginning, so that your existence will never, ever be the same? Who can predict it?

Not Charlie Dick, as he slicked his light brown hair back with Vitalis, and tucked a clean twotone shirt into his dungarees. He could check off in advance everything that tonight would bring him. Why should it be any different from any other Friday night date with Wanda Kimble? They'd do a little drinking, then a little dancing, then a lot more drinking, then they'd drive back here and jump on the mattress and he'd plow her pretty little ass for a few hours and they'd sleep like babies halfway through Saturday. What the hell else was a Friday night for? Isn't that what payday was all about?

Charlie regarded himself in the mirror with some satisfaction. Despite the fact that he was no six-footer, he was one handsome devil, with deep, light eyes, a warm, charming smile, a cleft in his chin, and mischief in his grin. Not too tall, but powerfully built, with a thick chest and strong shoulders, and muscles in his arms that had come from doing heavy work when he was younger. Now, at twenty some, he was a newspaper linotyper, skilled work. He didn't have to wrestle heavy sacks on a loading dock anymore, yet his biceps remained solid.

Taking out a fresh handkerchief, he rubbed a shine onto the pointy toes of his brand-new shoes, allowing his thoughts to drift to Wanda. Although he couldn't see it, a lickerish grin had settled over his face as Charlie pictured her cute little titties in that tight fuzzy pink sweater that left fluff like pink cat hair all over his shirt. Not that he minded. No, sir. In that sweater or out of it, Wanda was one juicy little piece.

He'd wanted to go juking tonight, hitting a few roadhouses in West Virginia, outside the state line, but Wanda had other ideas. There was a dance party at the high school, with a live local band, and a talent contest that had been scheduled after the all-day rummage and bake sale. Wanda complained that she was getting tired of slow-dancing to Patti Page and "The Tennessee Waltz." That song was already five years out of date, but it was still raking in the nickels on every jukebox in the South. And she wanted to dance the lindy to something besides Bill Doggett's "Honky Tonk." Good-natured Charlie had given in, but he'd taken the sensible precaution of picking up two illegal pints of bourbon whiskey, since the state of Virginia was as dry as a possum's bones when the hounds had finished licking 'em.

Giving himself a last approving glance in the mirror, Charlie tossed the now dirty handkerchief onto the pile of laundry in the corner. He knew his mother would take care of it. Charlie still lived at home, and sometimes it made things a little difficult. But Wanda didn't mind sneakin' in and out, and what his momma didn't know wouldn't hurt her.

He was tucking an extra pack of Camels into his shirt-sleeve when it occurred to Charlie that today was Friday the thirteenth. Friday, April 13, 1956. That meant bad luck, and Charlie was superstitious. For an instant he hesitated, one hand on his leather jacket. Maybe they oughta stay home tonight, just Wanda and him. Then his devil-may-care grin spread over his boyish face, and he threw his jacket over his shoulder and went off to meet his beginning.

In the boys' locker room that passed for the women's dressing room whenever the high school held live enter-tainment in the gym, Patsy Cline stood tapping her feet, impatient to get out there and sing. Of all the entertainers in the so-called "talent" part of the program, Patsy was the only real professional. Even the handful of men in her backup band were amateurs on loan for the occasion, just a couple of local pickers—a piano player, a fiddler, and a drummer. Whereas Patsy Cline appeared every damn week on the radio and on TV in Jimmy Dean's *Town and Country Jamboree* out of WMAL in Washington. She even had a recording contract with Four Star, although she had yet to cut a hit record. No fault of hers, she thought bitterly.

But even if she was a local somebody, that didn't make Patsy a star. She had to admit that to herself. For a profes-sional career, hers was going nowhere in one damn quick hurry; otherwise, why would she be pacing the floor in a smelly locker room in a lousy high school in her own home-town of Winchester, Virginia? Why wasn't she a regular on the Grand Ole Opry by now, if she'd been singing profes-sionally for eight of her twenty-three years? She'd never made the Opry even once, even though they'd given her an audition when she was fifteen. And why didn't she have a hit record, like Kitty Wells or any one of twenty real country-and-western stars she could name? She was still only a local girl making good, but not good enough.

But I am *good enough,* she told herself again. She could feel it when she sang, the way audiences responded to her voice. She sensed the electricity that happened between herself and the people she was singing to, a crackling connection that was entirely of her making. She could hold them in her hands using only her voice, and every time she did it, it gave her a sense of power, and of something more. Of a fulfillment that nothing else on earth held for her. It was as though Patsy Cline had been set upon this earth for one reason and one reason alone, to sing. It was a thrilling feeling, yet one tinged deeply and sometimes bitterly with loneliness. Her faith in herself was strong, but it was often hard going to keep it alive.

By the time that Charlie Dick gunned his battered little 1951 Chevy convertible into the high school parking lot, the dance had been under way for more than an hour, and the lot was already jammed with cars and pickups wedged in tightly side by side in rows. It appeared to be full.

They were late because Charlie had been nipping at the first pint on his way to pick up Wanda. When he'd reached her house, he was high and horny, and they'd ripped off a quick one in the back seat. But even a quick one took a good half hour, plus another fifteen minutes while Wanda made repairs to her face and hair, and Charlie picked the pink sweater-fuzz off his shirt and jeans. All the way to the high school, the two of them had taken turns with the bottle, passing it back and forth with giggles of enjoyment. Now they were happy and feeling no pain. All they needed was a parking space.

From inside the gym, the sounds of loud music came drifting out over the parking lot. Wanda wriggled in the front seat, impatient to get out and get down. Charlie's deepset eyes scanned the lot, and his foot came down hard on the accelerator, gunning the motor. The little car roared twice around the lot at high speed, fruitlessly seeking a home.

There was a space, but it was so narrow that other cars had wisely ignored it. Between the dark red Ford pickup that stood at the end of the row and the brick wall beyond it was a tiny parking space, hardly more than a crevice with not an inch of room to maneuver. Whoever tried to park anything bigger than a bicycle there must be purely a maniac. And that, of course, was Charlie Dick.

Backing the Chevy up a few feet, Charlie came barreling forward, heading straight for the crevice.

"Charlie, no! Don't!" squealed Wanda in terror, covering her eyes with her hands and shrinking down in her seat.

At the last possible moment, Charlie Dick gave the wheel a sharp turn, and the convertible, missing the Ford pickup only by inches, came to rest neatly between it and the wall. With a satisfied shout of laughter, Charlie turned off the engine and pocketed the key.

They were safe and they were parked, but they were wedged so tightly into the narrow space that they couldn't get the doors open to get out. This made Charlie only laugh louder, and he threw back his head, taking a deep swallow of the bourbon, emptying the small bottle.

"Tell ya what, Wanda, honey. You sit tight and I'll get us on out of here."

He rolled the window down on the driver's side, but there was no room to maneuver himself out from behind the wheel. Especially with more than half a pint of bourbon lining his insides. Pulling Wanda onto his lap, Charlie wiggled over to the passenger side, slowly, savoring the girl's strong perfume and the feel of her tight rump pressed against his crotch. It was with reluctance that he dumped her behind the wheel and rolled the passenger window down.

Since the car was a convertible, all he really had to do was put the top down and climb out easily. But Charlie was already too blasted to remember that. Besides, this way was more fun. It took him a few minutes to get out of the window, but only because he'd had three or four drinks too many. Still, with some grunting and scraping, he managed to get out.

When his feet were safely on the ground, he reached in

to haul Wanda out. This was even slower going, because she was wearing a skintight skirt, same as every other young woman in the year 1956. But finally, with a lot of pulling and pushing, with small squeals and giggles on Wanda's part, and a few surreptitious feels and ass pats on Charlie's, they were out. The piled-up fluff of Wanda's bleached hair was in total disarray, and her nylons were badly snagged, but they were out and ready to boogie.

Charlie reached back into the front seat for his leather jacket, which held the precious second bottle, and the two of them, swaying and laughing, made their way into the high school gym.

The dance was already in full swing, and the gym was crowded. It was a mixed bunch, everybody from teenagers to men and women in their thirties, on their faces the exhausted look that comes from marrying too young, working too hard, and playing too little. Almost all the boys were dressed like Charlie, in baggy dungarees and short-sleeved shirts; the girls, except for a few in crinolines and wide cotton or felt skirts, wore the standard outfit of tight sweater and skirt and wide imitation-leather belt wrapped snugly around their slender waists, very much like Wanda's. The Natalie Wood look. It was a typical Friday night crowd, determined to have a good time.

A flimsy, makeshift stage had been set up for the musicians at the far end of the gymnasium floor. The sound system was practically nonexistent, consisting only of a single microphone and the public address loudspeakers that were used for the hometown basketball games. No attempt had been made to be professional about anything; just as long as the music was loud, hardly anybody cared whether or not it was good. They were satisfied just to be dancing.

Up on the stage, a high school quartet was struggling through its rendition of "Down By The Riverside," complete with some fancy vocalizations and harmonizing that didn't quite come off. Still, nobody seemed to mind, or even pay the singers any attention. The floor was filled with swaying couples.

With drunken gallantry and a surprising grace, Charlie swept Wanda into his arms and pressed his body close to hers, leading her across the dance floor in a series of showy moves. All around him, people called his name in greeting, men giving him a friendly punch on the arm or thump on the shoulder, while girls cut their eyes at him behind their partners' backs. He was pretty well-known in Winchester as a good ole boy and a hellraiser. Charlie grinned happily at everybody; he was in a great, expansive mood, partly from the glow of the bourbon, but also from the comfort of familiar surroundings. He was among friends, and everybody seemed to be having themselves a party. With one hand he waved at his good buddy J. W. Woodhouse, who was dancing with his steady girlfriend, while he kept his other hand fastened tightly to Wanda's cute round bottom.

The song droned to a spiritless end, and the couples stopped dancing, waiting for the next number to begin. When the musicians struck up the introduction to a Hank Snow favorite, the upbeat "I'm Movin' On," there was an anticipatory buzz, and heads turned expectantly in the direction of the locker room, from where the talent would emerge. But nobody came out, and the musicians, hesitating, faltered to a stop.

Then, suddenly, there she was, without even an introduction. A tall, dark-haired young woman in a spangled western getup, strode forward, her long, shapely legs in their high white boots mounting the stage, the fringe of her short leather skirt swinging jauntily around her knees, and the white cowboy Stetson with its turned-up brim resting cockily on her dark curls. She stood quietly for a moment, not moving, just surveying her audience, grinning at the applause that came crashing up to the stage. Her dimples flashed, and she put her hands on her hips and her head to one side, checking them out, looking them over. They belonged to her, to Patsy Cline.

That's how Charlie Dick saw Patsy Cline for the first time in his life. He didn't even know her name.

That woman is my destiny, thought Charlie with a clarity that chilled him. *For good or for evil, that woman is my destiny, and my life from this very night is bound up with hers forever.*

In all his years he'd never seen anybody quite like Patsy Cline before. It wasn't just that she was pretty—although she was, very pretty—but there was a strength and an arrogance about her that attracted him instantly. It was almost masculine, although the full, rounded curves of her body, with its long neck and high, pointed breasts, were most definitely a woman's. When she grinned down at the audience, it was as though she was grinning only at him, sizing him up, daring him not be be attracted, warning him he'd better take care of himself. He became totally unaware of the crowd in the gym, or of Wanda Kimble standing by his side. He felt he was alone in this vast room with this dark-eyed woman and her long legs and challenging smile.

It occurred to Charlie suddenly that perhaps he wasn't the only man in the audience who felt that Patsy Cline was smiling directly at him, and a possessive anger gripped him hard. Instinctively, his hands balled up into fists. He was ready to punch out anybody who took one step in this girl's direction.

Patsy had the microphone now, but she wasn't singing, she was talking to them, and every word spoken in her clear, alto voice found its way directly into the secret places of Charlie Dick.

"I tell you what," she grinned down at her audience. "I'm gonna treat you right tonight. I could've sung any old thing that came to mind, but I said to myself, 'Lord, Patsy, these people took a bath and drove clear over to the high school. If you're gonna sing a song, sing a good one or stay the hell home.' So this is a *good* one. I picked it special to sing to you." She turned to the musicians. "Do it."

The introduction to the song struck up again, and Charlie held his breath. Although he was still a little boozed up, there was an untouched part of his mind that was responding clear as a bell. In that part of him, he felt that he had stood here before, many times before in many lives, waiting for the first note of that voice. And when it came, rich, clear, full, he recognized it instantly although he'd never heard it before. That voice had sung in his heart all his damn life.

There was nothing small about Patsy Cline's voice, nothing nasal or whiny. It came full from her diaphragm, from deep down inside her, to emerge with strength and purity. She threw herself headfirst into the beloved Hank Snow number, full throttle, tearing the stuffings out of the old song and turning it inside out. In country music, it was the men who were always movin' on, heading for some new horizon, and it was the women singers who were left to moan and weep over being deserted. Men called the shots, and the women were left behind to pick up the pieces.

But pickin' up the pieces was not for Patsy Cline. Watching her up on that nothing of a stage, which she dominated by the vitality of her presence, watching her shake her curls and stamp her foot and sing the living hell out of that song, alternately belting and growling it, Charlie found it inconceivable that anybody would ever dare to walk out on Patsy Cline. No, she was a woman who'd be doing the walking herself. That voice wasn't made for singin' the low-down blues. It was a happy voice, reaching deep down inside you and making you grin and tap your feet.

Out on the dance floor, nobody was dancing now. They crowded around the bandstand, listening to Patsy's music, loving Patsy's music. And they were in for a surprise.

Halfway through the song, Patsy gave a nod to the boys in the band, and the tempo slowed down. All at once, the song became a torchy ballad. The hardness, the masculinity disappeared entirely, and Patsy was all woman, threatening her faithless lover that she'd had enough, threats that the blue tones of her voice told you she could never carry out.

Now Charlie could feel her vulnerability, and realized that, along with her strength and a great potential for happiness, came a fragility and a great potential for unhappiness.

> *Someday, baby, when you've had your day,*
> *You're gonna want your mama, but your*
> *mama will say,*
> *I'm movin' on, I'll soon be gone . . .*

Then, just as quickly as it came, the sadness disappeared, and Patsy was tearing into the song again up tempo, bringing it to an exhilarated, joyous finish. She held on to the last note so long it felt like forever, and when at last she let it go, she brought her hands together in a mighty clap, as if to punctuate the song's ending. Then she stood beaming at the crowd, a film of sweat on her upper lip, her dark curls damp at the base of her neck.

They clapped hard for her because she'd made them happy with her music, but Charlie knew that the only person in the whole damn crowd who really knew what this woman was about was himself.

Taking her right hand off the mike, Patsy made a gun of her fingers and aimed it at the audience, all of them.

"I picked that one special to sing to you," she told them. Then, with a swirl of the fringe around her knees, she turned and left the stage.

Charlie Dick felt as though the wind had been knocked right out of him. Once, in a bar fight, he'd been punched out bad and wound up on the floor, desperately trying to catch his breath. He was feeling the same way now; the only difference was that he knew that the air he needed for life was this woman. All around him, boys and girls were slipping off the dance floor, heading for the parking lot, where their illicit bottles were stashed in their cars and vans. It was time for a drink, and maybe even a little grope, a few stolen kisses and some petting, before coming back to dance some more.

He looked around in desperation for somebody he knew,

somebody who maybe could give him the lowdown on this dark-haired singer. Across the dance floor he spotted J.W. Woodhouse cheek to cheek with his girl. Oblivious to Wanda's glares, Charlie darted toward the couple and pulled J.W. away.

"Who was that?" he demanded. "Singing just now. Who was that?"

"Patsy Cline. A Winchester girl."

Charlie shook his head as if to clear it. "Cline? Patsy *Cline*? From around here? Why don't I know her?"

His friend shrugged. "Damned if I know. She was in my brother's class till she quit school." He threw an uneasy glance over his shoulder at Charlie's date. "You better get back there," he warned. "Wanda's chewing her lip, and that means she's got her ass up in the air 'cause you left her standin' there. And she *sees* where you're lookin'."

But Wanda was the last person on Charlie Dick's mind right now. Recalling something that he'd once heard, he grabbed hard at J.W.'s arm as his friend started to dance away.

"*Wait!*" he pleaded. "She the one sings out on Rainbow Road? At the Rainbow Road Club?"

The last person on Charlie Dick's mind was dancing past them now, glued to another man and smiling up in his face. But Wanda took the time to hiss furiously at Charlie.

"Hell's gonna freeze over, boy, 'fore you lay another glove on me!"

Flinching a little, Charlie exchanged glances with J.W., the two of them shaking their heads in silent agreement. Wanda could be real mean when she was pissed.

But now Woodhouse's girl was getting ticked off, too, tugging at her boyfriend's arm, wanting to dance instead of having to stand here listening to the two of them jawing. J.W. nodded at her, and once more moved to take her into his arms, but Charlie grabbed hold of him again.

Impatiently, J.W. pulled his sleeve out of Charlie's grasp. He was bored with this bullshit, and wanted to get rid of

Charlie Dick once and for all. Using his fingers to count off the items, he rapidly went through everything he knew about Patsy Cline.

"She went to school with my brother. They always said, 'Don't dare Patsy if you don't want it done.' She's sung on the TV. She's made a record, and she's got *real* good tits."

Then he grinned at his friend and danced his girl away, yelling back over his shoulder, "And she's married, bozo. You lose."

Feeling drained and somewhat frustrated, Patsy dried her face and neck with a towel. *Come all this way and sing only one song. Seems almost a waste of time,* she thought, even though she knew that she'd had them going. Still, it was a dance, not a music hall, and she didn't want to step all over their Friday night out. Carefully, she removed her rayon satin western shirt, with the sparkly "diamonds" on the yoke and the silky fringe over the bosom, and folded it carefully into her bag, laying it on top of her leather skirt. Then she stepped into her street skirt and buttoned on a plainer blouse, slipped a string of beads over her head, and knotted a scarf around her throat. Combing out her dark curls, she tied a ribbon around her head and took a look at herself in the mirror, adjusting an earring. There. She was ready.

Hilda was waiting for her outside; Patsy had promised to go home with her right after her number, and she didn't want to keep her mother standing too long. Snapping her wardrobe bag shut, she made her way out of the locker room and into the crowded area behind the stage. Occupied in saying goodnight to the others, she didn't notice the man in the leather jacket approaching her until they were almost nose to nose.

Giving her his biggest smile, Charlie Dick turned the charm faucet on full. "I want you to get your coat," he said smoothly. "I want to drive you someplace for a drink. I want us to dance for a while, then I want us to get to know each other a lot better."

Patsy eyed him coldly. She was accustomed to drugstore cowboys hitting on her whenever she appeared on stage, and this grinning idiot was just one more of the same, with his slicked-back hair and the bourbon smell coming off him like cheap perfume. Jesus' own gift to the female sex, that's what all of them thought. *Well, I have news for you, buddy.*

He even had his arm up across the wall, barring her exit. Patsy turned to face him, her eyes dancing with mischief.

"You want a lot, don't you?" she asked him, showing him her dimples.

"Yeah, baby," Mr. Wonderful smiled back, flashing more white teeth than a piano.

Smoothly, Patsy ducked under his arm. Moving past him without a backward look, Patsy threw the last word over her shoulder. "Well, people in hell want ice water, but that don't mean they get it."

A loud laugh made Charlie turn his head. A young girl, one of the high school juniors, had heard the entire exchange and was laughing at him. Red-faced at the put-down, humiliated by the girl's laughter, Charlie just stood there and watched Patsy walk away. Yet, cutting through his embarrassment was a conviction that wasn't going to change, no matter how often or how publicly Patsy Cline rejected him. This was the woman for Charlie Dick, married or not, famous or not. Tonight was a beginning. She might not recognize that now, but she would in the days to come. He'd make certain of that.

But Patsy had dismissed Charlie from her thoughts as soon as she'd walked away from him. To her, he was just one more of those likkered-up peckerwoods who turned up everywhere she sang a gig. Nothing more on his mind than wanting to get into the singer's pants, so he could brag about it down to the factory or the garage on Monday morning. Well, *that'd* be the day!

Grabbing her coat off the hook, she struggled into it, eager to be on her way home. The rhythm of the dance had altered, as it always did when the evening wore on. Now there was much less enthusiastic lindying, fewer rapid two-steps. The music turned slower and more romantic, and young couples with nowhere else to go to make love stood glued together on the dance floor, bodies pressed tight against one another's, barely swaying, barely pretending that it was dancing they were doing. Romance mingled with frustration. Two by two they slipped away, looking for some less public place to show each other their affection.

Such a couple stood pressed against the wall near Patsy, within hearing distance. The boy wore his hair in long sideburns and a ducktail, in worshipful emulation of the great Elvis; the girl's curls were caught up in a ribbon. They couldn't have been more than fifteen or sixteen, scarcely more than children, but what they were feeling for each other was stronger than what many grown-ups will ever know.

As she buttoned her coat, Patsy couldn't help looking at them; they drew her eyes like a magnet. The boy's arms were tightly around the girl's waist, while she had put up one delicate hand to stroke his adolescent face.

Although she didn't intend to eavesdrop, the girl's words were carried clearly to Patsy's ears over the sound of the band.

"Crazy 'bout ya, baby. Love ya all the *time!*"

It was hardly Juliet's speech to Romeo, but something in the sweet, simple words touched a nerve in Patsy, and she turned her head away, her eyes stinging with sudden tears.

What the hell has come over me? she thought, fighting down a rising lump in her throat. *Actin' just like a little baby over nothing at all.*

Even so, it was with a strange sense of loss that Patsy went to find her mother. Suddenly, she'd had enough of this dance. She wanted to go home.

Two

MARRIED AT FIFTEEN, Hilda Hensley had been less than seventeen years old on September 8, 1932, when she gave birth to her first child, a daughter, Virginia Patterson Hensley. With so few years separating them, Hilda and Ginny would always be more like older and younger sister than mother and daughter, sharing a happy intimacy and a friendship that was precious to both of them. They even looked like sisters, both with the same thick, dark, lively hair and chocolate-brown eyes, both with the same soft, fresh complexions, both with the same touch of round plumpness.

There never would come a time when they didn't giggle together, never come a time when Ginny couldn't tell her mother everything, even after she'd changed the Ginny to "Patsy," for her middle name of Patterson, and embarked upon her professional singing career, even after her marriage to Gerald Cline.

Hilda's husband, Samuel Hensley, was a compact, muscular man, about five feet seven and one hundred and fifty pounds. When they decided to marry, he had been thirty-two, twice as old as Hilda, or so she'd believed. What she didn't know was that he dyed his gray hair dark brown in order to look younger. It wasn't until they went for the wedding license that Hilda discovered that he was forty-three years old to her fifteen, very close to three times her age; somewhere he had a daughter older than Hilda. A man of uncertain temper even at the best of times, moody, volatile, violent, he was at his worst when he drank. And he drank often.

Perhaps you couldn't blame him. In his earlier years Samuel Hensley had been a man of substance, a man of some education and even refinement. There had always been money until, one day, he found that it was gone, leaving him dirt poor. In 1931, he was a working man during the Great Depression, when there was no work for a working man to do. Every now and then he was able to pick up odd jobs on the railroads—his profession was blacksmith, working with steel in the railroad yards—but the family was always on the move, leaving one putrid cabin just a jump before they'd be put out of it, moving into another shanty, even more run-down. Until they finally settled down in Winchester in better times, they'd been forced to move on nineteen separate occasions.

Usually their pathetic little shack boasted no electricity, no indoor plumbing, and often no running water. Without screens in the windows, the wretched rooms would be alive with huge, vicious flies which tormented them with buzzing and stinging day and night, and with voracious biting mosquitoes which frequently brought on dangerous fevers.

Young Ginny Hensley would usually have to walk miles just to get to school, toting a lunch that was no more than a smear of lard on coarse bread. Her school dresses, more often than not, were stitched-up flour sacks. Small wonder Samuel Hensley drank. Small wonder that, when he drank, he would beat his wife and small daughter. To a proud man, God had sent the disappointments of the Depression, impossible to endure. Luckily for Samuel, God had provided women and children to bear the brunt of those disappointments.

He was a stern parent, and so solitary a man that he gladly forsook the company of neighbors, and insisted that his wife and child do likewise. He didn't want to live in town, he didn't want his daughter, Ginny, to make any friends of her own. It was enough she had a mother and father and, later, a brother and sister to look after. Samuel Hensley believed that family was all the friends a body needed.

To say that Hilda and Ginny were afraid of Samuel would only be to state the obvious. To them, he was as a god, all-powerful, stern, with a thick black beard and piercing dark eyes, a figure of authority and discipline in whose presence they trembled. Perhaps it was this—their mutual fear of Samuel Hensley—as much as mother and daughter's closeness in age that brought Ginny and Hilda together.

Yet, he could be tender. In his own way, he loved his daughter very much, perhaps too much. The thought that someday she would grow up and leave him made him crazy; if he could have his way, he'd lock her up and keep her for himself forever.

Oddly enough, Virginia, who was so close to her mother, inherited a great deal of her nature from her father: his moodiness, his stubborn streak, his sudden flashes of violent temper, and above all, his ferocious intelligence and unyielding strength of purpose. Once Samuel got an idea in his head, the U.S. Marines couldn't shake it loose, and, later in her life, Patsy Cline would be much the same way. She had almost none of Hilda's patience and abiding tolerance; she was her mother's friend, but her father's daughter.

When she was four years old, little Virginia fell seriously ill. Inoculations against child-killing diseases were unknown in the backwoods; every year or so a serious infection would strike some poor family, carrying off the youngest, the oldest, and the weakest. As Ginny's fever soared upward, the only sound to be heard in the cabin was incessant coughing, the harsh rasp of a little girl trying desperately to catch her breath, and the whispered prayers of her terrified mother.

Oh, dear Lord Jesus, save my baby. Don't let my Ginny die.

They'd had the doctor once, but he'd examined the child only briefly and diagnosed her illness as mumps. Since that time, the pain in Ginny's throat had become so excruciating that she kept going into delirium. But they couldn't afford to have the doctor again.

"How is she?" demanded Samuel, coming into the little cabin with an armload of logs for the wood stove.

"She's worse, I think!" sobbed Hilda.

Scowling darkly, he stepped up to the bed where the child lay struggling to breathe, and laid one callused hand on his daughter's brow.

"She's burning up," he muttered. Then he turned on his young wife, snarling with fury. "How in hell did you let her get so sick?"

In the pale light of the kerosene lamp, the tears on Hilda's cheeks glittered. "The doctor said it was only mumps. . . ." she faltered.

"The hell with those damn doctors! All they care about is the money! If my daughter dies . . ." He broke off, the threat, unspoken yet palpable, hanging in the air between them.

"I could go down the road and call the doctor again," Hilda suggested timidly.

"No, by God! No damn doctors!"

Ginny moaned weakly, tossing feverishly on the thin mattress. A sudden racking cough shook her tiny frame into painful spasms, and her thin body arched upward into a convulsion.

"Oh, Sam, she's going to die!"

"Not my daughter! I won't let it happen!"

"What are we going to do?" wailed Hilda.

"You got your egg money?" Sam asked suddenly.

"Y-Y-Yes."

"How much?"

"A dollar twenty, I think."

"That's plenty. Take the pail, go down the road, and get a dollar's worth of gas for the car. We're takin' her to the hospital ourselves. You hear? Run, now!"

On trembling legs, young Hilda obeyed, and fear lent swiftness to her feet.

Stripping the blankets off the bed where he and his wife slept, Samuel lifted his tiny daughter, now pitifully thin, from her cot. He wrapped her tightly in the blankets, almost stifling her, but keeping her warm. By the time he'd finished sponging her brow off with cool water from the pump, his big hands surprisingly gentle, he could hear his wife outside, filling the gas tank of their ancient flivver.

It was eighteen long, winding, bumpy miles down an unpaved backwoods road to the hospital. Samuel drove, his face grim as death, both hands gripping the wheel, while Hilda sat beside him, holding the tightly wrapped bundle that was their desperately ill daughter.

"It's diphtheria," said the examining doctor briefly, and they bundled Virginia onto a stretcher without another word and wheeled her away down the corridor, where Samuel and Hilda were not permitted to follow.

For two days and nights they battled the disease, while the child fought to hang on to life. She remained in that deathly limbo while her mother stayed down on her knees, begging God to spare her Ginny, and Samuel raged against the heavens.

On the third day, the fever broke.

"She'll be very weak for a while; give her plenty of rest and nourishing food. Then we'll see," the doctor told them.

"See what?" demanded Samuel.

"She was a pretty sick little girl. There may be some permanent damage to the larynx."

"Are you telling me that my daughter might not be able to talk again?"

But the doctor could only shake his head. "We just have to wait and see. Perhaps an operation. . . ."

For weeks after her recovery, Ginny could only whisper. Hilda kept her daughter's throat well wrapped and her own anxious eye on the child all the time. An operation! They could no more afford an operation than a grand cruise to all the capitals of Europe! Again, she prayed. It was just about all she knew how to do for Ginny.

Six weeks after Ginny came home from the hospital, the three of them went to Sunday services. It was the first time the child seemed well enough to come along. She sat quietly, drooping listlessly through the preaching, but when the singing began, she sat up straight. This was the part she always loved the best.

The hymn was a beloved favorite, "The Old Rugged Cross." As usual, Hilda's clear soprano and Samuel Hensley's tuneful baritone rose above the other voices. Suddenly another voice joined theirs, a strong, bell-like alto of unparalleled purity, yet childishly sweet. Hilda looked down and gasped.

It was Virginia Hensley's voice. The miracle that had saved Virginia Hensley's life had also saved her larynx. And it did more. The diphtheria which had nearly killed her had left her with the gift of a magnificent singing voice.

Ginny's brother, John, was born around her seventh birthday, and her sister, Sylvia, two years later. Now, instead of being an only child, Virginia Hensley became the oldest child in the family, the one expected to help raise her baby brother and sister. Responsibilities were heaped on the little girl's shoulders, but she was made of sturdy stuff, and she rarely minded the extra work. On the contrary, Ginny was glad and proud to help out her beloved mother.

Her father was often away for weeks at a time, looking for work on the railroads, but his absence was less of a hardship than a blessing. Mean when sober, he was cruel when drunk. When Samuel was away from home, the family could relax, even enjoy themselves with what simple pleasures they could afford. It was his return that they all dreaded; any reprieve from his harshness and his suspicions was worth any amount of doing without.

One thing, though, they never did without, no matter how poor they were. That was music. They all loved music, and had fine, strong voices, although none of the others was as good as Virginia. Wherever they lived, no matter how deep in the pine woods or how far from the town, they managed to find their way to some church on Sunday, usually one kind of evangelical sect or another, Pentecostal or the Church of the Holy Spirit, with a congregation as poor as they were. As long as there was signifying and sanctifying and praising the Lord in song. Especially song. And there the Hensley family would sing. People would turn their heads to hear Hilda's tuneful voice, and the clarity and sweetness in her daughter's. Frequently, they would be asked to sing duets of the beloved old gospel hymns.

At home they had an old Philco radio, battery operated, because they had no electricity in the cabin, and they kept that radio tuned to music until the batteries wore out. Hymns, country, dance music—mother and daughter loved them all. Ginny grew up singing along to the radio; that's how she learned the melodies and the lyrics of all the songs they played—mostly hillbilly and gospel, but some popular songs, too.

When Ginny was five, Hilda entered her in an amateur talent show in Winchester. These were common in the Depression; it was one more method of luring nickels away from people who could ill afford them. The local movie theater would stage these amateur nights for the kiddies between showings of the film, and the audiences would applaud for their favorites, who'd win some small prize or other. So for the same price of admission, you could see

Greta Garbo or Joan Crawford and a live show, maybe pick up some free glass dishes, and get to play judge when your applause picked the winner.

Thanks to a curly-haired moppet movie star named Shirley Temple, kiddie shows were all the rage; every doting mother was convinced that she had given birth to another Shirley. Families scrimped and saved to give their daughters fifty-cent dancing lessons, determined that their own little Ada Mae or Louisa would make them a fortune in Hollywood. The difference with Ginny, of course, was that she really *could* sing, and the song she chose to sing in her first amateur night was, of course, "The Good Ship Lollipop," Shirley Temple's biggest hit.

First prize in this particular contest was a large china table lamp, with a bright blue base and a frilly shade, donated by the local furniture store whose name had to be mentioned on stage at least twenty times in twenty minutes. There were five contestants vying for the prize, Ginny being the fifth in line.

Everything went routinely until it was the turn of the girl before Ginny Hensley. Dressed in a black leotard and a sweater, the girl was at least fourteen years old, and looked even older. First she played the banjo, and then she tap-danced. It was obvious from her dancing that she'd had years of lessons and practice, because her spins and fancy taps, and her tricky show-off steps were almost professional. Little Ginny stood mesmerized, watching those flashing, flying, tapping feet. As expected, the tap dancer got a big hand, and then it was Ginny's turn.

"And what are *you* going to do for us?" asked the master of ceremonies as he introduced the final contestant, five-year-old Ginny Hensley.

She opened her mouth to say, "I'm going to sing "The Good Ship Lollipop," but nobody was more surprised than she was to hear the words coming out as "I'm going to dance for y'all."

Dance! She'd never danced in her life! She wasn't even wearing dancing shoes, just her only pair of much-mended Sunday church shoes, the best she had. And they had no taps.

But the pianist had begun the music and there was nothing left for Ginny to do but dance.

At first, she tried to remember some of the steps and twirls she'd just seen, but those were hard to imitate with no practice and no lessons. And then she let the music take hold of her and she moved to it, naturally and gracefully, dipping and gliding and spinning around in rhythm to the piano. In her imagination, she was wearing a beautiful silky dress and a lot of jewelry, and tap-tap-tapping up there on the silver screen. But the reality was even more charming—a five-year-old with huge, sparkling eyes, thick, glossy hair, and chubby knees, wearing the only good dress she owned, ruffled and starched, and trying her damnedest to "dance for y'all."

So was it any wonder that those good folks put their hands together hard, and little Ginny Hensley received the biggest hand of anybody, and got to carry home that blue china lamp with the frilly shade? It was the proudest moment of her life. Even her terrifying father put his work-scarred hand on her dark head and told her it was well-done. As for Hilda, she couldn't get over it. Again and again, she said to her little girl, "You were supposed to sing! What in the name of the Lord Jesus possessed you to dance? I declare! I really do declare!"

Lordy, she was proud of that lamp! It sat smack in the middle of the room they all lived in, the only brand-new object among the other broken-down sticks of furniture and odd bits and pieces. And later, when the sheriff's men came to throw them out of yet another rented cabin, and to seize what few possessions they had, Ginny fought like a tiger for her beloved blue lamp.

"Sorry, little girl, but we have to take it. It's the law."

But the child had attacked the big uniformed men with her tiny fists, crying over and over, "It's not the law! It's mine! It's mine! I won it!"

The bailiff had looked at Hilda Hensley with a question in his eyes, and she nodded.

"Ginny won that lamp in a talent contest over to the movie theayter in Winchester. She danced a tap dance, and they gave her first prize."

So, when the three of them had piled into the ancient Ford automobile and driven off in search of a new home, little Ginny was tightly clutching her precious lamp.

Three

I haven't thought of that old blue lamp in at least ten years, Patsy said to herself as she walked with her mother into the parking lot of the high school. *Wonder why it popped into my head just now. And whatever the hell happened to it?* she asked herself nostalgically. *Musta got broken somewhere along the way.*

She was feeling a little depressed, which was unusual for her, because her energy and optimism generally knew no bounds. Part of her mood stemmed from the letdown that was the natural aftermath of a performance, part of it was the conviction that her career wasn't getting off the dime. But no small part of it was seeing those two kids, those teenagers all wrapped up in their puppy love, so passionate, so endearing, with their entire lives still ahead of them.

Hell, I'm only twenty-three, not so much older than they are, so what am I moaning about? But Patsy couldn't seem to shake the feeling that she was missing something, that life with all its excitement was passing her by. Never had she been touched by that kind of passion, that ecstatic electric current that she'd seen flowing between that boy and girl not ten minutes ago. It was a feeling that transcended sex; sex was nothing compared with passion.

As she climbed into the front seat of Hilda Hensley's 1953 Ford, Patsy shook her head to clear it of troubling thoughts. She didn't want her mother to suspect that anything was wrong. Patsy and her mother adored each other and were each other's best friends. As Patsy had grown into womanhood, she felt closer than ever to Hilda, understanding more completely the hard life her mother had been forced to lead and the burdens she'd been compelled to carry, even though Hilda rarely complained. There was a tight bond between them that formed a life-support system for them both.

Apart from the love they felt for each other, the strongest connection between mother and daughter was the laughter they shared. Both possessed the identical sense of humor, rich and earthy, and the same loud, free laugh that broke out whenever a situation or a person was ridiculous. Which, to Hilda and Patsy, was pretty damn often. The two of them loved nothing better than a good giggle.

Now, recounting to her mother the events of the evening, Patsy suddenly remembered the man who'd hit on her, deciding he was too rich a joke not to share with Hilda.

"Oh, Mama, you shoulda seen him," she laughed. "Could hardly stand up straight, drunk as a snake, but oozin' charm out of every pore. Wasn't hardly any bigger than me, but absolutely *con*vinced that I would drop everything and chase right after him. Well, I put him in his place. Told him that people in hell all want ice water, but weren't gettin' it."

"Oh, Patsy, you never did!" giggled Hilda, holding one hand in front of her mouth. She'd lost two teeth recently, and was still self-conscious about the gaps in her smile.

"I did, too," averred Patsy with a grin. "I looked him right in the face—did I tell you he was kind of a little fella?—and said, 'Buster, people in hell want ice water, too.' Betty Simmons was standing right there and heard me."

"Who was he?" her mother wanted to know.

Patsy shook her head from side to side. "I don't know. Probably some local good ole boy. Some clown with hot britches is all I know."

Putting on her shocked expression, Hilda gave her daughter a little smack on the arm as a light reproof. As a good Christian and a churchgoing woman, she never did like what she called "language." And Patsy used "language" just like any trucker. But her reprimand was tempered by a giggle; Patsy always did have a way of putting things that made her laugh despite herself.

Now Patsy sighed deeply, and a vertical line appeared between her feathery dark brows, a sure sign that she was annoyed at something.

"Lord God, but I do get tired of men sometimes, always pawing and snorting around." Tossing her curls in disgust, she turned to look at her mother. "Were they *at* you all the time when you were my age?"

Hilda gave a little shrug, refusing to meet Patsy's eye. "Oh, I don't know," she replied evasively.

But Patsy could smell that something was up. She knew her mother well enough to know when she was hiding something. And she was hiding something now. After all, Hilda had been a very pretty girl, and married at fifteen. So she must have ripened early, like Patsy herself, with a full-budded figure which more than hinted at maturity.

"Come on," she teased Hilda, "let's hear it."

"Well, back when I was in high school and had a nicer shape, there was this here boy named Teddy Welhoff. . . ." Hilda Hensley's eyes narrowed as she called up her memories. "He had the prettiest gray eyes, he did, with coal-black eyelashes. 'Course, this was way before I met your daddy—"

"And I hope he rots in hell with his back broken," interrupted Patsy without emphasis.

"Don't speak like that about your daddy," her mother replied automatically. It was an ages-old argument between them, one they carried on without even thinking twice about it.

"*Any*way," continued Hilda, "at lunch we'd all go into

the cloakroom, and ever' darn day this here Teddy Welhoff he used to brush his front up against me when I was bent over getting my dinner bucket."

Patsy uttered a scream of delighted laughter and began to wriggle around on the car seat, simulating adolescent sexual arousal, with little squeals and cries of "Woo woo!"

"Wait, now!" Hilda took one embarrassed hand off the wheel to slap feebly at her daughter, but it was obvious that she was enjoying herself as much as Patsy was. "That ain't all. This is the truth: one day it was so hot my thighs was lathered—ever'body was irritable. Well, the teacher told us to go get our dinner buckets, and I took my ink pen with me, and that thing had a *real* sharp point. . . ."

Patsy gave a high shriek and clutched happily at her sides in anticipation.

"And I stuck that dang pen down the back of my skirt so that the point was right down—well, you know where—and stickin' out, but covered with the skirt, see."

"Oh, Mama, no!"

"So anyway, I'm bendin' over and I'm waitin' and I'm waitin', and for the first time in a month o' Sundays, he's late. I'm feelin' like a pure-dee fool when finally along comes this Teddy Welhoff, and just like always, he pushes his front right up tight. . . ."

"Mama, *stop!*" begged Patsy, doubled over and out of breath from laughter.

But Hilda was caught up in her story now, and giggling so hard that her foot hit the gas by mistake and the car skidded slightly off the road onto the shoulder.

"Well, you never did hear such a holler in your whole life. Teacher came runnin', sure that one of us kids was kilt. I tell you, I never even looked at him the rest of the day, but my hand to God there was egg salad sandwich all over the cloakroom, and that boy walked funny for a week!"

Now the two of them exploded, Patsy slamming the side of the car with her hand, Hilda's eyes streaming. They laughed for at least three minutes while the car covered the last quarter mile to Patsy's house.

When Hilda put on the brake, the two women sat drying their eyes and wiping their faces, trying to catch their breath and regain their composure. But even after they'd calmed down, a sudden fresh burst of hilarity would catch one of them, sending the other off into peals of laughter.

Eventually, though, Patsy could talk again. "Come on in for a while," she asked her mother softly.

Hilda looked up at the house. There were lights on in the downstairs. Hesitating, she bit at her lip. "Is Gerald still up?"

"Looks like it," said Patsy shortly.

A silence fell between them, in which a great many significant words were left unspoken.

"Oh, honey, I better go home," said Hilda at last, uncomfortably, a worried expression on her face. She hated to see what was going on here, but she felt instinctively and deeply that her daughter had to work out her own domestic problems without a mother's interference.

"Chicken!" retorted Patsy with some bitterness.

"I'll come over for Sunday dinner," promised her mother gently.

"Chicken," said Patsy again, but this time it was an invitation delivered with a small smile. She reached into her purse and, as Hilda turned on the ignition, Patsy took some bills out of her wallet and stuffed them down the front of her mother's dress. Hilda opened her mouth to protest, but Patsy shoved her fingers into both ears, shaking her head vigorously from side to side. At last Hilda smiled, accepting the money, and drove off. But she still felt guilty, not about the money, but for ducking Patsy when her daughter needed her.

But it's not a mother's place, she told herself one more time in a long series of times. *Husband and wife got to work those things out for themselves.*

The smile fading from her face, Patsy stood watching Hilda drive away, then she turned and looked up at her little house. Immediately, her shoulders sagged, as though all the energy had been drained out of her, and she walked toward the house slowly. Now that she was home, she was burdened by the same feeling that lately was growing on her so heavily. That this house was strange to her, and that she was a stranger to it and had no business being here. Reluctantly, she turned the front door handle and walked in.

No surprises inside. Gerald was exactly where she knew he'd be, doing exactly what she knew he'd be doing. His bulk was occupying the living room sofa in front of the coffee table, and he was completely absorbed in messing with those goddamned clocks of his, just like a little seventy-year-old watchmaker. When he wasn't more than eight years older than she was. But he was like an old man already, and every time she was near him, she felt more and more like an old woman.

Patsy felt a stab of guilt; she knew she was being unfair to her husband. He was a good man, and he loved her. In the three years they'd been married, he'd never said a mean word to her. She knew that. But every time she saw him sitting there at the coffee table, intent on his repair work, all spread out so neatly on that towel, all those little springs and wheels with none of them missing, all those tiny little watchmaker's tools meticulously arranged in a row according to size, she felt so stifled and irritated she wanted to do something terrible. Scream, maybe, or pick up that towel with its dozens of cute little clock parts and fling it across the room, so that the tiny cogs and gears and wheels and winding stems would roll out of sight and be lost forever.

He was more interested in those goddamned tick-tocks than he was in her.

Gerald put down the tool he was working with, aligning it with the others with an almost military precision. Barely looking up, he asked Patsy, "How'd it go?"

"I only made twenty-five dollars, but I did good, I think,"

she said, and waited for some reaction. Right after they were married, he used to come along with her whenever she sang in public, but after a while, he just stopped. And Patsy missed that. She wanted to share with him her feelings when the applause came pouring like melted honey over the stage, and when the boys and girls stopped dancing and came crowding around just to listen to her sing. She wanted to relive the evening with her husband, who hadn't even bothered to be there.

But no interest lit up Gerald's face. He was totally concentrated on his hobby, and all he could find time to say was, "That's nice."

Patsy stood there looking at him, hoping for more, but nothing more was forthcoming. As usual, Gerald Cline sat hunched over his precious tools and his precious clocks, giving no thought to his precious wife. Without much hope, she tried again.

"I sang 'I'm Movin' On' tonight," she told him.

But Gerald had reached a tricky and very delicate part of the repair, and it was obvious that he wasn't listening. Patsy felt anger beginning to rise inside her, but she made an attempt to stifle it. If she got mad at him, it wouldn't get either of them anywhere. If there was anywhere still left to get.

"I been gone all evening. Don't you want to talk to me?" she demanded. "Say 'kiss my ass' or *some*thing?"

At the irritation in her voice, Gerald looked up at last.

"I'm sorry, honey. How'd it go tonight?"

Patsy sighed. "You already asked me that," she informed him. Then she toned down her voice, deliberately making it more gentle. "Ask me something else. Let's have a conversation."

For one startled moment Gerald looked nonplussed, even a little panicky, as though a conversation with his wife was totally beyond his capacity. But after a minute's thought, he fastened on something.

"Well," he began, "do you notice anything different?"

Patsy looked around the room. It was the same little living room in the same little tract house. Flowered draperies that were never drawn were pulled to the sides of the picture window that looked out onto nothing, and out of which nobody ever looked. There were two comfortable old chairs, and one uncomfortable new sofa, on which Gerald was perched in front of the coffee table. Two end tables held elaborate china lamps, and a whatnot shelf on the wall was filled with Patsy's beloved growing collection of salt and pepper shakers. On the wall above the sofa hung a pair of framed chromolith prints, bad reproductions of oil-painted landscapes that Patsy and Gerald had bought in the furniture store when they'd picked out their furniture as newlyweds, and hadn't looked at since.

Puzzled by the question, Patsy shook her head. Everything looked exactly the same to her. Nothing was new. Nothing was *ever* new in this house.

Proudly, Gerald held up one of the cuckoo clocks he was forever fiddling with. He showed it to her, eager to share his accomplishment.

"I got this one to working. See how this little door opens now?" He opened it and closed it, opened and closed it again, fascinated by its miniature workings.

An enormous weariness overtook Patsy, so that even her bones seemed to her to be tired. Her thoughts flashed back for one brief instant to the days when twenty-eight-year-old Gerald Cline was courting twenty-year-old Patsy Hensley, and the two of them were always finding so much to talk about, so many things that made both of them laugh at the same time. Everything was new then, all doors open, all hopes yet to be fulfilled, yet certain of fulfillment. What had happened to them? Why didn't they understand each other anymore? Why did she have to lower herself to beg for her own husband's attention? Did the simple act of marriage shut with a bang every door between a man and a woman?

How handsome she had thought Gerald then! And he had been handsome, with his barrel chest and his bright blue eyes. He was handsome now, still heavy chested and burly, still blue-eyed, still a young man. But the hot, bright ardency of his courtship he had thrown off like an old jacket that had become too shabby to wear. Instead, he seemed to be all one color now, a muted gray, with no brilliant flashes, no passionate rainbows. When had it happened? When had they stopped laughing together, stopped finding things to say to each other?

Suddenly Patsy felt so sorry for Gerald that tears stung her eyelids and threatened to fall. He seemed so pathetic, sitting there offering up his little cuckoo clock for her approval. He was too damn young to be pathetic! She smiled wearily at him and went over to the couch to give him a small kiss on his mouth.

"Patsy, why do you push at me so hard?" he asked her quietly. He had sensed the pity in her kiss and it annoyed him.

She shook her head. "I don't know," she confessed. "I guess I'm just hoping for a fight, or a laugh, or *some*thing."

"I don't want to fight with you," Gerald told her patiently. "I'm not *mad*."

Patsy nodded. How could she explain to her husband that he no longer made her feel alive, no longer seemed to be alive himself? She could picture him twenty years into the future, still squatting on the same goddamn sofa with those same goddamn tools and those pissant little wheels and screws and gears. What she couldn't picture was herself, still watching him, still nodding approval every time he put a spring in right. That wasn't going to be her future; she could swear to it. She'd die first.

Never going to live to thirty, anyhow, she told herself. She said it often, and sometimes she even believed it. Not that the thought of death ever bothered her; it was romantic and even thrilling to think of herself dying young and going to Glory. As to what was going to kill a girl who was healthy as a racehorse, Patsy never even gave it a passing consideration.

Now she smoothed Gerald's hair off his forehead, letting her hand linger for an instant on his brow, hoping that he might catch that hand in his, maybe pull her down on his lap. But he didn't, so she had no other choice but to leave the room. She couldn't stand to stay there and watch him play with those itty-bitty watchmaker tools a minute longer. It was enough to drive any sane person crazy.

In the bedroom, she went to the dresser mirror and pulled off her earrings, holding them in her hand for a minute. Patsy adored earrings. She collected them, had almost a hundred pairs. Like the salt and pepper shakers. She loved those little ceramic figures, the Indian brave and his sweetheart, the tiny black-and-white penguins and little green alligators, all paired up, one with bigger holes for salt, and one with smaller holes for pepper. Two by two. All paired up.

She, too, was paired up in a marriage, but her figure and Gerald's didn't match; they weren't from the same set.

Once they did match, back before they married, when they'd started going together and sleeping together and falling in love. Then Gerald's face would light up whenever he saw her, and he couldn't get enough of Patsy. He loved to hear her sing, and he would travel along with her to her gigs, taking her in his car, proud as could be. How excited they'd been when Four Star Records had signed her up! What plans they'd made, plans for the future, up to and including the happily-ever-after part.

Now, only a few years later, they had nothing more to say to each other. Each of them was locked away from the other, Patsy with her singing, Gerald in his little universe inhabited by ticking clocks and tocking watches, with a door so tightly shut that Patsy couldn't get in, no matter how hard she knocked.

It wasn't fair! If she was a married woman, then why

was she so lonely? You weren't supposed to be lonely, not when you lived with somebody else. Where had all the passion gone; where was the romance? Why were they like a pair of old married people in their fifties, with everything burned out of them? Was Gerald right? *Was* she pushing him too hard? Was it her fault that they were left with nothing to say? Had she talked so much that he was all talked out? When had he stopped listening, stopped caring, stopped being proud of her voice? Or was it because she wasn't yet a star, hadn't yet achieved that dream? Was it disappointment that had turned her husband off?

Yet, how could she actually fault Gerald Cline? There were many women who would line up for a chance at getting him, who would thank their lucky stars for a steady, reliable man like Gerald. He didn't drink, didn't throw his money away on cards or dice, didn't run around with other women. He was always home when she returned from a gig, always there. He never even raised his voice to her, let alone his hand. Patsy's father had beaten her mother, and had been brutal to his daughter in ways that didn't bear thinking about. Gerald was exactly the opposite; his temper was mild and yielding, and there wasn't an ounce of brutality in his nature.

Then why do I feel like I'm wrapped up in black velvet and smothering to death?

Automatically, her thoughts elsewhere, Patsy unpacked her cowgirl costume and put it away carefully. Her western outfit, with its white boots, little fringed vest all sparkled with spangles and rhinestones, and the bandanna around her long neck, had become the Patsy Cline trademark and she loved it.

Slowly she pulled off her everyday blouse and skirt and hung them up in the closet. Standing in her slip, she caught a sudden sight of herself in the full-length mirror on the closet door. It took her by surprise; for an instant, she wondered who the stranger was. Then she moved closer, curious, examining her reflection with a critical eye.

Staring at her from the mirror was a young woman whose

dark hair and eyes contrasted sharply with the whiteness of her skin, whose full body under the satin slip showed firm and youthful. The chin was strong and stubborn, but the mouth was soft and womanly, red lips curved. The shoulders were broad and the rib cage deep, the breasts large, high, and silky, tipped with small nipples of a deep pink. Narrow waist, hips rounded, legs long and well shaped, with slender ankles and full calves. She was desirable and she knew it; the expression on men's faces when they first laid eyes on her told her so. Even that drunken bozo tonight had desired her. So why didn't her own husband?

She thought suddenly of the boy and girl she'd seen earlier that evening at the dance, of how closely they had pressed their bodies together, oblivious of anybody who might be watching. Recalling what the girl had said, Patsy laughed out loud, tickled.

She turned sideways to the mirror, in a deliberately provocative pose, looking at her reflection over one shoulder. A vague feeling of sexuality, without focus, began to steal over her, creating a yearning, a need, that she couldn't quite define. Her lips pursed in a kiss and her eyes narrowed. In a near whisper, she spoke to the Patsy in the mirror.

"Crazy 'bout ya, baby. Love ya alla *time*."

The words felt strange on her lips, but good, and she giggled in embarrassment. What the hell. Might as well give it another try. What could it hurt?

Gerald Cline looked up from his work to find his wife standing in the doorway, regarding him with the oddest expression on her face. Her lips were pursed, and her eyes narrowed down to slits. For some reason he couldn't begin to fathom, Patsy was neither dressed nor undressed, but standing there in her slip, as though posing for a sexy girlie mag. Gerald's eyes were two question marks.

"Gerald," began Patsy, and her face was serious now. "What would you say if I said..." and her voice dropped down low and throaty, "crazy 'bout ya, baby. Love ya alla *time*!"

Embarrassed and uncomfortable, Gerald Cline cleared his throat. He had no idea what to answer, or what she wanted him to answer. He was simply at a loss where Patsy was concerned. Her very vitality was daunting to him, a challenge he found himself unable to meet, one that left him feeling impotent and, under it all, humiliated and angry. This wasn't what he'd expected out of his marriage. He'd wanted a well-kept home and hot meals.

Instead of being the homemaker he'd imagined she would be for him, Patsy was always thinking of her career. Singing was all that seemed to be on her mind, singing and making love, but Gerald had lost interest in both.

Instead of cooking his supper or ironing his shirts, she spent all her time with her mother, Patsy fitting on her western costumes and Hilda Hensley running them up on her sewing machine. When she wasn't at her mother's, she was on the phone with her mother, or rehearsing somewhere, or driving down to Washington, D.C., for Jimmy Dean's *Town and Country Jamboree* television show. God alone knew what she might be doing down there besides singing. She never did tell him.

Then, whenever she did finally come home, she challenged him in some way, threatening the even tenor of his life, trying to take his attention away from the only thing that brought him peace and pleasure, his clocks and watches. At least you knew where you were with timepieces. They were predictable. But you never knew from one minute to the next where you were with Patsy Cline. She wasn't a peaceful person. There was an aura of excitement about her that terrified him.

He was terrified now, as he looked at her watching him, waiting for him to answer her, daring him with her eyes. Her proud young body, outlined by the clingy satin fabric of the slip, made the palms of his hands go clammy. How could he satisfy a woman like that? Wretchedly, he turned his eyes away.

"Oh, Patsy, for heaven's sake...." he muttered weakly.

Gerald didn't see the look of pain cross his wife's face, followed by a wry smile and a poignant nod.

"I just wondered what you'd say," she whispered, more to herself than to him. *I guess I knew.* She forced a pleasant smile. "Good night, honey."

"Good night, Patsy," he replied, the relief showing in his face.

Slowly, she returned to the bedroom to finish undressing. Wearing her nightgown, she went to wash up. Without energy, she brushed her teeth. Listlessly, she pinned back her hair to clean the makeup off her face. As she wiped off the cream with tissues, she caught a glimpse of her face in the mirror; there was such a sorrow in those eyes, their expression so lifeless she wanted to cry.

"I can't stand it," she whispered to her sad-faced reflection. But only silence answered her.

There was only silence in the bed, too, quiet and lonely as the grave itself. Grabbing up her pillow, Patsy squeezed it hard, harder, pressing it against her own body as if to force the inanimate object to cry out, to speak to her. But the pillow said nothing. Salt tears began to flow down her cheeks, spilling hotly from her eyes.

"I can't stand it!" she wept into the heavy silence. "I can't stand it!"

How had it happened? How had she come to this loneliness when Gerald and she had once been so close?

Her thoughts turned inevitably to the way it had been at the beginning....

"Is this stool taken?"

Patsy looked around. The Brunswick Moose Club was usually full, but tonight was a slow night and the bar wasn't crowded. There must have been at least half a dozen other bar stools this big man could have chosen, but he'd deliberately picked the one next to her. Obviously, he must have something on his mind other than just a drink.

"Help yourself; it's a free country," Patsy shrugged,

watching him out of the corner of her eye as he sat down. She was having a soda between shows; the place would fill up later in the evening, and she might not get another chance to take a break.

He was on the tall side, and stocky, with a high-domed forehead and sandy hair. He had a pleasant face, and when he smiled across at her, it lit up and looked almost handsome. His age was hard to figure. Thirty, maybe, give or take a year.

Patsy herself wasn't twenty-one yet, but her life had been moving along at a pretty rapid clip in the last few years. Sometimes she felt like a child deprived of childhood; at other times, like a woman of forty.

She'd been sixteen years old when Samuel Hensley packed up and left home for good. That event made a grown-up out of her overnight. No way could Hilda Hensley support three children on her measly waitress job. Over her mother's protests, Ginny had left high school and gone to work full-time, down at Gaunt's Drug Store.

There, she tended the soda fountain, standing on her feet all day long, mixing ice cream into syrup and filling the glass up with foamy carbonated water, topping the soda off with a dab of whipped cream. These concoctions were placed on the marble counter for anybody with the price of a drink— fifteen cents, no small sum in those days.

Ginny made the sodas, Ginny washed the glasses, Ginny wiped down the marble counter with a wet rag and polished the spigots of the syrup containers until they shone. Ginny filled the tall glass jars with paper straws, Ginny lugged large vats of homemade ice cream out of the big freezer at the back. Ginny served up lime rickeys and lemon phosphates and banana splits and Coca-Colas with lots of crushed ice. It was tiring work, but at the end of the week there were two twenty-dollar bills to show for it, not to mention the nickel tips that were left for her from time to time. Her mother accepted the forty dollars gratefully; the nickels Ginny was allowed to keep as pocket money.

Two more important things happened at this time in her life. She began singing on weekends, almost professionally, with Bill Peer and his Melody Makers, at the Moose Club in Brunswick, Maryland. "Almost" professionally, because at first there was no money changing hands. But Bill gave her a start, and that was payment enough, for a while, at least. Later there'd be some money, as much as fifteen dollars an evening.

The second important thing was that she changed her name. After that awful evening with her father, which led inevitably to his leaving the next day, Ginny wasn't too happy about carrying the name he'd given her. Although at home she'd be known as Virginia and Ginny for some years to come, in the outside world she began to call herself "Pat," after her middle name, Patterson. Gradually, the Pat became "Patsy." Changing her name gave Patsy a sense of gaining control over her own life.

So, although she was only twenty now, she'd been working full-time for four years already. Working all week at Gaunt's, and all weekend with Bill Peer and the Melody Makers, singing country favorites.

For four years, men and boys had been hitting on her, at the drugstore and whenever she sang in public. At sixteen, she already had the ripe figure of a mature woman, with voluptuous hips and high, round breasts. Men just naturally gravitated to her, but she wasn't too keen on any of them. The vicious example of Samuel Hensley was always in the forefront of her mind, making her turn away from potential relationships, wary and frightened.

But this man on the bar stool next to her, the big man with the pleasant smile, he wasn't hitting on her at all. No propositions; his conversation was as much for the bartender as it seemed to be aimed at her. Patsy just sipped at her Coke and pretended not to listen, but her ears were perked by his stories of the war and the Battle of the Bulge. He was interesting; his conversation was intelligent, and he didn't sound like the rednecks she was accustomed to.

He didn't look like a redneck, either. This fellow was the closest thing to a gentleman that Patsy had seen in a while. He wore a jacket and a tie, whereas most of the men Patsy knew dressed in bib overalls and plaid flannel shirts. When he finished his drink and stood up to go, Patsy felt a real pang of disappointment.

"Who was that?" she asked the bartender.

"Name's Gerald Cline. His family's got some construction business over in Frederick."

"Is he rich?" she asked curiously.

"Family is. I don't know about him."

He'll be back, thought Patsy. *I'm sure of it.* But was she sure or was it just a wish?

He did come back, the very next Saturday night, and, joining her at the bar between shows, he smiled at Patsy as if they were already friends. This time, Patsy smiled back. She liked the fact that he was clean-cut and well-dressed; this time he had on a different sports jacket and tie.

"My name is Gerald Cline," he told her. "I really enjoy the way you sing. Do you live around here?"

"I live in the next state."

"Which one? There are three."

Patsy glanced slyly at him. "Oh, one of them," she said airily. No sense in making it too easy for him. Men didn't appreciate what they didn't have to work hard to get.

He offered her a drink, but all she would accept was a soda. Bill didn't like any of the musicians drinking between sets; besides, Patsy had discovered that she could get a little too fond of bourbon, so she kept herself away from it, drinking only cola or an occasional beer.

"I'd like to see you during the week," Gerald Cline told her. "May I?"

"I've got another job, so I'm usually pretty busy," Patsy said evasively.

She wasn't too keen on having this gentlemanly young man find out that she worked in a drugstore and that the Hensleys lived on the wrong side of the tracks. Ordinarily, that sort of thing never bothered her. Being proud and independent, Patsy Hensley expected the world to take her as she was, like it or lump it. But, sitting here sipping Coke with Gerald, she found herself suddenly shy and uncomfortable.

Not as uncomfortable, though, as when she looked up from scrubbing out the ice cream vat at Gaunt's the following Wednesday and saw Gerald Cline smiling at her from the doorway.

"How did you find me?" she gasped.

"I asked a few people who the best singer in town was, and they all said, 'The girl who works down to the drugstore.' So here I am, and there you are."

And that's how it began.

At the end of her working day, he came to call for her at Gaunt's, driving her home. What side of the tracks the Hensleys lived on didn't seem to make any difference to Gerald Cline. He made himself quite at home, sitting on the porch swing sipping Hilda's iced tea, being polite to Patsy's mother, and friendly to her brother and sister. He made no moves on Patsy, but asked if he could come again.

Suddenly, she found she had a boyfriend. Gerald was kind, serious, thoughtful. He brought little presents: a comic book for John, flowers for Hilda, a doll for Sylvia. He brought food and put it in the Hensley icebox, not out of charity, but as a gift of goodwill. Nobody had ever treated Patsy with such courtesy before, and she discovered that she kind of liked it.

Bill Peer was accustomed to picking Patsy up and driving her from Winchester to Brunswick to sing with the Melody Makers, but Gerald soon relieved him of that responsibility. Bill made no bones about not being pleased, but Patsy felt calm and secure with Gerald.

Calm and secure.

No man had ever made her feel that way before, unthreatened and peaceful. It was a new feeling, and one that would take some getting used to. And he sure was giving her the chance to get used to it. Gerald Cline was around all the time, seemed like. Every weekend, there he was, at the wheel of his Pontiac, waiting to pick her up and drive her to Brunswick, so he could sit and listen to her sing, with a proud smile on his face. During the week, he'd turn up in Winchester, sitting in the kitchen with the family or out on the front porch swing with Patsy.

By now, he was acknowledged by everybody to be Patsy Hensley's new fella. And everybody except Hilda presumed that the two of them were sleeping together. But they weren't.

Why weren't they? Gerald had yet to make his move; he was the perfect gentleman. Too perfect. On the night that he presented her with a beautiful silk blouse, Patsy made his move for him.

"I don't have to be home for a while," she murmured as she stepped into the car at the end of the evening at the Moose Club. And she looked hard into his eyes.

Almost by itself, the Pontiac headed for a quiet spot on the riverbank, where Gerald Cline took Patsy Hensley into his arms for the first time and kissed her full on the mouth. It was a long kiss and even a loving one, but there was little intensity in it, and no passion.

They kissed again, and this time Patsy took the lead. She opened her mouth and allowed her tongue to flicker across Gerald's lips until they, too, parted. Suddenly, passion flared up between them, and she felt Gerald's hand seeking her breast with an unaccustomed urgency. Gladly, she yielded herself to him, aware that they were standing on the threshold of something important to both of them.

Four

PATSY'S MARRIAGE TO Gerald Cline was a delicate subject between Patsy and Hilda. Having thrown her own life away at an early age, Hilda Hensley had not been happy to see her daughter rush into marriage only a few months after her twenty-first birthday. They had been married in the Clines' family church in Frederick, with Patsy all in white, her lovely dark hair covered in a lace veil, a corsage of lilies of the valley nestled fragrantly near her face.

Hilda had mixed feelings. Although she was glad to see her daughter happy, she was anxious about what would happen to her career. For sixteen years they had worked and sweated together, side by side, mother and daughter, to build Patsy's career. Ever since her triumph with the blue table lamp, both Patsy and Hilda had known what direction Patsy's life should take. She was going to be a singing star. It was what both of them wanted, Patsy even more than Hilda. Ambition ran in Patsy's veins like heart's-blood; she sometimes appeared to be not so much driven as consumed by ambition.

It had been little short of a blood sacrifice to dig up the money for dance lessons, but Ginny had been given dance lessons. The rest of the family might sometimes have to do without necessities, but on Virginia's seventh birthday her mother had presented her with a secondhand piano, bought on credit. Hilda considered it an investment.

Recognizing that Ginny's talent was not only a gift from

heaven but also a way out of hell, Hilda Hensley had turned herself inside out for the child, working extra long hours on her waitress job to pay for piano lessons and dance lessons, for pretty fabric to sew into little costumes, and anything else the budding star should happen to need. And Ginny also worked hard, learning new songs and new routines.

Just about every week, Hilda would gas up the battered jalopy and drive her little girl all over the state of Virginia so that people could hear her play the piano and sing. The two of them appeared at almost every church social in the state, every Elks Club benefit, every town meeting hall, and high school dance party. Never entertaining even the hint of a doubt, Hilda knew that her daughter was going to be a big star.

Wherever they went, audiences went crazy for little Ginny Hensley, responding to the big, strong voice coming out of that little curly-haired girl. There was a bluesy, torchy quality in Patsy's voice that set her apart from other country-and-western singers, particularly the women. In those days, "hillbilly" was almost the sole territory of men; there were very few women who'd hit it big in country music. You could name them on one hand and have fingers left over. Yet Patsy was determined to succeed, so determined that she never hesitated to walk right up to anybody, even the biggest of the stars, and ask them to listen to her sing.

When she was only sixteen years old, she'd marched into the studio at WINC, the local radio station, and asked— no, demanded—that Joltin' Jim McCoy put her on his show.

"I'm a singer and I want to sing on your show," she'd told him. "I ain't gonna ask you to pay me any money."

And big Jim had looked down at the child and asked her, "You think you're good enough to sing live on my program?"

"Yes, sir."

"Well, if you've got the nerve to ask for it, I guess I've got the nerve to give it to you." That's how Ginny Hensley began to sing on the radio, at least that's the story that made its way into the legend that was to grow up around Patsy Cline.

She'd done much the same thing with Wally Fowler when she was only fifteen, and already calling herself Patsy. A major country-and-western star, Fowler had brought his traveling show to Winchester and Patsy just snuck in backstage bold as brass and asked him to put her in his show. Took old Wally Fowler so completely by surprise that he didn't know where to look first, so he said yes, and Patsy had been given a great big hand by the folks who recognized her as the local girl who worked down to Gaunt's jerking sodas.

Fowler had been so impressed with Patsy's voice that he'd pulled some strings to get the most popular country show on television to give her an audition. The whole family had packed up and driven to Nashville, Tennessee, in a friend's car just to get Patsy on the Grand Ole Opry. They gave her an audition, and they liked what they heard. If Patsy had made it to the Opry right then, she would have been the youngest singer ever to do so. But there was a hitch.

The folks at the show, interested in using Patsy on the air, wanted them all to stay over another day, so that Patsy could audition again, this time for the people in charge. But the Opry people had no idea what they were asking. It was impossible.

Even though they'd all crowded into one cheap hotel room the night before, Patsy and Hilda didn't have a dime left in their pockets, after what it would take to buy gas for the ride home. And they had the two little kids, Sylvia and John, with them; there was that to think about. They had nothing to eat and nowhere to sleep, and you couldn't let little children go hungry. There was no way the Hensleys could stay. Probably, if the Opry show people had been aware of the situation, they'd have advanced the family fifteen or twenty dollars. But Patsy and Hilda were too proud to let the Opry people learn the facts of their poverty. It was their own problem. So home from Nashville they all went, and there went Patsy's first chance to sing on the Grand Ole Opry, and her only chance to be the youngest.

It could have made all the difference. There were so few chances for women to become country-and-western greats. In 1956, there was only Maybelle Carter, Kitty Wells, Jean Shepard, and one or two others. It was a man's world.

But Patsy had her dreams, and they were more powerful than the pale aspirations of other teenage girls. They gave her no peace. In her dreams, she wasn't the backwoods girl that the middle-class kids at school looked down on and made fun of. She wasn't the soda jerk at Gaunt's Drug Store, to whom the men and the boys who hung out there made leering propositions. She was somebody special. She was a star.

If she went to the picture show with her sister—and they went every single Saturday afternoon, after Patsy had finished work for the day, to Habell's Palace Theater downtown—the fire of her dreams were fed with new fuel.

For forty cents, you could see a movie and a stage show, local entertainers or even some second-class touring act. Patsy would watch and listen closely, and the conviction grew in her.

I'm better than that. I can sing better, dance better. It should be me *up there, not them.*

The movies were the only touch of glamour they had in their lives. She and Sylvia would sit in the dark, watching fascinated as Virginia Mayo or Betty Grable or Lana Turner would sashay across the screen dressed in a fabulous gown and decked out in jewels and furs. Patsy would imagine that it was herself up there on the screen, and a voice inside, a voice that was never silent, would tell her that she had what it took to be a star.

Becoming "a star" held many meanings for young Patsy Hensley. First, it meant that she would be able to take her mother and little sister and brother out of the crowded, shabby house on South Kent Street. She'd buy them the finest home in the Shenandoah Valley, with all the up-to-date labor-saving devices, like a toaster and a vacuum cleaner and even a refrigerator-freezer and washing machine. Hilda would never have to bend over a washtub again with a cake of yellow soap, a board, and a mangle. Hilda could be a lady. Sylvia and John would get good educations and make something of themselves. Neither of them would ever have to work in a drugstore, jerking sodas for a dollar and a quarter an hour.

It would mean that Patsy could dress in fine clothes, expensive clothes, and ride around in a Cadillac car. That's what she dreamed of, a big Cadillac, and a home of her own, with her own husband and children inside it, and yellow roses growing around it, climbing up the picket fence and sprawling in their fragrant glory upon the walls. She'd seen those roses once, growing on a rich man's red brick Federal-style mansion, and ever after those flowers spelled "luxury" to her.

It would mean, too, that the world was paying to hear *her,* Patsy Hensley, sing for them. They'd buy her records and line up to see her shows, because her voice made them happy. She wanted to get up there and make people happy, see their faces light up and their toes tap. She longed to entertain them, to make them forget their troubles, even for a little while, as she could forget hers when she listened to a song that she loved sung by a singer she admired.

But, perhaps most important of all, it would mean that Virginia Patterson Hensley was a "somebody." Not a poor white soda jerk from the wrong side of the tracks, but a *somebody.* And that meant more to her than all the Cadillacs in the world.

Meanwhile, though, all she could do was to go to the movies and dream.

In a favorite film of hers, Lana wore a fluffy sweater with a little black silk tie over it, and her hair tied up in a matching ribbon. For months, Patsy saved up her tips from Gaunt's until she had enough to buy an angora sweater at the local dress shop, and Hilda made her the tie and the ribbon to go with it.

Patsy's other passion was music. All she owned was a cheap little phonograph, but every penny she could scrape together was spent on records. She had Helen Morgan singing "Can't Help Lovin' That Man," and she'd sing along to the record again and again, never getting tired of it. She had Judy Garland, and "Birth of the Blues," which she loved, and brassy-voiced Kay Starr, singing "The Wheel of Fortune."

In her mind's eye, she saw herself, not Patti or Kay or Helen singing it on a giant stage. She cut pictures of Patti Page out of the fan magazines and pasted them on the wall of the room she shared with her sister. Someday, if she ever got any money, she'd go to a beauty parlor and have her hair done like Patti Page. And someday, she knew, she would be a country-and-western star.

Starting at sun-up, Saturday morning was "country time" on local radio. Weekdays were reserved for pop music and Sundays for gospel and hymns, but on Saturday morning WINC would broadcast country and western, with live groups. Every band in the area who was playing a gig on Saturday night would crowd into the radio station to claim a free half hour of promotion time to sell tickets to their shows. They'd play and sing their biggest hits, which were mostly imitations of Ernest Tubb or Kitty Wells, heavy on the guitar, the fiddle, and the bass.

One Saturday morning, early, Patsy tiptoed down the stairs.

"What are you doing up so early?" asked Patsy's mother. "You don't have to start work before eleven."

"I know that, Mama. I'm just going out for a walk."

It was a lovely morning in early spring, crisp and a little chilly, but with the promise of sunshine. Patsy walked up South Kent Street past the Mount Hebron Cemetery and turned north. Before long, she was out of town and in the countryside.

Only one building stood between her and the cornfields that stretched beyond. That was the low white shack with the transmitter tower, a little red light winking away on the top, sending radio signals and country music all over the Shenandoah Valley. WINC.

Walking up to the station, the girl pressed her nose against the large plate-glass studio window. Inside, she could see the pickers and singers waiting to go on the air, making easy good-ole-boy talk, rolling cigarettes or smoking ready-mades, comfortable and not nervous. In the control booth, the announcer was talking, the engineer making hand signals, as a new group got ready to go on the air. The first band had finished playing and was filing out, two fiddlers, a banjo and a guitar. Cars and vans kept pulling up to the station, and musicians would pile out of the vehicles, unpack their instruments, and head for the radio station.

It was the most exciting thing Patsy had ever seen. Her heart beat faster under her sweater, and she longed to join them. This was where she belonged.

Every Saturday morning after that, she came back to WINC to stand outside the station, looking in. After a while, the station personnel came to recognize the pretty little girl with the burgeoning figure and the huge dark eyes filled with yearning. They'd wave to her and smile, and she would wave back timidly, but never speak. It seemed to be enough for her to simply watch the country bands come and go.

But it wasn't enough. Patsy was only waiting until she felt she was ready.

At home, she had laid aside her Kay Starr and Patti Page records, listening instead to the so-called "queen of country music," Kitty Wells. Their voices were very different—Kitty's was high and thin, Patsy's full and contralto—but Patsy played Kitty's songs over and over, infusing herself with country.

One Saturday morning, she decided she was ready. With her heart in her mouth, she went down to the station as usual. While the last group was still performing in front of the single microphone, Patsy knocked at the station door.

The manager of WINC, John Morgan, opened the door.

"I was wondering when you'd say hello," he told her. "What do you want?"

Patsy swallowed hard. "I want to sing," she said, as steadily as she could.

The tall man looked down at the serious-faced girl. "We don't do auditions," he answered gently.

"But I can sing! I'd sound great with some of these groups. Why don't you give me a chance?"

Sammy Moss, the leader of the last group of the morning, had just played the last bars of his final number. In a few minutes, his band's instruments would be packed, and they'd be on their way to somewhere else, and this opportunity would be lost.

Morgan raised one eyebrow questioningly at Moss. "She's here every Saturday morning."

"I don't care if I don't get paid. I just want to sing," pleaded Patsy.

Moss returned Morgan's silent question with a shrug. "Fine with me," he said, and the members of his band nodded their agreement.

"What will it be, little lady?" Moss asked her.

"How about 'Slippin' Around'?"

The band spent a minute or two finding the right chords for Patsy's key, then they all trooped back into the control booth. One number. What did they have to lose?

As she heard her intro over the pounding of her heart, Patsy felt her legs turning to rubber. But as soon as she opened her mouth and let that voice of hers come tumbling out, rich and golden and happy, she knew it was going to be all right.

And it was all right. It was better than all right. It was toe-tappin', thigh-slappin' country-and-western music.

When the song was over, Moss asked her if she would come back next Saturday morning and sing with them again.

"I ain't leavin' here till then," laughed Patsy.

* * *

After all that hard work and slow progress, just as Patsy had struggled her way up to becoming a regular on local radio and had begun to appear on TV, she had to go and marry a boy she hardly knew. It got Hilda's goat, plain and simple, and it bothered her twice as bad that Patsy couldn't seem to settle down and take the bitter with the sweet. It didn't set well with Hilda that Patsy was doing all that moaning and hollering about Gerald after just a few years of marriage. So what if Gerald didn't drive her around anymore, or sit around and watch her while she sang? She wasn't alone, was she? Patsy still had Hilda, and Hilda Hensley would never let her daughter down.

Dragging herself out of bed early, Patsy fixed Gerald's breakfast, bagged him a lunch of baloney sandwiches and cookies, and watched him drive off to work. Tonight she was going to sing, as usual, at the Rainbow Road Club, but the rest of the day stretched out before her like a bleached desert with not a drop of water in sight. Every nerve in her body was raw and hungry, clamoring for something she didn't recognize and couldn't put a name to.

There were things she could do to keep busy. The laundry basket was full, for example. Or she might walk past the little community of tract houses and into the piny woods. Patsy loved the smell of the pine resin and the crunch of the sticky needles underfoot and the sight of her beloved mountains on the horizon. Or she could sit down at her old piano and rehearse a new song. She could iron a fresh costume for tonight and clean the spots off her white cowboy boots. Yet she couldn't bring herself to do a single one of these things. Instead, she went to see her mother, as she knew all along she would do.

It was no more than a ten-minute drive to Hilda's house, but Gerald was driving their only car. On foot, it was a good three-quarters of an hour of rapid walking, and Patsy arrived out of breath, because she had run the last quarter mile.

She found Hilda busy, as usual, cleaning up in the kitchen. When she saw the look on her daughter's face, Hilda laid down her mop and picked up a peck of fresh stringbeans. She knew she was in for a siege, and there was no use just setting idle. Handing Patsy two bowls, she led the way out into the backyard and sat herself down in the glider, filling the two bowls with the beans to string.

But Patsy Cline was in no mood to top-and-tail stringbeans. While her mother's hands kept busy and the bowl at her feet grew emptier, Patsy paced back and forth like a caged animal, puffing furiously at a cigarette. Whenever she was nervous or upset, Patsy would begin to chainsmoke, although, oddly enough, she never did learn to inhale. Because of the bout with diphtheria that had nearly cost her her life, Patsy was mortally afraid inhaling would give her sore throats and harm her vocal cords. But it never prevented her from turning the air blue with her cigarettes.

"I can't stand it!" she declared to her mother dramatically. "I just plain can't stand it one more day. It makes me want to scream and claw my face. What am I gonna do?"

Hilda looked a withered bean over carefully before discarding it.

"You didn't ask me how to get into this marriage," she observed dryly, "and I don't think you oughta ask me how to get out."

Patsy scowled deeply; the truth of Hilda's words bit into her and she shot her mother a black look. Yet it was an imploring look as well.

Hilda gnawed at her lower lip. Whether Patsy's griping was legitimate or not, her unhappiness was obviously very real. She relented just a little.

"He mean to you?" she asked Patsy, who shook her head no.

"He drink? Gamble?" Two more negative shakes.

"He chase the women?" Hilda demanded.

"*No!*" On that subject Patsy's denial was vehement.

"Then *what?*" Hilda was now out of mortal sins, and Patsy couldn't seem to come up with an answer.

"Come on, girl, tell the truth and shame the devil."

A profound sigh moved Patsy's shoulders. "As God is my witness, Mama, I don't know," she confessed. "I lay in bed last night and thought, 'Shit, what if I was blind? Or didn't have my legs or something?'"

"Watch that mouth," cautioned Hilda. She hated how Patsy could resort so readily to bad language; it was all them banjo and git-tar pickers she kept hanging around with. They all cussed as easily as they breathed.

But Patsy was so deep into her problems that she didn't even hear her mother's reproach.

"My life isn't so bad," she went on, her face troubled. "I look around and my life don't look so bad to me. I got a decent house, a man who loves me. I already sung on the television four times. So why do I have to force myself to get out of bed every morning of my life? Why, Mama?"

Hilda turned her face away from those beseeching eyes. "You always was hard to keep satisfied. Even when you was little."

"Oh, Mama, talk sense!" cried Patsy, irritated. "I'm not talking about when I was three—what am I gonna do *now?*"

Hilda shook her head. "Well, you might scream and claw your face—see if that'd help some," she advised dryly.

For an instant, Patsy's face crumpled as though she were going to cry. In truth, she did seem to be on the thin edge of tears a lot these days. But instead, she broke into a laugh and stuck her tongue out at her mother who, laughing, stuck hers back out at her daughter.

Then, feeling a lot better, Patsy grabbed up the bowl of beans and began to snap off the ends.

But she couldn't stay with her mother forever. Sooner or later, she'd have to go back to that house, to that husband, to that marriage. She'd have to come to grips with what was wrong between them. Was "lack of excitement" grounds for divorce? Was loneliness a legitimate reason for leaving home? Could she stand in front of a judge and tell him to his face, "Your Honor, there's just gotta be something more, and I can't seem to get my hands on it, and I need it to live," when she couldn't even say out loud what that something else was?

And if she told that judge, sitting up there so important in his black robe, that she ground her teeth in her sleep so hard she was getting a massive muscle in her jaw, that she didn't have to sprinkle the ironing because she was crying so hard her tears wet the clothes, wouldn't he chuck her out of his courtroom, ass first?

"But, Your Honor, I'm smothering. I'm choking to death!"

"Who isn't? Count your blessings. Next case."

Next case.

Meanwhile, life goes on. Friday night you sing at a high school dance, and your husband doesn't want to go to bed with you. Saturday afternoon you go see your mama, and she doesn't want to talk about what's ailing you. And Saturday night, while the whole world goes out celebrating, you gotta paint your face, plaster on a smile, and go sing your heart out at the Rainbow Road Club.

Actually, Patsy loved the Rainbow Road Club. It stood on a country road at the county line, just on the border between the two states, with enough of its premises in West Virginia to allow it to sell hard liquor. On Saturday night, it was the busiest dance party within miles, and its vast parking lot was filled to overflowing with cars and vans and pickup trucks.

You could always find the Rainbow Road Club because of the rainbow. A large electric rainbow, right out on the road, twelve feet high at its highest point and pretty as a speckled pup. Made up of hundreds of colored electric bulbs that switched on, stripe by stripe, red, yellow, green, blue, off, then red again, it lit up the dark with its colors, turning the night into something rare and beautiful. When you stood under it, bathed in its multicolored glow, you felt like you were on another planet, a place very different from plain old Earth.

Inside, it wasn't much different from roadhouses everywhere. A large bar, a small dance floor, a smaller bandstand, and a big neon-lit jukebox for when the band took a break. The lights were kept low for atmosphere; also, so you couldn't see the specks of dirt on the beer glasses.

What Patsy liked best about the club was the air of conviviality; hardly any fights broke out, because people were too busy having themselves a good time to pick quarrels. Another reason was that the drinks were expensive, and few men could afford to get really tanked up and argumentative.

It was a good thing she *liked* singing at the Rainbow Road Club, because it certainly wasn't her idea of the way to the top. Singing in the roadhouses on Saturday nights was a longer road to the Grand Ole Opry than could be measured in miles from West Virginia to Tennessee.

This was a real country-and-western club, Hank Williams style. Fiddles and a Jew's harp, along with the guitars and banjos, and no ballads in the repertoire. Patsy in her customary cowgirl getup, with sequins sewed to her western bodice, a full skirt of gingham trimmed in rickrack, a bandanna tied around her throat, and her Stetson pushed to the back of her curls, giving out with country. Singing full-voiced and happy, her head thrown back, her eyes shut tightly.

Patsy, opening her eyes, and seeing . . .

For a minute she didn't recognize him, even though he looked familiar. But with him standing there not five feet away from her, grinning, while the dancers pushed past him impatiently, it all came back.

This was the same damn fool who'd approached her last week at the high school dance! What the hell was *he* doing here?

Five

CHARLIE DICK COULDN'T get Patsy Cline out of his mind. Even the cold shoulder she'd shown him, even the fact that she was a married woman couldn't discourage him. This feeling was something new to him, this conviction that here was a woman who would be everything he ever wanted and more. And he knew he had to go with that feeling. If Patsy would just let him get close enough to talk to her, even for no more than a minute, he was sure he could make an impression. *Had* to! The magnetic pull she exerted on him was so strong as to be irresistible. And Charlie wasn't into resisting.

All he knew was her name, Patsy Cline, and that she sang at the Rainbow Road Club on Saturday nights, but that was all he needed to know right now. Thanks to his behavior last week at the high school dance, little ole Wanda had gone home with somebody else and still wasn't talking to him, but that proved to be a blessing. It left him without a date for Saturday night, which was exactly what the doctor ordered. Saved him from standing Wanda up, which he surely would have had to do.

He dressed for the evening with even greater care than usual, and Charlie Dick prided himself on being a snappy dresser. Picking out his most form-fitting shirt, a copy of an Italian style, he smoothed it over his chest and ribs and loved himself in the mirror. Then he put on his favorite sports jacket, a slubby Dacron tweed number with wide lapels, and pulled the collar of his shirt over the jacket, spreading it wide. His belt was studded with artificial jewels, his boots were polished to so high a gloss you could see every freckle on your face in 'em.

When he was fully dressed and looking fine, he had a few good, strong drinks to give him a glow like his boots and drove his sweet li'l self on out to the Rainbow Road Club, where he had a few more drinks while waiting for Mrs. Patsy Cline to make her appearance.

The minute he saw her, he knew he hadn't been wrong. Man, she dee-stroyed him, blew him right outa the water! Everything came together just right—the way she looked, that face and that body, and the way she sang, as though she was having the time of her life up there and would pay you to let her sing, 'stead of the other way around. She was so much woman that Charlie wondered what kind of man could have married her; he just bet she wasn't easy to live with.

Not easy, but a hell of a lot of fun.

As Patsy and the Kountry Krackers started making music, Charlie got up from the bar and pushed his way through the mob of dancers, a little surprised to find himself unsteady on his feet. When he was as close to the bandstand as he could get, he just stood there and looked hard at Patsy, grinning his damn fool head off. It didn't matter to him that he was blocking the floor, that he was the only person not dancing, that the dancers were giving him dirty looks as they had to shuffle in circles around him. Charlie Dick was happy as a clam. He wasn't more than five feet away from Patsy Cline. What more did the good life have to offer?

She hadn't seen him yet, because she was singing "Bill Bailey, Won't You Please Come Home" at full throttle, with her eyes shut, really digging the song. But she'd have to open up them baby browns sooner or later, and when she did . . . why, there'd she be, practically nose to nose with her future!

Then Patsy *did* open her eyes, and she found herself

staring into the grinning face of Mr. Hot Britches, her least favorite person! It actually made her miss a note, but she recovered quickly and continued with the song, trying to ignore Charlie.

But Charlie was impossible to ignore. As soon as he saw that flicker of recognition in Patsy's eyes, euphoria took hold of him and he became instantly high. First, he jigged in place, all by himself, but that wasn't enough fun. What he wanted was to get *into* the music, so he picked up his guitar and played the hell out of it, slapping it, twanging it, nodding his head furiously, and keeping time with his foot. When the dancers stared at him, he smiled cheerfully and gave the git-box another good thump.

Of course, he didn't have an *actual* guitar, just one made of thin air. But that didn't make no never mind to Charlie Dick.

When the song came to an end and the patrons burst into applause, Charlie cut loose like a madman, stomping his foot, whistling, cheering, and slapping his big plowboy hands together like cymbals.

"Goddamn, woman! You're good!" he yelled at Patsy. He turned to the crowd to inform them, in case they missed it, "I mean, that bitch can *sing!*"

He whirled back again to tell her, "You just put me away, darlin'," but the microphone stood empty. Patsy was gone, having stalked off the stage. What the hell?

Oh, good, there she was. He hustled his ass to catch up with those long legs striding away.

"I don't know if you rememb—"

"Take a walk," snarled Patsy over her shoulder, not turning around or even waiting for him to finish his sentence.

But Charlie was determined to explain himself. "No, listen . . . I really liked . . ." he sputtered to her back as she marched off.

Patsy whipped around to face him, and for the first time Charlie realized that she was mad, *good* and mad, in fact, Patsy Cline was madder'n hell. Her dark eyes sliced him to ribbons; the ice in her voice froze his bones.

"I don't know what you think you were doing while I was trying to sing," she told him angrily. "You think that was *funny*?"

"Hell," sputtered Charlie uncomfortably. "I was *listening*!"

A look of contempt crossed Patsy's expressive face. "I don't like the way you listen." She spat out her words with insulting clarity. "Take . . . a . . . walk!" Then she was gone.

Charlie Dick stood there as though somebody had taken a hammer and nailed his feet to the floor. His brain was racing. No woman had ever done him this way. Women were pliant, soft, agreeable creatures. They said, "yes, Charlie," and, "no, Charlie," according to his own wishes. Oh, sure, they got mad at him sometimes, and with good reason, like Wanda did just last week. But their anger was meaningless and soon over, a sun shower on a summer day. Then they'd be all soft and cuddly again and wanting their good-lovin' Charlie back.

But not this woman; this woman had backbone. This woman had balls as big as his, and he had big ones. More than that, this woman had no eyes for Charlie Dick.

Her rejection made him cold and then hot. For the first time in his life, he felt excitement like fire running through the veins of his body. He'd been hot for women before, but this ardor had cooled as soon as he'd possessed them and they held no more surprises for him. But this Patsy Cline was different from any woman he'd ever seen. The fever she raised in him wouldn't be quenched by the taking of her body. On the contrary, he could never drink his fill of those red-painted lips; just the thought of her hands and mouth made him hungry and thirsty.

He realized that she considered him a fool. Why not, when he'd behaved like one? And not merely once, but two times out of two. Shee-it! The thought of it went a long way toward sobering him up. She made him nervous, that's what. That's why he'd had to guzzle down a few before he could even face her. He stood in awe of her—her beauty, her arrogance, the fact that she was a little older, and above all, her talent. For the first time in his life, he felt his confidence waning in the presence of a woman.

Okay. That meant he had a long way to go just to get back to the beginning again. He had his work cut out for him, but that was all right. He'd show her what Charlie Dick was made of, that Charlie Dick didn't back off just because he'd been barked at and bit. Actually, he was one up on her, because he had some inside information that Patsy didn't have. Charlie knew that they were born to be together, the two of them. So all he had to do was convince Patsy.

Now that he'd seen her again, he was hotter for her than ever. He had to have her, had to taste her mouth with his, force his masculinity inside her so that she would know, would understand. The word "love" didn't occur to him, not yet. But it would. Even though he wasn't aware of it yet, Charlie Dick was in love with Patsy Cline.

His instinct was to go right after her, find her, and explain, but he realized on second thought that he'd better allow her to put daylight between them and cool down a little. It was obvious that right now she didn't want him in her face. And it wouldn't do *him* any harm to sober up. His foot had been in his mouth so often in these two meetings with Patsy that his breath must smell like shoe leather. He'd have a cup of black coffee, and *then* go find her.

He waited until the next break. When the band left the bandstand and the juke began playing, Charlie went in search of Patsy.

She was sitting having a drink with Mary Rose Dodds, the regular singer with the Kountry Krackers. Deciding on the direct approach, Charlie marched up smiling, hoping that Patsy wouldn't divine somehow that his heart was in his mouth.

She took one exasperated look at him and rolled her eyes up to Heaven. "Mer . . . ci . . . ful *GOD*!" she exclaimed.

"I wanna explain," began Charlie nervously.

"It's the Creature That Wouldn't Die," remarked Mary Rose with a sarcastic grin.

"He *won't go away!*" agreed Patsy. Neither woman was looking at him, and they were talking only to each other.

Now, by God, Charlie Dick was riled. There's just so much a man can take if he wants to stay a man. Patsy Cline had pulled this shit on him for the last time.

"Look, fool," he threw at her, stung. "I came over here to explain, to apologize for messing you up awhile ago. I was just enjoying your singing so much." The more he talked, the madder he got, pouring out all his frustration and longing into this one tirade.

"But now that I get a good look at Patsy Cline, she don't look so hot to me, anyway." He turned on his heel. "And I don't care if you *have* been on some half-assed television program, you don't sing *that* good! If you ever listened to a Kitty Wells record real close, you'd go home and slit your goddamned throat!"

And off he marched, carrying his indignation like a banner.

Patsy's eyes widened in astonishment. Nobody had ever dared mouth off to her like that before; nobody had ever had the balls. This little feller had balls, and he was... kinda cute. She liked the way his nose wrinkled and his chin dimple stood out when he got mad. And as for that remark about Kitty Wells, she'd make him eat those words stone raw before she was through, damned if she wouldn't.

No reason for him to stay sober now. Charlie headed straight for the bar and ordered himself a double bourbon.

"Seven and Seven," remarked a girl's voice from the bar stool next to his. He turned. Patsy Cline was just sliding that pretty ass of hers onto the stool. Charlie's jaw dropped in surprise.

Looking him straight in the eye, Patsy said, "At the high school last week, you said you wanted to buy me a drink. I want a Seven and Seven."

With those big, warm brown eyes of hers staring right at him, Charlie Dick's anger evaporated like a puddle on a windy day. Grinning, he signaled to the bartender. When the Seven Crown and 7-Up was placed in front of Patsy, and she lifted the glass with a little nod at him, Charlie felt such elation bubbling up in him that he was afraid it might boil right over and spill down the bar. All he could do was smile at her, his heart in his eyes.

"So," began Patsy pleasantly, "you've got the advantage. You know my name, but I don't know yours."

"Charlie. Charlie Dick."

She almost choked on the first sip of her drink, but managed to get it down with a great effort. *"Dick? Charlie Dick?"*

After all the years of smartass remarks, he still wasn't used to it. Where his name was concerned, Charlie had no sense of humor, just a sharp defensiveness. "That's right," he answered her shortly, defying her to make something out of it.

A dozen funny comments rose to Patsy's lips, but she pushed them back. Her instinct told her that this young man wouldn't find any of them humorous. She looked at him appraisingly, one feathery eyebrow cocked.

"So what do you want out of me, Charlie? I figure you didn't follow me to Rainbow Road just 'cause you're a fool for music."

The directness of her approach made Charlie uncomfortable. He wasn't used to women not acting coy. Here was Patsy Cline looking him straight in his face, just like a man.

"Hell, no," he bluffed. "I heard you always take a dare. I like that, and I wanna get to know you better."

But Patsy's innate bullshit detector was sounding the alarm, and the red warning light went on. "Okay, now what does that mean?" she challenged him.

Charlie shrugged. "It means I wanna know you better," he repeated evasively.

Patsy's level gaze bored into his face. She spoke softly, almost into her drink. "I figure when *you* say you want to know me better, what you really mean is you want a ten-minute screw in the back seat of your car."

He started as if she'd hit a nerve. The directness of her language and that mind-reading act of hers were too much for him. "Son of a *bitch*!" he cried, stung again. "You must think that thing you got between your legs is lined with gold! Damn it, woman, I can get tail anytime I want it. I don't have to come crawling after some mean-mouthed woman who's got a cob crossways? Hell, if I just want to bump uglies with somebody, I got lots of places to go for that!"

Patsy leaned back on her stool and regarded him with amusement. "'Bump uglies,'" she repeated with a grin. "What an awful expression. Jesus." Shaking her head, she said quietly, "You know who you remind me of? Me."

Her own words took her by surprise; the impact of them was like a blow. *That's the Lord's truth. This crazy peckerwood with the hot britches could be the other half of me. Now how 'bout that?*

Six

WHEN A MAN AND a woman are first attracted to each other, there is a physical and emotional tension between them that is so electric you can smell the ozone in the air. The two are drawn together like a magnet and a pile of iron filings, not because they want to, but because they have to, because nature won't have it otherwise.

The first time that Charlie Dick took Patsy Cline into his arms was only for a dance at the Rainbow Road Club, but just the sensation of her waist under his hand was enough to make him a lost man.

As for Patsy, she felt a humming along her veins like the singing of bridge wires in the wind. The touch of his hand at her waist raised something in her she hadn't known was there, and it left her gasping a little for air. She tried to fight against the feeling; Patsy Cline was nobody to jump into the rack with the first sweet-talking bozo who came down the pike. But there was something different about this Charlie Dick, something beyond his good looks and sharp clothes and fresh mouth. When he touched her for the first time, there was an inevitability about it that didn't bear fighting with.

At first Charlie held her as though they were strangers, steering her gracefully across the postage-stamp floor to Kay Starr on the juke, daylight between their two bodies. But after a few minutes, he tried to pull her closer. Without missing a beat, Patsy refused to yield, and removed herself firmly from the tightness of his clasp. Not that she wanted to.

She had to admit it to herself. The sheer physicality of this young man's presence had gotten to her, overwhelming her. She wanted to touch him, to wind her arms around his neck as they danced, press her cheek close to his, put one hand against the back of his neck, feel his belly hard against her own.

Being Patsy, she kept her cool and did none of these things. Getting laid was not what she was after; Charlie Dick had been right on the money when he'd told her that she thought that thing between her legs was lined in solid gold. Her sexuality was a big part of Patsy's personal fortune, and she guarded it like the legendary dragon guards his hoard, breathing fire at anybody who tried to steal it.

The world of country-and-western music could be a raw and raunchy place; all those horny banjo pickers and so few women singers. Patsy always had more propositions than she could number; sex was available to everybody. All you had to do was hold out your hand, and some dude would try to put his pecker in it. Patsy herself had done more than her share of hell-raisin', but that was before she was married, when there wasn't anybody gettin' hurt by a slow hello and a fast good-bye.

Since Gerald, things had been different. Patsy had fielded all propositions politely, thanks but no thanks, and the other musicians had respected her for it. No more drinking and hanging around with the boys after lights out. These days, she'd head straight home after every gig, usually with her mother driving the car. Maybe it was less fun than before, but it was what a woman agreed to do when she stood up in the church and repeated her marriage vows.

But Charlie had said he wanted to get to know her better, musical words to Patsy's ears. It was what she wanted more than anything in the world, somebody who'd know her better, care what she thought, listen to what she said. It put everything else in the shade.

Well, almost everything. When the record came to an end and the dance was over, Charlie removed his hand from around her waist and an actual physical pang of disappointment shot through her. But she didn't let him see it.

Dancing with Patsy was not like dancing with other women. There was a strong current of electricity flowing between them. It seemed to him impossible that she couldn't be feeling it, too. And yet she was so cool, friendly enough but distant. She didn't even want to dance close to him. He couldn't figure it.

By unspoken consent, Patsy allowed Charlie to lead her to an empty table and order drinks. He couldn't let her go now; he needed to be near her as a drowning man needs air.

"You know what gets me?" he asked as the drinks appeared. "That we grew up in the same town together and never even met. How was that possible?"

"Just lucky, I guess."

"You or me?" laughed Charlie.

Patsy took a long, cool sip and pressed the glass against her forehead to feel its icy refreshment on her skin. When could there ever have been a chance for them to meet? Here he was, sitting up so sharp and fine in his expensive jacket; how could she tell him about her early life in the cabins with their dirt floors and no running water, the privies in the backyard, the oil lamps in the kitchen?

"How come we didn't meet in high school?" persisted Charlie.

Patsy hesitated, finally admitting, "Well, I wasn't *in* high school all that long, you know. When my father walked out on my mama, I had to leave school and find me a job. I worked down to Gaunt's Drug Store for a few years."

"Did I know that, I would've come in and bought me a soda. Although if the truth be told, I was weaned on bourbon."

A great shout of laughter came from Patsy's lips. "I could have *guessed* that," she laughed. "I can read you like the morning paper."

A grin spread over Charlie's features and he tilted way back in his chair. "Read away, darlin', read away."

She cupped her chin in her hand and, closing one eye as if to study him better, gave him a long and searching look which took in the arrogant set of his shoulders, the cleanliness of his hands and fingernails, the neat part in his hair. This was no farmboy or mill hand.

"You got everything you wanted when you were a kid," she said finally. "Schwinn bicycles, a Bulova watch for your twelfth birthday. You were the apple of your daddy's eye, and spoiled *rotten*. You had it easy—shows in your face." She smiled. "How'd I do?"

Abruptly, the expression on Charlie Dick's face changed. His mouth hardened into a straight line, and the eyes became opaque. It was as though an iron gate had banged shut between them.

"Don't run out and buy no crystal ball," he said shortly. And changed the subject immediately.

"They told me that you make records, but I ain't heard any of them around."

"Then you ain't been listening," snapped Patsy. This was a touchy subject with her. In the two years since she'd signed with Four Star, she'd had only two sessions in the recording studio. And they hadn't led to any success at all.

In January 1955, they'd cut four songs, "Come On In," "I Cried All the Way to the Altar," "I Love You Honey," and "I Don't Wanta," three out of the four of which Patsy hated, and none of which she was allowed to choose for herself. "Come On In," had become her theme song, however.

Since none of them was a world-beater, Four Star had let the cuts sit on the shelf for a year, and her first single had come out only two months ago. So far, it didn't seem to be going anywhere at all.

Her second session had yielded up "Turn the Cards Slowly," "Honky Tonk Merry-Go-Round," "Hidin' Out," and "A Church, A Courtroom, and Then Goodbye."

"Hey, I heard that one!" said Charlie enthusiastically. "'A Church, A Courtroom, and Then Goodbye.' So that was you, huh? Pretty damn good."

But Patsy wasn't smiling. Her recording contract was a bone in her throat. She'd signed it back when she'd been singing with Bill Peer and the Melody Makers. Because Bill had given her her real professional start, he was sort of masterminding her career. His personal interest in her was pretty damn plain, but Patsy was a married woman and Bill a married man, so she kept him at arm's length. Yet, she allowed him to become her unofficial manager. Bill had the music business experience that Patsy still lacked.

When he heard from William McCall, president of the Four Star Record Company, based in Pasadena, California, Bill came to Patsy with their offer, all excited.

Four Star would agree to a three-year contract with Patsy, for a minimum of eight records. But there was a clause in that contract that Patsy didn't like the minute she read the fine print.

Four Star demanded exclusive rights to providing the songs to be recorded.

This meant that Patsy could not accept any songs—no matter how good or how suited to her voice—given to her by any songwriters not already under contract to or provided by the record company. She would therefore be totally at the mercy of Four Star's ability to recognize a potential country hit.

Also, her royalty was to be only 2.34 percent of the list price of the record, about half the standard royalty for a recognized recording artist at the time.

"I bet Kitty Wells has a better deal than that," she grumbled to Bill.

"I bet she does, too." Bill Peer grinned wryly back. "But Kitty Wells has already had some hits."

But what choice did Patsy Cline have except to sign? On September 30, 1954, she signed the three-year contract with Four Star; her witness, Bill Peer.

On the plus side, she was happy to have any record company signing her up at all. It meant that she was on her way at last. If you had a record label backing you, you could begin to feel successful.

But that clause—stipulating that she couldn't record any songs that weren't approved in advance by Four Star—had, as Patsy had feared it would, put a serious crimp in her budding career. Good songs were hard to find in any case, even harder for a country music woman than a man. Yet Four Star appeared to be more interested in having Patsy lay down cuts of music they already owned than in finding new songs and new songwriters for her special talents. And they hadn't backed her at all, not a dime for promotion to the all-important country music station DJs.

Charlie listened sympathetically, as though he understood completely the ups and downs of the music business. Patsy felt a warmth emanating from him, flowing toward her, and she was grateful for it. It was good to be able to talk to somebody besides her mother.

Her mother believed in Patsy so implicitly that she barely listened to her daughter when Patsy expressed disappointment with the slow way her career had been creeping along. Hilda was certain that anything left to Jesus couldn't fail, while Patsy was convinced that a few promotion dollars spent in the right places would be more effective than praying.

Hilda was too confident, and Gerald appeared to have lost all interest in his wife's career, but this here Charlie Dick was all ears and sympathetic attention. Patsy found herself talking compulsively, telling him every step she'd taken so far.

How after she'd sung for Sammy Moss, she'd become a regular over WINC on Saturday mornings, with Sammy and later with Jim McCoy. How when she was sixteen she'd joined up with Bill Peer and the Melody Makers, and how much faith Bill had placed in her. Because of Bill, Patsy had her record contract. Because of Bill, they'd had a second tryout with Arthur Godfrey. Because of Bill, she'd traveled to Hollywood for the first time, to cut her first record.

"I didn't care for Hollywood all that much," sniffed Patsy. "They treat us country-and-western singers like we was second-class citizens, and that William McCall, he was more of a businessman than a music man, seemed to me. And I *hated* the songs he picked. Lord God, I fought that man ever' damn step of the way!"

"Bet you did, too," grinned Charlie.

Patsy's pretty face fell as she remembered. "But I lost," she admitted. "I had to record all them turkeys he picked, and ain't one of 'em ever gonna be a hit."

"Tell me about the Godfrey show," urged Charlie. "I watch it ever' week, ain't never seen *you* on it."

"Nothin' much to tell, 'cause I ain't never *been* on it. Bill Peer kept pullin' strings until he got us an audition, so we drove on up to New York City to try out for the *Talent Scouts*. Never did get to see Arthur Godfrey; the man was just too busy, I guess. Was the furthest away from home I'd ever been up until then. 'Cept for that one trip to Nashville to try out for the Opry, I'd never been further away than Washington, D.C.

"We saw somebody they called a casting director, and they sent us into a studio to sing. We had only about fifteen minutes, and then they said they'd let us know, and that was just about all there was to it."

"Just about?" asked Charlie shrewdly, looking keenly at Patsy.

"Well," she said reluctantly, "they did call. Not Bill, though. They called me. Told me that I had what it taked but that the band was too hick and corny. Said that if I wanted to, I could come back without the band, and they'd put me on the show."

"And you said no."

Patsy smiled ruefully and offered up a little smile. "Yes, I said no. I ain't cut out to stab a person in the back, 'specially when that person's been good to me like Bill had been." She glanced at Charlie out of the corners of her eyes.

"Guess you must think I'm twenty kinds of a fool."

"Yeah, but an honorable fool. The kind of fool I'd like to have on *my* side."

A moment of silent warm feeling fell between them, and Patsy was almost embarrassed by it. Charlie's obvious admiration, while welcome, made her feel funny, especially after Gerald's coldness.

It was getting very late. The band had long ago finished its last set and packed up its instruments. The jukebox was silent. Everybody had gone home, including the bartender. Only old Mose was left to mop the floor, stack the chairs on the table, and lock up. And still Patsy and Charlie sat talking, oblivious of their surroundings, aware only of themselves and each other.

Once or twice the thought flashed across Patsy's mind that Gerald might be worried sick about her. She should have been home hours ago. But she dismissed the thought as quickly as it came; most likely he was so wrapped up in his clocks that time had no meaning for him except as something he could tinker with.

With all the things they'd talked about, Gerald's name hadn't come up once.

Now the floor was mopped clean, all the tables were stacked but their own, and Mose stood looking at the pair of them with a reproachful face that said he wanted to get along home to his own bed. It was time to go.

Reluctantly, they stood up, unwilling and unable to break away from each other, their friendship so new and fragile that it could snap like a twig with the first hard pull.

"Mose," Patsy said in a low voice, "let me take a bottle. And leave the sign on. I'll turn it off, okay? I promise." She slipped him a quick five bucks, which the old man pocketed with a nod.

They moved the party out of doors. It was a beautiful April night, cool and dry, too early in the year for mosquitoes. A high pale three-quarters moon was obscured by clouds that shone silver. The smell of pine resin was carried to them on the breeze, sweetening the night air.

Over their heads, the large electric rainbow still flashed, as Patsy had requested. The bulbs blinked—red, yellow, green, blue, off, then red again. Familiar though it was, it was nevertheless mysterious and beautiful, like some giant talisman symbolizing . . . what? A future, perhaps?

The only car left in the parking lot was Charlie's, the top down. Leaving the doors open, they climbed inside, and Charlie turned on the radio, fiddling with the dials until he found the station he wanted. Soft music filled the car.

The first nervous fever of their discovery of one another had passed, leaving them much more relaxed now. Sitting side by side like old friends, they passed the bottle back and forth, and quietly continued their conversation.

It never occurred to Patsy that, under Charlie's deft probing, she was doing almost all of the talking. He volunteered almost nothing about himself, while she was spilling out the story of her life.

". . . And then I just sort of . . . grew up. My daddy dumped us when I was sixteen." Her voice turned hard, and Charlie could hear in it a rage that would not die, a rage that went deeper than even she would acknowledge. The old man must have hurt her plenty.

"Anyway," continued Patsy, "Mama and I made out okay. She couldn't work too often, so I worked pretty steady since I was fifteen or so. Days at the drugstore, nights singing, whenever and wherever I could get the work."

"You made the livin' for your whole family?" Charlie gave a soft, respectful whistle.

"Well, Mama sewed for people sometimes, but basically, yeah, I did."

"Listen—all these things you said you wanted—answer real quick. Which do you want most?"

Patsy didn't hesitate even for an instant. The answer was always with her; it was what she ate and drank, what she breathed.

"I want it all, and I want it to be right. *Everything*. Ever since I was eleven or twelve, I've had my life mapped out. Maybe I haven't pushed too hard the last four, five years, but I'm gonna start."

She frowned as she saw Charlie grinning. "No, I'm serious. I'm gonna be a singer, make some money, then have kids and stop singing and raise 'em right. Have a big house with yellow roses all around." Her voice grew more gentle as her dream unfurled for him, as she showed him her innermost core.

"God knows *somebody* deserves to have a happy ending, and it might as well be me."

Charlie shook his head in admiration. "You know," he said softly, "I don't think I ever met a woman like you. I can *talk* to you just like a person. You know what that *means* to a man?"

Carefully, unhurriedly, he set the bottle down on the floor of the car and reached for Patsy. She flowed into his arms as naturally as she sang, and with the same unfettered joy. When their mouths came together in their first kiss, Patsy had a sudden sharp conviction that her fate had caught up with her at last. But all thought, all conviction, melted in the heat of the kiss, and she was lost.

It was a long kiss, by turns sweet, passionate, hungry. When at last they came up for air, Patsy was trembling, as much out of fear as desire. It seemed to her that somewhere during the kiss she had lost control of her life, she who had always fought so hard for her independence. Patsy who had always mapped out her next move like a general was now as timid and confused as the rawest recruit.

This man possessed a power that was overwhelming; there was mastery in his kiss and in the strength of the arms that crushed her against him. In the face of that power, Patsy felt herself growing weaker.

She expected him to kiss her again, to put his hands on her body, and she was ready for it, eager for it. Instead, he pushed her away from him and leaned forward to turn the volume up on the radio. The music swelled out, lush, full, romantic; the tune was an oldie, "Ebb Tide."

Taking her by the hand, Charlie led Patsy out of the car and pulled her into his arms for a dance.

It seemed like nothing more than a man and woman dancing to a car radio in an otherwise empty roadhouse parking lot. But in reality, there, in the sweet, fragrant coolness of an April night in West Virginia, under a rainbow of colored lights which shone so brightly they obscured the moon itself, two young people were fulfilling their destiny. As they slowly dipped and turned, the old world was turning right along with them.

Falling in love, Patsy Cline and Charlie Dick had found the center of the universe.

And this time Patsy surrendered her cool, allowing her thighs to press close to Charlie's, to feel with a sense of elation the hardness of his lean body tight against hers. With a sense of wonder, she brought her lips to his, asking without shame for his next kiss.

If it were possible, the second kiss was even more thrilling than the first. Their lips and tongues held a mutual acknowledgment of their desire, and a promise of fulfillment to come.

Shaky, breathless, Patsy broke the kiss, to look into Charlie's blue eyes with some amazement.

"I don't do this," she said, more to herself than to him. "But," she added firmly, "I'm doing it!"

This kiss held more ferocity than the others, more simple passion. Their tongues moved frantically, as though each needed to swallow the other up. Patsy could feel his teeth against her lips, but their painful pressure only added to the delight of the embrace.

This time it was Charlie who broke off the kiss, to lead Patsy by the hand back to the car. Rolling the top up, he pulled her almost roughly into the back seat with him and slammed the doors shut.

Now they were alone in their world. Now it would begin.

Never before had Patsy ever felt so ... *open*. With no one had she ever surrendered herself so completely to sensation, abandoning thought, care, everything. All she wanted to do was *feel*. She wanted to feel as though every nerve ending was completely and totally alive, as though she couldn't tell where she left off and Charlie began.

And she did; she felt exactly that way.

When it was over, and Charlie was kissing her chin, her neck, her eyes, it took Patsy a minute to come back into the real world. Her pulses were still racing, heart beating sixty to the dozen. Her body was covered with a film of sweat, and the curls at the back of her neck were soaked through.

The world as she'd always known it had been shattered forever, and something new and strange was unfolding to take its place. It wasn't the sex alone, although new doors had opened for her physically; it was the *rightness* of the two of them. They belonged together. All of a sudden, Patsy knew that with a conviction she had never felt about anything except her singing.

And now she knew what was lacking between her and Gerald. For the first time, she could see it, plain as a cloud on a sunny day. It wasn't that she didn't care for Gerald, or that he didn't care for her; it was that they didn't belong together. They weren't right. They didn't fit. Now she had found the man who fitted her completely, not only sexually but in every other way. Now, for the first time, she knew what was meant by the words "falling in love." You fell, you actually fell, off the top of a mountain and into a brand-new world. Well, she had fallen and her brand-new world was this funny, crazy, not-very-tall blue-eyed man she was clutching in her arms.

"Oh, Charlie," cried Patsy, and tears caught in her throat,

thickening her voice. "Oh, Charlie. I was starving and I didn't even know it!"

Above their heads, the prophetic rainbow flickered from red to yellow to green to blue and back to red again.

March 5, 1963

M AYBE SHE'D BEEN WRONG not to drive back to
Nashville with Dottie West instead of trying to fly. A good
friend, Dottie had urged her not to fly, anxious about the
weather, anxious about the small size of Randy's plane,
about Patsy's cold, and about Patsy in general. Two years
ago, Patsy had made a gift to Dottie of her precious scrapbooks, all the clippings of her professional life—the newspaper and magazine stories, the reviews, the interviews, the
press photographs, the programs from the Grand Ole Opry—
everything that Patsy and Hilda had pasted so lovingly into
the big books over the years.

When Dottie had protested that you couldn't just give a
record of your life away to somebody else, Patsy had just
laughed that full, big laugh of hers and said, "Hell, honey,
you might's well take 'em. I ain't never gonna live to be
thirty anyhow."

*Well, surprise, I have. I'm over thirty. Seems downright
strange to be thirty-one years old. Wonder why that is, when
I've had to be a woman near most of my life. Never did get
much of a chance to be a little girl.*

Dottie had sworn up and down that there was plenty of
room in her car, and if there wasn't they'd *make* room; had
pressed her to come along, promised her that they'd be in
Nashville long before Randy's plane ever left the ground,
but Patsy had been stubborn. It was a long drive, flying
was a lot faster, and she wanted to be home with her chil-

dren, with Julie and little Randy. Besides, it would upset Randy Hughes if she walked out on him now. It would show a lack of confidence.

At the mention of Randy Hughes's name, Dottie had fallen uncomfortably silent. Seems like everybody knew about their growing closeness. Patsy shrugged it off; she'd carried enough ugly secrets in her lifetime, and this one wasn't near as bad as some.

Now, Patsy looked at her watch. Six-thirty in the morning. It would be an hour later in Virginia, and her mother would be up and in the kitchen. It wasn't too early to call. She was eager to hear Hilda's voice, to learn some news of the children. Little Randy had been sick with a cold when Patsy had left for New Orleans; it was almost certainly where Patsy had caught her own cold.

She emptied her handbag for change, stacking up the quarters, nickels, and dimes and counting them. Not enough.

Looks like I gotta take up a collection.

The men groaned as she approached them with her hand out, because everywhere they went she kept throwing their money away in telephone booths, but they dug down and came up with all they had.

As she listened to the quarters banging and the dimes dinging into the coin slot, Patsy crossed her fingers that all was well at home. When she heard her mother's voice, sounding normal, she exploded into the phone.

"Mama? Patsy. We spent the whole damn night in the airport waiting for it to clear up. Yeah, that's right, we're still in Kansas City. How're the kids? Randy's cold? Yeah, well, I caught it, good and proper. Tell him that for me, he gave his mama a cold. I know, Mama, I'm antsy, too. Seems like forever since I seen y'all. First *spot* o' sunshine we see, we're takin' off. He did? He bought 'em ice cream? Well, that's okay, I knew he couldn't stay away from 'em. Yeah, I know, I know, Charlie's a doll. He's always a doll ... 'cept when he isn't. Give the babies sugar for me. I'll be seeing you real soon ... I hope. 'Bye, Mama."

Hanging up the phone, she rejoined the others. As she approached, Randy was grinning widely at her. Instantly, Patsy understood. They'd been cleared for takeoff. She ran to the airport lounge window. The rain had stopped, and a thin ray of sunlight feebly attempted to warm the still-watery sky.

"Hoooo-EEEEE!!" yelped Patsy gleefully. "We're goin' home! Race ya to the plane."

Grabbing up Julie's doll and Randy's teddy bear, she ran through the door and onto the runway, where the Comanche 250 sat fueled for takeoff. Hawk, Cowboy, and Randy, burdened down with the bags, couldn't catch up with her long legs and joyous spirit.

Laughing, they scrambled aboard, Randy in the pilot's seat, Patsy beside him, and the other two in the back.

"Hell, this sure beats drivin'," chortled Cowboy Copas.

For a minute or two, they sat there while Randy checked his flight plans and charts against the latest weather advisories. The storm had moved on, but it was vitally important that they stay clear of it, tracking it by radio from the ground. Then, satisfied, he got his instructions from the tower, started up the engine, and they taxied smoothly down the runway and set off into the sky.

Seven

GOING HOME MEANT that Patsy would have to face Gerald. This wasn't the first time she'd faced up to him. Two years ago, they had separated on her insistence, but after a few months apart, they'd gotten back together again. Gerald had pleaded to have her come back. The tears had stood in his eyes, threatening to fall, and melting Patsy's heart. Besides, she didn't have anybody else to be with, so it might as well be Gerald. But this time was different.

This time it would be for good. This time she had Charlie.

This time the separation would have to stick. Guilt was on her side. In all their married life she'd never walked in the door with a torn blouse at six o'clock in the morning, and she wasn't feeling too good about doing it now. But the sooner it was over with, the better it would be for everybody involved.

What Charlie wanted was to take her right home with him, home to his house, and never let her go.

"Come with me, Patsy," he'd begged, his lips tickling her neck just under her ear, his hand fondling her breast. "Let me take care of you from now on. You don't want to go back there. We belong together."

Patsy had recognized the truth in his words, but her mind was made up. Lover or no lover, she owed Gerald Cline the honesty of meeting him face to face and telling him she wanted a divorce. Furthermore, she had no intention of moving in with Charlie Dick, at least not yet. Not until she knew him a whole heap better.

"Where will you go, honey?" demanded the puzzled Charlie.

"Home to my mama." And she meant it.

So Charlie drove Patsy back to the house in Frederick she shared with Gerald, the house she had never thought of as her home. Promising to call him later, she gave Charlie a long, hard kiss good-bye, and went in to face her husband.

That Gerald was deeply angry was evident as soon as she clapped eyes on him. The muscles of his jaw were twitching, but Gerald didn't hit her, or carry on, or even yell, and that didn't make it any easier for Patsy. She knew that he loved her in his own way; the trouble was that Gerald's way was no longer Patsy's way. Most likely it never had been.

But to tell the honest truth, concern for Gerald was not uppermost in Patsy's mind. Freedom was. Being free and being with Charlie. She'd had a taste of something special, and had developed such a hunger for it that nothing and nobody could be allowed to stand in her way.

What she said to Gerald that morning she would never think about afterward, but she knew it was not her finest hour. She didn't mention Charlie's name, not once, but all Gerald had to do was look at her, sweaty, rumpled, the smell of another man's body still on her skin, to know what she'd been up to, even if he didn't know who she'd been up to it with.

"Patsy? That you?" The lights were on in the living room.

"It's me, Gerald." She drew a deep breath and squared her shoulders.

"Pretty late, isn't it?"

She nodded. "Later than you think, Gerald. I want out." She forced herself to look him right in the eye, forced herself to remain cool while she saw his face grow white and a stunned expression clouded his brow. His big hands doubled into fists, but he didn't utter a single word.

Perhaps if Gerald had shown her what was in his heart, perhaps if he'd acknowledged, there and then, that something had gone very wrong between them even before this night, she might have shown him a different face than this one of ferocity mingled with joy. Perhaps she might have been less obviously eager to be free *now,* right this very minute. Perhaps if he hadn't been so controlled, she wouldn't have been so wild.

Perhaps if he'd shown her how much she was hurting him, Patsy wouldn't have gone on hurting him so bad. But, as always, he hid his feelings from her, shutting her out. More than ever, she was convinced of the rightness of this move.

As it was, Gerald remained expressionless while a rumpled Patsy, her eyes blazing like the Archangel Michael's, expelled him from Eden with the flaming sword of her newfound passion.

"I can't take any more of this. This whole situation has made me crazy. You never talk to me anymore. You don't even care what I'm thinking or feeling. We're not a married couple, we're two strangers living under one roof. I don't want to live with you another day. You can have the damn house, you can keep the furniture; I'm going home to my mother. Please don't try to stop me. I want a divorce."

And all that Gerald Cline could do was open his hand and let the trapped bird fly free. If he hadn't, she might have pecked him to death in her frenzy.

"Well, Patsy, if it's your considered opinion that you want a divorce, I'll not stand in your way." His voice was as stiff as his words, stiff with unexpressed anguish.

It was over. She'd faced up to him, and he'd backed down. She told him she was leaving him; what was the point of staying a minute longer? She was free. All she had to do was walk out that door. *Thank you, Jesus.*

Her heart hammering in her chest so loudly it filled her ears, Patsy ran into the bedroom to pack. She grabbed a couple of suitcases down from the shelf in the closet and began flinging her clothes into it any which way. Shoes landed on top of dresses, her precious professional costumes were crushed in with her oldest dungarees, her bottles of cologne and jars of cosmetics thrown haphazardly into the pile. When the cases were loaded, she stopped. She didn't look into the closets or the drawers to see if she'd forgotten anything; she had everything she could carry, and that was enough. That and her freedom. That and her freedom and Charlie Dick.

She knew that divorce was not a pretty business, and that she'd have to face Gerald Cline at least one more time, in a court of law. There were things to divide up—the house, the furniture, the car. Despite what she'd told him just now, she'd earned them just as much as he had; money from her singing had gone to buy everything they owned in common, and she was entitled. But she didn't want to think about any of that now. Time enough when the time came, as her mother always said.

Her mother. Suddenly, Patsy wanted to see her mother more than anything in life.

She carried her suitcases past Gerald, and he made no move, not to help her, not to stop her. Once out the front door, she ran to the Buick and threw her bags into the back seat. The keys were in the ignition, praise the Lord. They'd have to have a discussion very soon about whose car it was, hers or Gerald's, but right now she needed it more than he did. Stepping on the gas, she peeled out of the short driveway and into the street. Gunning the motor hard, she sped away, not looking over her shoulder and not drawing a deep breath until she had reached her mother's house in Winchester.

Hilda was busy canning spring berries when Patsy came roaring up in the sporty Buick Roadmaster. It was Sunday morning; church bells were ringing all over Winchester, calling the faithful to prayer. But prayer had to wait when the fruit was ripe, because the Lord hated waste. The kitchen smelled like an orchard; syrup was boiling in the big old kettle on the stove, and rows of sterilized Mason jars filled with dark red fruit lined the scarred wood of the old work-table.

Hilda was so busy sealing a new batch of jars with a thin layer of paraffin that she didn't hear the car drive up. The first thing she heard was the front door slamming, then a clattering of feet like a herd of crazy elephants. She looked up, startled, to see a sweaty Patsy in the doorway with her hair all messed, her clothes torn, two great big suitcases in her hand, and a smile smeared all over her face like butter on a biscuit.

"What in the ever-lovin' world—" she began, but Patsy interrupted her.

"I feel so good, Mama, don't give me one of your dark looks. I feel so damn *good*!"

"What's them suitcases?" Hilda demanded, eyeing them suspiciously.

"I left him," grinned Patsy, her face incandescent.

"Patsy—" began Hilda, but her daughter wouldn't stop to listen.

"I don't care, I don't care, I don't care, I don't *care*!" she almost sang.

At that moment Hilda Hensley had one of those flashes of intuition for which mothers all over the world are famous.

"There's a man," she said flatly. It was not a question.

"No, I'm doing this for me," answered Patsy, but she didn't meet her mother's probing gaze.

"There's a man," Hilda stated again, her mouth set in a thin line of disapproval, a deep line appearing between her brows.

"No," said Patsy, this time more weakly. "Oh, honey, baby, dumpling, be *happy* for me!" she pleaded, grabbing her mother around the waist.

But Hilda wasn't buying any of this. She knew that there was a lot that Patsy wasn't telling her. She pulled herself away from her daughter and took up the arms-folded stance that Patsy always called "Mama's Bible-preachin' position."

"Does Gerald know?" she asked shortly.

Patsy nodded, and a pang of guilt shot through her. But she kept her voice and words light.

"I stopped by and told him on my way here. You know what he said?" Now she slumped her shoulders and put a hangdog look on her face as she imitated her husband. "He said, 'Well, Patsy, if your considered opinion is that you really want a divorce, I'll not stand in your way.'"

Her mimicry of Gerald Cline was so mischievously accurate that Patsy's mother had to fight back a smile. But the frown reappeared when she saw her daughter spinning around the little kitchen, barely able to contain her joy.

"There's a man," she said again accusingly. "You're too happy."

No longer could Patsy deny it. Her face turned a warm pink, and a small, embarrassed smile creased the corners of her full lips. "Yes, there is," she confessed almost shyly. "Well, there may be.... Hell! I don't know, but oh, sweet Jesus! It *feels* so right!" Turning to her mother, she pressed her hands together prayerfully.

"Oh, Mama, be *glad* for me!" she implored.

When she saw the incandescent face her daughter presented to her, saw the glow in those dark eyes, Hilda Hensley relented.

Tears shone in the eyes of both of them as they hugged each other hard.

Dear sweet Lord Jesus, prayed Hilda, holding her daughter tightly in her arms, *please let this be the right man for her, Lord, so she can stop hurtin', settle down, and be happy. But oh, Jesus, with two kids in the house already, where am I goin' to* put *her?*

And so Patsy Cline began her new beginning in her mama's house like a little girl. It would seem to her later, looking back, that she was laughing all the time back then, just after she took up with Charlie, and that the sun was shining every single day. No doubt she was right, because it was springtime, and spring in Virginia is as beautiful a season as you can find anywhere in the world. The Shenandoah Valley is a vibrant green, and the aroma of flowering bushes and shrubs—rhododendrons, mock orange, apple trees, magnolias, lilac, dogwood—follows you everywhere. On either hand, the mountains—to the east the Blue Ridge, to the west the Shenandoah Mountains of the Alleghenies—cast their majestic shadows on the valley. Covered with full-grown pine trees whose conical tops reach out to the heavens almost to the mountains' crests, in the late afternoon sun the summits glow dark green, with peaks showing pink above the timberline.

A country of bluegrass and thoroughbred horses, of apple orchards and rich bottomland for farming, watered by the Cacapon River, Winchester is an inspiring background for a young man and woman in love in the spring.

Patsy Cline and Charlie Dick were in love. Charlie had never thought twice about it, and Patsy had given up trying to deny it. It was official. They were in love.

It was less of a tight squeeze in Hilda Hensley's house than she had imagined. They made do. John had given up the tiny bedroom he called his own and went to sleep on the davenport in the parlor. Hilda and Sylvia went on sharing the larger bedroom, and Patsy was given John's room.

But it often didn't work out that way. There were many nights that Patsy didn't come home to sleep at all, and John wended his sleepy way back into his own bed. On such occasions, Patsy's mother forced herself to bite her tongue. First, because nothing she could say against it would mean a thing to that independent, stubborn mule of a daughter of hers. And second, because Patsy was so very happy.

The French have a saying: The more things change, the more they remain the same. Maybe rich folks can afford to be in love twenty-four hours a day, seven days a week, but poor folks have to earn a living.

It was glorious for Charlie to go to work now, to march into the offices of the *Winchester Evening Star* and join the other linotypers, knowing that they knew that the famous sexy singer Patsy Cline was Charlie Dick's lover. It made him feel like some conquering hero out of the history books— Alexander the Great, maybe, or General Robert E. Lee. Patsy Cline was his woman and nobody else's. She loved *him*, Charlie Dick, and nobody else. She lived for the moments that they were naked together in his bed.

Now it was Charlie, not Hilda, who drove Patsy to her singing dates—down to Washington, D.C., for Jimmy Dean's show, the *Town and Country Jamboree*, over to Springfield for the *Ozark Jubilee*, and to the place they first met, to the Rainbow Road Club, where she still sang with the Kountry Krackers. It was Charlie who, dressed up and looking sharp, sat at the best table in the house, nearest the bandstand, while his woman stood up there on the stage and mowed the people down with her singing. She made him proud. It made him proud, too, to accept the drinks that so many people offered to Patsy Cline's lover. Some evenings it was too many drinks, and Patsy had to drive the car home and put him to bed, but she never did seem to mind much. Because they were in love.

As for Patsy, she'd never sounded so good. Music came tumbling out of her mouth with a life of its own, and every note said, "I love you, Charlie." She'd never had so much energy in her life. Where she used to have to drag herself out of bed, she now bounded up first thing in the morning, ready for whatever the day might bring. But it was the nights she lived for. The nights with her music and her man.

Even her career was getting off the dime. In the summer of '56, Bill McCall sent for Patsy to come out again to Pasadena, to the Four Star offices. He played her a song over the telephone. Patsy hated the damn tune, but she agreed to get on a plane. Any action was better than none at all.

Four Star had signed up a new songwriter to a long-term contract. And Donn Hecht's first assignment was to find a hit song for a young country girl singer named Patsy Cline.

"I've spent a fortune releasing her," growled McCall, "and she hasn't earned me a dime. I'm getting ready to drop her, since she'd bombed out every single damn time. Why the hell is that?"

"Are you sure she's a country singer?" Hecht had asked. "I don't think she is at all."

Not too crazy over hillbilly music himself, Donn Hecht had heard a dark velvet in Patsy's voice, even in the technically awful, mediocre recordings she'd already completed. To Hecht's musical ear, Patsy Cline sounded more like a pop vocalist in the Patti Page tradition. Her lovely voice had none of the nasality he associated with country-and-western music. It was a voice that could take you apart and put you back together again.

There was a huge stack of yellowing unpublished material in the Four Star offices, and Hecht had dug through them, coming up with a song that had been written for Kay Starr, but she'd never recorded it. It was a pure B-flat blues called "Walkin' After Midnight." Donn Hecht performed what he called "minor surgery" on the song and had it demonstrated for McCall, who accepted it.

It was this song that McCall had telephoned Patsy about. When he told her the title, she said she hated it; then he played the song over the telephone to her, and she hated the song itself even worse than the title.

As soon as Patsy Cline got off the plane, the squabbling began. She didn't want to record "Walkin' After Midnight" because, as she said, "It's nothin' but a little ole pop song."

"And you ain't anybody but a little ole pop singer," barked McCall.

The cards were on the table, and McCall held the winning hand. If Patsy didn't agree to record "Walkin' After Midnight," she'd be in violation of the terms of her contract and could be dropped. No, damn it, *would* be dropped. On the other hand, if she *did* record the song and it flopped, that could also be the end of her career with Four Star.

Heads you win, tails I lose. It hardly seemed fair.

Surprisingly enough, Donn Hecht agreed with Patsy. To him it also seemed unfair to fault Patsy Cline for the failures of her records when the blame lay elsewhere. The songs were poor, the record quality was poor, and the advertising and promotion budget was totally nonexistent. Nobody should be asked to function under those conditions.

Of course, neither of them said a word of any of this until Bill McCall left the room to go for coffee.

Then, for the first time, they faced each other honestly, singer and songwriter, and discovered, to Patsy's surprise, that they genuinely liked each other.

By the time McCall came back into the room, Patsy and Donn had struck up an agreement.

"Tell ya what," proposed Patsy. "I still don't like this 'Walkin' After Midnight,' but I'll record it for you, if you'll let me back it with a song I like, 'A Poor Man's Roses.' If your side is the hit, I'll never complain about my material again. If my side is the hit, you have to let me pick my own songs. Deal?"

McCall looked at her hard. "What if neither one of them is a hit? What if we turn out another flop?"

Patsy shrugged, but a shadow crossed her face. "Well then, I reckon," she said slowly, "you better get yourself another singer."

"That's a deal!" cried Bill McCall.

Eight

NEVER WERE THERE TWO lovers like Patsy and Charlie. The more they bit into the apple of love, the hungrier they became. Too much of the good thing was never enough. It just kept getting better and better.

What Patsy liked best was Saturday night and all day Sunday. On Saturday night she'd always be singing somewhere, with Charlie right down front, his eyes shining with pride. That glow of pride in him made her so happy; she'd never seen anything like it in Gerald's eyes. Whenever the band took a break and the jukebox started playing music, he would take her into his arms and they would dance together, smooth and slow, pressed tight up against each other's bodies, Patsy's arms around Charlie's neck, his big hands around her waist, sometimes dipping to caress her buttocks, and who cared who was watching them? Let the whole damn world know that Patsy Cline was in love. It was nothing she was ashamed of.

Then, driving home, her head on his shoulder, watching his good-looking profile as he drove with one hand, the other arm wrapped around his lady. The pair of them knowing what was in store for them once they got to Charlie's house. Even Charlie's mother accepted Patsy, really liked the 'good old Virginia gal,' so there was no sneakin' around.

Some Saturday nights were different; those were the nights when Charlie had too much to drink and Patsy did the driving. When their lovemaking was awkward and over too

99

fast, thanks to the bourbon. When Charlie fell asleep like a rock and snored loud enough to wake up the dead in the Baptist churchyard. But Patsy bit her tongue against the harsh words that formed in her mind. She loved him; he worked hard; wasn't he entitled?

Still, most nights they got home in one piece. Patsy would be tired, but it was a good kind of tired, a tired that came from making people happy with her talent. She had been standing in front of a microphone for hours, tapping her feet and singing her heart out, but to her it was the only kind of life that was worth living. There was a rush that came from applause that nothing else in the world gave you, not even sex. But it left Patsy totally exhausted. She'd sink down on the couch in Charlie's living room, and her man would kneel in front of her and pull off those white cowboy boots that were part of her trademark and of which she was so proud.

Then, with the boots off and Patsy wiggling her cramped toes with a sign of luxurious relief, Charlie would begin, ever, ever so slowly . . . rubbing her feet, his hands on her calves, soothing the aching muscles, then up along her thighs, silk under his fingers . . . then Charlie scooping her up in his strong arms as though she were feathers, not flesh, Charlie carrying her up the stairs to his bedroom. . . .

Saturday night loving with her man. It was something to sing about. Falling asleep in his arms, a satisfied smile on her face and peace in her mind. And sometimes, hours later, waking up to find Charlie lying behind her, spoon-fashion, his strong body curled around hers. And she'd smile into the darkened room, both of them going back to sleep that way. Or maybe they wouldn't. Maybe they'd be wide awake all over again, hungry and thirsty for each other, grabbing and biting and kissing and loving.

But what she loved the most were the long, lazy Sundays. Getting up late, leaving her man still asleep in the rumpled bed. Running the bathwater so hot it could peel off her skin, but that was the way she liked it. A long soak in scented water, washing the aches and weariness from her round young body. A good energetic shampoo that left her curly hair shining. Patsy in a bathrobe, her hair wrapped up in a towel like a turban, down in the kitchen squeezing fresh oranges, making the coffee.

The smell of the coffee waking Charlie up, sending him ravenous into the shower. Charlie coming down all sweet and clean and shaved and starving, to find the bacon cooked and the eggs in the pan and the coffee steaming in the cups.

Patsy and Charlie, after breakfast, their bellies full, the day like a promise stretched before them, trying to decide what to do with their Sunday afternoon. Their time belonged to them. A picnic, a row, a swim, a drive, but first . . .

Ah, they did everything, those two! They made long, languorous love. They ripped off a quickie. They fucked like a pair of gladiators, punching and biting, each of them determined to vanquish the other, to hold out from completion the longest, to keep possession of the arena. Each of them losing, and winning by losing. And sometimes they laughed in bed, and sometimes they cried, weeping tears of surprise and happiness at the wonder that was the two of them together.

Patsy Cline and Charlie Dick were in love.

The first time he took her to his house, her eyes opened wide in astonishment. The disorder was catastrophic; sitting in the center of the living room, for example, was a car engine that Charlie had been working on in his spare time. A car engine!

"This place is a stone mess!" exclaimed Patsy.

Charlie grinned assent. He was used to hearing that from a woman; it always meant she'd turn up the next day in an old cotton work dress, her hair tied up in a bandanna, a broom and a paper bag full of clean rags and Bab-O in her hands. Whoever it was, she'd send him off somewhere out of the way, while she scrubbed and mopped and polished and cleaned the house from top to bottom. He'd come to expect that from his women.

"I mean, this place is a by-Jesus *pigsty*!" roared Patsy.

"Surely is," Charlie agreed in happy anticipation.

"Well, I'm gonna tell you something, Mr. Charlie Big-Dick. Afore I set foot in this place next time, you'd better have it cleaned up! Hard scrubbin'! I want to see it shine! Are you listenin' to me?"

He was listening. And he obeyed, because that was a big part of what he loved about her the most, that independence of spirit, the strength that set her apart from other women.

There was a down side to that independence, though. She wouldn't move in with him, not even after she started spending so many nights in his house. She'd always get up in the morning, cook him his breakfast and bag him his lunch, climb into her red Buick roadster, and drive home to mama.

The other thing was that Patsy wasn't so keen on letting Charlie into that other life of hers, Hilda Hensley's house on South Kent Street. She always seemed to turn evasive when Charlie pressed her to let him meet the family, as though she were ashamed, but whether of him or of them he couldn't be sure.

But Patsy wasn't ashamed; she was scared. Things were going too well in her private life; it made her nervous. She didn't want to rock the boat in any way, shape, or form. She just couldn't feature Hilda looking Charlie over with those all-seeing eyes of hers, checking out all his faults and his flaws. She didn't want Charlie not to cotton to Hilda. She needed them both so much, and she needed them to love and respect each other, not only for Patsy's sake, but because they honestly did.

Patsy was between a rock and a hard place, with Hilda hammering her on one side and Charlie on the other, and both of them demanding the same damn thing: "What's the matter? Are you ashamed of me? Ain't I good enough to meet your mother (your lover)?" She knew she couldn't hold them off much longer. The day would have to dawn pretty soon when they'd have to meet.

The day that Charlie Dick first came to supper at Patsy Cline's mother's house nearly sent poor Patsy over the edge. She woke up with a nervous headache, had stomach cramps all day, and smoked two packs of Lucky Strikes without inhaling once. It astonished her that this ordinary occasion was so important to her, and it astonished her even more that it seemed to be so unimportant to Hilda.

But while Hilda Hensley remained tranquil on the outside, going about her daily duties as though this evening's meal would be no different from any other, inside she was as nervous as her daughter. Charlie Dick seemed to mean so much to Patsy; it was vitally important that the two of them be friends, too, if only for Patsy's sake. She *wanted* to like him, but she had her doubts. For one thing, he drank, and Hilda had bitter memories of her marriage to Samuel Hensley. Samuel was a drinking man, and the thought of it made Hilda shudder. That miserable kind of life wasn't what she wanted for her Patsy.

For another, Charlie Dick was a well-known hellraiser, and evidently catnip where women were concerned. Of course, he was still young; that was surely in his favor. Many men changed when they settled down and gave up their old wicked ways. But was Charlie ever going to settle down with Patsy, or were they just going on doing what they were doing, which didn't bear thinking about by a good Christian woman?

So far, Charlie's behavior hadn't shown Hilda much. If he was so all-fired in love with her daughter, why didn't he come courting to her house like a respectable man, instead of always dragging her home to his place to spend the night?

Tonight was the night that Hilda would see what Charlie was made of. Tonight he'd be coming to supper, and he'd have to answer for his behavior to *her*, Patsy's mother. Just because Patsy Cline was jumping around like a barefoot cat on a hot greased griddle didn't mean that Hilda Hensley wouldn't be taking a long, hard look at this here Charlie Dick. Even if Patsy had long forgotten, Hilda Hensley still remembered that the first time Patsy had laid eyes on Charlie, she'd called him "a clown with hot britches."

Patsy had set the table with the best they had—the good china, the lace tablecloth they used at Christmas, and as many matching knives and forks and spoons as she could find in the kitchen drawer. But all they had for the lemonade was jelly glasses, and Patsy was still moaning about it.

"Any man not too proud to drink moonshine whiskey out of a fruit jar shouldn't be too proud to drink fresh lemonade out of a jelly glass," averred Hilda with some stiffness.

"Mama!"

When the doorbell finally rang at six o'clock sharp and the clown with hot britches stood grinning on the doorstep, smelling to high heaven of Vitalis and Mennen Skin Bracer, Hilda Hensley's first impression was that he'd be cutting no ice with her. Oh, he was good-lookin' enough for a little feller, with his dimples and the cleft in his chin and them deep-set blue eyes and them muscles. She'd grant him that much at least. But beauty is as beauty does, and a man needs a lot more than a pretty face to make a good woman respect him.

Charlie was holding on for dear life to two bunches of flowers, and Hilda gave a silent scornful sniff when she got a look at them. One was a big, beautiful bunch of bright-colored snapdragons for Patsy, while the other was this mingy, measly little bunch of field daisies wrapped up in tinfoil, no doubt an afterthought for her.

But there was Charlie, smiling and bowing and presenting Hilda Hensley with that big, beautiful bunch of flowers, while the little bunch of nothing was handed over to Patsy. Well, Hilda just had to smile in spite of herself. I mean, the boy had some class to him after all.

"I know I ought to call you Mrs. Hensley," said Charlie, with a twinkle in his eye, "but you're not much older than

Patsy here, and you two look so much alike that my tongue gets tied up around the words."

"I reckon," conceded Hilda, "that you can call me Hilda."

"Thank you, Hilda, I will. And may I tell you right here and now that my hand to God I ain't never eaten no fried chicken lighter nor crisper nor tastier than this."

"Mama's famous for her fried chicken. She fries it in lard," put in Sylvia, blushing. She was already in love with Charlie, from the first minute he'd grinned at her and asked her where she went to school.

"Take another piece, Charlie," urged Hilda. "You don't eat enough to keep a bird alive."

This was a patent lie, since Charlie had done more than his share of filling up his mouth, and wasn't done yet.

"Hilda, if I eat any more of this dee-licious bird, I'm likely to sprout feathers and fly away. But if you'll permit me I'll try to manage another one of these fluffy biscuits of yours."

"There's peach pie for dessert, so you better save room," advised John. He, too, had fallen under the Charlie Dick spell when it transpired that both he and Charlie rooted for the same baseball team, the Baltimore Orioles. Orioles fans were a very special band of brothers. They were strong men and no summer soldiers or sunshine patriots; their team hadn't made it to a single World Series since the first one was played back in 1903. In the last seven years, the Series had been dominated by the New York teams, the Yankees and the Dodgers, and even though it was early in the season, it already looked like it was going to happen again in '56. But if they'd learned nothing else, Orioles fans had learned patience. They'd wait until Nineteen *sixty*-six if they had to.

"Now how did you know peach pie was purely my downfall, Hilda?" dimpled Charlie.

"Mama is famous for her peach pie. She bakes it with lard," offered Sylvia, again yielding up the lard bucket, apparently the culinary secret of the Hensley kitchen.

During this love feast, Patsy sat almost silent, mixed emotions holding her back from saying much or eating more than a mouthful or two. She had dreaded this first meeting for so long, and here it was coming off a thousand times better than she'd expected. Charlie was on his best behavior, with all his charm and good manners spread out on show. Mama was being the perfect hostess; the kids were acting like human people instead of teenagers. Everybody was cosying up to everybody else. So why this lump as big as a basketball in the pit of her stomach?

Maybe because she saw a big part of her precious hard-won freedom going down the tubes, disappearing like the fried chicken right off the platter. Keeping the two parts of her life separate and distinct from each other had given Patsy a measure of control that she now stood to lose.

Patsy liked to make her own decisions. She could stand up to Hilda when her mother criticized her; she could stand up to Charlie when he second-guessed her. But could she stand up to the two of them if they were to unite against her? What if they joined forces "for her own good"—and she wouldn't put it past either of them; just look how they were practically smooching over the peach pie, Charlie stuffing his face and rolling his eyes in ecstasy, Mama giggling just as coy as a kitten? She wouldn't stand the chance of an icicle on the Fourth of July.

They took their coffee in the living room, to give Patsy and Sylvia a chance to clean off the dining room table and wash up the dishes, but mostly so that Hilda and Charlie could sit side by side on the sofa and get better acquainted.

Out in the kitchen, Patsy could hear her mother and her lover laughing fit to be tied over the best joke in the big wide world. Was it something about her?

I must be going loony. First I'm scared out of my britches that Charlie and Mama won't get along; now I'm feeling left out because they're hitting it off fine as wine.

When the door closed behind Charlie, it was close to eleven o'clock, and Patsy was as tuckered as if she'd sung three shows. Hilda, on the other hand, was as fresh and as bright as a newly opened flower.

"Well?" demanded Patsy. "What do you think? Be honest with me, Mama."

Her mother smiled. "Well," she said slowly, "that there boy thinks the sun don't rise till he gets up in the mornin', but he surely does know how to charm a lady."

At Patsy's shocked look, Hilda laughed. Then her face turned serious, even a little grave. "Be careful, honey. He's a powerful lot of man and you're a powerful lot of woman. I wouldn't want to see my child get hurt."

"I love him, Mama," said Patsy softly.

"I know you do, candy lamb, and he loves you. I only wish that love was enough to make people happy. I'll ask Jesus in my prayers tonight to bless Charlie; I always do pray for *you*."

Patsy's divorce came through without a whole heap of trouble. Gerald had filed for it, and Patsy hadn't contested it. She got to keep the Buick, which had been her Christmas present in 1955 anyway, and Gerald had asked for the house. Surprisingly, he had found himself another girlfriend and wanted to get married again right away. *So much for a broken heart*, thought Patsy, not without a small pang of something very like jealousy.

But, truth to tell, Patsy had no eyes for that goddamn house. Between Hilda's house and Charlie's, she had two roofs over her head. Besides, she'd always hated that tacky little place where she'd never spent a truly happy day, so she said yes. It didn't occur to her until later that what they should have done was sell the house and split the profits. But that was Patsy; she gave everything away.

The divorce was granted *a vinculo matrimonii*, which is fancy lawyer Latin for 'a release from all matrimonial vows,' and Patsy found herself a free woman. Right back to square one, only a few years older and, she hoped, some small bit smarter.

The night her divorce became final, Patsy and Charlie celebrated in the best way they knew how. First, they drove to a Chinese restaurant and pigged out on chicken chow mein and spareribs. The setups there were only a dollar apiece, and Charlie sneaked in a bottle of the best—Jim Beam's, a Tennessee sippin' whiskey guaranteed to put hair on the balls of your feet. By the time they left, they were feeling mellow. A late summer moon, almost a harvest moon, hung low and hugely orange in the night sky. It lit up the world.

"See that moon, darlin'?" Charlie put his arm around Patsy's shoulder and hugged her tight. "Well, that's the moon you hang for me."

Blinking back tears of happiness, Patsy kissed her lover on the first place she could reach, which happened to be the back of his hand. Maybe it wasn't romantic, but it was heartfelt, if slightly tipsy.

Then they went home to Charlie's house and went to bed.

Her fingers were a little shaky on the buttons, from one drink too many, so Charlie reached over to help her undo them.

"No." Patsy pulled away. "I'll do it myself."

"Go ahead, sugar. You do that." Fully clothed, Charlie threw himself onto the bed, boots and all, his arms folded comfortably under his head, propping him up.

"You do that," he said again. "And I'll just lay here and watch you."

He was serious. He really was serious. For an instant, Patsy considered refusing, but the warmth that began rushing through her veins told her otherwise. Slowly, teasingly, she began to remove her clothing, keeping her eyes fixed on Charlie, who stared back, fascinated. The blouse. The skirt. The slip. She stood there in garter belt, stockings, panties, and strapless bra, feeling his eyes burning her skin.

"Leave the stockings and shoes for last," he whispered.

The bra. Her nipples puckering in the chilly air of the

bedroom. The panties. All she had on now were the high heels and stockings and the garter belt.

"Turn around," he said with a catch in his voice. "Yeah, like that. God, you're gorgeous! C'mere, sweetheart."

But Patsy held up a warning hand. "No. Now it's my turn. Get up. That's right. Now get undressed. Slowly."

She took his place on the bed and watched Charlie take his clothes off somewhat bashfully and awkwardly. The jacket. The shirt. The undershirt. The belt. The Levi's. He didn't know whether she was kidding or not, but he was starting to get as heated up as a cast-iron stove.

"Leave the boots for last," she told him, and kept her eyes on him as he pulled his jockey shorts over his boots. "Now turn around. Yeah, like that. God, you're gorgeous! C'mere, sweetheart!"

By the time he reached the bed, they were so ready for each other that not even an Indian attack could have stopped their immediate joining. It was the hottest, most furious sex they'd had so far, and when it was over it left them both breathless and gasping for air.

"Hooo-EEE, baby, you're the best there is!" breathed Charlie.

"Well, who'd know better than you, cowboy?"

"Love me?"

"Didn't I just prove it?"

"Wanna prove it again?"

"Charlie, if you don't beat *all*!"

And he did.

Nine

THE GRANITE QUARRY hadn't been mined in more than forty years. Since its abandonment, fertile nature had worked such changes in it that it had been transformed from a hideous scar on the face of the planet to a thing of surpassing beauty. First, brush had sent out its tentative, windswept roots; next scrub, then trees and bushes had grown up around it, covering its rawness with the verdant softness of foliage. Rain had fallen into the quarry over the decades, filling it to a great depth and turning its harsh rocky surface into a cold, dark lake. Numerous caves had been carved into its sides, first by the quarriers' picks and dynamite, later by the persistence of the water, which rounded the entrances, deepened the caves themselves, and turned them into caverns of mystery.

The banks of the quarry were a favorite picnic spot for the ten thousand or so people who lived in Winchester. But today, a weekday in early September, Charlie and Patsy had it all to themselves. Charlie had taken the day off from work to be with his woman. It seemed to him that these days, ever since he'd made friends with the Hensleys, he and Patsy scarcely had a minute to themselves anymore. Outside of bed, of course. Not that he didn't enjoy their company. Hilda Hensley had become almost like a mother to him, and the kids were great; it was like having a younger brother and sister. Still, sometimes a family of that size heaped on him all at one time was a little too much for a man of his tender years.

But anything to make his Patsy happy, and Patsy had never been happier.

Life with Charlie was so different it seemed unfair to compare it to life with Gerald. For one thing, they laughed all the time. Charlie always knew how to break her up, so that she held on tight to her ribs and begged him to stop. He could be such a clown, with his idiotic juggling tricks that left broken eggs all over the kitchen floor, with his crazy imitations of good ole boys out on a toot. Patsy was always in stitches.

They'd even sing together, just the two of them, and while Charlie Dick's voice was nothing to make Ferlin Husky nervous, it didn't break any mirrors, either. It was a pleasant baritone, harmonizing well with Patsy's clear alto.

She just loved when he came along with her on her singing jobs. He always looked so proud, setting there down front where everybody could see him and know that Charlie Dick was Patsy Cline's man. He fitted in well with the musicians, too, and was everybody's good buddy, so that the two of them would often go out drinking with the boys in the band, which gave the pickers an even better rapport with Patsy when she was up there on the stage with them.

And it was a real treat to Patsy to see how well Charlie took to Hilda, Sylvia, and John, and how much her family meant to him. In only a few short months, he'd become a part of them. Even her mother, watching her daughter's happiness on the increase, had relaxed somewhat in her suspicion of Charlie's charm.

Incredibly, even the sex was better. Now that the first ferocity was burned out and over with, the first hunger pangs allayed, and they were both certain that there was plenty more in the larder when they got hungry again, the sex had altered somewhat.

Knowing each other's bodies so well, each had learned

every little touch and kiss that excited the other, every secret place that held ecstasy. They became more experimental, trying things with each other that both had hardly dared to even fantasize about alone. Their rhythms became slower, more leisurely. Even so, Patsy still felt a strong thrill at the very thought of making love with Charlie. Once, putting some clothes into the washing machine, she had a sudden sharp vision of his naked body, and she became so dizzy she had to grab on to the washer for support.

That was the time she spent half an hour cleaning up spilled Oxydol soap powder off the washroom floor, all the while sneezing her head off.

Yes, Patsy Cline had just about everything she needed in the world for perfect happiness, thank you, Jesus. Now if only the Lord would help her get her career to rolling. . . .

It was on one of the most glorious days of late summer that they brought their picnic to the quarry. The first frosts were at least a month away, and the earth was radiating back the warmth it had been soaking up from the sun all summer. Wild flowers were everywhere in profusion—large clumps of daisies and tall Johnnie Pye weed, late-blooming day lilies, black-eyed Susans, purple loosestrife crowding the others out down by the water. Mallard ducks, their eggs hatched and ducklings nearly grown, were still basking inside their nests in the tall cattails, and pale green willow shoots, hanging low, admired their reflections in the inky depths of the bottomless tarn.

If only one could put up such a day, the way Hilda Hensley bottled her ripe peaches, to keep forever in some magical preserving syrup, to be taken out and tasted again, like the peaches, all through the sunless, cheerless winter! How imperfect a syrup is human memory!

Yet Patsy would always remember every small detail of this day—the insistent humming of the bees among the wild flowers as they gathered the last of the season's nectar, the dazzle of the sunlight on the water, the shape of the clouds floating like cotton bolls in the windless air, the coarse texture of the sunburned grass, the clean mother-smell of the earth. This day would be preserved in the deepest part of her memory for as long as she lived.

Leaving their picnic basket and blanket on the grass, they went for a row, Charlie at the oars, Patsy lying back in the wooden boat, admiring alternately the shapes of the clouds and the bunching swell of Charlie's biceps through his thin cotton shirt as he pulled back smoothly on the oars. In her ears, the thin splash of the water beneath the blades and the creaking of the ancient oarlocks were summer's music.

"Nice day," remarked Charlie.

"Great day," Patsy agreed.

A thin edge of annoyance was perceptible in Charlie's words.

"What do ya wanna do, top me all the time?" he demanded. "Just say, 'Yeah, it's a nice day.'"

Patsy was too blissed out to argue. "Yeah, it's a nice day," she echoed amiably.

His annoyance vanished. "This water's *cold*. We used to swim in here clear up into November. And back in them caves the water's got *ice cubes* in it. A guy in my class—Jimmy Byers—said he saw an eight-foot water moccasin surface, with its mouth all open and showin' white."

"Charlie!" she protested.

Patsy was mortally afraid of snakes, even harmless little green garden snakes, but a venomous water moccasin was deadly enough to frighten the bravest man. It didn't bear thinkin' about, and it certainly wasn't a topic she wished to discuss on a beautiful day like this one.

But Charlie was wearing his most mischievous expression; he dearly loved to stir up trouble.

"How much would it take for you to swim back in one of them caves?"

Patsy only shuddered in reply, but Charlie was persistent.

"No, I'm serious. How much?"

She sat up in the boat and looked at him hard through narrowed lids. He *was* serious; he was issuing a challenge.

Well, Virginia Patterson Hensley Cline had never refused a dare in her life.

"Three hundred," she said shortly.

"Damn!" laughed Charlie. "You'd really do it?"

Patsy stood up in the rowboat, tipping it perilously.

"You got the cash?" she demanded, ready for anything. Her hands found the buttons on the waistband of her capri pants, and made to pull the slacks off.

"I love it!" howled Charlie. "I wish I had three hundred!"

"Well, until you *do* have it, fool, keep your damn mouth shut and don't you dare me!" growled Patsy, settling back down into the rowboat.

"What a woman! All balls," sighed Charlie admiringly.

Mollified, Patsy returned his grin. "You're just finding that out? Hell, hoss, you should *know* it by now!"

Leaning forward, he laid one gentle hand on her ankle. "I do know it, Patsy. I'll always know it."

A feeling of such sweet rapture filled Patsy at that moment that tears sprang to her eyes. This was what happiness was all about; this was what she'd been waiting for all her life. Nothing she could think of was as wonderful as passion mixed with tenderness.

Later, they made languorous love under the open sky. Afterward, famished, they threw themselves at the picnic basket, wolfing down ham sandwiches, cold chicken, sweet pickles, washing the food down with icy lemonade from a thermos. Then, their bodies satisfied both inside and out, they lay down together to nap in each other's arms like a pair of innocent children.

When they woke, two hours later, the sun was hanging low in the western sky and it was getting colder. Patsy stood up and picked up the blanket to shake off the crumbs, but Charlie put one restraining hand on her arm.

"So. You wanna have other nice days like today?"

"Sure," said Patsy without thinking, giving the blanket a good hard shake.

"No, I mean lots of 'em."

"Sure," answered Patsy again, unclear as to what Charlie was driving at.

But Charlie was looking at her earnestly, his blue eyes seeking her brown ones. It was imperative that she be made to understand.

"No, *lots* of 'em. Good days all the time, Sunday to Sunday."

Puzzled, she could only stare at him, waiting for the punch line.

And then it came.

"You wanna get married?"

It took a second or two for Charlie's words to sink in, and a second or two more to see that he wasn't just kidding around; he was in dead earnest. Patsy had never seen his face so serious before.

For a long minute, time stopped for Patsy, frozen in the moment. With dazzling clarity, she saw it all, felt it all.

On the one hand, she wasn't sure that this was the right time to get married; she was determined to make her singing career get up and get going at last. Besides, neither one of them had a dime to set up housekeeping with. Also, she'd already *been* married, and being single was a whole lot more fun. This was the first time in her life that she'd felt free. New though it was, it was a vital and necessary feeling. She didn't want to be without it ever again. Marriage meant responsibility, a serious commitment, a settling down. Was she really ready to undertake it? Charlie was not an easy-going man, like Gerald had been. His energy was wonderful in a lover; in a husband it presented the potential for danger. She could hear her mother's warning echoing in her ears.

On the other hand, she loved Charlie Dick with a passion she'd never before thought possible, a passion of which she hadn't known herself capable.

On the other hand, what had happened to that dream of the house with the yellow roses all around, and the children she longed to "raise right"? Didn't she want them to have Charlie's blue eyes, Charlie's quick grin and sense of fun?

On the other hand, she loved Charlie Dick so tenderly she thought that some day she'd explode from the sheer joy of it.

On the other hand, he loved her back enough, he really loved her back enough to ask her to be his wife.

On the other hand, she knew suddenly and chillingly that if she turned him down, she'd stand a good chance of losing Charlie. A man like him had his pride, and didn't take to rejection easily. It wasn't likely he'd hang around long after Patsy had said no. The thought of being without Charlie froze the marrow in Patsy's bones. It wasn't possible to live without him.

And all of this went through Patsy's mind in the split second before Charlie said, "I dare you," and she gave a whoop and a holler of glee, threw her arms tightly around his neck, and kissed him so hard she nearly knocked him over.

Patsy Cline in the early days of her career. (From the personal collection of Patsy Cline's family.)

Jessica Lange as Patsy Cline in the movie *Sweet Dreams*.

Patsy as lead singer with the group Kountry Krackers. (From the personal collection of P. Cline's family.)

Patsy performs with the group Kountry Krackers.

WELCOME Patsy
Here to the Star that likes
to Shine—Winchester Ohh
Patsy Cline!

ABOVE AND RIGHT:
Patsy and Charlie on
their wedding day,
Sept. 15, 1957. (From
the personal collection of
P. Cline's family.)

Welcome
Patsy
Sep 15

LEFT AND · BELOW: Patsy and Charlie, played by Ed Harris, just after their wedding. (© 1985 Tri-Star Pictures, Inc. All rights reserved.)

JUST MARRIE

Patsy and Charlie stop for a photo before embarking on their two-night honeymoon. (From the personal collection of P. Cline's family.)

LEFT: Publicity photo of the legendary Patsy Cline. (From the personal collection of P. Cline's family.)

BELOW: Patsy Cline— a star! (From the personal collection of P. Cline's family.)

Ten

So Patsy Cline and Charlie Dick made up
their minds to live happily ever after, starting with their
wedding day, September 15, just one week after Patsy celebrated her birthday, and not very long after Patsy had first
laid eyes on the "clown with hot britches" who was to change
her life so dramatically.

To say that they were a nervous bride and groom would
be to put it mildly. Both of them smoked one cigarette after
another before and after the ceremony, and if the reverend
would have given them permission, they'd have chain-
smoked right through their "I Do's."

It wasn't a large wedding or an elaborate one; who could
afford it? It was held at home, in the brick house on South
Kent Street. Both Hilda and Patsy had spent a solid week
scrubbing it and scouring it from top to bottom, so that on
the morning of the wedding day the odor of furniture polish
was stronger than the perfume of the bride's bouquet.

About forty people were invited, many of them pickers
and singers and Charlie's friends from the newspaper where
he worked. Patsy invited Mary Rose Dodds from the Rainbow Road Club, who was tickled silly that Patsy Cline was
actually hitching up with the Thing That Wouldn't Die.
Wasn't it wonderful how Fate worked out sometimes?

Neither Charlie nor Patsy had a large family, but what
kinfolk they had all turned up to see them get married. All
except Samuel Hensley, Patsy's father.

When they'd first settled on the date for the wedding, Hilda had brought up the subject of tracking down Samuel and inviting him—after all, he was the bride's father—but Patsy had whirled upon her mother with such a black look of fury that Hilda had dropped the subject immediately, knowing when she was licked.

Patsy had already been married once in white, so this second time around she chose pink, white being too hypocritical. Besides, everybody at the wedding knew that the couple had already been on a honeymoon.

During the last week before the ceremony, Charlie hadn't seen hide nor hair of his Patsy. She'd moved back in with her mother to get the house ready for the wedding. But more than that, she needed some time to herself, to sleep alone and deal with her apprehensions. Sleeping with Charlie could always make them go away, but what Patsy needed to know was, would her fears go away when Charlie wasn't around?

Meanwhile, across town in Charlie's little house, the bridegroom was so horny he was biting the pillow. Man, how he missed her! Why the hell had he ever given in and let her go back to her mother's house for a whole goddamned week?

Seeing his suffering, the boys down at the paper offered to take him out and get him laid, sort of a good-bye–to–bachelorhood present. And Charlie had been mighty tempted, too, because the whore they had in mind for him had titties out to *there*, and an ass that just wouldn't quit.

But, damn it, he was in love with Patsy, and he wasn't going to start out by cheating on her. Besides, there wasn't a woman in the world who was equal to her in the bedroom, so why go for second best when he had the best at home, or would have in a few days more?

"Be patient, hoss," she told him when she'd headed on home to Hilda's. "Just keep it warm for me."

"Sweetheart, it ain't warm for anyone else on this here earth *but* you," he'd answered sadly, and it was true. She'd been halfway out the door when he'd grabbed her suddenly into his arms, and she was two and a half hours late getting to her mama's house. Two and a half *well-spent* hours.

Now, dressed in a new beige suit with a white flower in his buttonhole, beige suede shoes, an uncustomary necktie, and a new white shirt so full of starch that he was choking in the collar, Charlie Dick stood next to the minister, waiting for his bride.

To say that he wasn't having last-minute doubts would be to tell a lie. Everybody wants to git to heaven, but don't nobody want to die. If only he could have Patsy for his wife without having to get married! Not to mention that he'd kill his own mama for a cigarette right this minute! And for a drink, he'd happily knock off half the population of Winchester, Virginia!

Upstairs, Patsy adjusted the veil on her feathered hat and took a long, critical look at herself in the bedroom mirror. The pink knitted two-piece suit was very becoming, hugging her hourglass figure and showing off the contours of her breasts. She'd bought it a week ago as her wedding dress, in one of the best stores in Winchester; that was her something new. The something old was her favorite pair of pearl earrings from that collection of hers that kept growing. The something borrowed was her mama's prayer book to carry, and the something blue was hidden underneath her clothing, next to her body; nobody but Charlie would ever see it.

Stepping back from the mirror for a longer view, Patsy took another long drag on her cigarette and stubbed out the lipsticked butt. *I'm as ready as I'll ever be, so I may as well get the hell on with it.*

Downstairs, a chord was struck on the piano, and Patsy could hear the first notes of the beloved hymn, "Lead Kindly Light," her mother's lovely contralto soaring. It was time to go. A knock on the door; her brother, John, had come to take her down the aisle.

She took John's arm and the two of them headed gravely out of the bedroom toward the stairs. Patsy's knees were shaking so badly that she stumbled, and her brother had to catch her to keep her from falling.

"Hey, easy," he whispered. "This is a wedding, not a hanging."

Patsy smiled at him gratefully, and he grinned back. *He's right,* she thought. *This should be the happiest day of my life. Damn it, it* is *the happiest day of my life. Oh, Lord, I'm going to work so hard to make Charlie happy.*

Coming down the stairs she could see the people waiting: the girls she'd grown up with and gone to school with; her sister in a new blue dress with her hair pinned up like a grown-up and lipstick on; Charlie's best friend, J. W. Woodhouse; and her mother, singing with tears in her eyes. Suddenly, she wanted to turn around and run right back up the steps.

But when she got to the foot of the stairs and saw her Charlie standing there in his new suit, looking so handsome and so terrified, all need for reassurance left Patsy's heart immediately. Suddenly, she was totally at peace. This marriage was what she wanted; she knew it for certain. They were blessed in this union.

And when Charlie saw Patsy walking toward him in her pink bride's outfit, her hair a crown of glossy black under the soft hat and veil, her eyes shining with love, her lovely face transfigured, all his doubts went out the window. If the two of *them* couldn't be happy, then who could be happy in this vale of tears? God had given him a real blessing when He'd sent him Patsy.

So the words were spoken over them that made two people one flesh, and there they stood, a married couple. Hilda cried, and Sylvia cried, and Charlie's mother cried, and Patsy's unmarried girlfriends cried, but everybody else was smiling.

It was a wonderful party; the guests kept running back and forth to the table, loaded down with plates of chicken and ham and turkey and potato salad and biscuits and black-eyed peas, and home-baked cherry cobblers and pies.

In the center of the table, standing by itself in a wreath of roses, was the tall white butter-frosted wedding cake with the miniature bride and groom on top of it. The little children at the party regarded it with awe, counting the minutes until Patsy Cline Dick would make that first cut and everybody would get a piece.

Hilda had set out pitchers of lemonade and milk and iced tea and hot coffee, but some evil-minded villain had sneaked whiskey into one of the tea pitchers, and the men crowded around it until it was empty. Then, by a miracle, it was filled up again, and, later, again. Hilda Hensley must have known what was going on, but for the sake of peace she chose to ignore it.

And then there was that last-minute flurry of getting ready for the bride and groom to leave. Patsy cutting the wedding cake with Charlie's hand guiding her wrist. Posing for the pictures—Patsy stuffing cake in Charlie's grinning mouth; Patsy holding up her little wedding bouquet of freesias and white roses, and turning her back so that none of her girl-friends could accuse her later of deliberately tossing it to somebody else. Patsy throwing the bouquet high over her head, behind her. And who do you think caught it? J.W.!

Not that he was allowed to keep it, with every unmarried girl in the place trying to snatch it out of his hand!

Suddenly, it was over, and the newlyweds were running out to the car, to the rear bumper of which somebody had thoughtfully added a string of tin cans and a "Just Married" sign.

"Hey," yelled J.W. after Charlie, "if you forget how tonight, just give me a call."

"That's okay!" Charlie yelled back. "I got a book I can look it up in."

And Patsy, about to climb into the car, suddenly running back to her mama's arms for one last tear-filled hug and kiss.

"Be happy, honey!" whispered Hilda.

"I will, Mama," she whispered back. "You're my very best friend in the whole world."

"Bless you, child, you got a husband now. Make *him* your best friend and you'll never need another."

"I'll always need *you*, Mama."

And Charlie's car pulling away with a rattle of tin cans and a lot of good-natured hootin' and hollerin.' And there was suddenly nothing left to do but to wrap up the leftovers and wash the dishes. The wedding party was history.

"It's scary, isn't it?" asked Patsy softly. She came out of the motel bathroom dressed in a new nightgown, freshly bathed and with her hair brushed and shining.

Charlie was already in bed, lying naked under the covers. It was a funny thing. For the last seventeen months she'd been sleeping with this man every damn chance she got. His body was as familiar to her as her own. Now, suddenly, she was as shy as a fifteen-year-old virgin.

"I don't know why you're scared," lied Charlie, nervous himself and feeling much the same awkwardness as Patsy.

Searching for the right words, she bit her lip. "What I mean is, you buy a dress, you stand in front of a preacher, say a few words, and everything looks different. Scares the hell out of me, I can tell you." She searched his face with earnest eyes. "I want this to work out, Charlie. I want it to be *right*!"

He gave her one of his loving smiles. "I know what you need," he told her, patting his shoulder. "You need to put your head right there."

Coming to the bed, she lay down beside him, nestling close to him on top of the covers, enjoying the comfort and strength of his masculinity. His broad shoulder under her head felt like safe harbor, just as he'd promised.

Charlie nuzzled at the curls on her forehead, all the while stroking her upper arm lightly, then his mouth moved down to her cheek and sought her lips. The kiss was long, deep, and satisfying. As he slipped his hand inside the nightgown, encircling her breast with his fingers, Patsy stiffened and pushed him away.

"Wait. It's my wedding night, Charlie. I want the words. Say the words."

He'd said many loving things to her since they met. How wonderful she was, how sexy, how talented, how beautiful, how smart. He'd told her he loved her this and was crazy about her that, how much he needed to see her and hold her and make love to her. But those three little words— *exactly* those three little words—the ones that make the world go around, those exact words had never left his lips. They made him uncomfortable, as though there was something unmanly about saying them right out loud.

But Patsy was waiting for them, waiting for those words, and while she was waiting he could look at her sweet, round body, but he couldn't touch.

So . . . if he knew what was good for him . . .

Well, what the hell. He owed her that much, didn't he? Besides, it was nothing but the Lord's truth anyway.

But it wasn't easy. "I . . . love you," he said, the words sticking in his mouth like peanut butter.

"Oooohhhh," purred Patsy. "That's *nice*! Say it again."

Now she had Charlie laughing, and the laughter made it easier the second time.

"I *love* you, damn it!" He hugged her more tightly, realizing for the first time that this wasn't just Patsy anymore, but his wife. Not his lover, but Mrs. Charlie Dick, and his responsibility was to protect her and care for her and make her happy.

"Look," he began, his face serious, "I want this to turn out right, too. I'm gonna try, 'cause I've seen too many marriages just . . . what?" He groped for the word, found it. "Just . . . disappear, sort of. Marriage is *hard*."

Patsy nodded solemnly, her face as serious as his. But the twinkle in her eye ought to have warned him.

"Then let's *practice* so it'll get easier," she advised him deadpan.

With a low growl, Charlie seized her and pulled her on top of him, pinning her to his body, discovering the "something blue" that Patsy was wearing just for him.

One weekend—two days—was all they had for their so-called honeymoon, two days and two nights in which they never left the Sweet Repose Motel, Color TV in Every Room. Thank Jesus for small favors. Another day or night might have killed the two of them altogether.

They ate takeout chicken from a greasy bucket; killed two quarts of sippin' whiskey and endless bottles of 7-Up; smoked so many cigarettes that they had to open the windows just to see each other's faces; and they made love.

After the first thirty hours, Charlie's pecker was sore; the thing lined with gold between Patsy's legs was aching, and still they couldn't let each other alone. They had invented this new and wondrous thing called sex, and if they didn't keep doing it over and over, they'd forfeit it and somebody would come and confiscate it.

When they were too tired and too achy to do it any more, they retired to the bathroom and took a long, hot, soaking bath together, drowsing off in the steamy heat of the tub. It made them feel so much better that they straightened the sheets, fluffed up the pillows, and went at it again.

But for every action, there is an equal and positive reaction. Drink enough booze, smoke enough cigarettes, screw your butt off, and what you have is action. Equally and positively, Monday morning is going to roll around, bringing with it a punch card, a timeclock and the hangover that ate the world. That's reaction.

When at dawn on Monday the honeymooners left their rose-covered motel cottage in the pines for the grim realities of the outside world, they individually and collectively resembled ten pounds of shit in a five-pound sack. Especially Charlie Dick.

As the first rays of daylight hit him, Charlie winced,

groaned, and closed his puffy eyes.

"I'll drive," volunteered Patsy, who was feeling somewhat better than Charlie, having drunk a great deal less.

"Drive what?" croaked Charlie.

"It's that bad, huh? Are you sure you're up to going to work?"

"Work where?" moaned Charlie. "No, I can do it. I'm really not as bad as I feel. I couldn't be. Patsy, honey, can you drive the car without moving it?"

"I'll put the top down. You'll see. The fresh air will do you some good."

"Talk sense, woman. Ain't *nothing* gonna do me any *good*."

He was a little less gray in the face by the time they reached his house, but not a whole bunch less. With trembling hands, he managed to brush those funny little things they call teeth, and run a comb through his hair, but any attempt at shaving would have been downright suicidal. He hadn't shaved since Friday; one more day wasn't going to make a damn bit of difference.

"And *shave*!" Patsy yelled up the stairs to the bathroom, just like she had ESP. "You look like something the cat forgot to bury."

When Charlie came gingerly down the steps fifteen minutes later in a clean shirt, there were little bits of toilet paper sticking all over his face to stop the bleeding, but he'd shaved. More or less.

"I'm going to die," he announced in a hollow voice.

Laughing, Patsy didn't look up from packing his lunch.

"Go ahead and laugh, but I mean it. I will die before I get to work today. Nobody can live with pain like this," he whimpered, flinching as his new wife chucked a lunch-meat sandwich and an apple into a paper bag and handed it to him. He accepted his lunch with two shaky fingers and began to hobble stiff-legged to the door.

"You will never see me alive again," he prophesied over Patsy's screams of laughter. "I'm . . . dying . . . now. . . ."

The kitchen door slammed behind him and the car engine started up. Charlie was gone, but Patsy was still laughing.

"You look like you need this more than I do," said J.W., handing Charlie a paper cup full of sweet, scalding coffee.

"God bless you, mister." Charlie's trembling hands and thin, reedy voice were an uncanny imitation of an old rummy.

"Big night?" asked Woodhouse, grinning like a wolf.

"*Real* big," admitted Charlie ruefully.

"So how was the honeymoon, nice?"

"Oh, *hell*, yes!" He spat the words out scornfully. "Two days at a cut-rate motel with beaverboard walls. It was great. Real uptown stuff."

"Patsy didn't like the place?" J.W. wanted to know.

Charlie's lips twisted bitterly. "Patsy never said a word. She wouldn't. I didn't like it. *I* didn't like it," he repeated harshly. His face was a savage mask of anger.

"Well, Je-*sus*!" commented his friend. "You're in a pretty mood."

"I got twelve dollars to my name," Charlie admitted sullenly. "Twelve dollars between me and payday."

He looked around the large linotype room, with its huge keyboarded typesetting machines and its rolling cabinets filled with metal slugs, as though he hated the place.

J. W. Woodhouse had known Charlie Dick a good many years, and he read Charlie's facial expression unerringly.

"The money ain't so bad here," he said defensively.

"Or so good," growled Charlie.

Woodhouse laughed derisively. "What? You wanna be like that old fart Lawrence? Wear a suit and run the place?"

Charlie shook his head, but the expression of discontent remained on his face.

"Hell, no, but don't you ever wanna do somethin' different? *Better?* I'd like to get me a place, maybe . . ."

His voice trailed off as he allowed his imagination to carry him away for a minute, then he became aware that his friend was looking at him oddly, at this side of Charlie Dick he'd never seen before, and he closed himself off immediately.

"Ah, what the hell. . . ." He wasn't going to take this bullshit job much longer, anyway.

Things were different now, him a married man and all. He deserved more respect. Not to mention more money. This was a nowhere job; he hated it. He wanted to keep his hands clean, wear nice clothes, instead of getting dirt under his fingernails every damn day. Charlie hated the feeling of no money in his pockets; it demeaned him and made him out to be worthless. He thought about Patsy, with her voice like an angel. Now, *there* was a life! *There* was a career. Maybe what Patsy Dick needed was new management. . . .

Eleven

THE FIRST MONTHS of their marriage passed swiftly and blissfully. Autumn came and carried the leaves off the trees, leaving only the pines to reign as forest kings. For Thanksgiving, Patsy and Charlie went over to Hilda's for a big family feast of turkey with all the trimmings, and Christmas followed Thanksgiving so rapidly it seemed like no more than a week had come between them.

Patsy's own Christmas tree was a tiny little tabletop affair hung with tinsel and topped with the only ornament she had, a big star. Charlie had suggested one of those pretty white aluminum trees that lasted forever, but Patsy had given him a vehement no. If it wasn't real, it wasn't a Christmas tree. She loved bringing the smell of pine into the house.

Hilda knitted a sweater for Charlie, a soft blue wool that matched his eyes. For Patsy, there was the most beautiful cowgirl vest you could imagine—Patsy's mother had embroidered big stars on the front and had filled them in with red, white, and blue sequins. Long silk fringe hung down all around.

"Mama, it's a masterpiece!" enthused Patsy, her eyes shining. "It's the best one ever! I'm gonna wear it to sing on the *Town and Country Jamboree*, so the whole world can see it!"

"I got news for you, darlin'," said Charlie a little sourly. "Washington, D.C., ain't hardly the world."

He was bitter because he couldn't afford to give Patsy any of the pretty things he'd seen in the store windows downtown, and because, more and more, he hated his job.

This was a busy season for Patsy. There was lots of entertainment around the holidays, everybody going out to have a good time, and she had almost more one-night gigs than she could handle. Charlie envied her, because she loved her work so much, riding off happy in that Buick to Berryville or Clarkson or the Rainbow Road Club, leaving him behind at that shit job at that shit newspaper.

New Year's Eve, though, was a humdinger, just the best there ever was. Patsy went out to the Rainbow Road Club with the Kountry Krackers and they had themselves a jamboree. Charlie put on his brand-new sports jacket—Patsy had surprised him with it at Christmas when the two of them were finally alone together—polished up his silver-plated belt buckle, slipped on his best pleated pants with the creases stitched right in, and went along for the party.

What a party it was! Patsy, her curls bouncing and a dimple showing in her cheek, introducing him from the bandstand as "My darlin' new husband, Mr. Charlie Dick, and I don't want to hear none of you sniggerin', neither."

And everybody clapping and cheering for him, and lining up to buy Charlie drinks.

Patsy was in the best voice he'd ever heard, stronger, yet more womanly. Married life seemed to be good for her. She announced that she would sing the new songs she'd just recorded for Four Star's Coral label, "Pick Me Up on Your Way Down," "A Poor Man's Roses," "The Heart You Break May Be Your Own."

When she told her audience about her label, Coral Records, the sides she'd cut, she sounded so proud, but Charlie knew what was really in her heart—bitter disappointment that Four Star had done nothing with the records: no promotion, no advertising, no pushing them to the all-important country-and-western deejays, and precious little distribution. The sides had sunk without a trace. It only proved to Patsy that her own record company had little or no faith in her future.

But this was New Year's Eve, time to celebrate and look ahead, not behind. And Patsy Cline had a lot to celebrate, living with and loving her own man.

In each other's arms, Charlie didn't think about the boring hell of a job he was trapped in, and Patsy forgot her heartache over her ignored records. All they knew was that they were young, married, in love, and in a few hours would be back in bed together.

And then it was midnight, and everybody was yelling, "Happy New Year!" and kissing everybody else, and the band was playing "Auld Lang Syne" and "Dixie."

Patsy came down off the bandstand and gave her husband a great big kiss while everybody applauded like crazy and Charlie had the grace to blush. Then she climbed back up and sang her curly head off and Charlie danced with the prettiest girls there, and neither one of them had a care in the world that they'd talk about.

"I won't do it!" cried Hilda Hensley for the third time. "I just won't do it, Patsy! It's *wrong*, plain *wrong*!"

Desperation made the muscle in Patsy's jaw stand out. "Mama, please, this could be the most important thing in my whole life! I'll never ask you for anything again, but you've *got* to do this one thing for me!" She raised her voice, as much demanding as imploring. "*Please*!"

But Hilda was adamant, a woman with principles so strong they couldn't be shaken by any kind of argument.

"I won't do it! The idea, asking me to go on television and tell a lie!"

Fighting for control in the knowledge that losing her temper would gain her less than nothing, Patsy fought to bring her voice down to a reasonable level.

"You don't have to lie," she pointed out. "Just say, 'Mr. Godfrey, I'm Hilda Hensley, and I've brought my friend

Patsy Cline, and I'm her talent scout.' That's no lie. You *are* my friend."

But Hilda kept shaking her head stubbornly from side to side. "I ain't gonna do it, so you might as well quit flapping your jaws at me." She shot a keen look at her daughter, who was now on the verge of exasperated tears.

"That man from the show," Hilda continued, "*told* you that talent scouts can't be a relative." A sudden thought struck her, and she narrowed her eyes suspiciously.

"Is that why you give me that housecoat of yours with the little cap sleeves, just so you could turn around and ask me this?"

"I gave you that housecoat 'cause you said you liked it!"

"Well, I won't lie on television," argued Hilda, her train still on the same track.

Now Patsy couldn't control her temper another second, and it flared into an explosion.

"You don't have to *lie,* goddamn it! Just don't spill your guts is all I'm asking," she shouted, her face reddening.

"Watch that dirty talk," sniffed Hilda.

Patsy could see that this yelling wouldn't get her anywhere. You can catch more flies with honey than with vinegar, everybody knows that. She changed her tone to a cajoling one.

"Oh, please, Mama! I *want* this. Think what it can mean for me to be on national television! It's Arthur Godfrey's *Talent Scouts*! Everybody in America watches it. Look, all you have to say is 'Mr. Godfrey, I'm Hilda Hensley and I've brought my friend Patsy Cline, and I'm her talent scout.'"

It seemed so little to ask, to gain the possibility of so much. But Hilda staunchly avoided her daughter's pleading eyes. A bitter lie was a bitter lie, and no amount of coating it with honey could turn it into the sweet truth.

"What the hell do you want?" demanded Patsy, at the end of her rope as she saw this golden opportunity slipping through her fingers. "You want me to get down and beg, I will."

Before her mother's shocked eyes, Patsy fell to her knees and clenched her hands together in an attitude of prayer.

"Please help me to be a singer and have my house with the yellow roses," she begged, looking soulfully at her mother. "Please, please, please, goddamn it, *please*!"

Hilda waved one exasperated hand at her daughter. "Oh, that house with the yellow roses. I'm sick of hearing about it. And get up off your knees, for land's sake. What's Charlie say about it?"

Hesitating a fraction of a second, Patsy answered carefully.

"He can't afford to miss a day's work, or he'd go with us. But he thinks it's a terrific idea."

Well, that's not exactly a lie, is it? He is tickled. But how can I tell Mama that he's not too happy that I'm still using the name "Cline," when I'm married to him now? How can I tell her it pisses him off to think about me going up on national television as Patsy Cline? I wish I could make him understand a little better. There's all my contracts, and the shows I been doing for years. Everybody knows me already as Patsy Cline. It ain't got nothing to do with Gerald. It's only a little thing, anyhow.

Hilda didn't miss that beat of hesitation in Patsy's voice; she never missed a thing where her daughter was concerned.

"Well, I ain't gonna do it," she sniffed, but the conviction in her voice was weaker than before.

And Patsy discerned that little hint of weakness, because she knew her mother so well.

"Is that a smile I see starting on Hilda Hensley's mouth?" she teased. "You're gonna do it for me, aren't ya?"

It was true; in the long run, Hilda had never been able to deny Patsy anything.

"Oh, get up, you silly," she said now, flustered and embarrassed to have given up her principles so easily.

But Patsy didn't get up. Ecstatic, she threw her arms around her mother's waist with a whoop of happiness. She'd won! She'd won! It was green lights now, all the way!

* * *

The first time that Patsy ever went up north was to audition with Arthur Godfrey. She was Patsy Hensley then,
and singing with Bill Peer and his Melody Makers, strictly
country. The whole gang of them auditioned for Godfrey,
but were turned down because the talent coordinators who
booked the acts for the show reckoned that country was too
"hillbilly," too regional for a national audience.

They may have turned down the band, but they liked
Patsy enormously, hearing, as Donn Hecht would hear later,
in the smoothness and magic of her voice the potential of
a great popular singer like Patti Page or Kay Starr. In fact,
they had approached Patsy with a separate offer. Leave the
Melody Makers and we'll put you on the show as a regular,
as our girl singer. We want you, but not them.

Sweet Lord Jesus, but that had been a murderous decision
for any young, ambitious girl to make! Here was a chance
to make it to the big time, the chance that she'd always
dreamed of. And all she had to do was get rid of a few
musicians who could always find themselves another girl
singer!

But it was more than that; it was a matter of ethics and
honesty and loyalty to a man who had given an unknown
teenager a chance. Patsy just couldn't find it in her heart
to stab Bill Peer in the back.

So she'd said no very politely, no thanks, but I have to
stay with my band. The toughest decision of her life, but
she felt good about it. Most of the time, that is, although
many was the time she'd wondered what might have happened to her singing career and her life if she'd told them
yes. Especially after she left the Melody Makers anyhow.
Still, regretting was a foolish and painful way to spend your
time.

And look here. Bread cast on the waters might be coming
back buttered. They'd never forgotten her, those New York
City people. They'd kept her on file, and now that Arthur
Godfrey's *Talent Scouts* was one of the biggest programs

on television, they'd phoned her up and invited her to come on and try for first prize.

"Are you still with that same band?"

"No!" Patsy had cried joyfully. "No, I'm not. I'll be happy to come."

"Just get yourself a talent scout, and we'll send you a couple of plane tickets. Just as long as it's not a member of your family."

And now she had her talent scout, her best friend, Hilda Hensley. Who *was*, in fact, a member of Patsy's family, but that was just a technicality, wasn't it? The important thing was to go to New York and sing on prime-time television. She went around in a daze, but happy for herself.

Others were less happy for Patsy Cline. Jimmy Dean, for example, who wasn't too pleased that Patsy would be missing from her regular stint on *Town and Country Jamboree* while she was in New York. Patsy had built up quite a following on that show, and Dean was ticked off to have his nose rubbed once again in the fact that his program, popular as it was, was local and not national. Back in 1957, country-and-western music was looked down upon as "hick" and "rube" by the rest of the world of entertainment, and hardly any country artist had "crossed over" into making it big in pop. Even Kitty Wells, the reigning queen, was almost unknown outside of the country charts.

Then there was Charlie, who had very mixed feelings about his wife turning up on national TV. Funny, when they were just dating, he was proud as a peacock to have the name of Patsy Cline's boyfriend. But now that they were married, he surely didn't want to be known as Patsy Cline's husband. He wanted her to move forward, but at the same time he wanted her to stand still, to be his wife first and a singer second. He knew it didn't make good sense, but there it was. Not that he had told his thoughts to Patsy; his mama hadn't raised no stupid children.

Nevertheless, Patsy had caught the vibrations, and when

she had time to think about it, she knew a little of what was on Charlie's mind.

But she didn't have a lot of time to think about it. Here it was the second week in January already, and the broadcast was January 21. There was yet so much to do. She had to pick out songs and arrangements to take with her to New York, and stand still for fittings in the brand-new cowgirl costume that Hilda was sewing for her. They had to make airplane reservations and hotel reservations—they were going back to the Dixie on Forty-second Street; it was cheap and, besides, they liked the name. And both she and Hilda had to get new permanents and manicures—the first manicure in Hilda Hensley's life—and pick out a dress for Patsy's mother to wear on TV, and Jesus only knew what-all else.

It was a busy time and a happy time. Patsy rehearsed until her throat started to get sore. Panic-stricken, she stopped rehearsing. Didn't stop smoking, though. Couldn't.

The first thing that struck Patsy and Hilda when they got off the plane at LaGuardia airport after their very first airplane ride was that they were surely going to freeze to death in this city.

New York in January is considerably colder than Virginia. Manhattan, an island surrounded by water, catches icy winds from both the Hudson river and the Atlantic Ocean, and those winds went looking for the marrow of the Hensley bones. Their winter coats, warm enough for Winchester, were barely enough to keep Hilda and Patsy from shivering uncontrollably until they climbed aboard the overheated Carey airport bus with sighs of relief.

"Honey, we're gonna need sweaters," said Hilda.

"Can't afford them," answered Patsy, through chattering teeth.

"Well, we will surely have to wrap up your throat, so at least we can buy you a woolen scarf. Now, don't you shake your head at me. Do you want to lose your voice?"

"Mama, I'm so damn cold, I don't care if I lose my *head*!"

The next unpleasant surprise came at the meeting the following morning with the Godfrey talent coordinator.

Arthur Godfrey was more than a man; he was a show business legend. That old redhead had parlayed a mellow voice, a relaxed delivery, a down-home folksiness, a Hawaiian shirt, and a four-string ukulele into a multimillion-dollar industry. One of the sharpest negotiators around, he presented only a warm, benevolent image to his adoring public. He seemed to be everybody's father, when in fact he was one tough businessman.

There were three Arthur Godfrey shows running on the same network back in 1957. CBS had them all, the morning show, *Arthur Godfrey Time*, the Wednesday night show, *Arthur Godfrey and His Friends*, and, of course, Arthur Godfrey's *Talent Scouts*, on Monday nights, which introduced new talent. The man was a one-person industry.

Every would-be singer or dancer or juggler or acrobat or ventriloquist or child-prodigy violinist or Swiss bell ringer or accordion player or Irish or Italian tenor wanted to be on the *Talent Scouts*. It was really the big chance to hit the big time. So, of course, it wasn't an easy show to break into. The selection process was a careful one. There was a lot more to it than just talent.

Anybody who made it to the show had to have a certain quality besides talent, a kind of humanity and sweet vulnerability that made you root for him or her to win, even to win out over more talented performers. When the talent coordinators had seen Patsy first, years ago, she was a natural, because she was still so young, only a teenager. That big voice coming out of that little girl was a real startler.

But now Patsy was a woman, and even though the voice was better, more mature, more assured, the shock value of it had lessened. Nobody expected a girl to have a woman's voice, but it was no big surprise coming out of a tall, beautiful, curvy thing like Patsy Cline.

Still, her talent was undeniable. It was her material that was so dreadful. They hated all the songs she'd brought with her, and that was the big, unpleasant surprise.

"Don't you have anything else? These are mediocre at best."

"Well, those are the ones I recorded, but maybe that's why they didn't sell any records," answered Patsy unhappily.

"One more song? Anything?"

Patsy sighed deeply. There *was* one more song in her repertoire, a new one, but it had been forced on her by the people at Four Star, and she hated it.

"It's nothin' but a little ole pop song!" she'd yelled at the stone-hearted Four Star executives. Now she said it again.

"It's nothin' but a little ole pop song, but I do have another one. It's called 'Walkin' After Midnight.'"

"May we see the arrangement? Hmm. Would you be good enough to run through it for us?"

Reluctantly, Patsy sang it through once, realizing that this was her only chance. It was uptempo, a song sung by a lonely woman who goes out walking after midnight in search of her lost lover. Of all the material that Four Star had force-fed her, she liked this song the least. But if the Arthur Godfrey people didn't go for it, she had no chance to get on the show at all. There was nothing else left in her box of tricks.

The talent coordinator listened critically.

"Yeah, that's not bad," came the decision. "It goes with your style. Okay, you'll sing that one."

Hilda Hensley had rehearsed what she was supposed to say on TV at least a thousand times, and most of the time she got it wrong. Instead of "I've brought my friend Patsy Cline," it kept coming out, "I've brought my *daughter* Patsy Cline," which would be a disaster. But it slipped out so natural, and it was nothing but the plain God's honest truth.

Now, standing backstage waiting to go on, Hilda was in a sweaty funk of stage fright. *I just know I'm gonna get it wrong, and then where will we be? Why did I ever let Patsy talk me into this foolishness? It's gonna be the death of me, I know it is. Sweet Jesus, help me, please, amen.*

And Patsy was looking so beautiful in her country calico dress with the ruffles and the rickrack piping, her hair tied with ribbons, and her white boots on her feet for good luck. *Please don't make me let her down*, prayed her mother.

All around her backstage were other acts just as nervous as she and her daughter, but Hilda never noticed them. She just held herself in a dread-filled suspension until a man with an official-looking clipboard beckoned to her. Then, taking a deep breath, a trembling Hilda Hensley crept out onto the stage, under the hot lights, to face a live audience and a live TV camera.

"Hello there, and welcome," said a redheaded, freckle-faced man who looked astonishingly like Arthur Godfrey. "Where you from?"

That wasn't the question that Hilda had expected would be first. But she was already programmed. Off a dry tongue and out through parched lips came the much-rehearsed words.

"Mr. Godfrey, I'm Hilda Hensley and I've brought my friend Patsy Cline, and I'm her talent scout."

Backstage, Patsy relaxed for an instant. *Thank you, Jesus, she got it right.* But she was still shaking like a leaf as she waited for her intro.

Now a giggle ran through the audience at Hilda's answering the wrong question. They recognized an advanced case of stage fright.

"Well, good," smiled the Old Redhead. Nervousness never bothered him; in fact, he encouraged it. His audience loved to see people quaking in their boots; it added a down-home authenticity to the program, and contrasted nicely with his own relaxed style. "And, like I said, where're you two from?"

Now that the lie was out and over with, Hilda Hensley

felt a little better. For the first time, she actually heard the question.

"Winchester, Virginia."

"That's mighty pretty country down there," Godfrey went on smoothly. "Now. What's Patsy talent?"

"She sings," answered Patsy's mother.

"Is she good?"

"She's *wonderful!*" beamed Hilda. Lordy, but it felt good to tell the truth!

"Let's bring her out. Ladies and gentlemen, welcome Patsy Cline!"

There was a burst of music and some polite applause. Backstage, Patsy Cline took one deep breath and slammed her hands together hard. Then she virtually marched out there on the stage, smiling broadly, her dress swirling around her knees.

The studio orchestra broke into Patsy's arrangement of "Walkin' After Midnight" and Patsy Cline tore into the song headfirst. Her shoulders shook, her feet tapped, her beautiful dark eyes snapped and blazed. Her voice, that magical instrument that was uniquely Patsy's, filled the studio, bouncing off the rafters. If she hated that song before, she surely loved it now. It was hers, nobody but hers, it had been given to her, and now she made it completely her own.

Back in Winchester, Charlie sat glued to the little black-and-white television set, not taking his eyes off Patsy for one solitary second. On the sofa next to him, John and Sylvia sat rapt, thrilled out of their minds to be seeing their mother and sister on live TV. Sitting on the floor, J. W. Woodhouse took a swig of his beer and envied Charlie Dick.

And then the song was over, and the audience went insane. The show stopped cold as they clapped and cheered. Patsy just stood there, grinning all over her face, looking by-God beautiful. Charlie, watching it all in Winchester, let out a bloodcurdling rebel yell, loud enough for his wife to hear it in New York City.

"You lucky sucker!" shouted J.W., pounding Charlie on

the back. "She could make it big!"

And then the show was coming to an end, with every act brought out to do a little reprise, and the audience to pick the winner. There was an eight-year-old accordion player who got a big hand, a violinist who had played "The Hot Canary," who did only so-so, and then it was Patsy Cline's turn.

As she heard her music start up, Patsy stepped forward, opening her mouth to sing a bar or two, but the audience cut loose before she could make a sound. As one, they rose to their feet, clapping furiously. The meter shot all the way up to the top and froze there. The applause went on and on and on, long after it was apparent that Patsy Cline was the easy first-prize winner.

It was no longer applause, it was an ovation. On national television. In front of all of America. Patsy couldn't help it. She burst into tears.

In the wings, Hilda Hensley stood with happy tears running down her cheeks. *Thank you, Lord, for letting this happen for my Patsy. Thank you for her beautiful voice, and for giving her this moment. Keep on blessing her, Lord. Amen.*

In Winchester, even with all the yelling going on in the house as Patsy was named the winner, the kids jumping around and hugging each other, J.W. grinning and thumping him, a thought flashed across Charlie's mind, cutting coldly through his excitement and pride.

That shoulda been Patsy Dick up there, not Patsy Cline. Damn it, she's married to me now, and she should be givin' me the credit, not him.

As for Patsy Cline, now crying unashamedly, her heart was hammering so hard in her chest that she could hear it above the tumult of the applause. *This is it. Lordy, lordy. Finally. This is what I worked for for so long. All those years. And now it's here, it's mine. And I ain't never gonna let go of it. Never. This is my time; it's come at last.*

March 5, 1963

*T*HEY FLEW AN INDIRECT COURSE, always keeping out of the path of the storm, which was still raging. Randy knew that the storm was somewhere on his five-hundred-mile flight path, but he stayed in constant touch with the ground, talking again and again on the two-way radio to Atlanta for their weather station's updates and briefings. Hughes wasn't an instrument-rated pilot, but, hell, he had no intention of flying through that mess on instruments, anyway. It was better to avoid it entirely.

As he flew across Missouri and headed into Arkansas, the storm was ahead of him, and the danger of catching up with it became greater. No fool, Randy Hughes set down three or four times to wait it out and let the front pass. At Little Rock it was particularly bad, with head winds carrying icy sheets of sleet, and they had to sit on the ground for a couple of hours.

Their intention was to refuel at Dyersburg, Tennessee, which wasn't far from Nashville, no more than ninety miles by air. But it was much safer to take on extra gasoline toward the end of the trip than to run the risk of an empty tank. He might have to zigzag even more than he expected.

When they landed at the Dyersburg airport, everybody took a deep breath. Only ninety miles from home, now. On the last leg. The tension had been close to unbearable, although all four of them had put the best possible face on it, keeping quiet in the rough spots, each of them frightened but unwilling to communicate it to the others.

Randy was the only one who had insider's knowledge of just exactly how dangerous the flight had been. A small twin-engine craft caught up in a thunderstorm was like a cardboard box in a whirlwind. But he certainly didn't want Patsy to know that; she was worried half out of her mind as it was, fretting to be home with her babies.

But now, on the ground, so close to Nashville, they could relax and drink coffee in the airport lounge, swap lies and tell jokes, smoke cigarettes, laugh and feel human. Now they could try to top one another with tall tales about how terrified they had really been.

"Man, I was so scared," laughed Hawk Hawkins, "I was afraid I was gonna shit!"

"That's nothing," Cowboy Copas scoffed. *"I* was so scared I was afraid I was *never* gonna shit, 'cause it froze right up my bee-hind."

"Hoss, *I* was so scared," put in Patsy, "that I was afraid I was gonna *turn* to shit, bee-hind, boots, and all!"

Their coarseness and vulgarity was somehow comforting; it was evidence that they were alive, had pulled through it, could make rough jokes about it.

But another question had come up. The Tennessee weather reports weren't favorable, especially over Camden, where a front just hung there and didn't seem to be moving. Camden was between Dyersburg and Nashville, and there was no flying around it.

The airport manager proposed that they stay overnight in Dyersburg; he'd see to it that the stars of the Grand Ole Opry were made comfortable. It would be an honor.

No way was Patsy going to listen to *that* proposal, not when she was so close to home she could almost smell the apple blossoms.

"Well, how about this? Take the airport car and *drive* to Nashville. We got a nice 'sixty-one station wagon here, and somebody can fly the plane home for you when the weather clears. Maybe even tomorrow. It's a lot safer driving than it is flying."

"How far is it by car?" asked Randy Hughes.

"'Bout a hundred and twenty miles. Ninety by air, hundred twenty by road."

"Hell," exclaimed Patsy, "that's at least three hours driving in bad weather. Maybe even more. I vote no."

It's possible that the other three might have voted her down, but two things worked against it. First, Patsy Cline could be a well-known terror when she was crossed. Then, too, how would it look for three good ole southern boys to admit they were uncomfortable about flying when a little lady had already said she wasn't afraid?

The decision was made. They'd take the chance; if the weather proved too much for them, they'd turn right around and come back to Dyersburg. It seemed to satisfy everybody.

Randy Hughes radioed ahead to Nashville, informing them that his twin-engine Piper Comanche 250 was taking off from Dyersburg, and asking them to turn on the runway lights at Cornelia Field.

At a little after six in the evening, they took off for the last time. They were all in a happy frame of mind. After all, they'd be home in Nashville within the hour.

Twelve

NOTHING WAS THE SAME for Patsy after she sang "Walkin' After Midnight" on Arthur Godfrey's show. The whole world did a 110-degree spin, and when it came back to rest on its axis, Patsy Cline was on her way to being famous.

The first thing that happened to her was right after the program, when a whole mess of people came crowding around her and Hilda to congratulate them and wish them luck. Patsy had always heard stories about New York City people—how nasty they were, how coldhearted, how indifferent and mean-spirited and critical. But these here people were giving that story the living lie.

Of course, what she didn't stop to figure out as she shook all those hands and accepted all those compliments was that even New York City people like to cosy up to a winner.

But then this tall, distinguished-looking man with obviously expensive clothes and silver-touched hair, like Andy Hardy's father in the movies, pushed his way through the crowd and came right up to the two of them.

"Miss Cline? Mrs. Hensley? I'm Bill Shawley, and I've got a question for you. How'd you like to make a record of that song you just sang?"

Out of his vest pocket he took a business card rimmed with gold, and handed it to Patsy, who accepted it, dazed. Craning her neck, Hilda Hensley could make out the word "Decca," which she recognized as a top label.

Patsy's first hot burst of ecstasy was extinguished by a sudden splash of the cold water of recollection.

"Oh, I already got me a recording contract, with Four Star. I cut some sides on the Coral label."

"Believe it or not, I'm aware of that," answered Shawley smoothly. "It poses no problems for us, nor should it for you. We retain a staff of lawyers who can easily negotiate around it."

Patsy grabbed he mother's hands tightly, squeezing them in her joy.

"Do you always sing like that?" continued Shawley.

Patsy looked at Hilda, puzzled. What other way was there for her to sing? "Uh . . . yeah."

The tall man smiled in satisfaction. "Excellent. I've got a feeling I can do you quite a bit of good." He leaned forward confidentially and lowered his voice so that the crowd of onlookers couldn't hear him.

"I think you can make me a lot of money," he smiled, "and some for yourself along the way."

Unable to suppress her excitement, Patsy's mother gave her a sharp nudge in the ribs.

"Oh, God," laughed Patsy to Hilda, "just wait till I tell Charlie!" She turned back to Bill Shawley, and her face became more serious.

"I made records before, but they were pretty bad. The sound and all. . . ." She shook her head, then was struck by a sudden reminder.

"Oh, I wanted to tell Mr. Godfrey something. This lady here, who said she was my friend? She's really my mother."

The two women held their breath, waiting for the sky to fall on their lying heads. But Bill Shawley didn't bat an eye. Putting one arm around Patsy's shoulders and the other around Hilda's, he led them away.

"Not to worry. I'll take care of it," he promised easily. "Arthur and I go way back."

But Patsy shook her head firmly. "'Twouldn't be right, Mr. Shawley. It was my doin' and I'll undo it myself."

Hilda nodded her approval. The tall man shrugged.

"It's up to you. Come on, let's you two and Big Bill Shawley go talk contracts over a daiquiri."

Behind his back, Hilda Hensley mouthed silently to her daughter, "What's a daiquiri?"

"Damned if I know," Patsy mouthed back.

"Hello? Charlie? Charlie, is that you? It's Patsy, honey."

"Hey, darlin', you were fantastic! I was so damn proud of my little girl, winning out over all them others. I knew you would. We were all here rootin' for you, John and Syl—"

"Charlie, I can't talk too long, 'cause it's long-distance and mortally expensive. So listen, because there's a lot happening that you have to know about. Mr. Godfrey wants me to stay another week and go on his morning program *three times*! And I'm gonna come right out and tell him about Mama being Mama and not a friend. Oh, and Charlie, there's a man from Decca Records who wants me to cut a record of "Walkin' After Midnight" right here in their sound studio in New York where they got good sidemen and good acoustics and—"

"When are you comin' home?" Charlie interrupted brusquely, his elation evaporating.

"Well, soon, honey, but I can't say exactly when. But Mama's here with me and—"

"When the hell are you coming home?" he demanded. "And what the hell am I supposed to do with myself while you're farting around in the big city?"

"Charlie, that's not fair and you know it." Patsy sounded genuinely hurt.

"This is what we've been waiting and praying and hoping for. I've worked real hard for this. And I'll be getting paid. Mr. Godfrey is going to pay me union scale for singing on his morning program, and I'll be getting some money from Decca real soon. I already borrowed twenty-five dollars from them against my advance, and they said they'd be happy to make it two hundred and *fifty*! So, listen, honey, why don't you fly up here and be with me? I got me a nice hotel room, and they're payin' for it. We could have us a real good time together. I miss you, baby."

But Charlie, disgruntled and lonely, refused to allow himself to be cajoled.

"Somebody has to keep a steady job, and you know it. You could get paid by Arthur Godfrey today and be flat on your ass tomorrow, so don't go talkin' about me flying up anywhere."

What Charlie didn't tell Patsy was that he was already in trouble down at the paper. After Patsy had won the *Talent Scouts*, he and J.W. had gone out celebrating, and he hadn't shown up for work the next morning. Old fart Lawrence had read him to filth and creamed his ass; now he was on probation.

But there was something else troubling him. The note of bubbly happiness in Patsy's voice was something he had heard before only when the two of them were having one of their play parties. She'd *never* been happy about her career, not since he'd known her. Always moaning about the screwing she was getting from the record company, and how she was never going to be a star at the rate she was going.

Now he felt suddenly pushed aside, made out to be of lesser importance. She was happy about something, very happy, and it had nothing to do with Charlie Dick.

"Listen, I can't talk anymore, it's costing too much. I'll be home before you know it. So eat good and take care of yourself. It's cold as a witch's tit up here, honey, so you're probably better off in Winchester anyway. Good-bye, Charlie, I love you."

And before he could say, "I love you" or "I miss you" or "I'm hurtin', don't do me this way," all he had in his ear was a disconnected telephone line.

* * *

Patsy and Hilda had an appointment to meet Arthur Godfrey himself the following morning, before the show went on the air. Patsy was determined to tell him the truth about her "talent scout." If he fired her before she got a chance to sing on his morning show, well then, so be it. But she couldn't continue this masquerade a minute longer. With her heart in her mouth, she faced the famous entertainer, who greeted her with his celebrated broad grin.

"Hello, Patsy, you were terrific last night. How do you feel this morning, after your big win?"

"I'm fine, sir," said Patsy nervously, clasping the hand that Godfrey held out to her. "But there's something I've got to tell you, and I got to say it now, before I lose my nerve. Mr. Godfrey, this lady here is my mother. She's the best friend I have in the world, so I never lied about that, but she's also my mother. To tell the honest truth, that was the only way I could get up the nerve to come on the show, to have my mama with me."

A look of puzzlement appeared on Arthur Godfrey's freckled face.

"Why didn't you just bring your mother along as your talent scout?"

"Well, they told me I couldn't bring a relative, anybody else *except* a relative."

Godfrey's eyes narrowed, and his jolly mood evaporated; Patsy had heard backstage that he could be a bully when he was angry, firing anyone who displeased him. "Who told you this?" he snarled.

Determined not to get anybody in trouble, Patsy murmured, "Somebody from the show called me. I don't remember the name."

He shot her a keen, penetrating look, but Patsy kept her eyes down, and Hilda just stood there silent, her fingers nervously twisting the handles of her pocketbook.

"Well," drawled the redhead with a mock sigh, "I surely don't know *what* to do in a situation like this one. Here you are, a good Winchester girl, and here's your fine mama, a good Winchester lady, and the audience doesn't know it. If it were me, I'd be ashamed to show my face back down there if I didn't acknowledge this fine lady as my mama."

Stunned, Patsy raised her eyes to Godfrey's and saw the twinkle in them. Before she could gasp out a single word, the Old Redhead continued.

"You're gonna work with me this week, and I want you to come on back next week, too. And today, when we're on the air, I'll ask you, 'Patsy, how's that nice mother of yours?' and you'll tell me she's fine, hear? Then I'll tell the audience that your talent scout was really your mother. The truth will be out, and I'll be in the clear. What do you say?"

What *could* Patsy say? She said thank you, Mr. Godfrey. And, no more than two hours later, on coast-to-coast radio, that's exactly what he did.

Shawley was as good as his word. Recognizing a potential gold mine, he made an immediate deal with Four Star, in which Decca would supply the recording technology and the distribution and split the profits from "Walkin' After Midnight" with Four Star. As for Patsy Cline, her contract continued to be with Four Star; it still had a couple of years to run. And her royalty would still be the pitiful two-and-a-fraction percent. But time was of the essence here. Patsy Cline had taken America by storm with her singing, and he wanted to get her record out in the stores while people were demanding it. He had Patsy's signature on the agreement faster than a coon hound can tree a raccoon.

She didn't get to read much of the contract, and she didn't have a lawyer to go over it with, but Big Bill assured her it was fair, and she was as eager to sign it as he was to have her sign it. So it was signed, and Patsy Cline was now nominally a Decca artist, along with such stars as Bing Crosby, Peggy Lee, Judy Garland, and Ella Fitzgerald.

The recording sessions were like nothing Patsy Cline had

ever experienced before. They were totally professional, with no expense spared to get the best possible sound out of the musicians and the vocalist. What she'd had before on Coral was merely shoestring production with ancient equipment, unrehearsed musicians, and a muddy, amateurish sound. Her previous recordings had been of the worst possible quality.

Decca's studio was state of the art. When she saw all those sound boards, with their dials, flashing lights, and meters, Patsy's eyes grew round with wonder. There were *three* engineers in the control booth, and one producer, and they all wore headphones. The whole thing was more wonderful than she'd ever dreamed possible.

And yet . . .

"Perfect!" called Shawley, as she finished her fourth take of "Walkin' After Midnight." "That's the one. That's a wrap."

The musicians groaned in relief. It had been a long session, and they were frazzled. Shawley's words were what they'd been waiting for, merciful, blissful relief.

"Can't we try it just one more time?" called Patsy. "I think I can get it some better this time around."

When the musicians groaned again, it was not with relief. And that, too, would become part of the Patsy Cline legend. "One more time," she'd always beg her producer. "Let's try it just once more. I'm sure I can do it better next time."

When Patsy returned from New York City, it was to find herself not only a Winchester celebrity, but *the* Winchester celebrity. She was front-page news in the very newspaper that Charlie worked for, and he even got to set the type for the story himself, which made him proud and pissed him off at one and the same time.

Newspaper clippings then started pouring in from everywhere—Richmond, and Roanoke, and Lynchburg, from Washington, D.C., and Frederick and even Baltimore, where Patsy had a big following, thanks to Jimmy Dean's TV show. There was so much coverage of Patsy's *Talent Scouts* first prize that Hilda started to fall behind in the scrapbooks she had pasted up for Patsy ever since her career began. Newspapers were piling up in Hilda Hensley's otherwise tidy house, waiting to be gone through for pictures and stories of Patsy.

A few requests for interviews began to trickle in from magazines, but when Decca released "Walkin' After Midnight" and it started getting air play, the trickle increased to a flood.

And then—the accolade that was the hope and prayer of every country-and-western singer—an invitation to sing on Grand Ole Opry. Singing at the Opry was the equivalent of playing the Palace to a vaudevillian—it meant you'd made the big time. After years of not giving her a tumble, Nashville was suddenly mighty interested in Miss Patsy Cline. An appearance on the Opry meant only one thing—that Patsy had a hit record.

Grand Ole Opry had been a country music institution since 1925, when it started as *Barn Dance* over radio station WSM. By February 16, 1957, when Patsy Cline made her first solo appearance, the Opry was what everybody listened to on Saturday night. Since 1950, they could watch it on television, too.

Folks would begin lining up early Saturday outside the Ryman Auditorium in "Music City, U.S.A.," hoping to get seats for the show. The Opry went on the air at seven-thirty in the evening and lasted until midnight, but it wasn't unusual to see lines forming for tickets as early as ten in the morning.

When Patsy Cline heard her introduction, she came out on the Opryland stage in her western outfit, bold as brass, but quaking inside. This was a country audience, the most critical in the world, and they had been accustomed to listening to the best. At the Opry, they expected the best. Would she measure up?

The applause was deafening, even before she reached the microphone.

All she could do was stand there and pray she wouldn't cry again, like she'd done on the Godfrey show. God keep her from becoming known as Patsy Cryin'! But her heart was fuller than it had ever been.

These were her people—country people—and they knew her! They recognized Patsy Cline as one of their own, and they loved her for it! She launched into "Walkin' After Midnight" with joy and abandon, singing her heart out for her country friends. And, when the song was finished, the audience at the Grand Ole Opry was even more enthusiastic.

Listening to the stomping and cheering, the clapping and whistling, Patsy couldn't help but let the tears roll down her cheeks. How could she stop them?

She'd come home.

Money was starting to trickle in, too. Not a whole lot, barely enough to buy some of the furniture that Patsy had been wanting for the house. A new house, a new car— these were still just dreams. One appearance at the Opry and one grand prize on Arthur Godfrey and one record out from Decca, these didn't yet add up to "star."

Everybody assumed that Patsy Cline was getting rich from "Walkin' After Midnight." In fact, her royalty checks were pitifully small, considering how well the record was doing. Four Star was charging her for every expense possible in connection with the record—not only distribution costs, but promotion, publicity, advertising.

Patsy never saw any advertisements for her record, and as for the publicity, the best of it—the Godfrey show and the Grand Ole Opry—they were free as air.

The list of expenses that arrived with the checks floored Patsy. On the sheet were hundreds of dollars for things like telephone calls and postage stamps and "entertaining disk jockeys." Sometimes Patsy would call the record company to complain.

"What's this for?" she'd demand.

"Promotion," they'd answer blandly.

"What the hell did you promote and where the hell did you promote it?"

"Oh, it's impossible to itemize all of it," would come the evasive reply. "It's standard business practice."

Standard business practice. Sure, they were giving her the business, and they'd had a lot of practice. And there wasn't a damn thing she could do about it. If you took their figures as valid, the damn company was practically *losing* money on "Walkin' After Midnight." What the hell would they do if they had a number-one hit on their hands? Go out of business?

Her friends couldn't understand why Patsy and Charlie didn't have a big house and a Cadillac car and a swimming pool, and nothing that Patsy could tell them about the royalty system and record company bookkeeping made any sense to them. Well sure, why not? It didn't make any sense to Charlie and Patsy, either.

Still, it was better than what they'd had before. Only thing was, the new money was all earned by Patsy Cline; not a dime of it by Charlie Dick.

Patsy had everything she wanted now—a career that was beginning to take off, some money coming in, a man she was passionately in love with, and her dream was still intact. The house with the yellow roses and the children with Charlie's blue eyes were closer to becoming a reality than ever before. So, if there were subtle warnings of trouble to come, little danger signals that flashed off as quickly as they flashed on, how could she be expected to pay them any mind?

Patsy hummed as she put the chicken in the oven. It was a good, plump, fresh-killed local bird; none of your plastic-wrapped supermarket trash. The stuffing was sage and on-ion, Charlie's favorite. She was looking forward to this meal, sitting down at the new kitchen table with the lace cloth, her hair done, Charlie sitting across from her enjoying the chicken.

It seemed to her that she had less and less time alone

with her husband these days; she was always on call for this or that. A rehearsal, an interview, a series of one-nighters with a well-known country band—everything seemed to be pulling her in a different direction from Charlie. She'd make it up to him, though.

She glanced at the kitchen clock. Almost five. Charlie would be home by six-fifteen, hungry as a bear for his supper, and she still had a lot to do. Put up the beans, make the salad, set the table, take a shower, and for Jesus' sake get her hair out of those rollers.

On her way to the bedroom, she stopped to survey the living room, and a smile touched the corners of her full lips. Pretty, damned if it wasn't pretty. Her gloating eyes took in the new sofa and chairs, the red velvet drapes, the knickknacks on top of the new "entertainment center," a floor-model television set with a big screen and a built-in radio and hi-fi phonograph. All bought with singing money. Now, *that* was satisfaction.

By six-fifteen everything was ready except Charlie. He wasn't home by seven, nor by eight. The chicken sat cold on the table, a thin film of grease congealed on its breast. The stuffing was already turning sour, coming in second to Patsy, whose facial expression by now was pure vinegar.

At twenty minutes after eight, the sound of Charlie's car. A door slamming. The front door opening. And here's our hero, strolling right in, a mite unsteadily, king of the castle, a grin on his face from one ear to t'other.

"Where you been?" demanded Patsy.

"I had a drink on the way home." His tongue was thick.

"*Or* five. *Or* seven. Damn it, I worked my hump off making you baked chicken tonight, and you come home this late!"

Charlie waved one careless hand. "I'll eat it. M'hungry."

Patsy screwed her eyes up and gave him her dirty look, which bounced right off his oblivious hide. "You got a finger?"

He looked at her, puzzled as to her meaning. "What? Yeah."

"Well, *use* it!" she shouted. "Put the goddamned thing in a telephone and dial me when you're gonna be late."

What the hell was she talking about? One little drink. . . .

"I said I'd eat the damned thing, didn't I?"

Flopping down at the table, he was reaching for the platter of cold chicken when he caught full sight of Patsy's face. She had her mean mouth on, and it was enough to make any man react. Instantly, he flared up.

"Hey, lady, I got a message for you," he snarled. "Screw your baked chicken and screw *you.*"

"Well, it's the last time I try to cook anything special for you," sniffed Patsy.

Now it was Charlie's turn to get mean. Cocking his head to one side like a coy maiden, he mocked her in a mincing falsetto.

"Oh, poor Patsy! Oh, boo hoo."

That was downright unfair. She didn't deserve that, and it made her see red, him making fun of her like that, when all she'd tried to do was please him. She had been trying to keep her temper under control, but this was just too goddamned much.

"You dumb redneck son-of-a-bitch!" she yelled, and swung into action.

With one sweep of her arm, Patsy slammed the platter of chicken hard against the kitchen wall. The platter shattered, sending shards of china and pieces of greasy chicken everywhere, making a hideous mess of the wallpaper and a slippery booby trap of the floor.

For an instant, Charlie sat shocked, but he bounced back almost at once, with a ferocity that matched her own.

"Oh, you wanna play?" he shouted, grabbing up the bowl of green beans and hurling it against the farther wall. It, too, broke, and the holy mess those beans made sliding down the wall was truly awesome to behold.

Now it was Patsy's turn. Furiously, she grabbed hold of the new lace tablecloth, and plates, glasses, lettuce and tomatoes, knives and forks went flying everywhere to the crashing sound of mass breakage.

But Charlie wasn't to be topped so lightly. There was still his end of the table to be cleared, and he cleared it. And *how* he cleared it!

There wasn't anything left to throw now; everything was tangled up or broken or lying wetly and greasily and greenly on the floor. The two of them sat regarding each other furiously, breathing hard, each one waiting for the other to make the next move. Suddenly, surprisingly, Charlie grinned.

"You wanna start on the living room?" he asked.

Patsy tried to scowl, but she couldn't do it. A snort of laughter escaped her lips, to be stifled only when she surveyed the hideous wreckage that had once been a chicken dinner. Covering her mouth with her hand, she gasped.

"Oh, Lord, Mama and I just papered these walls last month. She'll have a *fit*!"

"Come on," laughed Charlie. "We'll go for a pizza. I'll help you clean up later." He headed for the bathroom, whistling, to start up the shower.

Patsy stood looking around at the debris in the kitchen, half rueful, half in wonderment. In less than two minutes, her nice, normal kitchen had been turned into World War Three. Then she shrugged.

"Well, I *told* Mama I wanted a little excitement," she reminded herself, and went in search of her husband.

As usual, he'd left a trail of discarded clothing all the way to the shower. Sighing, she followed the trail, bending to retrieve shirt, socks, trousers, underdrawers. In the bathroom, she stuffed the dirty clothes into the hamper.

The water was good and hot, and Charlie was under it. Patsy slipped out of her good dress and underthings and joined him in the shower. He moved over to make room for her.

There was a liquor bottle on the edge of the bathtub,

because her husband dearly loved to have himself a little drink while getting clean. Charlie picked it up and took a long pull, then handed it to Patsy, who took a somewhat shorter swallow.

"Here, hon." He handed her a washcloth and a bar of soap and presented her with his back. As she obligingly scrubbed it, he grinned happily and took another drink.

"Just sip it slow and the world stays sweet."

"My daddy used to say that," said Patsy reminiscently. "He was something, my daddy—used to eat cold navy bean sandwiches for breakfast ever' morning of his life." In a very different voice, she added, "And I hope he has arthritis in both those nasty, grabbin' hands of his."

Charlie turned his head to peer curiously at her. "What do you mean?"

Patsy gnawed her lip as the ugly memory surfaced, but she kept her tone neutral. "Oh, he tried a little somethin' with me a few times. . . . And once, not long before he left, he tried somethin' more." There was a catch in her voice as she said these last words.

Now Charlie turned himself right around and looked Patsy straight in the face.

"You tellin' me he tried to mess with you?"

Patsy nodded, her expression grim.

"Jesus," breathed her husband, horrified. "How come you never told me that before?"

Handing him the soap and cloth, Patsy turned to have her own back scrubbed. "How come *you* never talk about *your* family?" she countered.

He refused to meet her questioning eyes. "Aw, hell. Not when I'm in such a good mood. Do my back some more."

Before she could take the cloth from his hands, the telephone rang. Grabbing up a towel, she raced downstairs to answer it, dripping water on the new scatter rugs.

Charlie picked up the bottle and took another swig, hoping Patsy would come right back and not stand there jawing with her mother while she soaked the floor through. But when she came back to the bathroom after several minutes, her footsteps were slow. He looked out through the steamy water to see her standing there in the doorway, a stunned look on her face, like she'd just been hit on the head.

"Patsy?" he asked, concerned.

"Charlie—" and her voice quivered. "Oh, my God, Charlie, that was Decca Records. "Walkin' After Midnight" jumped all the way to number sixteen! I'm on the son-of-a-bitching *charts*!"

It took a second for it to hit home, but when it did, Charlie yelled like an Indian and, grabbing his wife, dragged Patsy, towel and all, into the shower with him. They kissed and hugged and carried on like idiots, slipping and sliding around in the porcelain tub, yelling, laughing, holding on tightly to each other.

"Oh, honey, let's get two pizzas. Hell, *five*! We've got the world by the tail with a downhill pull!"

He kissed her wet face, her eyelids, her lips. And then he was bending his head to kiss her breasts with their erect nipples.

Patsy threw back her head and closed her eyes, feeling Charlie's lips tracing fire patterns on her body. This was something worth celebrating, and she and her man always knew how to celebrate.

Thirteen

IT WAS THE NEXT MORNING that the blow fell, and from a quarter that took both of them totally by surprise.

The night before had been something for the record books. First, that glorious food fight, then Patsy finding out that she had a hit on the record charts, next, making love in the shower and then again on the bed, still damp and a little soapy. Then Charlie, ravenous and howling for food, driving six miles to pick up pizza. Patsy had half the mess cleaned up by the time he returned with the large, flat, fragrant boxes, and they fell like wolves on the savory pies, eating them steaming hot and washing them down with Miller's.

Then the two of them pitching in and getting the kitchen as clean as it could possibly get, never mind the permanent stains on the brand-new wallpaper. That had left them so messy themselves that there was nothing else for it but another shower.

Which led, inevitably, to more lovemaking, this time long and slow and as sweet as honey in her veins. Holding her man on top of her, both of them satisfied and exhausted, two cigarettes in the ashtray, what more could a woman want? They had so much energy, these two, so young and so strong, juice in their bodies and fire in their brains. Was it any wonder that every now and then their juices would bubble up and over, and all their energy would turn to anger and come rushing out at each other?

They made up. They always made up. They had developed a pattern of fighting and loving and fighting and loving that came naturally to both of them, easy and familiar. It was simple for Patsy and Charlie to react emotionally and erupt into a fight, rather than sit down and talk over their problems.

What was love all about, when you came right down to it, but fighting and making up with kisses and passion? Put a strong man together in a marriage with a strong woman and what you wound up with was TNT. The only difference was the length of the fuse.

When Patsy opened her eyes the next morning, it was to hear birds singing, early in the season, spring not due yet for three whole weeks.

The first thing she remembered was the loving, because she was still tingling inside and out. The next thing that came back to mind was that "Walkin' After Midnight" had hit the country charts at number sixteen and was climbing, according to the A&R man at Decca. The record company was going to take ads out in *Billboard* and *Cashbox*, the music industry trade journals, announcing that a new star had appeared like a comet in the sky, Miss Patsy Cline. Her photograph and everything. She was on her way.

She could hear Charlie brushing his teeth in the bathroom, and she stretched her naked body luxuriously in the bed, hating to leave it, while at the same time eager to get started on this magnificent day. She was so lucky. *Thank you, Jesus*, she said silently. She had her man and her singing and her mama was still young and healthy.

As soon as her husband had vacated the bathroom, Patsy dived into the shower. She was dressed before he was, because all she pulled on was a pair of Levi's and a simple shirt. She loved going barefoot and never wore shoes around the house if she could help it. Only when company came, and sometimes not even then.

Practically flying around the kitchen, Patsy put coffee up to perk, at the same time frying bacon in the pan, cracking eggs into a bright blue bowl. She had big plans for this day;

she was going to clean out every shelf in the house and put down new contact paper, then drive over to Hilda's and help her with the precious scrapbooks. Hilda was baking today, and had promised her daughter a lattice-topped cherry pie to take home for Charlie's supper.

Speaking of Charlie, he was walking in the kitchen door right now, the morning paper tucked underneath his arm, riffling through the mail.

"Got a letter from Washington, D.C.," he announced. "Probably from that fool Eisenhower wantin' to know why I didn't vote for him this time around...."

He broke off, a horrified look on his face as he read and reread the brief letter. "Shit *me*!" he gasped, his eyes wide as they met Patsy's. "I've been drafted!"

Stricken, Patsy could only put one hand to her mouth and stare at Charlie in disbelief.

"I can't be drafted! I'm in the friggin' National Guard!"

The bottom had just dropped out of their life, and neither one of them could fully comprehend it yet.

"Well, old big-shot you," retorted Patsy with pathetic sarcasm, "you said they'd never miss you at those meetings."

They stared at each other again, frozen, then Charlie suddenly sprang into galvanized action, pacing around the kitchen and slamming his fist into his open palm.

"I ain't going!" he said with finality. "I'll tell you that for sure and certain. I'll shoot my toe off. I'll tell 'em I'm a homo. I *will*!" He turned to his wife and looked her right in the eye.

"I. Ain't. Going!"

He went.

Charlie Dick passed his physical with flying colors. He didn't shoot his toe off or try to tell the Army psychiatrists that he was a fairy. Instead, he quit his job at the newspaper and waited morosely at home for his induction notice. He didn't have to wait long. His orders came. First basic training, then Fort Bragg, Fayetteville, North Carolina.

It was a lovely spring day when Patsy and Hilda took Charlie down to the station and put him on the bus, but it was winter in the newlyweds' hearts. Only Hilda seemed to be philosophical about the situation.

As the bus pulled away, taking with it a disconsolate Charlie, unhappily waving from a window, Patsy's mother took her sobbing daughter into her arms.

"Well now, it ain't the end of the world. Fort Bragg's not exactly a million miles away. And you got that tour coming up...."

Patsy pulled away from her mother, exhibiting resentment on a face already stained with tears.

"Why don't you just tell me every cloud's got a silver lining?" she sniffed miserably.

But Hilda, recalling what it was like to be Patsy's age, took no offense.

"You just come on and move in with me, honey. No sense in paying rent on your place, too. And you'll be seeing him when he's done with basic training. That's only six weeks."

"Oh, Mama!" Patsy wept. "Six weeks! What am I gonna do *tonight*?"

Patsy moved back in with her mama, putting her lovely new furniture and all her salt and pepper shakers into storage. It wasn't much of a home without Charlie there, anyway. At least with Hilda she had company, and that was something. It seemed to her that the good times were over.

The Army had assigned Charlie to something they called "L&L," which stood for "loudspeakers and leaflets." Patsy had never heard of it before, but Charlie was really proud of it.

The Radio Broadcast and Leaflet Battalion was the only one of its kind in the services—it was set up to deal with psychological warfare. In a crisis, Charlie's unit, according to Buck Private Charles Dick, was supposed to jump out of airplanes and drop leaflets on the enemy. Patsy couldn't make any sense at all of it; the way Charlie explained it, it sounded insane, but the mere thought of her precious husband jumping out of a moving plane over enemy lines was enough to take the curl right out of her hair.

For Charlie the Army was both better and worse than he was afraid it was going to be. Fort Bragg was made up mostly of good ole southern boys like himself, hard-drinkin' and hell-raisin' shitkickers, and he fit right in. He was even something of a celebrity, being married to the woman whose "Walkin' After Midnight" was such a big hit. Basic training had been hell on earth, but Charlie was in prime condition, and it was a lot easier for him than for the fat-assed northerners with glasses, who couldn't climb a rope or throw themselves over a ten-foot wall. Even the chow wasn't bad; he was used to grits and greens with pot likker and chicken-fried steak and pork chops cooked in lard; hell, he'd grown up on food just like that. All in all, Charlie found himself a man in a man's world, and it had its up side.

But it had its down side, too, the side he hated with a ferocious passion. The contempt with which the enlisted men were treated by the officers, the subservience officers expected—and got. The chickenshit inspections, with demerits for the smallest infractions, for dumbass things no real man cared about. All that sweeping and dusting and polishing was woman's work. It was for faggots, and Charlie Dick was no faggot. Not the way he missed his wife.

Patsy missed Charlie every waking hour of the day, and dreamed about him during the sleeping hours of the night. She slept badly. Accustomed to the warm weight of him curled around her in the bed, she felt robbed and violated without him. The other half of her was missing.

And making love wasn't all she missed. Patsy missed the closeness, the "two-ness" of them. They'd developed a genuine and precious camaraderie through fucking and fighting, and because they loved each other so much. Twenty times a day, she'd turn to tell Charlie something, to share with him a joke or a piece of good news, or a grievance. And he wasn't there. She had her mother, of course, but she couldn't tell her mother everything; Hilda was just too upright a Christian woman.

Telling Hilda just wasn't the same as telling Charlie and watching his reaction, those blue eyes which would light up in joy or darken in anger, his quick grin, with the strong teeth and the dimple in his chin. She had to push his face out of her mind a thousand times a day, or the image of it would drive her crazy.

On Patsy's wedding day, her mother had told her that her husband should be her new best friend, and that she'd never need another. As usual, Hilda Hensley had been right.

Patsy missed her husband, her lover, her best friend.

She had quit the *Town and Country Jamboree,* much to Jimmy Dean's loud and public disgust. He accused her of ingratitude, of getting too big for her britches, and the son-of-a-bitch had said so on the air. Well, screw him. Patsy was so busy getting ready for her tour with other country artists that she no longer had the time to drive down to Washington and back on the weekends. Besides, she used to have so much fun there with Charlie, and going down there just reminded her of what she was missing.

Busy as she was, she still found time occasionally to drive out to the Rainbow Road Club and sing a set or two with the Kountry Krackers. The roadhouse was a sacred place to her, where she and Charlie had met and fallen in love. Patsy had conveniently buried the memory of their earlier meeting at the high school dance, where she'd read him his beads and put him down. The Rainbow Road Club was far more romantic; it was there that they'd made love for the first time.

Yet, after she'd completed her sets, she went straight back home to her mother, even though she was Patsy Cline the celebrity now, and they begged her to stay and have a drink, sign an autograph, dance with this one or that one.

But there was no heart left in Patsy to party. Work was her only solace these days.

She had to drag herself out of bed again, just as she used to when she was married to Gerald. There hardly seemed any point to it.

This morning, Patsy's bathrobe was wrapped around her and fastened with a pin where the belt loop had ripped. Somehow Patsy hadn't gotten around to fixing it. Or putting her hair up in rollers either, so that it stood up around her head like an untamed mop.

That goddamned song was on the radio again; she was getting damn sick and tired of hearing it. When was she going to hear another of her sides being played? Was she going to be a one-hitter, a flash in the pan, forever?

"Good morning," called Hilda cheerfully over the music. Hilda was dressed, as usual, in a spanking-clean housecoat, her hair neatly combed and arranged, already washing up a sink full of John's and Sylvia's dishes.

"Says who?" retorted Patsy sullenly.

"For heaven's sake, girl," her mother replied with just a touch of impatience, "sit up and take some nourishment! Charlie will have his first leave in three weeks, and you walk around with your lower lip dragging on the floor in front of you, big bawl-baby."

Hilda turned away to pick up the coffeepot and pour Patsy the first cup of the day, obviously much needed. Behind her back, her daughter gave her the scornful finger. As Hilda turned back around, Patsy put her hand down quickly, but not quickly enough, because Hilda caught a glimpse of it and knew what she'd done. Her face reddened with anger.

"You're still not too big for me to smack your jaws, you know that?" threatened Hilda Hensley. "You make that sign to me again, and I'll leave the print of my hand across your face! I'll make your teeth rattle!"

But the sight of Patsy's morose mouth and sad eyes made her soft-hearted mother relent.

"Oh, I know you're upset, sugar. You had a check from the record company this morning. Why don't you go spend some money; it'll make you feel better."

"Says who?" said Patsy again, her chin sunk in her hand.

"Well," huffed her mother, "you are just too mean to live!"

But Hilda Hensley's advice was always wise and well-meaning, and later in the day, Patsy actually took it. She moped out of the house like a worn-out old coon hound, but came driving back a couple of hours later a frisky pup.

The first thing Hilda heard was a loud blaring auto horn, like somebody had his hand pressed down hard on it and wasn't letting go, and the sound of a car's wheels stopped right outside the door. She ran to the kitchen door to have herself a look.

"My land!"

There sat her Patsy, big as life and grinning like a coyote, behind the wheel of a turquoise-and-white two-tone Packard convertible with tail fins a city block long.

"My land, Patsy!" said her mother again, wiping her hands on her apron as she went out to the car.

"I think I hate it," stated Patsy.

"You're a sour, mean thing," scolded Hilda.

A strange look crossed Patsy's face, and a twinkle suddenly appeared in her eye.

"You're right, I am," she told her mother. "But I know how to get sweet again."

"What in the ever-lovin' world are you talking about?"

"I'm going down to see Charlie. I'm driving down in this very car! Day after tomorrow I'll be going on the road with the band, and I won't have a chance to. So this is my chance, and I'm taking it."

"But, Patsy, Fayetteville's three hundred and fifty miles! You can't drive down there all by yourself!"

"Better believe it," said Patsy with a stubborn set of her mouth that Hilda recognized of old.

When Patsy looked like that, there was nothing to do but

give in. Besides, now she was happy. Look at her sparkle! Just the thought of seeing her husband had given Patsy a zest she hadn't had since the bus had driven off taking Charlie Dick with it.

"I'm going to pack," she called over her shoulder as she ran into the house. "Is everything washed and ironed? Where's my new nightgown?"

"Now, honey, you just calm down and I'll take care of everything. You've got nice clean clothes, and all your underwear and things are folded in the drawers. How long you going to be gone anyway? What about the tour?"

"If I leave right now, I'll be back tomorrow night."

"Patsy Cline, are you standin' there tellin' me that you're planning to drive seven hundred miles there and back just for one night!"

"One night with Charlie," said Patsy so softly that it shut her mother right up.

When the road was clear and wide, she did eighty miles an hour, loving the feel of the wind around her as she drove with the top down. She avoided the big cities, skirting Charlotte, Durham, and Raleigh in order to save time, but whenever she had to slow down to sixty in traffic, impatience made growling noises in her guts. *Charlie*, sang the convertible's wheels as they kissed the road. *Charlie. Charlie.*

Once she reached Fort Bragg, Patsy had to go through a lot of frustrating and delaying red tape, applying for a pass at one office and carrying it to another office just to find out where she could inquire for Charlie Dick. It seemed endless, but at last she was standing in front of the right desk, actually in the office of the Radio Broadcast and Leaflet Battalion, actually talking to a sergeant who knew her Charlie.

"Yeah, he works in this building, but he's off on Sundays. You could maybe catch him on his way to the mess hall around now."

Patsy had been forced to leave the car in the base parking

lot. Now she hurried along on foot, in her high heels, suddenly desperate. The base was so big, and all the men were dressed alike. What if she couldn't find him? What if she didn't recognize him? What if he'd left the post to go to a movie or something? She passed dozens of soldiers, but none of them were Charlie Dick. Many of them whistled at her, called after her, but once she knew that a man wasn't Charlie, she paid no further attention to him.

There! Ahead of her! Could that be him? No, that man was thinner, but still there was something about him. . . .

"Charlie!" called Patsy.

The man turned. It was Charlie.

He was about seven pounds lighter, and his beautiful hair was cut very short in the GI crew-cut style, but it was unmistakably and miraculously Charlie.

Charlie was staring at her as though he couldn't believe his eyes. Patsy? Patsy! And then they were running toward each other, hearts pounding, her high heels clattering on the cement walk, running, running, until they came together at last. At last, holding tightly, tightly, not wanting to let each other go long enough even for a kiss.

And then, incredibly, Charlie getting permission to leave the base overnight, a pass obtained without delay or hassle from a sergeant who had bought a copy of "Walkin' After Midnight" and who thought Patsy Cline was the greatest lady singer in country music.

Charlie loved the Packard; laughed fit to kill the minute he laid his eyes on it, and that was the very minute that Patsy stopped hating the car.

They drove into the first motel with a vacancy sign, and could barely wait to lock the door and pull the curtains before they threw themselves on each other, starving, each ready to chew the other one up.

The ferocity with which they made love knew no human bounds. They coupled like frenzied animals in rut, grunting and clawing at each other's bodies, wanting to do everything, touch everything, be everywhere at once.

When they stopped at last, pulling away from each other, gasping, their bodies soaked in sweat, it was not so much that they were satisfied but that they were too exhausted to continue. They had reached the limits of what endurance could bear, had taken each other to the outer edges of space and brought each other home.

Cigarettes. They had to have cigarettes.

Patsy moaned as she left to pick up the Chesterfield pack and the Dixie lighter Charlie had given her, the one with the Confederate flag enameled on it. She could barely stand up. But, oh, the joy of that first wracking puff; contentment began to flow through her, through them both. They were finally beginning to believe that they were together again.

After a moment, Charlie put his arm tightly around Patsy and pulled her close against his body, not for sex, but for comfort. Instantly, she sensed the difference in his mood.

"What?" she asked softly, pillowed on his chest.

"Ah, I don't know. . . . Felt sad for a minute." He sighed deeply, and his next words were spoken in a voice filled with bitterness.

"God, *God*, but I hate this Army. I get up mad ever' mornin' and go to bed madder ever' night. I'm tellin' you, I could just fight a buzz saw with my bare fists."

His tone became mockingly servile. "Yes, *sir*! No, *sir*! Can I kiss your ass, *sir*?"

Charlie shook his head. "And the other guys in the office," he went on despondently, "they're either smartass college kids or they're so stupid they can't find their ass with both hands. Ah, hell, *I* don't know . . . I miss you."

Surprised, Patsy raised her eyes to look at his face. "You telling me Good Time Charlie feels alone?" she asked.

He turned his face away from her gaze. "I got my share."

Now Patsy raised herself onto her elbow above him, so that she could look plainly into Charlie's eyes.

"Let me tell you something, Charlie," she said with great earnestness. "You're *not* alone. You can't go to your grave saying you weren't ever loved, 'cause no matter what happens to you for the rest of your life, by God, right now somebody loves you."

She pulled him close to her, and they lay together calmly, not speaking. Something had passed between them, something crucial, something that marked a change of which they were not yet aware.

They had ceased to be boy and girl. They were now man and woman. They had ceased to be newlyweds. They were now husband and wife.

Fourteen

Within days, the visit with Charlie was no more than a treasured memory, and Patsy Cline was on the road.

The tour had been put together hastily, to capitalize on the success of her hit record. It was scheduled to cover a lot of territory, because all over the South, country-and-western fans were curious to hear the new singer. It was only a small group that set out: the Kountry Krackers—banjo picker, a drummer, two guitarists and a fiddler—a singer, Johnny Widdoes, because it was unheard of to tour without a male vocalist for the Hank Williams and Hank Snow songs, and Mary Rose Dodds, who'd been on the bandstand with Patsy at the Rainbow Road Club.

They didn't even have a bus or a trailer; they drove off in three separate cars with the instruments tied to the roofs with hunks of rope, like Okies in the Dust Bowl.

A lot of ground would have to be covered in a short time, so almost everywhere they went it was for a one-night stand. They played in school auditoriums and Rotary lodges, at the VFW, in armories and in churches, and, once or twice when the gate was sizable enough to warrant it, a big tent was set up out of doors and they played and sang under canvas like revivalists, hardly able to hear themselves over the howling of the wind.

It was grimy and exhausting work. The only reason they

kept on going was that the Krackers wanted and needed the money, and Patsy wanted and needed the exposure to new audiences. It was, admittedly, exhilarating to stand up in front of a group of foot-tapping people and sing their hearts out, but to drag halfway across the southland, one little town at a time to do it! There were moments when it seemed insane.

By the third week of the tour, even Patsy's vitality was giving out. She was feeling ill, maybe coming down with something.

The first symptom was a nagging queasiness; nothing seemed to set right in her stomach. At first, she took to drinking Alka-Seltzer after every meal, then *with* every meal as a beverage. But after a day or two, the queasiness turned to nausea, and the Alka-Seltzer didn't help anymore.

She thought she might have a touch of food poisoning, not impossible with all the greasy spoons they'd been stopping at, so she gave up cheeseburgers and pork chops and switched her diet to bland, tasteless, innocuous foods like Jell-O, rice pudding, baked potatoes, and a small steak every now and then, if the diner was clean enough. It was obvious that road food didn't agree with her, not after growing up on Hilda's fresh home cooking.

But the nausea got worse, not better, and soon Patsy couldn't keep anything down. They kept having to stop somewhere on the road and find a ladies' room, so that Patsy could puke her guts up. Sometimes she couldn't make it to a toilet, and had to let go on the side of the road. Mornings were especially bad. She had to have that one cup of coffee, *had* to, but once it was down, it came right back up again, leaving Patsy sitting on the bathroom floor beside the bowl, wracked with the dry heaves.

If her ass was dragging behind her before this, she was twice as exhausted now and looking like shit, dehydrated and sallow, not to mention getting skinnier by the minute, with nothing in her stomach. She couldn't even take a drink anymore, she was so hollow. It wasn't fair.

By the second day of this, Patsy just couldn't seem to get up off that bathroom floor at all. She sat resting her head against the cool tile of the ladies' room wall, wishing she was dead. Every few minutes, she'd retch again, her entire body shaking with the effort of bringing up nothing. She had nothing left to give, and still she went on giving.

Outside, in the motel coffee shop, the Krackers were wolfing down ham and eggs, fresh biscuits with sorghum syrup, hot corn cakes and grits. Even the thought of it made poor Patsy go for the bowl again, hanging her head over it in the worst misery she'd ever known.

"Patsy?" It was Mary Rose Dodds, putting her head around the ladies' room door, a look of concern on her pretty face.

"Patsy? You okay?"

More retching. "Oh, I'm sick enough to die," moaned Patsy.

"You didn't even have anything to drink last night." Mary Rose winced as Patsy heaved again. *"Jesus!* Sounds like you're strangling a cat in there."

"Tell the guys they'll have to wait for me," answered Patsy weakly. "I can't get up. Leave me be, I'll be all right soon."

In a few minutes she emerged from the ladies' room, her face white, her hands trembling, but feeling a little better. She'd washed up and combed her hair back and rinsed her mouth out with cold water, but her knees were still made of rubber and she took very small, hesitant steps.

The boys called out to her as she approached.

"Hey, girl, you okay?" "How're ya feeling, Patsy?"

"I been better," she said briefly, sitting down and averting her eyes from the smears of grease and ketchup on the dirty plates. Picking up her coffee cup, she took one sip and set it down hard in the saucer.

"God in heaven!" she exclaimed. It had just hit her.

All eyes turned toward Patsy.

"I bet I'm pregnant!"

It all fit, the sickness in the morning, the queasiness all

day, the sore and aching breasts. She was going to have a baby.

A sudden swift elation carried her aloft, then her mood changed just as abruptly and tears filled her eyes as cold realization struck her.

"I *can't* be pregnant! I just had a hit record. My husband's in the Army! Oh, my God, how can I tour if I'm pregnant?"

The others sat stunned, not knowing what to say as Patsy went from joy to despair in nothing flat. Without Patsy, there *was* no tour. They'd all have to pack up and go home.

Now her mood changed again; Patsy's rich, hoarse laugh rang out and she shook her head at the sheer ridiculousness of her situation.

"Talk about your bad timing," she marveled. "What the hell do I do now?"

There wasn't a hell of a lot *to* do. They had to cut the tour short, and were all back in Winchester by the end of the month. Visiting her doctor, Patsy learned that her baby was due by mid-August.

Hilda was ecstatic at the advent of a first grandchild, even if she was still a little young to be a grandmother. She fussed over Patsy as though the girl were made of glass, making certain she was eating right, drinking lots of milk and fruit juices, and taking vitamins. Mercifully, the nausea passed in less than a month. Left to her own devices, Patsy might have existed solely on cigarettes and mint chocolate chip ice cream, for which she had developed an insatiable craving.

When she phoned Charlie to give him the news that he was going to be a father, there was a single moment of stunned silence, followed by a rebel yell into the telephone that pretty near busted Patsy's eardrum.

"You're sure?"

"'Course I'm sure. Would I be calling up long-distance just to make stupid jokes?"

"Hell, that's the best news I've heard in years! Know

what, darlin'? This means we can live off base! Together!
Now, how 'bout that?"

There was a dependent housing unit for the wives and
children of the enlisted men at Fort Bragg, and Charlie
moved Patsy in with some of their furniture as soon as the
next apartment became vacant. Then the tedium began.

Even with the curtains hung and their old familiar things
in place, the apartment was depressing as hell. It hadn't
been painted after the last tenant had moved out; there were
greasy handprints and crayon markings all over the walls,
and no amount of scrubbing with Spic and Span or Bab-O
would take off the dirt. The walls themselves were made
of little more than thin plasterboard, and the apartments
were all connected, with common walls between them on
either side. So you could hear every fart, every toilet flush
on the other side of the wall, and, as far as making noises
while making love, forget it. You had to fuck on tiptoe,
with one finger on your lips.

Patsy could hear babies crying at every hour of the day
and night, and smell what every wife was cooking for every
meal. The cooking smell was always mingled with the odor
of shitty diapers. The place just wasn't worth fixing up
pretty; nothing would get the stink out of the walls.

There were children everywhere, underfoot, yelling in
the odorous corridors and alleyways. The complex was built
in the shape of a U, around a central "playground," a pitiful
thing of concrete with not a grass blade in sight, except for
a few pushing up in the cracks that had already appeared
in the cement. A slide, a handful of swings, and a rusting
jungle gym were always occupied by noisy children, but
they were everywhere else, too. Wherever you walked, your
feet crunched on broken bits of toys and headless dolls.
Their debris was everywhere, abandoned like the wreckage
of a home hit by a bomb.

There was a world unknown to Patsy, a world inhabited
only by women and children. All her life, Patsy Cline had

associated freely with men. Country music was a man's world, and she roamed through it without self-consciousness, calling them, one and all, "Hoss." She drank with men, partied with men, laughed with them, sang with them, danced with them, and had affairs with them. Even after her marriages, when the affairs had stopped, she was still an accepted, welcomed member of an essentially masculine community, the hard-drinking, hard-loving world of pickers and singers.

Here, in the dependent housing unit of Fort Bragg, Fayetteville, North Carolina, she was just one more woman among a hundred others. Worse, she wasn't even Patsy Cline; she was Patsy Dick, Private Charles Dick's wife. Nobody knew otherwise, or would have cared if they'd known. The women were totally caught up in raising their snotty-nosed babies and doing for the husbands in the evening. They never had a moment to think about themselves, and nobody seemed to want Patsy Dick for a friend.

The men came home at night, most nights anyway, one per apartment. Once inside, they stayed there, dog tired, and let their wives wait on them hand and foot. It made up for some of the chickenshit Army crap they had to take all day.

Seeing Charlie, being with Charlie was the one and only bright spot in Patsy's endless pregnancy. On the one side, here she was, bored and lonely, getting uglier, puffier, and more bloated every day. Decca Records kept sending her angry letters about her not making any more records. She was far from any of their recording studios, and was unwilling to get on a plane in her condition. She was missing her mama and Winchester and all her friends, not getting any younger, not getting any richer, not singing, not doing much of anything but trying to keep three miserable little rooms clean and fill out the rest of her time reading fan magazines, smoking, and eating mint chocolate chip ice cream by the pint.

Patsy Cline had left her career to raise Charlie Dick's babies right, as she always had sworn she was going to do.

But where was the joy, where was the house with the yellow roses? She'd never expected to be living in the next thing to a barracks.

On the other side, here was Charlie, lean and handsome in his uniform, with his cute little crew-cut, marching into the apartment to take her into his arms. It didn't make up for everything, but it sure made up for a lot.

Their lovemaking was much different now, partly due to the fact that you could hear every sound through the cheesy walls, partly due to the awe with which both of them regarded Patsy's belly. There was a little baby in there, and it didn't do to rough him up too much.

Only, they didn't make love *all* the time, not the way they used to. Of course, Patsy knew that married couples don't go on and on about sex, the way single couples do. When it's right there every time you stretch out your hand, that hand doesn't stretch out too often. Besides, Charlie was tired most evenings, and depressed a lot, too, hating the Army. But Patsy harbored the secret suspicion that Charlie was less interested in sex because Patsy was getting a big pregnant belly and flat feet, and looked like hell in those stupid shapeless maternity tops.

You couldn't blame either one of them. Charlie had so much to do all day, taking orders. No wonder he just wanted to lie around at night doing nothing. Patsy had virtually nothing to do during the day except mope and be uncomfortable; she looked forward to having her man home with her for a little excitement. But there was very little excitement. They were out of synch with each other.

And the weeks dragged on. Patsy was in her seventh month now, her legs swollen with the heat of a North Carolina June, her back aching. She avoided mirrors as much as she could, but every once in a while she'd catch a despairing glimpse of herself, blown up like a zeppelin, and she'd groan.

"I look awful, don't I?" she'd moan to Charlie.

"Naw, honey, you look just fine to me." But how the

Patsy and her mother, Hilda Hensley, played by Ann Wedgeworth.

No sign here of the stormy times ahead in the passionate, but rocky, marriage of Patsy Cline and Charlie Dick.

Fighting and loving were the cornerstones of their marriage.

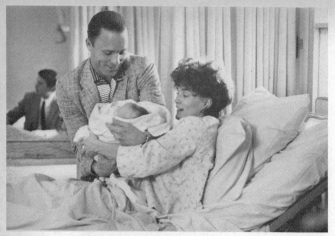

Charlie visits Patsy in the hospital after the birth of their first child, daughter Julie.

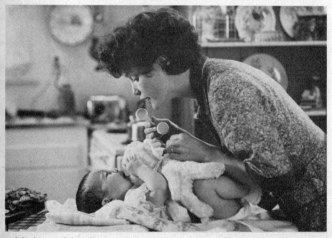

Mother and daughter.

Patsy performs at the Grand Ole Opry, a dream come true that marks her as a legendary country singing star. (© 1985 Tri-Star Pictures, Inc. All rights reserved.)

Patsy performing on the road. (© 1985 Tri-Star Pictures, Inc. All rights reserved.)

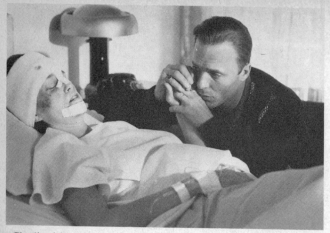

Charlie visits the unconscious Patsy after her near-fatal car accident.

A still hurting Patsy, back in the recording studio after the car crash.

Charlie spends a lonely night in jail after Patsy calls the police on him.

RIGHT: Patsy sings in the haunting, lyrical voice that brought her to the top of both the country and the pop charts. (© 1985 Tri-Star Pictures, Inc. All rights reserved.)

BELOW: Charlie, holding daughter Julie, attends his wife's funeral. (© 1985 Tri-Star Pictures, Inc. All rights reserved.)

recall them, knowing exactly what Charlie's reaction would be.

"Nobody asked you to come," he told her sullenly.

Her temper flared. "The hell you didn't—you begged!"

"Well, I didn't mean it."

Patsy didn't want to fight; she was too worn out. "Oh, Charlie, let's don't fuss. I'm makin' chili for dinner, you like that. Let's just be nice," she begged him wearily.

But Charlie wasn't willing to let it go. He was in a mean-red mood, and needed somebody to dump it on. All the bitterness and the hatred he had stored up in him against having to take orders came pouring out now, and standing right there in the way was Patsy.

If he hadn't been drinking, he might have thought twice. But he was half lit, and his judgment was none too sharp.

He yanked off his uniform tie, and his face contorted into a scowl. Then, putting on a mincing expression, he mocked her in a high, ladylike voice. He was good at mimicry, too good, too hurtful.

"Oh-h-h-h, my," he simpered, pretending to be Patsy. "I make him chili and want to be nice, but my hus-band is *so* rude and nasty."

"Shut *up*," grated Patsy, furious.

But Charlie was on a roll, too caught up in his sarcasm to stop. "P-o-o—r Patsy," he falsettoed.

"I'll hit you with the first thing I lay my hands on, Charlie," she threatened. Her voice was dangerously quiet.

"Try it," he growled through angrily clenched teeth.

Patsy's head snapped up, and her eyes blazed with a sudden fire. "Don't ever dare me, Charlie. I've told you that."

Charlie hesitated, but he'd gone too far to back down, and the liquor was talking.

"I *dare* you!"

Instantly, she slapped him across the face. With the instinct of a fighter, he slapped her back, not very hard, because she had taken him by surprise. At the sting of her husband's palm across her cheek, Patsy took a step backward. Then she raised her hand and hit him again, hard.

The slap made a noise like a pistol shot when it connected. Charlie reeled for an instant, then he saw red, dark red. If he could have stopped to think, even for a split second, he would have stayed his hand. Patsy was smaller, lighter, weaker than he was, and she was in her seventh month of pregnancy.

But that split second of thought never took place. Instead, he cocked his fist back and hit her with all his strength, slamming her into the opposite wall, and knocking her down.

As he saw Patsy fall, Charlie was as shocked as she was. What the hell had he done? His brain was still foggy with bourbon, but he took a step forward to help her up.

"Patsy . . ."

Shaking her head, she waved him away and regained her feet by herself, awkward as she was. Her lip was cut open and bleeding; it had already started to swell. There was a cut on her brow, too, dangerously close to her eye.

Slowly, she started for the bedroom, turning her back on the stricken Charlie, whose eyes were filling with remorseful tears, wishing he could have cut his hand off before he'd punched her. At the bedroom door, she turned to face him. There was no anger in her face, no sadness; in fact, there was no emotion in it at all. It didn't matter to her that Charlie was deeply sorry for what he had done. Nothing mattered. Her face was cold and still, and Charlie felt a chilly fist close around his heart.

"You know the part I remember?" said Patsy softly, without expression. "I remember the part where you said over and over again how you'd protect me, how you'd keep anybody from hurting me. Remember all those times you used to say that?"

She looked Charlie up and down, and now contempt crept into her face, scorn twisting her lips. Her husband stood silent and trembling under her disdain, afraid of her, hating himself. Patsy's contempt was killing something inside him.

"Mr. Wrong," she said quietly, and went in to the bedroom to pack.

Fifteen

GOING BACK HOME to her mother was both a comfort and a humiliation to Patsy. It was an admission of defeat. When she climbed out of the Packard in front of the house on South Kent Street, her mother flew out of the door, a worried look on her face. As soon as she saw Patsy's swollen lip, Hilda stiffened, but said nothing. Inside, though, Patsy's mother was bleeding for her daughter.

Sweet Lord, not her, too! Why are men born to do women this way?

Placing one comforting arm around Patsy's shoulders, she drew her into the house. John and Sylvia, out of school for the summer, swiftly unloaded the suitcases from the car and carried them inside. Within hours, Patsy had settled in just as though she'd never been away.

But she *had* been away. Something earth-shattering had happened between her and her husband. Was it over between them for good? Not wanting to pry, Hilda asked no questions; Patsy volunteered no information. All Hilda knew was that Charlie telephoned again and again, but Patsy's voice on the phone during these very short conversations was cold and noncommittal.

Now they had only to sit and wait for the baby to be born. These last two months of waiting were the longest Patsy had ever known. As the days of June vanished over the edge of time, followed by July, and the rich, humid heat of August arrived to hold Winchester in its grip, Patsy found it all but impossible to breathe.

She was so bulky that she couldn't even drive her car; she stayed indoors with her mother, with the electric fan on full, as much breeze as was stirring blowing into her face, watching Hilda sew the baby's layette, and listening to her own records. Patsy was forming a new determination.

"I'm gonna start singing again, Mama, just as soon as the baby's born."

Hilda looked up from the quilt she was stitching.

"I was hopin' you'd stay home for a while," she replied mildly.

But Patsy shook her head, her mouth set in a straight line.

"I'm gonna start singing the same *week* the baby's born." She struggled to her feet, her voice rising.

"I can make it, damn it, I know I can. All I need is one good song, just one good song, just *one* good song to put me over the top. Then, when I make enough, I can retire and raise the baby." Her dark eyes looked earnestly at her mother. "I want it to be *right*."

"You forgot the part about the yellow roses," her mother answered softly.

Then, one day, Patsy woke up in the morning to find that her belly was inches lower.

"The baby's dropped," her mother told her. "It's getting ready to be born. Could be any day now."

"The baby's dropped," her doctor told her. "Could be any day now."

The news that her waiting was about to come to an end gave Patsy a new energy; she got back behind the wheel of her car, and even managed to do a little grocery shopping.

"On the day you were born, I got up at five and scrubbed the kitchen floor, just 'cause I felt so full of go," said Hilda. "It's natural. If you get a craving to polish all the furniture, we'll know you're about to start your labor."

But when the first pain struck, sending Patsy with a gasp down onto her knees, she wasn't scrubbing or polishing, but carrying sacks of groceries. The pain hit her not in the belly, where she expected it, but deep in the small of her back, making her cry out with the force of it. Cans and boxes spilled out of the sacks and onto the road in front of the house.

Charlie tore off the bus the instant the doors opened. Rumpled and sweaty, he took off, running the three-quarters of a mile from the depot to Hilda's house, his legs pumping, racing past stores and office buildings and warehouses, deserted now on a Sunday evening. Arriving out of breath, he threw the front door open and burst into the living room.

To find Patsy and Patsy's mother sitting calmly and comfortably in two easy chairs, watching the *The Ed Sullivan Show*. Patsy's belly was bigger than ever. He couldn't believe his eyes. Hadn't they phoned up Fort Bragg only this morning and said the baby was on its way?

"What the living hell?" gasped Charlie. "They told me ..."

"False alarm," said Patsy dryly.

He threw himself onto the sofa, exhausted. "Oh, Hilda, I know you're probably mad at me, but I like to died trying to make that mothering bus go faster. I'm wore out. Put a star in your crown and go get old Charlie a beer," he pleaded.

Smiling in spite of herself, reluctant to respond to his charm but unable to help it, Hilda got up and went to the refrigerator.

The second she was out of the room, Charlie leaped from the couch and went over to where Patsy was sitting.

"Can I have a kiss?" he begged.

She nodded, glad to see him, yet holding some part of herself in reserve, wary. They kissed, lightly.

"Can I have a *decent* kiss?" he asked again.

The second kiss was warmer, more like old times, and it seemed to satisfy Charlie.

"Did you miss me?" he asked.

Patsy inclined her head. "Yes," she admitted grudgingly, "I didn't know it till I saw you, but I did."

He smiled at her broadly; these were the words his soul had been craving ever since she'd packed her bags and left him in Fayetteville.

Hilda came back into the room with Charlie's beer. With a light kiss on his mother-in-law's cheek, he took the brew, kicked off his shoes, and stretched himself out luxuriously on the couch.

"I got ten days' leave, two good-looking women to spend it with, and a baby on the way," he announced with a wide grin. "Hog *heaven!*"

But hogs in heaven don't mind being crowded together in a bristly heap. Hilda's little house wasn't built to take another person, much less a full-grown man in civilian clothes with nothing to do but lie around bored, watching TV and drinking beer. By the following afternoon, Charlie was so much in the way that Patsy and Hilda had to step over him each time they went into or came out of the kitchen.

So, when she stepped over him yet again and he reached a hand up under her dress, Patsy couldn't help but get real annoyed.

"Oh, Charlie, for the love of God get out from under our feet! Go have a drink. Have *nine*. Supper's at five-thirty."

He didn't have to be told twice. Up like a shot, happy, he was out the door before she put a period on her sentence.

He had a lot of catching up to do, first looking up J.W., so they could hang out together. His old haunts were beckoning him, saying to him, "Why, Charlie Dick, where you *been*? It just hasn't seemed the same around here since you been gone." A man needs to hear those words every once in a while.

They went to shoot a few games of pool. The usual good ole boys were sitting around the pool hall, wearing dungarees and Cat Tractor mesh caps, watching what passed for action in Winchester. J.W. and Charlie racked up a table, and Charlie broke.

"Charlie here say he loves the Army," joked Woodhouse.

"Oh, *hell*, yes," agreed Charlie. His audience guffawed.

"Says he's going to reenlist when his two years are up."

"That's the Lord's truth; they may even make me a corporal," he answered derisively, clearing the table. Charlie glanced at his watch. "I gotta get on home."

"Didn't know they made apron strings as long as all that," challenged Woodhouse softly.

Charlie shot him a dark look, but he couldn't ignore the dare in his best friend's words. "Let's shoot another game."

They moved the homecoming to The Wild Turkey, one of Charlie's old favorite bars. By now the party had grown, as the news of Charlie Dick's leave had spread around. Girls had joined the fellows, among them Wanda Kimble, Charlie's old girlfriend.

Now Wanda wasn't a girl to whom men said good-bye lightly. What she had, she liked to hang on to; and she'd had Charlie Dick. All she did was turn her back on him for five minutes, and off he'd gone, sniffing like a bloodhound after that band singer. To this day, Wanda was convinced that if she herself hadn't gone off mad, Charlie would have come crawling back to her instead of marrying that Patsy Cline.

It was good to see him again, even though he'd grown so thin. She'd missed him. Charlie Dick had a way with him that a girl got used to. The lovers she'd had since didn't measure up to his skill and enthusiasm; he could always get her going.

At first, the two of them only eyeballed each other from opposite sides of the booth. But as the long summer afternoon wore on, turning to evening, and they'd both had a few drinks, then more than a few, Wanda began to feel warmer and warmer toward Charlie.

"I really do have to go now," Charlie said, his speech

slurring. His words were met by a chorus of "No!" and by Billy Bob Auslander clucking like a chicken, telling Charlie he was too chickenshit scared to stay on.

"Hell," protested Charlie, trying to focus on his watch, "it's getting dark out. I'm late for supper already!"

But before he could stand up, Wanda Kimble had planted herself on his lap and wound one soft arm around his neck. She smelled good, all lipstick and cologne. He just didn't have the heart to protest; 'sides, it would hardly be the act of a gentleman to stand up and throw a lady off.

This was no false alarm. The contractions were coming so close together that Patsy's doctor, over the phone, had ordered her into the hospital right now. Patsy had wanted to wait for Charlie, but Hilda was not listening to any arguments. "Now" meant *now!*

And as a pain washed over her that was more excruciating than the others, Patsy didn't have the breath to argue. She gave in, and Hilda kept her foot on the gas pedal all the way to Winchester Memorial.

The pains were bad, very bad. Especially in her back, which was giving her mortal agony. The baby was lying in a reverse position, pressed up inside against Patsy's back, which was going to make for a difficult labor. They might even have to do a caesarean, but that was a decision the doctor would make later, if Patsy couldn't deliver normally. Meanwhile, he'd have to let her go on laboring, because it would be better for both of them—mother and child—if she didn't have to have the surgery.

If only they'd give her something for the pain! But it was too early to dope her up; she still had a long way to go. The baby, needing all the oxygen it could get for the long journey ahead, would not be benefited by painkillers.

Hilda was with her daughter as they transferred her to a gurney and rolled her swiftly down the corridor to the labor room. A nurse with a clipboard trotted by the stretcher's side, filling in the necessary forms.

"Is the father around, so I can get the rest of the information from him?"

Hilda shook her head, worried. Her own three childbirths had been easier than this.

"Well, what's his name?" the nurse inquired.

A long contraction caught Patsy up in its agonizing wave, and she cried out from anguish and fear. Her hair was soaked with sweat, and there was a glassy look in her eyes. She rode the crest of the pain for a minute, then it mercifully passed, and her laboring body relaxed.

"Oh, *God!*" she yelled. Then, as the pain left her, she said to the nurse, "Charles Dick . . . the son-of-a-bitch."

"Watch that dirty talk," responded Hilda automatically, so out of her mind with worry that she didn't realize what she was saying. "He'll be here soon," she told the nurse, but in her heart she doubted it. And, as she thought about that low-life son-in-law of hers, the words came bursting forth.

"The *son* of a *bitch!*"

Never in her life had Hilda used language like that; never in *her* life had Patsy known her mother to cuss. It was the funniest thing she'd ever heard, and a yell of laughter escaped Patsy's lips, to be followed by a yell of pain as another fierce contraction hit.

Her face creased by anxiety, Patsy's mother took her daughter's hand in hers. Patsy squeezed it gratefully and hard. When would this ordeal be over? When the hell were they going to give her something for the pain?

After an eternity of unrelenting anguish, a pain so all-encompassing that Patsy didn't remember a time it wasn't there, they moved her from the labor room into the delivery room and stuck her feet into the stirrups, strapping her down. The straps were more terrifying to Patsy than the pain had been; they proved to her that she was a prisoner here, and that nothing would release her until pain itself was finished with her.

"Push!" they told her. *"Push!"*

Between her legs, looking down the pulsing mound of her swollen belly, Patsy could see the doctor moving feverishly, beads of perspiration running down his brow and over his mask. *What the hell is* he *sweating about?* I'm *the one doing all the work!*

"Be a good girl and help us," the delivery room nurse urged her. "Push down hard!"

What do they think I'm doing, moaned Patsy to herself, pushing and pushing until she thought her guts would pop out along with the baby.

Charlie, where the hell are you, Charlie?

Charlie had to have a few more drinks before he could make love to Wanda. After it was over, he'd fallen asleep, thanks to the combination of bourbon and sex. He couldn't believe it! He'd fallen asleep! He had no idea how long he'd been snoring by Wanda's side, but it was dark when he pulled on his clothes hurriedly and raced out of the apartment and back to Hilda's house.

The house was dark, and would have been totally quiet except for the ringing of the telephone.

"Answer the phone, somebody," called Charlie, but there wasn't anybody, and the phone went on ringing. Groggily, he reached it and picked it up.

His mother-in-law was on the line. It took him a minute to grasp what she was saying—that she was calling from the hospital, that Patsy had already given birth.

"I'll be right down," he told her, sobering up a little.

"No, you won't be right down," retorted Hilda in a passion. "You just keep your miserable self away. She had a hard time and she's finally asleep. She asked for you fourteen times tonight. I *counted.* Oh, damn your soul, Charlie Dick, *where were you?*"

The receiver slammed hard in his ear, leaving him suddenly cold sober. Oh, God, he was in for it now! He'd fucked up by the numbers, he surely had. Or else why would a forgiving Christian woman like Hilda Hensley talk to him like he was dirt under her shoes? And Patsy, he'd failed her! She'd been calling for him while he'd been screwing Wanda Kimble, drunk out of his gourd. *I* am *dirt,* he thought. *No better than the lowest piece of trash who ever lived. My wife was off having our baby, while I was tomcatting around . . . . Our baby!* For the first time, it sank in. They'd had a baby, Patsy and Charlie. A baby!

Damn if I didn't forget to ask Hilda, boy or girl?

I can't believe it's over, thought Patsy. Seems to me like I'm gonna have to go through it all over again, today and tomorrow and ever' day for the rest of my life. . . .

She looked down at her stomach, half expecting to see it still mountainous, but the blanket tucked over her was flat. They say that women forget the pains of childbirth once they're over them, yet Patsy Cline was certain that nothing could eradicate the agony she'd gone through last night. Nothing. She'd remember it as the longest day she ever lived.

When the nurse brought in her baby, though, wrapped in a soft cotton blanket, and laid it down on the pillow next to Patsy, by the time Patsy had finished examining the incredible beauty of each tiny feature, the little curled fists and the soft down on the baby's head, the fat little button of a nose, she had forgotten almost everything about her ordeal. This was what it was all about, this tiny body nestling in the crook of her arm, asleep, long eyelashes brushing its downy cheeks. This was love and this was trust and this was responsibility, next to which pain was as fleeting as a snowflake on a warm windowpane.

With a trembling finger, she touched the infant's brow very delicately, and the little head stirred in response. Patsy caught her breath; never had she felt anything so soft as that forehead!

Funny, now that she was holding her baby in her arms, Patsy completely forgot that she had once told Charlie she didn't want children right away.

"I don't want to have kids until we have a nice house and can support 'em," she'd said when the subject of children first came up between them.

"I want to make some more money, travel and go places, and have us some fun before we settle down to raise a family. But after all that, I *do* want children, lots of 'em. I want to give our kids the things I never had when I was a little girl. A nice house, bicycles, toys, friends. And the most important thing, Charlie, is, I want my children to have a mother and father happy together. I want them to see that, grow up with that. I want to prove to them that it *can* be done.

"And I want to buy a nice house for Mama, just to thank her for all she's done for us."

And Charlie had put his arm around her, hugging her tight, telling her in a husky whisper, "Yeah, we'll do all o' that. I promise you, Patsy, we will."

Well, so much for what either one of them had wanted; now the baby was here, and the reality must alter the shape of the dream.

Holding the biggest bunch of flowers he could find, Charlie Dick walked into the maternity ward, his blue eyes scanning the beds until they lighted on Patsy. He hurried forward, his face eager, and stooped to give his wife a kiss.

She turned her mouth away, and all he got was the corner of her cheek.

He put the flowers down on the table and reached for his child, thrilled when Patsy handed the baby over.

"They said downstairs she's a girl."

Patsy nodded.

"You still like 'Julie' for a name?"

Patsy nodded again; thus far she hadn't spoken a word to Charlie. He gnawed at his lip, and his words came out softly, anxiously.

"She's beautiful. I wish I'd been with you."

"Where were you?" she asked him evenly. She didn't even bother to raise her voice.

His eyes sought hers imploringly. "I could tell you a hundred lies, but I ain't goin' to," he lied. "I got drunk."

There were many things Patsy could have said to him, sharp and angry words, argument-provoking charges and accusations. Perhaps if she'd said a few of them, and they'd had a fight, it might have cleared the air between them. Instead, she shrugged and let it go. She didn't believe him. Of *course* he'd been drunk; that went without saying. But he never did answer her question about where he'd actually been last night when she needed him, and she knew deep down it was because he didn't dare to.

He'd failed her, and that was all she really cared about. Nothing he could say or do would wash away that stain. Charlie Dick had failed her.

So, all she did was shrug indifferently and say, "Well, that's whiskey under the bridge."

Charlie reached out to touch Patsy's hand, to unite the three of them as a family—husband, wife, child. Almost absentmindedly, Patsy pulled her hand away from his, giving Charlie a little pat on the arm, like an afterthought.

In that simple little gesture of hers, Charlie heard a door slam.

Sixteen

CHARLIE'S LEAVE FLEW BY; the ten days were up almost before they were aware of time passing. On the sixth day of his furlough, Patsy came home from the hospital with baby Julie. Patsy was pale, very thin, and it still hurt her to sit down, but she appeared to be radiantly happy.

All of her attention was focused on the baby. Charlie felt a chill wind blowing from the east, a wind that whispered to him that he might no longer be at the center of his wife's universe. It was Julie this and Julie that, and "Hush, the baby has just gone to sleep," and "Don't smoke that nasty cigarette around this precious infant," until he like to thought his face would turn bright blue.

Julie's grandmother was in a state of total euphoria; no baby in her recollection had ever been as good, or as beautiful, or as potentially intelligent, brave, religious, dutiful, or virtuous as her little granddaughter.

Not that Charlie didn't love his daughter. Who couldn't love so beautiful a morsel of humanity, all rosy and cuddly, nestled in her cot or in Patsy's arms or Hilda's? It was only that a man couldn't really be expected to spend more than five or ten minutes in the presence of a sleeping infant without running out of adjectives. How much was there to say about a child still only a few days old? After a few minutes, Charlie would get restless and want to be somewhere else.

He wanted to be with Patsy. Alone with Patsy, but that appeared to be damn near impossible. First of all, there seemed to be no place at all in Hilda's house where they could be alone, even for an hour or two. The little house was bursting at the seams, with a mother, a father, a grandmother, an aunt, and an uncle all doting on one small baby. The baby itself, while weighing no more than seven and a half pounds, took up fully half the damn house with her bassinet and bathinet and crib, and diapers hanging everywhere you turned, hitting you wetly in the face.

Still, if Patsy had wanted to, she could have found a way for them to be alone together. She was smart, and she could manage anything. But she didn't want to. She wanted to be with Julie. Hilda was allowed into the circle, because she knew so much about babies that Patsy was still learning. But there was no time or room for Charlie.

It wasn't sex he was after. He knew that it would be weeks, maybe even months, before his wife was allowed to have sex in the usual way. It was the closeness he missed, the friendship they used to share. That was gone.

Patsy never alluded to that night, but he had the feeling that she never forgave him, either. She was polite, even friendly, like meeting the people next door for the very first time. They oohed and aahed over the baby together, but that was about all she'd share with him. Her attention was elsewhere.

It drove Charlie crazy. Patsy had never looked more beautiful or desirable to him, and he loved her more than ever. There was a new softness to her, in her voice and in her manner, that was feminine and appealing, but the softness wasn't for him. It was all for the baby. She'd smile down into Julie's sleeping face, her own face so radiant with joy that Charlie wanted to yell or bite down on something. She'd never looked at him that way.

Once, when Patsy was nursing the baby, Charlie reached out his hand to touch the satin of her bare breast. It wasn't a sexual gesture, or an aggressive one. He simply felt the instinct to share with his daughter the touch of Patsy's breast. There was such beauty in the act of nursing that he wanted to have some part in it, too.

But Patsy had pulled away from him so vehemently, and had given him such a look from under her brows that he'd pulled back his hand as if it had been burned, and said nothing. She had totally misunderstood his gesture, and he didn't have the words to set her right. All he could do was nurse his pain and tell himself that he did, after all, deserve it in some measure. But when would she forgive?

The one time they were together with nobody else in the house for a full five minutes, he taxed her with it.

"When are you gonna let up on me, Patsy?" he demanded.

She turned an expressionless face to his. "I don't know what you're talking about."

It would have been better for Charlie if she'd hollered at him or even hit him, but this passive, silent treatment was more than he could bear.

"I *told* you a thousand times I'm sorry. When are you gonna break down and forgive me?"

"I don't hold any grudges, Charlie," she said softly, but there was no pardon in her face, and he didn't believe her.

Then, almost without warning, the furlough was up and Charlie's bag was packed. Hilda would drive him to the bus station, and he'd be riding those long, lonely miles back to the hated Fort Bragg.

He still hadn't straightened things out with Patsy. She hadn't given him a chance.

Even now, when they were saying good-bye, and when they wouldn't be seeing each other for God only knew how long, she wouldn't put the baby down even for a minute to throw her arms around him. Instead, she kissed him good-bye as though he were little more than an acquaintance, turning her face at the last minute so that his kiss only grazed her lips.

With the whole damn Hensley family standing around

watching, there was nothing Charlie could do except say good-bye, kiss the baby on her head, pick up his bag, and walk on out the door.

Once back at camp, he began to miss her and the baby ferociously. If only he could get her away from her family, all to himself, maybe everything would be just as it was before the trouble started. Better, even, because they'd have the baby, and because they could start their lovemaking again. Charlie Dick was a true believer—he placed a lot of faith in the power of making love. Just give him one good night in the sack with Patsy, and all that sweetness would come bubbling back. Nobody could please her like her husband; there wasn't a man on earth who knew her body the intimate way that he did.

He wasn't much of a hand at writing letters, but he called her once a week, and every week she had some other excuse for cutting the conversation short—Julie needed this or that, or was crying or hungry, or it was time to put the baby to sleep. Always Julie, always something.

But not this time. This time he had news. He dropped a large handful of coins into the telephone slot, one after the other, until his hand was empty. As soon as he heard her voice, Charlie started talking fast, very fast, pitching her hard so he wouldn't lose the sale.

"Hi, honey, it's me. Guess what! I found a terrific apartment. It's got a room for the baby and it's cheaper than what we had before. Got a big kitchen, too. I know how you hated that other one we had down here. What d'you say? Come on down."

"Can't do it, Charlie. Sorry."

"Oh, come *on*, baby!" He sounded desperate. "I really miss you, and I wanna see my kid." He listened for a minute, but what she said turned him red with frustration.

"God *damn*, why are you so *polite* anymore? Can't you just talk normal? I feel like I'm talkin' to Eleanor Roosevelt. . . ."

"Charlie, I can't talk to you anymore right now. The

baby just woke up, and I have to go and warm her a bottle—"

"Okay," he answered morosely. "If Julie woke up. Yeah, 'bye." He hung up, depressed; she hadn't even given him the chance to tell her he loved her.

Patsy hung up the phone, depressed. She could hear the desperation in Charlie's voice, even under the cheerful, persuasive words. Why couldn't she react to it? How long was this leaden feeling going to stay with her?

In her deepest heart, Patsy knew that Charlie loved her with all his soul, so why was she so unforgiving? She'd known when she married him that liquor would always be his big temptation, and liquor was usually followed by other things, like women. He was an attractive man, and she'd been out of sexual commission for months. What did she expect? Charlie Dick couldn't walk the path of the righteous on the best day of his life; what made her think he'd be an angel after two months of no loving?

No, it wasn't the drinking or the whoring that had gotten to her and turned her heart to stone. It was the fact that he had placed her second to himself at a time when she needed to come first. She had been in agony, terrified out of her mind, and he had let her walk alone into the Valley of the Shadow when he should have been walking right beside her, holding on to her hand.

Now he thought that if he talked fast enough, she'd pack up a newborn baby and drag her three hundred and fifty miles to the ass end of the earth, an Army camp, so the three of them could be together in boredom and irritation. Well, you can just think about that twice, Charlie Dick!

Patsy was in her bed and sound asleep when the light was snapped on in the bedroom, waking her immediately.

Still groggy, the light hurting her eyes, she sat up and stared, one arm up to shield her from the glare.

"What on earth?"

"Put somethin' on, I want to take you someplace," said Charlie.

"What!" She squinted at the clock, barely making out the time. "It's two-twenty in the morning!"

But Charlie was holding out Patsy's bathrobe, and his tone brooked no argument.

"Come on, it's important."

Wrapping herself tightly in the robe and stuffing her feet into slippers, she followed him out of the bedroom, her awakening brain beginning to race with questions. How the hell had he gotten here? What was he doing here, when she'd spoken to him on the telephone no more than six hours ago? Why was he so covered in mud and dirt? And where in the *hell* were they going at this hour of the night?

With disbelief written on her features, Patsy followed her husband out the front door, dressed only in a nightgown and bathrobe. It was raining—not heavily, just a fine, misty rain—but the evidence of the puddles showed that it had been raining very heavily indeed.

Charlie's Harley-Davidson was parked in the driveway, close to the house. His motorcycle and the rain accounted for the filthy condition of his clothing; he had ridden his motorcycle all the way from Fort Bragg to Winchester and, judging by the time he'd turned up in her bedroom, he must have been going eighty miles an hour most of the way.

Silently, he climbed into Patsy's Packard, and she got into the passenger seat next to him. The rain was tailing off, but the air was still soft gray, heavy with moisture.

He turned on the engine.

"Where are we going?"

But he smiled and said nothing. They drove in silence for long minutes, Patsy growing more and more curious.

"I wish you'd tell me where—"

"You'll see," was all he would say.

And then, suddenly, they were rounding a curve, and there it was, lighting up the sky. An electric rainbow, emerging in all its polychrome glory from the misty night. Red, yellow, green, blue, off. Red again. He had driven her all the way out to the Rainbow Road Club. He parked in the lot, very near the rainbow, the same spot he'd chosen that first night, the night they'd made love for the first time.

"My God, Charlie—"

"Shh."

He switched on the car radio, looking for a station, finding it. Soft dance music, a romantic theme, came out of the night as if on cue. Opening the door, Charlie reached down for Patsy's hand, pulling her from the car and into his arms.

For a long minute they stood there, body pressed to body, then they began to dance, slowly, like lovers. It began to rain again, very softly, the shimmer of the drops making the rainbow look even more mysterious and yet at the same time more real. As they moved in the glow of the lights, their faces changed colors with the changes in the rainbow.

"I need something from you," said Charlie. "I need you to look me in the face and say, 'You screw up a lot, but I still love you, Charlie. I always will.'"

Patsy pulled back a little to look at her husband. "I told you before you left I'm not holding any grudges."

"I need something from you," said Charlie once more, pressing her more tightly against him. "I need you to look me in the face and say, 'You screw up a lot, but I still love you, Charlie. I always will.'"

Patsy stopped dancing. Her dark hair caught the raindrops and reflected them back as she thought it over, looking hard at Charlie, assessing her feelings. At last she looked him straight in the face and said, "You screw up a lot, but I still love you, Charlie. I always will."

Charlie heard a door somewhere far away click open, and Patsy felt a leaden lump deep inside her begin to dissolve.

March 5, 1963

*T*HEY WERE ONLY NINETY miles from Nashville; within the hour they'd be home. Patsy looked anxiously at her watch for the thousandth time and did her thousandth calculation. Sixteen hours since they took off from Kansas City, what with all the starts and stops, the landings to wait out the storm, the refuelings. Dottie West was probably home right now, snug in her bed. *And if I'd rode along with her in the car like she asked me to, that's just where I'd be, too.*

Well, no sense in fretting about it anymore. She'd learned her lesson; next time, she'd drive, take a bus, or even walk. No more of these dumbass private airplanes.

The weather front was still hanging over Kentucky Lake near Camden, Tennessee, and it was turbulence all the way. The little plane, suddenly seeming no bigger than a toy, bounced and bucked, rocked by the constantly changing air currents.

Patsy shifted the weight of the big doll on her lap, hugging the teddy bear to her like a child. Little Randy was just going to love this here bear, it was pretty near as big as he was. Only two years old, Randy hadn't had as much of Patsy as Patsy wished she could have given him. But since she had become a star, her time was not her own to give. Somehow it all got swallowed up—in television studios, recording studios, in rehearsals, on stages. If she didn't have Hilda to help her with the children, she didn't know

202

what she would do. She thanked God again for her mother's unwavering support.

When they'd taken off from Dyersburg, Patsy had given up her seat in front to Hawk. Randy said he needed him to "ride shotgun," to look out his window and see if he could spot a break in the weather for them to fly into. Visibility outside the plane kept shifting, but it wasn't what you'd call real good at any time. Hawkins, six feet five inches high without his boots on, had a better chance of seeing something than little Patsy, if there was anything to see.

The sky turned black. A sudden burst of turbulence rocked the Comanche, worse than anything they'd encountered up to now. The wind, catching them up, shifted the plane violently, tossing it from side to side. Rain spattered on the windshield, heavy drops that made pistol-shot noises as they landed. They were flying directly into the weather.

Patsy's knuckles were aching from clutching the toy bear so tightly, but she didn't notice. The nervousness in the little cabin was palpable, as thick as the weather outside, yet nobody spoke. What was there to say? They all wanted the same thing—to get the hell out of this.

Without warning, the engine sputtered and coughed. And died. Three yelps of fear cut through the silence.

"Relax," said Randy Hughes. "One tank's empty. I've just got to switch to the other, is all."

He flicked a switch, changing the fuel system over to the full tank. Then he turned on the engine ignition to restart the motor.

It wouldn't start. It had stalled out. It choked, coughed, didn't ignite. The three passengers exchanged horrified glances. You didn't have to be a pilot to know when a motor hasn't turned over. The sound was unmistakable, terrifyingly unmistakable.

Suddenly, the nose of the plane turned downward. The Comanche began to plummet out of the sky like a bird caught by the blast of a shotgun. Down, down. As the wind buffeted it, the Comanche was even more like a wounded bird, caught up and rocked sideways in its fall, at the mercy of the storm and the inexorable pull of gravity.

"Randy!" shrieked Patsy in terror.

But Randy's attention was focused entirely on the ignition switch. Again and again he switched if off and on, off and on, begging it, cursing it, praying to it.

"*Turn*, damn you! *Turn*! Oh, God, *turn*!"

Seventeen

"HE'S REAL SICK, PATSY," said Hilda again. "He needs you." She waited, a strained expression on her face, for her daughter to respond.

But Patsy, bending over Julie's crib, fussing with the baby, continued to refuse to reply or even to react, pretending to herself that Hilda wasn't even talking. Inside, though, her feelings were in turmoil.

It was plain, however, that Hilda wasn't about to let this go. Uncomfortable though it made her, she had to persist.

"Patsy," she said, more firmly, "your father called me last week. I just didn't know how to tell you. He wants you to call him."

Unable to hold on to her silence another second, Patsy jerked her head up and scowled at her mother.

"Fine," she grated between clenched teeth. "He left home—what—twelve years ago? Now he strolls back and expects everybody to jump."

"Don't tell me the man's faults," snapped Hilda, losing patience. "I was *married* to him." She hesitated for a moment, attempting to gauge the depth of her daughter's anger, then added softly, "I think he's dying, Patsy."

Don't tell me that! I don't want to hear it, I don't want to know it! What the hell has it got to do with me? Why are you standing there telling me that? Don't you know how I feel by now? When is the hurt supposed to stop? It never stops, Mama, never! Don't you know that by now, after so many years?

Out loud, she snarled, "Mama, I don't want to see that son-of-a-bitch . . . *ever!*"

"Why not?" asked Hilda painfully, avoiding her daughter's eyes.

"Don't you ask me why not!" exploded Patsy. "You know damn well why not!" The wound her father had dealt her was as fresh and soul bleeding today as when she was an innocent of sixteen, a girl confused by the changes in her own adolescent body, and terrified by her father's violent reaction to those changes.

Her yelling woke up little Julie, who began to bawl. Snatching her up out of the crib, Patsy held her tightly in her arms, glaring at her mother over the baby's head.

Hilda, sighing deeply, was silent for a moment. When at last she spoke, her voice was taut, as though she were fighting back tears.

"I don't excuse him, honey, you know that. All I'm saying is, you've grown up with a lot of sweetness in your nature. Can't you give him a little of that sweetness?"

For years, they had not spoken—not out loud—of the secret they'd shared unwillingly between them, the sudden, violent act that had put a stain on Patsy's young life. Each of them had carried the memory like a scar on their hearts, but Virginia the child had learned a bitter lesson: hate. This was a heavy burden for a forgiving Christian woman to bear, this wrath of Patsy's that ran deep inside her veins. If Patsy had a fault, it was that her nature was unforgiving. It wasn't the Way that Jesus had taught; He had preached tolerance and love and, above all, forgiveness. Hilda worried sometimes about Patsy's immortal soul.

Conflicting emotions were now struggling for mastery over Patsy. Her mother's goodness and patience always made her feel a little guilty. Why couldn't she have inherited a touch of that goodness instead of her father's stubbornness that was so central to her nature? She let out a deep breath, handing the baby over to her grandmother.

"What else?" she demanded sourly. "My husband's in the Army, my career's in the toilet. Maybe I'll get struck by lightning. Maybe I'll get run over by a bus. Hell, why don't *you* go?"

A look of sorrow crossed Hilda Hensley's face. "He asked for you," she said quietly.

She went; all along Patsy had known she would have to go and see her father, but it was in her nature to fight, so she'd fought. She had no peace to make with Samuel Hensley. It was up to *him* to make his peace with her. She hadn't sinned against him; it was he who had sinned against her. After what he'd done . . . even today, the gorge rose up and she tasted bile in her throat at the thought of what her father had done to her.

The fear of him was still in there somewhere, a darkness that cast a shadow over her spirit to this day. Woman though she was, she had never outgrown that child's fear.

For the first time in years, she allowed the memory of that night to come back in its hideous totality, a memory she had kept at bay for so long. . . .

Hilda was working as a waitress; anything to make ends meet. Sometimes she worked days, other times she was on the night shift. Tonight was one of those nights.

"I'll be home around two," she told Virginia. "Put the children to bed for me. Don't let 'em sit up too late."

The girl heard with a sinking heart; she hated to be alone in the house with her father. He was never in a good mood anymore; his temper veered between anger and a brooding melancholy. Of the two, Ginny preferred the anger. She could deal with a slap or even a punch.

But, when Samuel Hensley was in one of his dark, bitter, sad moods, he became oddly affectionate, turning to his daughter for the kind of comfort only a wife should be asked to give. He'd put his arm around her, nuzzle her, even try to touch her.

Virginia had blossomed early; her figure had taken on the round contours of a grown woman—large breasts, narrow waist, big hips. It was almost a torture to her, this ripeness. All at once, the boys at school had become conscious of her and leered at her, making snickering remarks. As though big breasts automatically meant that she was easy.

But the worst part of it was the way her own father looked at her voluptuous body. He seemed to be torn between loathing and desire. As a misogynist, he hated all women, his wife included. Now that his daughter had developed into a woman, he hated and feared her, too.

But Samuel was also drawn to her, and eaten alive by jealousy, certain that behind his back Ginny had boyfriends, and that she allowed those boys to touch her.

Please, God, don't let Daddy come home before Mama tonight.

He did come home, and his face was scowling dark.

"Where's your mama?"

"At work, Daddy."

"Damn it, a woman should be there when her man comes home."

"She left you supper on the stove."

But Samuel Hensley wasn't hungry. Instead, he took a fresh jar of moonshine whiskey out of the kitchen cupboard and swallowed hugely. The smell of whiskey had already been on him when he'd walked in the front door; now it was even stronger.

"Come over here and set by your daddy." He patted the sofa invitingly.

She didn't want to go, but she had to. Above all, she didn't want to make him angry, because she was never sure from one minute to the next what he might do. As soon as she sat down, her father wrapped an arm around her tightly.

"You're a big girl. You're growing up fast." He gave her a squeeze.

"Yes, Daddy."

"Bet all the boys are after you." He squeezed harder. "Is that how it is? Are they all sniffin' around after my daughter? By God, I'll shoot 'em dead if they try anythin'!" Samuel's voice rose to a roar of anger.

"No, Daddy, honest!" She tried wriggling out of his grasp, but it was too strong. Her upper arm and shoulder ached where his fingers were digging in.

"Daddy, let me get you your supper. It's gonna be all cold."

He released her, pleased to have her waiting on him. Ginny ran to the kitchen and took down a plate, filling it from the pot on the stove. She kept one eye on Samuel, waiting for her chance, waiting for him to take his eyes off her.

And then it came. He leaned forward to turn on the radio, and Ginny moved quick as a bolt of summer lightning, dashing for the stairs, running up to the bedroom she shared with Sylvia. Once inside, she slammed the bolt across the door and sat down on the bed, breathing hard, her pulses hammering in her ears.

"Ginny! You come on down here, girl, y'hear?"

She didn't move, hardly daring to draw another breath.

"Ginny!!" The roar was louder. "Hear me? I said, come on down here."

It took all her courage to defy him. "No, Daddy, I'm staying right here. And I've got the door locked."

Heavy footsteps sounded on the stairs. The child trembled; she'd never been this afraid in her sixteen years of life.

"Open that goddamn door, or I'll break it down." The voice was oddly flat, yet filled with menace.

Ginny's quick eyes darted around the darkened room. On the bureau, her mother's sewing shears. She leaped off the bed and grabbed them.

"Go away, Daddy. The door is locked, and I've got a big pair of shears. I mean it, Daddy. I'll use 'em if I have to. Now, go on away and leave me alone. Just leave me be."

There was a silence outside the door, followed by the gurgling sound of whiskey being swallowed from a Mason jar. Then Samuel spoke again, and his words made the nape of Ginny's neck prickle with terror.

"I got John, ain't I? Your baby brother is out here, and not in there. And I'm mad now, daughter, good and mad. If you ain't out here by the time I count up to five, I'm gonna start beatin' on somebody. If it can't be you, it'll have to be John, won't it? And if I hurt him bad, whose fault is that? Yours, Ginny, not mine. Yours. Now take your pick, you or him. One . . . two . . . three . . ."

She threw the bolt, came out shivering and sobbing, to those hands—those terrible hands. How could she ever be asked to forgive or forget?

The next morning, he packed and he left. With no word to anybody. Samuel Hensley abandoned his wife, his tormented daughter, and two small children with not even a backward glance. Was he afraid of what he had done? Ashamed? Sorry? Patsy would never know, because Samuel had never said.

After that, the family only saw him one more time.

They'd heard he was back in Winchester, and they all lived in mortal fear of his coming back home. Things were easier for them now, with Ginny working full-time at Gaunt's Drug Store, and bringing all her money home to Hilda. Hilda had put some insulation into the back room, fixed it up a little, and rented it out to a Mr. Purdy, a quiet bachelor who drove a taxi. Mr. Purdy kept out of everybody's way and paid fifteen dollars a week for his room, so they were getting by.

They had no need of Samuel Hensley, but he came anyway, his face as dark as a rain cloud.

"You got another man living under your roof," he shouted at Hilda. "And we're still man and wife. You're nothing but a whore!"

"Don't you call me names!" yelled Hilda, standing up to him for once. "You walked off and didn't send your own kids a penny. Ginny had to leave school to go to work."

At the mention of his daughter's name, he looked uncomfortable and, suddenly, old. With a shock, Hilda realized that Samuel must be over sixty. He had stopped dying his hair, and it had reverted to gray; the stubble on his chin was more white than black. But his eyes were angry and his mouth mean. Samuel Hensley was still a dangerous man.

"Where the hell *is* Ginny?" he demanded, looking around.

Hilda didn't answer. John and Sylvia were locked in upstairs, but how could she tell him that Ginny had run down the road to call the police?

As she saw her husband's hand snaking toward his jacket pocket, saw the bulge there that could only be a gun, Hilda prayed that Patsy would keep out of Samuel's sight. Although Patsy hadn't told her everything that had happened the night before Samuel had left home, she'd said enough, and Hilda had guessed the rest of the sorry story. It wasn't something you could talk about out in the open.

"Who the hell is that?" Samuel hissed when he heard a knock at the door. He thrust his hand into his jacket pocket.

"Police! Open up!"

"Don't you open that goddamned door!" he threatened his wife. "And you let me get a five-minute start, or you'll wish to God you had!" He pulled his hand out of his pocket, but Hilda caught a glimpse of a .38 revolver.

And then he was gone. That was the last time the family ever saw Samuel Hensley.

Now he was very sick, dying probably, according to what Mama said, and he wanted to see the daughter he'd wronged.

How could Patsy bring herself to go and see him? Once, she'd thought him a giant among men, almost a god. He had loved her like a father should love a daughter, with protectiveness and pride. And she had loved him back, as her protector. Even when he was in one of his terrifying moods, she had respected him.

But he'd destroyed that love and that respect in one terrible night, with his bare hands.

Still, she went. Everything had to come full circle or there would be no order in the universe. If Samuel Hensley was indeed dying, it was time for the circle to close.

She was a grown woman now; what was there to be afraid of? Even so, as she climbed the rickety steps of the seedy, dilapidated rooming house where her father was living, Patsy felt something very like panic tugging at her throat. Yet, Patsy being Patsy, the panic made her all the more resolute. She had a reputation to protect; Patsy Cline never refused a dare.

Reaching the landing, she searched among the numbers on the shabby doorways. Ten. Eleven. Twelve. There it was. Number twelve. She raised her hand to knock, hesitated, put her hand down again. All those years came rushing back at her at the same time, a torrent of memories strong enough to drown her.

In her mind's eye, Patsy saw a man whose strength was almost legendary, whose scowling brow had been a thundercloud, whose voice had been the thunder and whose quick wrath was lightning itself.

And those hard, heavy hands. Brutal hands. Angry hands. Shuddering as she remembered the weight of those angry hands of his on her, she almost turned and ran. Quickly, before she could lose her nerve, she knocked at the door.

"Come in," said a voice she didn't recognize.

She opened the door, but didn't come into the room, standing instead in the doorway. The light in the room wasn't good; it was late in the afternoon and the window faced east. The sun had long departed for the other side of the house.

What she could see of the room itself struck her as unspeakably shabby. A sink in the corner, but no toilet. A dangling light cord hanging from the ceiling, its bulb burned out. No closet, but a few nails hammered into the wall, holding a tattered jacket, an ancient coat. One old wooden chair. A rickety iron bed. And, on that bed...

Patsy's eyes peered into the gloom at the figure on the bed.

It was a stranger.

This couldn't be her father. This shrunken, gaunt, feeble, pathetic wreck couldn't have once been the giant that was Samuel Hensley! *That* man had been domineering and had always inspired dread; *this* man couldn't inspire any emotion more powerful than weak contempt.

The figure, dressed only in faded khaki pants and a torn undervest, raised itself on one elbow.

"Is it Virginia?" he asked, barely audible.

"Yes," answered Patsy.

"Call yourself Patsy now, I hear." His voice, once like thunder, was now a reedy croak.

She merely nodded, not trusting herself to speak.

"Come sit down where I can see you," her father invited her. Patsy didn't budge.

"Oh, it's gonna be like that?" asked Samuel dryly.

"Yeah, more or less," said Patsy curtly.

A silence fell between father and daughter, broken only by the sound of Samuel's ugly hacking cough, coming up from his very bowels to rack the thin, miserable frame. He put his hands up to his mouth in a futile gesture of politeness.

His hands. They were emaciated into feeble claws, almost too weak to cover his mouth. Patsy tasted bitter bile in her throat, recalling those very hands on her body. Those hands, so strong that nothing she could do would stop them, had dominated her adolescent body—hitting her, fondling her, then, abruptly holding her down. She shivered, thinking of her own little daughter's precious unsullied flesh. How had Hilda borne that memory all those years? How had Patsy?

"You grew up pretty," remarked her father.

"Mama says you're sick. What's wrong?"

The emaciated face struggled for an instant, and managed a grin. It was a horrible sight, as though a skull were fighting to return to life.

"Oh, I abused this old body for years, and now it's getting back at me. You name it, I got a touch of it."

"Do you hurt?"

"Oh, yeah." Another fit of coughing shook him like an autumn leaf in a windstorm, leaving him gasping for breath.

"Can't you sit down, for the love of God?" he pleaded.

Patsy shook her head hurriedly. "I gotta go."

Samuel fell back onto the thin mattress, breathing with great difficulty. "I'd spend a year in hell for a drink," he pleaded.

You'll spend eternity in hell anyway. Out loud, she said coldly, "I'm not buying you any liquor."

They eyed each other, father and daughter, and something like a spark of the old Samuel returned to his glance to challenge her.

"I mean it. I'm not!" repeated Patsy. She walked over to the sink and turned on the cold tap, running the water until it was less than tepid and most of the rust was out of it. Taking a chipped and dirty glass off the sink, she rinsed and filled it and handed it to her father.

He drank it thirstily, with such abject gratitude that Patsy had to turn her eyes away from the wretched sight of him. She'd hoped for years never to see him again in this life; she was unprepared for this assault on her emotions.

This dying thing on the bed had nothing to do with Samuel Hensley. This pitiful thing couldn't be her father.

But it was.

"Like a cool breeze in August," he told her, handing her back the glass.

"You used to say that when I was little." The words just slipped out of her, but the memory came back strong.

There *had* been a time when she'd loved her father, even worshiped him. There *had* been a time when his strength had been a source of pride to Patsy, before disappointment and drink had turned him from a forceful husband and father into an embittered and vengeful wife-beater and child abuser.

That time still had some claims on her; it rose up again from the deepest part of her to claim Patsy now. But she fought against it and, losing, sought retreat.

"I gotta go," she told Samuel, heading for the door.

"I used to stand by your crib by the hour when you were born, just lookin' at you." His voice, cracked and weak though it was, was suddenly gentle.

"Don't." She shook her head to keep his voice from entering her ears.

"I thought the sun rose and set in you."

"Don't!"

With enormous effort, Samuel Hensley pushed himself up on his elbow again. "If it means anything at all to you, I loved you all my life, and I love you now."

She turned, suddenly savage. "I can buy that," she said without emotion.

The reference to their past was aimed at him like a blow, and when it struck, Samuel gasped and flinched as though the words were fists.

"You turned out to be a cool one, didn't you?" he said bitterly.

Without replying, Patsy left, closing the door behind her. She managed to get all the way down the stairs and out into the street before she let go of her control and allowed the tears to flow. They came and they came, pouring out all the emotion she had kept bottled up for so many years. All the hatred she felt for her father, all the love she felt for her father, gushed out in a storm of weeping.

And Patsy let it gush. She wanted it out of her system, wanted it over with. She wasn't going to let Samuel Hensley see that she'd been crying when she climbed back up the stairs again with the bottle of whiskey she was about to buy for her daddy.

Eighteen

STAYING HOME WITH LITTLE Julie was both a pleasure and a pain. Patsy had never felt so much love for another
human being in her life; she simply doted on her baby
daughter. But there were just so many hours you could hang
over a crib where a baby was sleeping. The rest of the time
she was almost out of her mind with boredom.

She *had* to get back to work. For more reasons than one.
Charlie had come out of the Army with seven hundred
dollars severance money, and had taken up his old job as a
linotyper, still hating the work and the level of pay. They
had almost no money. "Walkin' After Midnight" had done
well on both the country and the pop charts, yet the record
had so far earned her less than a thousand dollars total in
royalties. The company was screwing her and there was
nothing she could do about it.

There was a clause in her contract that said she didn't
get paid a penny of royalty out of the gross, only out of the
net, *after* all their expenses had been deducted first. Patsy's
most recent royalty check, covering a six-month period, had
netted her exactly $215.59.

What was happening to her life? She'd been in the spotlight for exactly five minutes, and now everything was dark
again. She and Charlie didn't have two nickels between
them, so the buffalo didn't even get a chance to mate.

Broke, bored, stifled; it was an old story to Patsy Cline.
When was it going to get any better?

I'm coming out of retirement, she told herself grimly. *I'd rather go back to playing the Berryville Armory dances and the Elks Club benefits than to sit on my ass doing nothing at all.*

She phoned Bill Shawley. "Get me back into the recording studio," she pleaded. "Get me some songs. I'm coming back to work."

He put her back in the recording studio, but *this* one was sure not going to be a hit. Patsy sang the last few notes of the last take. When they wrapped, she turned to Peter Jameson, the producer, who doubled as the head sound engineer.

"That song is a piece of shit," she told him flatly.

Jameson shrugged. "Well, Bill Shawley knows what sells, and he picked it."

"Tell your boss he's pickin' songs blindfolded lately," growled Patsy. She was deeply dissatisfied with her material; all her songs were for bland, nasal hillbilly singers. Not one of them had bite, and Patsy Cline was a singer who bit into a song and chewed the stuffings out of it.

Jameson looked down at her and smiled. He was a handsome man, but a smooth article, and too aware of his good looks.

"Aw, it's too pretty a day to talk business," he suggested. "I know a place where they serve a *real* good steak. We could have a couple of drinks . . . just a little social lunch. . . ." His meaning was quite plain.

Patsy looked him up and down. Then she looked him down and up again, real slow. Then she spoke.

"I'd rather die," she said, and sashayed out, taking her sweet time about it. *Eat your heart out, cowboy.*

Outside the studio, in the recording company waiting room, Hilda was sitting with baby Julie. Although her shoulders were drooping with fatigue, Patsy happily took the baby into her arms, cuddling her for a moment.

"Honey, your mama's life is not working out. Trust her. It's not working out." To Hilda, she said, "I'm going up to Nashville tomorrow. I gotta change some things."

There were three major items on Patsy's agenda. First, she needed to confront Big Bill Shawley; she had to have something decent to record, not the piles of crap he was handing her. This deal was no better than Four Star. Second, she needed to talk to Owen Bradley, the Decca Records production executive. Bradley was always willing to listen to Patsy and give her his good counsel; sensitive to the plight of the artist, Bradley was a man much admired and much respected in the country music business.

Most important, she had to see about new management. A good manager could make all the difference to a musician's career, and Patsy had never been given good management. Some of it was well-meaning, like Bill Peer's, because he took such a personal interest in her, but Peer never had the clout Patsy Cline needed. Shawley had more power than Peer, but he had apparently lost interest in doing anything for her. Also, as Patsy had learned, his reputation in the business wasn't the most savory. Charlie talked sometimes about managing Patsy's career, but that could be a disaster. They had enough to fight about already, cooped up as they were in a tiny apartment with hardly a dime coming in.

No, there was a certain person Patsy already had in mind. Someone with clout and savvy and a good reputation. Now, if she could only persuade him to see her and listen to her sing. . . .

Big Bill Shawley was not too happy to see Patsy Cline. He'd heard about her angry phone calls to the Four Star accountants, and Jameson had reported to him her nasty comments about the songs she'd just recorded. This gal was too damn big for her britches, carrying on like she was an honest-to-God recording star instead of a cracker bitch who'd got lucky once.

Now here she was, bigger than life, sitting on the other side of his desk, telling him how to run his business!

"Don't give me that crap!" he shouted angrily. "I've handed you good, solid songs."

"Oh, Jesus Christ!" Patsy cried in disgust. She held up her fingers and ticked the titles off, one by one, her voice dripping sarcasm.

"'Barnyard Boogie'? 'I'm the Queen of Broken Hearts'? 'I Wonder, Lawanda'?"

Shawley stood up suddenly, looming as big as a wall. All traces of his smoothness vanished; he was big and mean and scary.

"Don't you tell me songs!" he growled at Patsy. "You don't march into my office and tell me nothin'! You didn't follow up the Godfrey show, you didn't follow up "Walkin' After Midnight"—you just went off and got yourself knocked up."

With one swipe of her hand, Patsy slammed a fancy pen-and-ink set off Shawley's desk. It went flying across the room, to shatter on the floor. Ink spilled everywhere.

"Don't tell me how to live, man!" she yelled back, her face darkening with rage. "I'll put my baby on my back and *walk* if you'll just get me a decent song to sing in a decent club!"

Shawley spun on his heel and opened a drawer of the cabinet behind him. He pulled out a document and waved it furiously at Patsy. It was the contract she had signed with him in New York, in that first excitement after she had won first prize on Arthur Godfrey's *Talent Scouts*.

"You want this? Huh? Who the hell *are* you? I can walk out on the street and whistle, and a dozen just like you'll come arunning. You lucked into one hit, baby."

Shawley rapped his knuckles on the desk to emphasize his words. "You're a *one-shot-singer*! Now, I'll carry you for another year if—"

But Patsy had reached over the desk before he could finish his sentence and snatched the contract out of Shawley's hand. Ripping it into pieces, she threw the contract into the air, sending it flying after the inkwell.

"You are ugly, you're a liar, and you're no damn good at your job, but you know what I hate about you the most?" she roared. "You are as ignorant as dirt, because the one thing you haven't got in your office today is a *one-shot-singer*!"

Then, pulling herself coldly together, she marched out the door of Big Bill Shawley's office.

Once out on the street, she began to tremble violently, partly from the strain of the scene she'd just been through, partly from apprehension. Now what was she going to do? Almost at a run, she headed for Owen Bradley's recording studio, hoping that Bradley would see her.

Owen Bradley listened patiently and sympathetically, just as he always did.

"What am I gonna do? I can't get songs, I can't get decent club dates, I've got a new baby, my husband is just out of the Army. Can't you do something for me?" pleaded Patsy, crying. "I'm trapped! No money, no management, not a damn thing!"

"Now, Patsy, you know I would if I could. We'd love to sign you up directly with Decca Records, you know that. Paul Cohen has told me that many times. But your contract with Four Star has another year to run, and they won't even let me find songs for you."

He reached over and patted her hand soothingly, "But I do have one piece of advice for you, honey. I think you're making a mistake staying down there in Winchester. The country-and-western scene is here in Nashville. This is Music City, U.S.A. If you're not around Nashville, things are just naturally gonna be slim pickins. Here you could meet the songwriters, get on the Opry now and then, keep yourself generally visible. Out of sight, out of mind, and it doesn't take long for people to forget you. But I can't say more than that, Patsy. The rest is up to you and your husband. You both have to make that decision."

"You really think I got a chance to make it?" she asked him earnestly.

"I've always said so, Patsy. You've got something special. There's only one voice like yours."

"Thanks, Mr. Bradley. You've given me a lot to think about."

She was thinking hard as she walked up the hilly street from Owen Bradley's office. Many producers and record companies had their office buildings on Lower Broadway, the busy Nashville street near the Ryman Auditorium, home of the Grand Ole Opry. Just being so close to the heart and soul of country music gave Patsy a thrill; it made her feel a genuine part of it.

She opened her handbag and smiled at the precious slip of paper bearing the name and address of the person she had come to see. Only two or three doors down now.

Patsy had met Randy Hughes several years ago when he was still a musician and hadn't yet gotten into big-time management. The two had remained friends, following each other's careers with interest. In a few short years, he'd become manager of some of the top names in country and western—Ferlin Husky, Billy Walker, Ray Price, Wilma Lee, to name only a few. He had once told Patsy to look him up if she ever made it to Nashville, and that was exactly what she planned to do now.

As she headed up to his office, she saw him walking down the stairs. He looked vastly different from the old days, more like a banker with his dark, pin-striped western-cut suit, silk shirt and dark tie, and conservative black boots.

"Hey, Patsy," he greeted her, "what are you doing here?"

Patsy grinned up at the tall man. "Well, we just moved here with my baby, and I haven't been singing much, but now I really want to—"

Ramsey "Randy" Hughes looked down at her with an amused smile. "You don't have to sell me," he replied easily. "I think you're maybe the best country singer in the world."

Patsy put one hand on Randy's shoulder. "I like a man who knows how to start a conversation good!"

He escorted her into his office which was large and bright, and furnished like a living room with sofas and comfortable chairs. He listened patiently as Patsy told him about the poor material she had to sing and how she wanted to get her career moving again.

"Before God, I'll make us both money. I'll do you proud. You won't be sorry. You know why not? 'Cause when the song's right and I'm feelin' good, I've got power! I can see from lookin' at people's faces that I've reached right into 'em. You got any idea what that *feels* like?"

Randy tilted back in his swivel chair. "You want to be Kitty Wells, right?"

"*Hell*, no!" exploded Patsy. "I want to be Hank Williams!"

"All right, then. Sit own and listen to me!" he ordered, and Patsy heard an authority in his voice which made her sit on command, like a trained pooch.

"I got a story to tell you," continued Randy. "I heard you sing one night in a dump in Virginia; twelve tables, watered-down drinks, and a dance floor the size of that coffee table. And you were good. The crowd liked you, just ate up all that yodeling and growling stuff. You did six or eight uptempo numbers, and then, all of a sudden, you let go with 'Walkin' the Floor Over You.'

"But you did it slow, like a ballad, and I'm tellin' you, the hair on the back of my neck stood up. I mean, there I was in this dive in Virginia, and I was listening to . . ." He paused, searching for the right word, not finding it. "Well, something *real* special. You get my drift?"

"*No!*" exclaimed Patsy, although she *did* know what Randy Hughes was driving at. She'd heard it before, from the talent coordinators on Arthur Godfrey's show, from the songwriter, Donn Hecht. Heard it, and dismissed it without giving it a second thought.

"If we're gonna work together," Randy said softly, looking closely at Patsy, "I want you to move away from the hillbilly stuff and toward something softer. Ballads."

"But I'm *country*!" protested Patsy.

Now Randy Hughes raised his voice, and it had an edge of steel in it. "I don't care if you take off your shoes at night, and you got cow shit between your toes. I'm talkin' *voice*!"

Patsy shook her head. "Man's crazy as a loon," she muttered to the air.

"You got a certain kind of voice that needs a certain kind of song. *Nature* did that!" he insisted.

"Mad as a hatter," whispered Patsy, half to herself.

Randy Hughes leaned forward in his chair. "You're real slow, aren't you? Listen to me; I'll make it simple. Patsy Cline has a voice that was made to sing love songs. If I work with Patsy Cline, we take advantage of that fact."

He sat back; he'd finished what he had to say. The ball was now in Patsy's court. For a long minute or two, she said nothing, but sat mulling his words over in her mind, her head swimming with the possibilities, the options that had opened to her. Although Patsy Cline as pop singer was no new concept, it was the first time she'd ever given it any actual consideration. At last, she spoke.

"You got anything to eat around here? Peanut butter, anything? I'm just starving!"

Laughing, Randy Hughes stood up. "Come on, I'll buy you the best damn lunch in town."

"The best damn lunch in town" was a hot dog and a root beer, but Patsy didn't mind. She was so elated that she had no idea what she was eating or drinking, anyway. They walked together down the street, and Patsy was thrilled that almost everybody who passed them said "Howdy" to Randy. He was famous. She liked that.

"Well, you know where I stand," Randy told her as they headed back to his office.

"Yeah, with your foot on my neck."

"Nobody wants you to be Doris Day. I just want you to

put another string to your bow."

"You said that already. Twice," Patsy reminded him.

"And you could use a different look, too," he suggested mildly.

Stung, insulted, Patsy whirled on him, scowling. "The *hell* you say!" Patsy, who liked a bit of flash and razzmatazz in clothing and judged it accordingly, had no idea how expensive his suit and fine leather boots really were. Where was the top stitching? Where was the embroidery?

"You're no Tony Curtis yourself!" she threw at him.

Randy smiled down at her, seeing a lovely dark-eyed young woman wearing dark lipstick, bright earrings, fringe on her shirt, both a necklace and a scarf tied around her neck.

"Why are you all decked out like a Christmas tree, anyway, with that scarf and all? And why don't you buy yourself a *pretty* dress?" he demanded.

For an instant, tears of anger and humiliation stung Patsy's eyelids, but her sense of humor won out.

"You *sure* you want to manage me?" she challenged him. "You don't like my songs, my scarf, my dress. Hell, you sure you talkin' to the right woman? Patsy Cline? Sort of a pretty girl from Virginia? Big voice?"

"You make me laugh," grinned Randy, pushing open the door to his office building.

"Well, *you* make my *ass* ache!" retorted Patsy, her hands on her hips.

"Come on in, let's make a deal," invited Randy.

She put her head to one side, pretending to be thinking it over, while he waited patiently, pretending to believe her. Then she gave him a nod and a smile. Randy Hughes threw the door open wide, and ushered Patsy Cline in like a duchess.

"I'm glad you're home," Charlie said gloomily, as she walked into the tiny apartment that was all they could afford. "It's so goddamn lonely here without you. Little Julie cries all the time for missing you, and so do I."

Patsy threw her arms around her husband's neck, hugging him tightly. "Aw, what's got my Good Time Charlie so down?" she murmured.

He pulled himself away from her. "It's that shit-eatin' job. God, how I hate it and all the crap they hand me down at the paper."

"Well then, I got the sure cure for those blues of yours."

"What the hell do you mean?"

"I mean, Mr. Charlie Dick, let's wipe our feet on this here town and head for the big time. Charlie, what would you say if I asked you, can we move to Nashville?"

"Nashville? You kidding? Just pick up and move to Nashville, Tennessee? Just the three of us, you, me, and the baby?"

But Patsy wasn't kidding; she was nodding happily, and her face was alight with excitement and anticipation. Charlie could feel the energy flowing right out of her at the very mention of the word 'Nashville.' And the excitement was contagious; he felt himself caught right up in it with her. Throwing back his head, he uttered his famous rebel yell, waking up his baby and causing his wife to put two delighted hands over her ears.

"Well then, Patsy, honey, I'd say, let's do it! Let's get our asses on out of here!"

Nineteen

EXCEPT FOR THE TIME that Patsy had spent living in married quarters with Charlie at Fort Bragg, she and her mother had never been apart. Even when she'd lived in Frederick with Gerald, it had only been a hop and skip away from Winchester, just a short drive that mother and daughter made constantly back and forth.

Moving to Nashville was another matter entirely. Hundreds of miles would be separating them, and this time, Hilda would be parted from her beloved grandchild, too. If Hilda could have foreseen the future, and guessed that Patsy would become pregnant again in only a few short months, she might never have let Patsy go so easily.

"It's your life, honey. Go live it the way you want."

So, in September of 1959, Patsy and Charlie rented a trailer, packed everything they owned into it, and drove west to Nashville, Tennessee, to begin a brand-new life.

Using the seven hundred dollars of Charlie's mustering-out pay from the Army, they rented a little house on Marathona Drive, in Madison, a suburb of Nashville. Its only claim to fame was that Hank Snow's house was right across the street from theirs. Charlie got a job right away, as a linotyper for the Nashville Newspaper Printing Corporation, which owned two newspapers, the *Nashville Tennesseean* and the *Nashville Banner*.

At first it was a struggle, but Patsy was never one to mind hard work. Randy Hughes got her a gig traveling with

Ferlin Husky, the country singing star he managed. She would sing a few songs to open the act, and later, a duet or two with Ferlin. There was a club date now and then, but the most important thing of all still eluded her. She couldn't seem to get her hands on a hit song.

Meanwhile, though, she had fallen in love with Nashville. How on earth had it taken her so long to figure out that this was where she belonged? This place was where she was understood, where her ambitions were shared by others. Not like Winchester, where she was often looked down on as being too pushy. In Nashville, she felt at home.

Nashville, Tennessee. The mecca for every would-be country-and-western picker and singer and songwriter. In Nashville, Patsy recognized kindred souls, men—and a few women—who had left their homes in little towns and on farms in Kentucky and Georgia and West Virginia and Texas to travel to Music City, U.S.A., hoping to make it. Most of them didn't; you only had to look in the windows of the pawnshops, and count the number of abandoned guitars and banjos, to know the truth of that.

But for those who were making it, or on the verge of making it, for those who hadn't given up yet, Nashville was a paradise of camaraderie. The pickers and singers would congregate downtown, near the Opry, at the Orchid Lounge, Linebaugh's Cafeteria, Ernest Tubb's Record Shop, where they could have a cup of coffee, or a drink together, swap a few lies, and give one another good tips on jobs. A support system.

Patsy fitted right in with them, one of the boys. She could cuss with the best of them, and drink beer like any cowboy. Bourbon, too, when she could afford it. She was drinking more these days, partly to allay her anxieties, but also because she enjoyed it. You could always hear the sound of her laughter, rising above the other noise in whatever bar she was in.

When he got off work, Charlie would often get a local sitter for Julie, then join her for a couple of drinks. More often than not, they'd fight, right there in public. Patsy was touchy about being second-guessed, and Charlie was touchy about being thought pussy-whipped, so when they'd had a few they went at each other hammer and tongs.

But no matter how often they fought or how violently— Patsy once hit Charlie over the head with a bottle, and Charlie once doused Patsy with a schooner of beer—they were welded together in love. They bitched and moaned about each other, but that was okay. Let anybody from the outside make a remark about either of them, and the other was ready to kill.

Under the management of Randy Hughes, Patsy Cline was going through changes. She was even beginning to look different, and Charlie hated the changes in her. That was what they seemed to fight about most.

Randy was toning down Patsy's appearance; she was on the way to becoming a class act. He made her get rid of all the flashy things she was so fond of—the big, chunky, glittery earrings; the white boots; the fussy accessories. At first, Patsy had kicked like a mule. She was crazy about clothes, about buying soft scarves, wide belts, costume jewelry, dresses with ruffles and tucks and shirring.

But after a while, she began to look at clothing with an eye that Randy was training, and she saw what he was getting at. All that froufrou was less than becoming to her rounded figure, making her look shorter and wider and— confess it, Patsy—dumpy.

The new things that Randy was urging her to buy, even fronting the money for, were simpler and sleeker, with classic lines and unfussy details. They were flattering and slenderizing.

Looking at herself in the mirror with a critical eye, Patsy had to admit to herself that she was looking better than she'd ever looked before. Even her makeup was softer and more natural, giving her lovely complexion and large, dark eyes a chance to be better seen and more appreciated.

For the first time in her life, Patsy Cline found herself

surrounded by people who understood her, liked her for what she was, wanted to be her friends. Her natural warmth and generosity bloomed like a flower opening up to the sun. Patsy and Charlie began to see other couples for the first time.

One of their new friends was a young man who'd recently arrived in Nashville, Hank Cochran. Twenty-five-year-old Hank and twenty-seven-year-old Patsy were both broke, but both were determined to make it, Hank as a songwriter, Patsy as a singer. And both were looking for a hit.

Hank had a song he was trying to peddle; he'd written it together with Harlan Howard, and it had been turned down just about everywhere, including Decca Records. Roy Drusky of Decca said no to it, but Owen Bradley heard it and liked it, and tried to get Roy to change his mind. No go.

When Patsy got wind of it, learning that there was a song floating around Nashville that Owen Bradley had his eye on, she acted right away. She phoned Cochran at his boardinghouse on Boscobel Street.

"Hoss, I hear tell you got a song for me to listen to. I'm ready anytime you are. Let's make us a record."

"But, Patsy, you ain't heard it yet. You don't even know what it's called."

"So, what the hell's the problem? All you have to do is tell me the title."

"'I Fall to Pieces.'"

"Not a bad title. Not a great title, but not a bad one. I'll take it."

But when Hank played the song for her, Patsy changed her mind. "I don't like it, hoss, sorry. I can't sing that; a song like that wouldn't do me a bit of good. Not one damn bit of good atall."

But Owen Bradley liked the song; Randy Hughes liked the song, so nobody cared if Patsy Cline hated it. She was going to record "I Fall to Pieces," like it or not.

She didn't like it, and a series of shouting matches ensued that rocked the city of Nashville. Everybody in the business seemed to know that Patsy was yelling at Randy and Owen, and that they were yelling back at her. Had Patsy stopped to consider that this was her chance to have an innovative Owen Bradley–produced record? If she had, she sure didn't appear to be grateful for it.

In the end, they wore her down, both of them being too strong for her. She agreed to record "I Fall to Pieces" backed by "Lovin' in Vain." Pregnant with her second child, she went into the studio, and instantly got into another fight.

The arrangement of "I Fall to Pieces" was different from anything Patsy had ever had before. It was softer, with lush strings and a full, romantic sound; a strong rhythm line was laid down by the plucking of a bass fiddle, not a guitar. It was far more what Randy had told her he had in mind for her—a ballad.

But what Patsy hated most when she walked into Owen Bradley's recording studio was the sight of a second microphone, with four men behind it, going "doo-doo-doo" while she was singing, and echoing her words at the end of a line. She felt like she was being followed, and she blew her stack.

"I don't care what Owen Bradley wants! I don't want four son-of-a-bitchin' men drowning me out!" Glowering at Randy Hughes, she tapped one impatient foot. "Did you tell Mr. Bradley what I said?"

Randy shrugged lightly. "Owen's the producer," he pointed out calmly.

"I'm the *singer*!" retorted Patsy furiously.

"So sing," said Owen Bradley from behind her. He had overheard her tirade, but remained unruffled. "You got a big bank account, Patsy?"

She shook her head.

"You *want* a big bank account, Patsy?" he continued pleasantly.

Jesus, what a question! "Of course," she mumbled, unwilling to meet his eyes.

"Then do the world a favor," said Bradley. "Use your voice to sing with, not yell with."

"But—" began Patsy, who wasn't finished protesting yet.

"*Sing!!*" chorused Bradley and Hughes.

"Well, all right, if I have to, but nobody's ever gonna be able to hear me with all that doo-doo-doo shit."

Famous last words.

On January 26, 1961, five days after Patsy and Charlie's son was born, Decca released Patsy Cline's new single, "I Fall to Pieces."

The last few months had swirled past her like a nightmare. She was five months pregnant when Charlie had an automobile accident that left the car totaled and Charlie himself in a wheelchair for six weeks. The thought that her husband might have been killed nearly caused Patsy to have another miscarriage. She'd already had two—one when she was married to Gerald and another before this pregnancy. And she wanted this baby so badly! It cost her an effort to hang on to it, but hang on to it she did. Her mother flew in from Winchester to help her out with Julie, and Patsy stayed off her feet as often as she could, although she visited Charlie in the hospital every day.

Charlie improved rapidly, and thank God there would be no serious aftereffects. Except, perhaps, for one. When he was in the hospital, she found herself leaning more and more on Randy Hughes's shoulder. Patsy was a woman who needed to have a man around, somebody to talk to, somebody to look up to and rely on. With Charlie smashed up and out of reach, Randy came to mean more to her than ever.

Not that there was anything physical between them. A growing attraction, certainly. Patsy had never looked so beautiful in her life as she did with the new appearance that Randy had led her to so gradually. Randy Hughes was a most attractive man. But it went beyond the physical. Patsy Cline was in need of continual reassurance; she hungered and thirsted for the admiration and respect denied her as a girl. Randy Hughes supplied them in full measure, and she was grateful.

"I Fall to Pieces" was slow in getting started; DJs on country stations were not certain they liked or approved of Patsy Cline's new sound. It was more pop than country.

But then she got her first real break since moving to Nashville. The Grand Ole Opry asked her to come on the program as a regular. She'd appeared from time to time, but this was different; this was one of the highest honors a country music star could aspire to or achieve. It was an accolade, the official stamp of approval by the country-and-western establishment. Appearing regularly on the Opry meant you were accepted by your peers, reassured by your colleagues that you were one of them.

It wasn't all gravy. The Grand Ole Opry didn't pay their regulars a whole lot; you were supposed to do it for the honor, and everybody did. It also meant that you couldn't take any other Saturday night singing engagements, even though they were far more profitable. On Saturday night, you belonged, body and soul, to the Grand Ole Opry. The only Saturday night that Patsy was able to take off was January 21, 1961, when she was in the hospital giving birth to her son.

When the baby was born, she named him Allen Randolph, just so she could call him "Randy." Charlie wasn't too happy about that, but there seemed to be nothing he could do. After all, "Allen" was Charlie's own middle name; besides, Randy Hughes's real name was Ramsey, not Randolph. Still, calling his son "Randy" stuck in Charlie's craw.

Even with Patsy a regular on the Opry, the Dicks were broke. And then the miracle happened. By April 9, three months before little Allen Randolph cut his first tooth, "I Fall to Pieces" was number one on the country charts. *Number One*.

By September, the record had climbed up to number twelve on the *pop* charts, a total crossover hit. And it stayed on the country charts for thirty-nine weeks. "I Fall to Pieces" was a milestone, not only for Patsy but for the country music business. The recording was an innovation, a new sound, designed by Owen Bradley and created by Patsy Cline. Half country, half ballad. The gamble had paid off big.

Patsy was forced to eat crow, to apologize to Owen Bradley and Randy Hughes and Hank Cochran. They'd all been right, and she'd been wrong. Embarrassing though it was, it was a glorious moment for her, too. How could she mind admitting that she'd been mule-headed when everything had turned out so wonderful?

The night that she sang her number-one hit on the Grand Ole Opry was one for the record books.

When the orchestra broke into the opening bars of "I Fall to Pieces," the audience went stone crazy, yelling and stomping and clapping and whistling. The announcer had to hold his hand up to plead for silence.

"Yes, you all recognize that song, don't you? And we got the little gal here tonight who made it the number-one hit. Ladies and gentlemen, Miss Patsy Cline!"

And there she was, striding into the spotlight, wearing a two-piece gold suit and high-heeled shoes, a class act, even if Randy Hughes had snatched her big fluffy orchid corsage off her shoulder as she'd come out of the wings.

Patsy smiling, Patsy in command, Patsy dominating the stage by her mere presence, all confidence and happiness. Patsy giving and giving and giving the best of herself, singing her heart out to make the people happy, leaving them yelling the house down for more.

And Charlie, his face beaming with pride, down front, where she could see him grinning and hear him cheering. And afterward, on the drive back to their little rented house in Madison, where the children were carefully watched by a baby-sitter, Charlie telling Patsy how wonderful she was, just like old times.

"God, they like to went crazy over you. One woman was

cryin' like a baby. Patsy, honey, I like ever'thing you sing, and your voice just makes me fall down. But when you sing them slow ones . . . well, I just purely love it!"

"That's what Randy says, too. He wants me to concentrate on the ballads."

In the dark of the car, she didn't see Charlie's face grow set as stone at the mention of Randy Hughes.

The first part of Patsy Cline's dream had finally come true. She was, at last, an undisputed star. Now she could finally start living like one.

Twenty

*T*HEY MOVED FROM A RENTED house into one of their own, a tiny house on Hillhurst Drive in East Nashville, across the Cumberland River. It wasn't the house of Patsy's dreams, with the yellow roses growing around it, but it was still a big step up from South Kent Street, and surely a step in the right direction. The dream house would be theirs eventually; Patsy and Charlie were certain of that. Meanwhile, she splurged on some new clothes for her and for Charlie and the kids, and fulfilled another dream. She went right out and bought herself a Cadillac. A white convertible with red upholstery, at least a block long. It might have been secondhand, but it was still a Cadillac.

All over the United States, radio stations were playing "I Fall to Pieces" by listener request. Country music fans were buying the records as fast as they could be pressed and distributed, and even music lovers with no enthusiasm for other country-and-western songs were lining up to buy Patsy Cline's new hit.

On the Grand Old Opry, Patsy had become more than just a regular. She was now a star. And, now that she could begin to afford it, Patsy began to give full rein to the generous part of her nature. Even as a kid, if she had two lollipops, she'd give away at least one, and sometimes both. Now she was busy shopping for her friends, distributing gifts left and right.

But, more precious than anything money could buy, time

was what Patsy Cline was most giving of. Never forgetting what it was like to be on the bottom, and how especially tough it was for female singers, she took the girls who were just starting out in the business under her wing.

One night, backstage at the Opry, a very pretty young girl came up to her and thanked her for an encouraging letter Patsy had written to her years before, in answer to the girl's fan letter telling Patsy how much she enjoyed "Walkin' After Midnight."

"You said that if I ever came to Winchester I should look you up and we'd get together, and you wished me luck on my career."

"I did?" replied Patsy amiably. "Well, we're both in Nashville now. You a singer too?"

"I'm hopin' to make records," came the answer.

"Well, good luck to ya. What did ya say your name was?"

"Dottie. Dottie West."

"Well, Dottie West, how'd you like to come over to my house for supper later?"

And that's how their friendship began, a relationship marked by the closeness of sisterhood. Patsy was rising toward her zenith, and Dottie just at the beginning of her career, but they never let that difference get in the way. When Dottie wasn't busy with singing jobs of her own, she'd ride along with Patsy in that big white Cadillac, hanging on for dear life, because Patsy behind the wheel was a daredevil.

It wasn't only Dottie West whom Patsy Cline befriended. Jan Howard, wife of Harlan Howard, co-author of "I Fall to Pieces," was just starting to appear now and then on the Grand Old Opry, while Patsy was a star. But Patsy took her on as protégée, showing her the ropes, making her a friend.

Little Brenda Lee, too, became one of Patsy Cline's "chicks." So did Barbara Mandrell and Roger Miller. To her friends, Patsy's generosity was unbounded. She gave everything away—clothes, money, even bags of groceries, when she knew that it had been a long time between singing engagements. How could she ever forget what it meant to be poor? Even now, she was far from rich, but that never fazed her.

"Hoss, why should you go short when I'm tall?" she'd say, stuffing some money into the pocket of a pal in need.

Patsy was determined that success would not change her, that she'd still be the good ole country girl from Winchester, Virginia. But stardom was already changing her, in subtle ways of which she wasn't even yet aware.

Always the perfectionist, she began to drive others as hard as she drove herself. She'd second-guess Owen Bradley, who had proved more than once that he knew exactly what he was doing. She began to gain the reputation, in some quarters, of being a bitch to work with.

Now that she was an Opry star, she hung out more and more with the other stars, mostly after hours at Tootsie's Orchid Lounge. She and Tootsie became famous pals. Patsy would come in wired after her Friday night performances on WSM's *Friday Night Frolics* and Saturday night at the Ryman Auditorium. She'd be breathing hard, almost hyperventilating with excitement. There was a rush she got from singing in front of an audience that nothing else could give her. She had come to depend on that rush, like an addict depends on a fix.

And she'd head straight for the bottle. Now that she could afford it, she'd drink bourbon, not beer, and often pick up the tab for a dozen or more serious drinkers.

Most of the time, Charlie would be with her—a babysitter minding the kids—and, more often than not, the boozing would lead to trouble. Patsy was naturally high-spirited, and was used to the company of men. After all, she'd made it in a man's business and in a man's world. That should count for something.

And Charlie was just naturally jealous. Still working down at the printing company, he felt stifled, even diminished by Patsy's sudden success. Oh, he was proud of her and no mistake, but he hated sharing her with the whole goddamned world. And it seemed to him that the whole goddamned world was right there in Tootsie's Orchid Lounge, all of them wanting to sit down next to his wife and drape an arm across her shoulder.

It led to fights, then more fights, some of them violent. Patsy's friends worried that Charlie might do her some real physical damage one day; they urged her to call the police on him, have him put away to cool off. But she couldn't find it in her heart to lock up Charlie Dick.

For years the two of them had followed a pattern of fighting and loving. But these days there was more fighting and less loving. Instead of making up right away as they used to, now they would allow the coolness to grow between them for a longer time, even to fester.

In great demand now, Patsy drove or flew everywhere, appearing on television programs locally and nationally, visiting deejays, being an honored guest at the all-important disk jockey conventions, singing at county fairs and rodeos. The money was good, but something was eating at her. She was always on the go, always in a car or a plane, and it began to make her nervous.

The press was calling her "the Female Hank Williams," but there was a dark side to that nickname. Hank had died of a cerebral hemorrhage just short of his thirtieth birthday. For the first time, Patsy began having premonitions that she, too, would die young.

"Hell, I ain't never gonna live to be thirty," she'd say, and try to pass it off with that big laugh of hers.

But what if she *did* die young? What would happen to her precious babies? Julie wasn't even three years old yet, and the baby Randy only three months. Would Charlie be able to cope with them, with those violent moods of his and his drinking?

She was on a commercial flight from Kansas to Nashville when she decided it was time that she made her wishes known. She'd write out a will.

"Miss?"

"Yes, Miss Cline." The stewardess smiled at her brightly. "What can I get for you?"

"Honey, you got any paper and pen? I need a heap o' paper."

A minute later the girl was back, holding a pad of lined yellow paper and an airline pen.

"Will this do?"

"Sure will. It'll do fine. Thanks a heap." Letting down her meal tray, Patsy took up the pen and wrote out her will in longhand. At first, she wrote slowly, still thinking about what she would say, but soon the words crowded her mind so thick and fast that her hand couldn't keep up with her thoughts. She wrote:

> *To Whom It May Concern:*
> *I Virginia Hensley Dick (known in my profession as singer Patsy Cline) being of a sound mind and body, leave (and it is my wish) to Hilda Virginia Hensley, my mother, my children, Julie Simadore Dick and Allen Randolph Dick, to be cared for and raised to the best of her ability until they are eighteen years of age. If in this time Hilda V. Hensley would pass away, my wish is that my sister, Sylvia Mae Hensley, take care and raise my children as if they were her own.*
>
> *Also to Hilda V. Hensley, I leave all money which is in my possession at the time of my death or any income to follow coming from my work or record recordings in any way. I leave this to Hilda V. Hensley to use in any way to benefit and educate my children, Julie and Allen Dick, as she sees fit.*
>
> *I, Virginia H. Dick, having royalties of 5% from each recording sold of the said Recording Company to whom I'd contracted with at the time of my death, or any royalties paid to me thereafter, I wish the money to go to the care and education of Julie S. & Allen R. Dick.*

Their father, Charles Allen Dick, being also of sound mind, and body and good income, can visit, help in raising, clothing and educating the children, Julie and Allen Dick, in any way, but I, Virginia H. Dick, wife of Charles A. Dick, wish that the children remain in the home of my mother, Hilda V. Hensley, and in case of my husband remarrying, that the children still remain in the home of my mother, Hilda V. Hensley or Sylvia M. Hensley, until they themselves can choose otherwise.

If my home in which I reside is paid for, or if the insurance finishes paying for the home at the time of my death, I, Virginia H. Dick, leave the home to my children, Julie S. & Allen R. Dick.

My personal insurance on myself is to be used to put me away and to be put in a savings account by my husband, Charles A. Dick, in Winchester, Va., to be used for the education of Julie & Allen Dick.

My awards of which I received for my work as a singer and all pictures, I leave to my daughter Julie & son Allen Dick.

The children's bedroom furniture is theirs. One oil painting of myself, I leave to my mother, Hilda V. Hensley, until her death and then be passed on to Julie & Allen Dick. My diamond ring I leave to Julie Dick. To John Hensley, my brother, I leave one blond bedroom set and one Polaroid camera and a table model television set.

To Sylvia Mae Hensley, I leave all my jewelry and one black bedroom set. To my mother, Hilda V. Hensley, I leave all clothes, a dinette set, a Kenmore kitchen stove, Kenmore washer and refrigerator. Also to Hilda V. Hensley, I leave all dishes and kitchenwares.

To my husband, Charles A. Dick, I leave my western designed den furniture, hi-fi stereo record player and radio, all records and albums, and a tape re-

corder and blond floor model television set. To my husband, I leave whatever make cars we have at the time of my death.

Whatever household property I may purchase between now and my death, I leave to my mother, Hilda V. Hensley.

I wish to be put away in a white western dress I designed, with my daughter's little gold cross necklace and my son's small white Testament in my hands, and to be buried in the resting place of my husband's choice, and my wedding band on.

I, Virginia Hensley Dick (Patsy Cline), wrote this myself on April 22nd, 1961.

Virginia H. Dick.

When she had finished, she wrote out a second copy, word for word, like the first. Now she felt better, as though she had tied up the most important of her loose ends.

Patsy's sister, Sylvia, was being graduated from high school; Patsy made up her mind to throw the biggest damn graduation party she could afford. The whole family drove in from Winchester to stay with them. Hilda was ecstatic, because it gave her a chance to see her precious Julie and the new baby, little Randy. But she wasn't too thrilled by some of the changes she saw in Patsy.

Her daughter, while acting the life of the party, appeared more reserved and withdrawn than Hilda had ever seen her.

I know that girl better than anybody else in the world knows her. And she's different. She may be actin' happy, but inside she's coverin' up somethin'. I don't like the way she's always got a glass in her hand, either. She'd take a drink now and then, sure, but now you can't ever see daylight 'tween her hand and that glass.

They'd thrown Sylvia a big barbecue at their new house, with Charlie at the coals, grilling the hamburgers. The backyard was crowded with musicians and other friends, all clamoring for burgers and beer. The sky above was heavy with dark rain clouds, but so far the bad weather had held off.

"Listen up, ever'body," called Patsy. "I want a big round of applause for the very first high school graduate in the family. So put your hands together for Miss Sylvia Hensley!"

Sylvia, shy and proud at the same time, wearing a new real silk dress that Patsy had bought her, blushed with mingled joy and embarrassment as she accepted the box that her sister held out to her.

Inside was a beautiful gold wristwatch, with a card that read: "Congratulations and much love from Patsy, Charlie, Julie, and Randy." Tears filled Sylvia's eyes; this was the proudest, happiest day of her life.

Patsy regarded her sister fondly. It did her right proud to know that she could give her family nice things now; this watch was only the beginning.

"Is there any more ice?" yelled a voice near the house. Charlie was busy at the barbecue grill, Hilda was busy inside the house, so Patsy went to see about the ice. But before she had reached the house, Randy Hughes stopped her.

Taking a small black velvet box out of his pocket, he handed it to Patsy. She gasped in surprise and delight when she opened it. Inside was a lovely pin in the shape of an orchid. The body of the flower was a large amethyst, and the winglike petals were rimmed in tiny diamonds.

"It's to make up for the one I yanked off you the other night," explained Randy, reminding her of the orchid corsage he refused to let her wear on stage. Then he leaned over and kissed her lightly on the lips.

Neither saw Charlie's scowling eyes watching them.

Patsy, carrying little Randy, joined Hilda in the kitchen, where her mother was filling bowls with homemade potato salad and cole slaw. As soon as she laid eyes on her grandson, Hilda Hensley held out her arms for the baby, who snuggled up under her chin.

"It kills me that I don't see 'em more," she said with a

sigh, kissing the top of the little boy's head.

"Don't I know?" groaned Patsy. "I wrote the *book*. Seems like I'm always on the road these days. Never seem to get enough of the kids."

"How is it with you and Charlie?" Patsy's mother wanted to know. Patsy shrugged and turned her face away.

"Up and down?" asked Hilda.

"Yeah," answered Patsy, a little secret smile touching the corners of her lips. "There's lots of up and down."

Hilda flashed her daughter one of her disapproving looks that stated plainly how she hated that kind of talk.

"Charlie drinks some," continued Patsy with a small sigh, "but I knew that when I married him. Other than that, things are silk-smooth. 'Course, when he drinks, he's got him a temper."

"Does he hit you?" Hilda asked bluntly.

Involuntarily, Patsy's hand flew up to her eye, even though there was no mark there, and that reflexive gesture told Patsy's mother the entire story.

"No, just that once," lied Patsy, uncomfortable.

"Yo, Patsy!" Her brother John stuck his head in the kitchen door. "We're out of hamburger buns. Can I have the keys to the car? I'll run get some."

"I'll come with you," said Patsy quickly, eager to be out from under her mother's reproachful eye.

They hadn't been together in such a long time, she and John. Laughing, they called up the old days, teasing each other about schoolyard crushes and teenage heartbreak. Then, it was the end of the world; now, it was just another cause for whoops of laughter.

The rain clouds, which had held off for so long, changed their minds and opened up fully, pouring down water by the bucket. John switched on the windshield wipers, and the two of them sat in silence, listening to the heavy drumming of the rain on the roof of the car and the swish of the wipers. The sky had turned black, although it was only about four-thirty in the afternoon.

They were going along Halls Lane, which rose and dipped into little peaks and valleys. It wasn't the safest road even in the best of weather, and it was a double yellow line all the way. No passing.

Coming toward them were two cars on the other side of the yellow line. Suddenly, inexplicably, the second car pulled out and tried to pass the first one.

Now the driver was crossing the double line, intruding into the wrong lane, coming out of nowhere to head straight for Patsy's Cadillac. John put his foot desperately on the brake, flooring it.

The other driver, a woman, perceiving the Caddy for the first time, gunned her motor and tried to get around it. But it was too late. A head-on collision—at fifty miles an hour on a slick, wet road—was unavoidable.

Patsy screamed.

With a grinding crunch of tortured metal and a shrill shattering of glass, the other car rammed the Cadillac head-on. John Hensley's torso hit the steering wheel, puncturing a hole in his body and breaking several ribs, but Patsy Cline, helpless as a rag doll, was flung headfirst through the windshield.

Twenty-one

CRITICALLY INJURED AND BLEEDING copiously from her head and face, an artery severed, Patsy remained conscious throughout her excruciating ordeal, even insisting, when the ambulances arrived, that the others be taken to the hospital first. Lying in her own blood, she watched the passenger in the other car die, her little boy removed to the hospital near death.

John, not as severely injured as Patsy, remained with her while her head wound was sewed and her broken hip was set.

Because of her severed artery, Patsy had lost a great deal of blood; the medics gave her three pints when they stitched her up, but she was wide awake through the sewing. She didn't receive general anesthesia until they took her into the operating room to set her hip.

The extent of her injuries was still not known, but her face was as raw as chopped hamburger, and it looked as though her eyesight might be involved. A long, deep gash in her forehead was dangerously near her eye, and there was a distinct possibility that some vital nerves had been severed.

It was touch and go. More than once, she started to slip away from her doctors, weakened by shock and the loss of blood and the terrible trauma her body had undergone.

I knew I'd never make it to thirty, she thought once as the anesthesia began to take hold. *First Charlie and now me. Thank God I made out my will when I did. At least my babies will be looked after right.*

The hospital telephoned Charlie, would tell him nothing apart from the fact that his wife had been in a serious accident, a head-on collision. Fear was behind the wheel of the convertible along with Charlie Dick; fear kept his eyes straight ahead of him on the slick road as he wove in and out of traffic at a perilous speed.

Roaring into the hospital parking lot, he screeched to a stop and was out of the car and running almost before the engine was turned off. He was in such a hurry he even left his keys in the ignition.

There was nobody sitting at the information desk when a wide-eyed and breathless Charlie came pounding through the door. He dashed past the desk and down the hallway, passing departments with signs he couldn't even understand—Radiology, Nephrology, Pathology, Pediatrics. He was looking for anybody, somebody who could tell him what he needed to know.

Alive or dead? kept hammering at his brain. *Alive or dead?*

Who could tell him the truth?

The corridors seemed deserted; no, here came a youngish nurse carrying a tray of nightly medicine, each dose measured out in a little paper cup.

Desperately, Charlie ran up to her.

"My wife's been in an accident—Patsy Cline. . . ."

The nurse kept right on walking, no change of expression on her face as she spoke. "Check with Information. I don't have information on individual cases," she told him without emotion.

"But there's nobody there!" cried Charlie, following her

down the corridor. She was his only hope. "Can't you call somebody? Oh, lady, *please*! Maybe somebody at the switchboard."

But the nurse had no intention of breaking her routine. "I don't have any information on specific cases," she told him again, not even bothering to look at him.

Charlie's hands balled into fists, and a large vein in his neck stood out, pulsing. "My God, I'm desperate!" he cried hoarsely. "I don't even know if she's alive! Can't you just *try*?" he pleaded.

"I've *told* you," she informed him in a cold voice tinged with annoyance. "I don't have any information on—"

This was it, all Charlie Dick could take. He'd reached the breaking point. Grabbing the young nurse's arm in a grip of iron, he sent the medicine tray flying. All the tiny cups landed on the floor, oozing sticky pink medicine. Without letting go, he dragged the girl down the corridor to the deserted nurse's station, grabbed the phone, and slammed the receiver into her free hand.

"Listen, bitch, you make that call or I'll drag your ass up and down these halls until you *get* some 'specific information'!"

With one look at his terrible face, eyes red with fury, lips drawn back from his teeth like some ferocious wolf's, the nurse had little choice but to surrender.

"The name again?"

"Cline. Patsy Cline. C-L-I-N-E."

The girl dialed the phone with trembling fingers, asked a question in a low voice, heard the answer, hung up, and turned to Charlie. There was respect in her eyes now, along with the fear, and even something very much like sympathy.

"Your wife's in the operating room, sir. She's alive. They say she'll live."

She turned away so that she wouldn't see his face crumple or hear the long, terrible, shuddering sobs that racked him.

From his depths came a low, muttered prayer of thanks to God. Some things were just too personal to watch.

They'd been sitting together all night, but they hadn't spoken a word to each other. What was there to say, with each of them locked in a private hell? Hilda Hensley looked old, suddenly, and very fragile, as though she would break at a touch. She prayed silently but continually, asking Jesus for the same thing over and over—to let her Patsy live, to bring her child back from the edge of the grave.

Charlie, having wept, was now silent, shut away with his thoughts. What if Patsy were to die? What would he do without her? Every harsh word he'd ever spoken to her, every time he'd raised his hand against her were coming back now to stab hot needles of guilt and self-loathing into his tortured brain.

All he knew was that he loved her, loved her terribly, and there she lay, drugged, unconscious, unrecognizable. His Patsy, her head completely swathed in bandages from the crown to the neck. They'd left eyeholes for her to see through, and no more than an inch or two of mouth and chin showed. He couldn't even see if she was breathing.

The two people who loved Patsy Cline most in the world sat miserably side by side in a dark and silent hospital room, while the hours crept slowly past them, and the angel of death brushed black wings across their hearts.

The night finally ended, and daylight entered Patsy's room. Hilda was dozing lightly and fitfully in a chair, her head thrown back, her hands still clasped tightly together in an attitude of prayer, as though even sleep couldn't relieve her of her assignment.

Charlie stood by the window, looking out, seeing nothing.

There was a sound from the bed, faint, weak, but without doubt a sound.

Hilda woke up as though a gun had gone off, and Charlie reached Patsy's bedside in two seconds flat, putting his ear close to her mouth to hear her.

Patsy was mumbling, almost incoherent. ". . . The babies. Where are the babies?"

"They're fine," Charlie assured her. "John's all right, too." He made a major effort to keep his voice light, but it cracked with the strain and unshed tears.

"Hell," he tried to laugh, "you had us scared there for a little bit."

But Patsy's half-drugged voice still held anxiety. Her hands fluttered weakly on top of the blankets.

"Charlie, tell me. Are they alive?" she pleaded.

"You mean the kids?" asked Charlie. Then he spoke as clearly as he could, and loudly, to penetrate the fog enshrouding his wife.

"Patsy, Julie and Randy weren't with you. *John* was with you, and he's okay! Patsy, can you hear me? Do you understand? The kids are okay; they were at home all the time."

He must have gotten through to her, because she uttered a small sigh of relief, and drifted back into a drugged sleep.

Hilda tugged lightly on Charlie's sleeve. "Come on, Charlie, let's go home now. You could use you some rest. She's gonna be okay. You'll see."

But Charlie shook his head violently.

"You go, Hilda. You're good with the kids, and they need you. I'm not going anywhere. Patsy just might wake up again, and I mean to be here when she does."

"It won't do you any good to wear yourself down like this. The time Patsy is gonna need you is when she's awake. If you haven't got anything left to give her, you won't be doin' her or yourself any favors. Now, come on home, honey, and let Hilda fix you something to eat."

But Charlie wouldn't budge. He could no more leave his

wife's side than he could sprout wings and fly away. This was the only place he belonged. His very life was in that bed, his heart and soul wrapped up in those bandages.

Twenty-two

A T FIRST, PATSY CLINE was not expected to live. Her head injuries alone might have proved fatal to another person, one not as young or strong as she. But Patsy was a born scrapper, and she wasn't about to quit the most important or difficult fight of all. She battled so hard that her doctors were able to take her off the critical list in only two days, although her condition was still listed as only "fair."

Getting better was a slow and very painful process. Patsy's injuries were more complicated than they had first appeared to be. Her hip had been dislocated, and she was going to be in a wheelchair and then on crutches for a long time. The miracle was that her vision hadn't been destroyed; the long, deep gash on her forehead hadn't severed any of the nerves or muscles of the eye.

Her biggest worry was her face. Still hidden under thick wads of bandage, Patsy's face was a terrifying mystery. It had been sliced to ribbons when she'd gone headfirst through the windshield, and none of the doctors was willing to make any promises on the outcome. The bandages would have to remain in place and there could be no looking underneath them.

The worst part was not knowing! The bandages wouldn't come off for weeks, not until the healing process was complete. Meanwhile, all she could do was lie in that hospital bed and fret, imagining the worst.

Everybody had been wonderful. Cards and letters and telegrams kept pouring in from all over the country, sent by friends and strangers, wishing her well, telling her that she was remembered in the prayers of thousands of people. Patsy's fourth-floor hospital-room looked like a flower garden, piled high with bouquets and floral arrangements. So many flowers, so many baskets of fruit, so many boxes of candy were delivered to her room that she sent most of them on to the children's ward.

The switchboard of the Madison Hospital was jammed with phone calls every hour of the night and day from concerned fans, friends, and colleagues in the music world. Ferlin Husky and Faron Young, Maybelle and June Carter and the Carter family, Roy Acuff, Tex Ritter, country music station WSM, were only a few among many others who sent messages and floral tributes.

Dottie and Bill West, Jan and Harlan Howard, Brenda Lee, Owen Bradley, Randy Hughes, Hank Cochran, Tootsie Bess from the Orchid Lounge, Roger Miller and the other members of Patsy's inner circle called two or three times a day, begging for the latest news of her.

Patsy sent them all messages of love, through Charlie. She kept saying that she had never really appreciated her life until she'd almost lost it.

"Some people die with their song still inside them. How grateful I am that God has let me sing mine, and that I'm gonna live to sing it again. Sometimes the pain is so bad I want to cry, but I still thank the Lord Jesus that I'm alive to feel the pain. I miss you all and I wish I could see y'all and hug and kiss ya."

But they were forbidden to visit, because Patsy's doctors had restricted her visitors to immediate family only, at least for a while. Hilda had of course stayed on, not only to see her daughter every day, and to help Charlie with the babies, but also because John was in the same hospital. His injuries had required surgery, and John had only recently graduated from the bed to the wheelchair.

As for Charlie Dick, his new home was the side of his wife's bed.

"I Fall to Pieces" was now number two on the country charts and climbing to that all-important number-one spot, so the story of Patsy Cline's near-fatal accident was still hot news. The newspapers carried updates, and the DJs, whenever they played the song, would remind their listeners that Patsy was still flat on her back in Madison Hospital, and to "keep them cards and letters comin' in, folks."

At the Grand Ole Opry, they missed her enormously. The night of the accident, the whole Opry group—staff as well as stars—had driven down to the hospital and sat in the waiting room, some of them until two in the morning, just waiting to hear if Patsy Cline was going to make it. While she was in the hospital, the Opry always said a very special good-night to Patsy on the air before the show ended. When she heard it, heard those fans cheering her name and wishing her a speedy recovery, she broke down and cried.

Across Broadway from the Ryman Auditorium, where the Opry was broadcast, was another country-and-western legend: Ernest Tubb's Record Shop. Every Saturday night, right after the Opry program was over for the week, radio station WSM would air the *MidNite Jamboree*, live from Tubb's record store. It was another Nashville institution; fans and stars would gather there, and pickin' and singin' would go on like a play party. Many had been the time that Patsy herself had crossed the street from the Ryman to the record shop to sing some more.

Now, all she could do was lie in her hospital bed and listen to the radio. On this particular Saturday night, she heard a voice she'd never heard before. The girl was a stranger to her, new to Nashville, and her voice was nothing like Patsy's. It wasn't big and gutsy, but high and sweet in the country tradition. Boy, could that gal sing!

The song she had chosen was, of all things, "I Fall to Pieces." And she made it completely her own, not following the Patsy Cline rendition, but giving it little original twists and turns. Patsy listened, her eyes dancing, her smile half hidden under the bandages.

When the song ended, the singer announced, "I want to dedicate this song to Patsy Cline, who made it a number-one hit, and who, as you know, was in a pretty bad car wreck. She's still layin' over there in the hospital. So, if you're listenin', this is for you, Patsy. Get well soon."

Well, ain't that the sweetest thing, thought Patsy.

Turning to Charlie, Patsy said urgently, "Go get her, honey. Drive on down and pick up that little ole gal before she leaves Tubbs' store, and bring her here to me. I wanta meet that . . . what's her name again? Loretta Lynn?"

When Charlie returned with Loretta and her husband, O. V. Lynn, in tow, Patsy saw a shy girl in a western outfit, with long dark hair and the biggest pair of eyes in the world. Those eyes were staring at Patsy Cline in awe.

At first, when Charlie Dick had come up to her at Ernest Tubbs' Record Shop and introduced himself, Loretta hadn't known who he was. But when he'd identified himself as Patsy Cline's husband, and said that Patsy wanted to meet Loretta, she gave one whoop of joy and threw her arms around Charlie's neck and planted a big kiss right on his face. That's how thrilled she was.

The girls hit it off right from the jump, and sat chattering away like old friends five minutes after they'd been introduced. Even with her face bandaged, you couldn't stop Patsy from talking, and Loretta's stories of the hard times she'd been having getting started on her career struck such a chord in Patsy's heart that they became friends on the spot.

Loretta Lynn's husband was nicknamed "Mooney" or "Dolittle" and answered mostly to "Doo," which was what Loretta called him. After that first meeting in the hospital, Loretta and Doo became an important part of Patsy's circle of friends.

With all the anguish and all the suffering, Patsy was learning two important things from her near-fatal accident: the importance of friends and a new faith in God. These days she was praying as she'd never prayed before, thanking God for sparing her life.

As soon as she was allowed visitors apart from the immediate family, they came pouring in to see her. Loretta came every day, and so did Dottie. But her most constant visitor, apart from Charlie and Hilda, was Randy Hughes.

She hadn't realized exactly how much she'd missed him until he walked in through the door, handsome in a silk shirt and dark suit. For the first time, she felt her heart acting funny in his presence, and suddenly, she wished that he hadn't come. She didn't want him to see her this way, bandaged up like a mummy, and helpless.

In the next moment, she dismissed her feelings as foolish. After all, he was her manager, and they had a lot of business to discuss.

But the look in Randy's eyes was not the look of a business associate. There was so much care and concern that she had to turn her own eyes away; it was too much.

"Patsy," was all he said, and he took her hand in his and held it very tightly.

"Hi, Randy," she managed to reply, but tears spilled from her eyes down her cheeks under the bandages, where they stung her sensitive, unhealed skin.

After that first meeting, he came every day, and things between them grew easier and more natural.

The doctors came and cut the bandages off, replacing them with new, smaller ones, exposing her forehead above the eyebrows. But they still wouldn't let her see her face.

What she could see was bad. A wide, stitched-up gash near her brow, and bright yellow-and-purple discolorations, as though she'd been beaten violently.

The itching of the new skin that was growing was driving her crazy; it was almost as bad as the pain. She had an ointment that went halfway to relieving it, and she would spend at least an hour every day rubbing that ointment into her skin to promote the healing.

Now that she could put on lipstick and comb out her

hair, she had Charlie bring her cosmetics and a couple of her favorite wigs from home, so that she would be more presentable when visitors came.

She looked forward to visitors now, especially Randy Hughes. He'd been busy lately, on her behalf, settling her present engagements and negotiating them into future ones.

"Not to worry," he reassured her, taking the tube of skin ointment from her hand. "All the hell you have to do is lay on your ass and get well. I've got *everything* covered."

Very gently, he began to spread the ointment onto Patsy's face, the tips of his fingers delicate and . . . loving.

"I canceled the personal appearances, and told the record people to sit on their thumbs till I tell 'em different. *We'll* know when you're ready. So you got yourself a vacation here. Relax. *Smile*."

Charlie came into the room, but stopped in the doorway as his eyes took in the intimate scene. His mouth hardened, and his deep-set eyes took on an opaque look. Abruptly, he held his hand out for the tube of ointment.

"I can do that," he said flatly.

"That's okay," Randy answered lightly. "I'm almost finished."

"I said I'll do that," Charlie repeated, his voice tight.

Randy stopped rubbing the ointment on Patsy's face and straightened up, but made no move to hand over the tube. For a long minute the two men eyed each other like a pair of dogs preparing to fight, each waiting for the other to make the first move.

But it was Patsy who made the first move. Sensing that the rivalry between them was about to erupt, she interposed herself hastily.

"Charlie, what about the scars? Randy won't tell me anything."

Now the two men exchanged a very different kind of look, a complicity of silence, agreeing without words to keep the bad news from Patsy.

"The doctors said it'll take time, but it'll be okay," Charlie answered evasively.

Patsy looked from Charlie's face to Randy's, but their expressions revealed nothing. That alone told her almost everything she needed to know.

Thirty-five days after Patsy Cline was admitted to the emergency room of Madison Hospital in critical condition, she was allowed to go home. It was a front-page story in all the newspapers, and it went out over the wire services. DJs announced the good news hourly on their programs, like bulletins. Patsy's fans waited outside the hospital entrance with bunches of flowers, holding signs saying, "We love you, Patsy." One or two of them read, "God loves you, Patsy." Photographers snapped dozens of photographs of Patsy being wheeled out by Charlie, her face still swathed in heavy layers of gauze, but her grin showing wide where the bandages left off.

The day, weeks later, when the bandages came off Patsy Cline's face, was the day she needed all her newfound faith in God. She was out of the wheelchair but still on crutches when she came into the doctor's waiting room, flanked by Charlie and Hilda. All three sat together nervously, waiting for the doctor to call them in. There seemed little to say; Patsy was locked into her own thoughts and fears so tightly that she barely looked up when the nurse called her name.

The three went into the office together, Patsy holding tightly to Charlie's hand. Swiftly, expertly, the doctor cut off the bandages, and they fell away, revealing Patsy's face for the first time since the accident.

It was worse than either Charlie or Hilda had expected. Patsy's face was crisscrossed by scars, angry red, puffy, swollen scars. On her forehead was a deep gash at least two inches long.

Despite all her self-control, Hilda Hensley couldn't help the tears that welled up in her eyes, and Charlie's fingers closed over Patsy's so tightly she let out a little cry of pain.

"That bad, Mama?" asked Patsy softly, seeing the answer mirrored in her mother's tears.

"No, honey," lied Hilda, "it don't look so bad."

"Give me a mirror."

"The scars will lessen in time," the doctor said in a soothing professional voice. "And you can have plastic surgery if you want."

"Give me a mirror," said Patsy again. The doctor nodded, and the nurse offered her a large hand mirror.

For a long time Patsy looked into it without saying anything. Only the slightest trembling of her lips gave her emotions away. At last, she handed the mirror back.

"Well," she said briskly, "you cut your suit to fit your cloth. If this is what I got to work with, okay. Hell, *yes*, I want plastic surgery! All I can get!"

She turned to Charlie and gave him a lopsided smile. "Maybe I can get to look like Grace Kelly."

Charlie returned the grin. "Grace Kelly who?"

If she couldn't sing in public yet, she could certainly go into the recording studio. And that's what she wanted, what she needed, to lose herself in work. She'd been idle too long.

With her usual energy, Patsy pulled herself together as much as she could. She plastered makeup thickly over the scars, hiding the worst of them. She hobbled around on her crutches as though they had racing stripes. So eager was she to get back to work that she could hardly think or speak about anything else.

Because of this, and maybe because of the growing intimacy between them, she was on the phone to Randy Hughes at least twice a day. Patsy had a momentum going that she couldn't afford to lose, a number-one hit on the country charts. "I Fall to Pieces" was still the nation's favorite.

"I got a running start now. I wanna grab hold and make me some good money. But first, I gotta find me—"

"The right song. I know that, Patsy. Owen Bradley's got something he wants you to listen to. It's a tape by a new song writer, a kid named Willie Nelson."

"Hey, I know him. Isn't he the one who wrote 'Funny How Time Slips Away' for Billy Walker?"

"That's the boy."

"I wanted that song, Randy. You should've got it for *me*."

"Water over the TVA, honey. Here's another chance. He's written a song called 'Crazy' and Owen has a demo tape of it."

"WaHOOO! I'm on my way down."

Patsy, hearing the demo tape, ran true to form. She had despised "Walkin' After Midnight" and loathed "I Fall to Pieces"; she had recorded both of them under protest, and they'd both been monster successes for her.

As soon as she heard "Crazy," she shook her head vehemently from side to side. Not for her. It didn't matter what anybody else thought of the song; "Crazy" wasn't for her.

Willie Nelson had recorded it in his own style, as a song meant to be half sung, half talked. When Patsy heard it for the first time, the tenth time, the twentieth time, she couldn't conceive of it being done in any other vocal style.

This time she had all three of them lined up against her— Owen, Randy, and Charlie.

Owen had given her the demonstration tape to take home and listen to. Charlie loved the song, and played the demo over and over again until Patsy was so sick of it she hollered.

"I can't sing like Willie Nelson, damn it! How many times do I have to tell you that!"

"Honey, nobody expects you to sing like anybody in this world except Patsy Cline. Do it, darlin'. It's a great song."

"It's a *terrible* song!" she wailed to Owen Bradley. "I can't sing that man's songs!"

Convinced that he was right and Patsy wrong, Owen shrugged mildly. "Take it away from him. Make it yours."

"Yeah," put in Randy, grinning. "The hell with the demo. *Steal* the son of a bitch!"

"You think I could?"

"Easy as pie," Owen told her, knowing he'd won.

But it wasn't easy as pie. In mid-August, 1961, Patsy hobbled into the recording studio on her crutches, her body still one gigantic ache, and laid down the first tracks for a Decca album. She recorded "True Love," "San Antonio Rose," "The Wayward Wind," and a newly arranged remake of "A Poor Man's Roses (Or a Rich Man's Gold)."

They also rehearsed a new single, "Who Can I Count On" and "Crazy." No matter how many times Patsy did the song, she couldn't get it right. Not to *her* ears, anyway.

"Let's try it one more time," she'd beg. "Just once more." It was what she always said, every time she recorded, but this time she was right. The song wasn't going well because her ribs were aching so badly she couldn't hit the high notes she was capable of yodeling before the accident.

Four days later, she came into Owen Bradley's studio again, determined to get the better of "Crazy."

"Okay, let's have a little atmosphere in here. Let's try and relax. This damn song ain't gonna bite us. Turn off some of those lights, and somebody bring me one of those beers."

Owen handed her a cool brew, and she took a long pull. Then she hoisted herself painfully up on the stool in front of the microphone and let her crutches fall with a clatter.

"Ready?" asked Bradley.

"*Hell*, yes!"

The exhausted, perspiring musicians struck up. And Patsy Cline, fresh from the hospital and still in pain, Patsy Cline, who couldn't read a note of music, Patsy Cline, who had fought against damn near every worthwhile song handed to her, Patsy Cline clutched her bottle of beer and made musical history.

She stole that demo and made it her own. Whatever the song might have been if a man had recorded it, it now became a woman's song entirely. It now became Patsy's, forever and ever, the definitive Patsy Cline song.

As the last notes died away, a silence fell in the studio. Randy and Owen held their breath, just staring at Patsy, almost unbelieving.

"My Lord," whispered one of the musicians in awe. "My dear Lord."

Patsy could feel it thrumming through her veins, the knowledge that this was it, this was the perfection she'd been seeking for so long. One look at their faces told her she wasn't wrong.

She broke the silence, broke it big. Slamming the beer bottle against the far wall, she let out a yell of triumph that made her ribs holler in protest. And all at once, everybody was yelling, stomping feet, slapping one another on the back, carrying on as though they were loony.

"There it is!" yelled Patsy happily. "That's the by-God *Patsy Cline version* of that song!"

And, of course, the rest of the world would soon agree. Patsy Cline would have another number-one hit on the charts.

Twenty-three

BECAUSE THE COMPANY didn't want to cut into the success of "I Fall to Pieces," Decca Records waited eight months after the release of the previous single to release "Crazy." But word flew around the industry that Patsy Cline had another monster hit, and the deejays were champing at the bit, waiting impatiently to get their hands on the demo.

The release date was targeted for Monday, October 16, 1961, just a little more than a month after Patsy Cline's twenty-ninth birthday. On the Saturday night before, October 14, Patsy introduced the song on the Grand Ole Opry.

She came out on the stage, leaning on her "sympathy sticks," as Faron Young had dubbed her crutches. The nickname had stuck and become an insider's joke at the Opry.

"Patsy, lend me your sympathy sticks for my next number so's I'll get a good hand," her colleagues would say with a grin.

The doctors had told her that she'd be on crutches for at least six months. But that didn't put a crimp in Patsy Cline. She'd get herself all dressed up in some stunning new outfit, put a ribbon on the curly black wig that covered the forehead gash, and tie matching ribbons on the sympathy sticks. It was her way of winking her eye at the audience, of making light of the pain she'd been through, and was still going through.

Tonight was different, though. Tonight was the first time

a national audience was going to hear Patsy Cline sing her new song, a song in which Decca Records had made a big investment, a song on which Patsy's own hopes were riding.

And she sang it with everything that was inside her, sang it bluesy and torchy and filled with throbbing low notes. Even as she sang, she could feel the audience reaching toward her, their hearts striving towards hers, becoming a part of her and the song.

It was that feeling that kept her going always, that incredible rush that she got from bringing her music to people and *feeling* them receive it. It was an exaltation as good as—no, better than—sex. It was pure love, washing over her in waves, and she could never get enough of it. These people were her family, and she held a kind of mystical communication with them. They exchanged gifts, and every day was Christmas.

It was this feeling that frustrated Charlie so much. He couldn't seem to break through it anymore. It appeared to him that it was the audience's love that Patsy needed, not his. Her need for him had sunk almost to zero, and it was tearing him up inside.

In the back of his mind had been the thought that when they moved to Nashville, he'd have his wife more to himself. Not that he was jealous of Hilda, exactly. She'd done so much for them and went on doing it. But he had thought that Patsy would turn more to her husband now that she was separated from her mother.

But it hadn't worked out that way. Here in Nashville, with Patsy's star on the rise, and her a regular on the Opry, she had made so many new friends that they could only snatch a few minutes alone together. There was always Dottie and Bill, Loretta and Mooney, Jan and Harlan, and the others who flocked around Patsy to enjoy her good cooking, her motherly concern, her quick laughter.

They went out a lot, too. Not that Good Time Charlie minded going out. He was such a regular at Tootsie's Orchid Lounge that he never even had to order his first drink;

Tootsie had it waiting for him as soon as he ambled in the door. He loved the place, with its checkered tablecloths and its famous wall of autographs, and he and Patsy were proud as punch the night she wrote her name up there on the wall with the other country greats.

No, it was mostly a good life and no mistake, but it had its disadvantages. One of them was the fact that it was Patsy making the big money, not Charlie, which meant it was Patsy calling most of the shots. Another disadvantage was booze. Patsy and Charlie socialized with a traditionally heavy-drinking crowd; Patsy herself was drinking more and more, getting so that she relied on it to mellow her out, and God knew that drink had always been Charlie's special curse.

He could be an ugly drunk, mean and violent, quick with his fists. Patsy was quick with her mouth, and that often led to trouble. They fought, and Charlie hit her. Afterward, when he was sober, he was sorry as hell, but that didn't make Patsy any quicker to forgive him. Every now and then she'd sport a shiner to rehearsal, and one of her friends would ask her, "Did Charlie hit you again?"

"Well, *somebody* did," was all she would say.

The Dicks had gained the reputation of being a hard-fighting couple. Hard-loving couple, too. Everybody knew that the two of them were in their own way inseparable, but it was no secret around Nashville or in the enclosed little world of country-and-western music that Charlie Dick often beat up on Patsy Cline.

Not since the accident, of course. He hadn't lifted a finger against her since that terrible day. Ever since then, Charlie had stood by Patsy's side, being loving and supportive, thanking God every day for sparing his Patsy's life. On the other hand, so had everybody else. It was like a DJ convention in her hospital room as soon as the doctor had allowed visitors, and, at home, Loretta or Dottie or both were over to the house every damn day, or Patsy was busy taking them shopping and buying them things, or sitting answering all the loving cards and letters that had poured in from sympathetic fans.

It wasn't only that Charlie was feeling closed in by so many people chasing after Patsy, it was also that he was feeling left out. Loretta Lynn, for example, never made a move without Mooney, who watched over every aspect of her career; Dottie's husband, Bill West, was a musician himself, and they worked together. But Charlie was of less and less use to Patsy, who now had Randy Hughes to rely on. Between Hughes and Owen Bradley, she had all the expert advice she needed, and Charlie was getting to feel more and more like the second shoe on a one-legged man.

Look at her up there now, on the stage of the Ryman Auditorium, bringing "Crazy" to a smash finish, experiencing the outpouring of so much love from her audience. She ate and drank that love; she needed it to survive, like air.

She thinks that what I feel for her is just a drop in the bucket to that, thought Charlie bitterly, as the audience rose to its feet in a crescendo of applause and cheering. *I can't make that damn much noise, but I love her more than all of them put together.*

Patsy came off the stage now, moving slowly on her crutches, hearing them calling for more, more, more. "Crazy" was a sensation. The audience adored it.

They wouldn't stop cheering; they couldn't. Again and again the audience called Patsy Cline back to the stage, not permitting the show to continue. She sang three encores, before she begged them to let the show go on. Tears were flowing freely from her eyes, but a smile as big as a wheat field made her scarred face beautiful.

They love me! Just listen to them! They love me!

Out loud, she wisecracked to her audience, "Well, I guess that's gonna have to be my song from now on."

But inside, all the hurt and rejection of those early years was washing away in a flood of happiness. The middle-class kids who'd looked down on her as a redneck who jerked sodas, the men and women who thought she'd never make it out of Winchester, the people who poked fun at her dreams and her ambitions—they were all washed away forever by this great outpouring of love welling up from the audience.

Standing on crutches in front of a microphone, looking down through her tears at the thousands of faces yearning to her, Patsy Cline knew that she had reached the summit. Everything else that was going to happen would be gravy, delicious, luxurious gravy.

But this night at the Grand Ole Opry was meat and drink. This was the glorious realization of an ambition she had held all her life.

When she came off the stage at last, she was trembling all over, white-faced and exhausted. Charlie rushed to her side.

"I need a drink," she told him brusquely, her voice low.

The energy had been drained out of her, given away freely to her audience. There was nothing left for her husband.

"Crazy" came out in October, and began to move quickly up the charts. In November, Patsy Cline was named "Favorite Female Vocalist" in a disk jockey poll conducted by *Billboard* magazine and "Female Vocalist of the Year" by *Music Vendor* magazine. That last honor was especially precious to Patsy, because it had been the exclusive property of Kitty Wells, the "queen of country music." Kitty had been winning it year after year. Patsy Cline was the first woman to take that award away from Kitty Wells and, Lordy, how it tickled her and did her heart good! By then, "Crazy" was number two on the country charts.

"Darlin', we're gonna be in high cotton," announced Patsy, grinning with delight. "I just got off the phone with Randy, and you'll never guess."

"Then I suppose you'll hafta tell me," Charlie answered sullenly. He had grown to hate the sound of Randy Hughes's name, hated the eagerness with which Patsy always answered the phone, hated to hear her lowering her voice as if Charlie Dick was eavesdroppin' in his own home.

"We're goin' to New York City! To Carnegie Hall!"

"Who?" demanded Charlie. "You and him?"

Patsy laughed merrily. "Yeah, me and him and about a thousand others. Faron Young, Minnie Pearl, Grandpa Jones, Marty Robbins, Jim Reeves, The Jordanaires, Bill Monroe—"

"Whoa!" interrupted Charlie. "You tryin' to tell me that you hillbillies are gonna play in that fancy Carnegie Hall in New York *City*?"

"Yup, we've been invited to put on a country music extrav-a-*ganz*-a for them city folks."

"Lemme get this straight," said Charlie dubiously. "You expectin' to actually sell tickets to this thing? In New *York*?"

"To tell you the God's honest truth, hoss, I was wonderin' that very thing myself."

For a while, it seemed as though Patsy's fears would be justified. Advance ticket sales were practically nil. By the morning of November 29, 1961, the night of the Carnegie Hall program, the twenty-seven-hundred-seat concert hall was only half sold out. It looked like all the nay-sayers and doubting Thomases and jeerers and Miss Dorothy Kilgallen might be right after all. New York City wasn't ready for what Kilgallen had nastily called "the Carnegie Hillbillies."

But what they didn't take into consideration was a very simple fact of life. Country music fans weren't the kind of people to make advance reservations. They were in the habit of simply showing up to hear their music.

And show up they did, filling the hall, overflowing it, standing room only. The box office had to turn away hundreds of disappointed last-minute ticket buyers who would have been more than willing just to hang from the chandeliers if anybody had let them.

The show itself was supposed to last about two hours, but it ran to over three. The audience interrupted it so often with prolonged bursts of applause and requests hollered out from all four tiers of seats that the performances just went on and on.

Carnegie Hall was the most beautiful theater Patsy had ever played, and she marveled at the wonder of it, at the red velvet, the elegance of the bronze and crystal chandeliers and, most of all, at the acoustics. Famous for its magnificent acoustics, Carnegie is a concert hall that almost doesn't need microphones. Even a whisper from the stage can be heard in the last row of the topmost balcony.

And Patsy Cline was no whisperer. She really belted out a song, and when she gave them "I Fall to Pieces" and "Crazy," she brought down the house. The audience cheered for all of them, but especially loud and long for Patsy; not only because of the courage she showed during those long, pain-filled months, but also because she had a number-two hit with a bullet, meaning that the number-one spot on the charts was only a whisker away. The whole world loves a winner.

What a surge of emotion! Here she was, standing on the very stage that had housed so many great performers of music, of all *kinds* of music; she could feel her predecessors' spirits, their personas, possessing her own, lending her renewed inspiration.

Jesus, what a feeling!

Afterward, she told Dottie West about it.

"As I walked from the dressing room to the stage, up this flight of stairs, all I could think of was that so many great and famous musicians had walked up these very steps, had held on to this very railing. Dottie, it gave me such chills I broke out in goose bumps. You gotta play Carnegie someday, hon. It's a dream come true."

In December, "Crazy" was number nine on the pop charts, the biggest crossover hit Patsy had ever had. She was now known all over the U.S.A., not only by country-and-western fans, but by everybody and anybody who bought records.

She'd been on the road forever, it seemed, traveling first on a two-week tour with Johnny Cash, Johnny Western, Carl Perkins, and Bill Monroe. She was off the crutches now, and standing on her own two feet. After that tour, Patsy came home to Charlie and the kids, but only for a few days, then off on the road again.

Even when she was home, it was as though she was still away somewhere. The phone would be ringing all the time, with requests for personal appearances, charity benefits, publicity tours, interviews, photo sessions. Patsy was in constant demand, and the little time she had left with Charlie often ended in a quarrel.

He felt so left out of things, and Patsy didn't know how to make it up to him. The fact was that Charlie Dick *was* being left out of things. Anything he was able to do for her in a business way, Randy Hughes could do faster and better. Randy was beginning to walk in Charlie's shoes. And Patsy was all business now. Her career was steamrolling along, and she was steamrolling with it.

More and more she began to depend on three things— first, the incredible love that poured over the stage toward her, love she could feel, love she could count on, love that never got jealous or angry, love that never called her filthy names or slapped her face or punched her in the ribs. Next, she was leaning on Randy Hughes more and more, reading in his face his all-too-evident feelings for her. For the first time, she wasn't turning those feelings of his aside. She'd come to depend on them; more, to *need* them.

And, last, Patsy Cline had come to need the alcohol that she once merely enjoyed. Her hectic life, the demands made on her, the pain she still experienced, the pace she insisted on keeping, all drained her of the vitality she'd always possessed. A drink—or two, or five—relaxed her, unwound her, and, eventually, began to take her over.

God knows she wanted to keep her marriage together, if not for her sake and Charlie's, then for the children. She never did get to see enough of them, and Hilda would often come to Nashville and stay awhile, just to help out when Patsy was on the road.

But it was fight, fight all the time. Anger seemed to be always crackling in the air between them, like green lightning in the sky on a hot summer night. In the old days, the power between them was equally balanced. Their goals had been the same goals, their need for each other's support the same need.

Now, a star, pulling in big money, Patsy had the upper hand; she was queen of the world. All poor Charlie had were his two fists, so he used what he had. Which meant that the star often had to layer the makeup on extra thick to hide the bruises.

At first, Patsy would make excuses. "I put the brakes on too fast and my head hit the steering wheel," or "I wasn't lookin' where I was goin' and I didn't see the kitchen cabinet door open, and wham!" But, after a while, she came to realize that nobody believed her anyway, so she stopped.

Hank Cochran, bless him, had noodled around on his git-tar and come up with another song for Patsy, "She's Got You." When he played it for her, a miracle occurred. Patsy Cline actually liked it! Liked it well enough to call up Randy Hughes on the telephone and sing it for him then and there. Randy liked it and told her to call Owen. Owen Bradley listened to it and brought Patsy Cline in to his recording studio. A third top-of-the-charts hit was in the making.

At last it was time for the dearest of Patsy Cline's dreams to come true, the one she had held in her heart for so many years. She had money coming in now, and the little house on Hillhurst Drive was bursting at the seams. Every time they turned around, Charlie and Patsy were stepping on one of the kids or Loretta testing out a recipe in the kitchen, or Dottie trying on clothes in the bedroom, or some new young singer or picker in Nashville having another free meal under Patsy's generous wing.

"Where we going?" asked Charlie for the fourth time. He couldn't figure out what the hell they were doing driving around Goodlettsville, about fifteen miles out of Nashville.

"Never you mind. You'll see. Turn right, here."

The sign read Nella Drive. A big brick house, really big, with many rooms, was still under construction, but almost completely finished. It stood back from the road up a driveway, on a good-sized piece of land with beautiful old trees.

"This is it, baby, this is my dream house. What do you say?" Patsy turned toward her husband with a hopeful smile.

Charlie blew out his breath, and his forehead wrinkled in a worried frown.

"It's a mighty big house, Patsy. And it's just gotta cost the earth."

The smile dimmed a little, but Patsy fought hard to hold on to it. She didn't want to get into an argument with Charlie, not today of all days.

"C'mon in. Let me show it to you. You ain't never seen *anything* like this place."

Following her from room to room, Charlie grew ever more uneasy. The house was enormous, especially since it was standing empty, with no furniture to take up space in the vast rooms. It was more house than he felt comfortable with, but what was eating at him most was that Patsy seemed to be so familiar with the layout, as though she'd been here many times before. She went dancing from one room into the next, showing the house off to Charlie.

"I want carpeting—pale, pale blue, and over here, two big divans to make a sort of conversation area," she called over her shoulder.

He didn't remember ever seeing her so happy, at least not for a while. Patsy was like a kid with a new toy, all excitement and pleasure. A suspicion formed in his mind, but he was afraid to put it into words, afraid that it might be really true.

"Look here," Patsy called happily from the kitchen. "It's even got a dishwasher and an oven built right into the wall. . . ." She pulled the oven door down to demonstrate.

"I just open the door like this, the Queen of Sheba. No more bending over to check the roast and—"

"You bought it," said Charlie flatly. It was a statement, not a question.

Turning to him, Patsy met his eye and didn't flinch. "Paid down on it."

"Why didn't you tell me?" *For God's sake, Patsy, why didn't you ask me? Why didn't we make this decision together?*

"I wanted to surprise you," she answered, a little more subdued.

"You surprised me," replied Charlie without expression.

Perceiving instantly what he meant and what he felt, Patsy felt her heart tighten against him. This house had been her dream all her life; she had earned it, and nobody was going to take it away from her!

Then she softened a little; Charlie would come to love it once they'd moved into it. How could he help but love it? A house like this could make all the difference in the world. Maybe they'd even stop fighting and try staying home nights together. Maybe it would help to save their disintegrating marriage.

She turned to lead the way up to the bedrooms, to show them off to Charlie. The bedrooms were huge; the master bedroom was bigger than their whole downstairs on South Kent Street.

"Randy says the best thing we can do with our money is put it into bricks and mortar," she told him.

"Well, if Randy says . . ." retorted Charlie sourly.

Patsy called to him from the bathroom. "Come and look at this marble sink, Charlie. It's got *real gold* in it, and oh, look at the view of the lawn from up here." She was in the master bedroom now, leaning out of the large bow window.

Charlie walked into the bathroom and stared down at the

sink with its veinings of gold. It was meaningless. He looked into the large lighted bathroom mirror, and a meaningless face looked back at him. What the hell was he doing here? He didn't belong in a showplace like this, and he never would. He never could.

"I'm gonna plant two hundred yellow rose bushes come next spring," he heard Patsy call out, but her words might have been in a foreign language for all he comprehended them.

Only one thing was clear to him. Patsy had achieved her heart's desire; she had every goddamn thing in the world she'd ever said she wanted, including her precious house with the precious yellow roses. What was that she always said?

"I want everything, but I want it to be *right*."

But it wasn't right; there didn't seem to be room in her dream house anymore for Charlie Dick.

March 5, 1963

"*T*URN, JESUS GOD, *TURN*!" gritted Randy, totally focused on the dead ignition.

My babies, thought Patsy. *Oh, my God, my precious babies!* Thank heaven she had made out her will. That presentiment of hers...always expecting an early death. *Wrong about so many things all my life; wouldn't ya just know this would be the one damn thing I'd be right about?*

There was a sudden loud cough, a choking and sputtering noise. The ignition had caught; the engine had actually, miraculously, caught. The nose of the plane was no longer pointed at the earth. The engine was pulling it up, up... they were flying, not falling!

Flying!

"Hallelujah!" yelled Hawkshaw Hawkins. "We ain't gonna die! Thank you, Jesus!"

Patsy burst into tears of happiness, doubling over as Cowboy Copas pounded her on the back in his jubilation.

It was true, they were flying now, parallel to the earth. Randy had leveled the aircraft off, flying at a fairly low altitude because of the lack of visibility. It was his plan to land again, on a highway maybe, or in a field, somewhere he could set down and wait out this unmoving front.

He couldn't see a goddamned thing. He knew he was very close to Camden, Tennessee, maybe even right on top of it. Somewhere there had to be a highway wide enough to land a small craft on, anywhere where there were no houses. Outside, the storm still raged, rough winds and driving rain beating at the fuselage of the Comanche.

But inside all was joy and gratitude. They were going to live! It didn't seem possible, not after that hideous tumbling dive through the implacable heavens.

Randy turned his head to smile at Patsy in the back seat, and she smiled feebly back at him. The adrenaline that had been coursing through her had subsided, leaving her weak as a newborn kitten.

Home. She wanted only to be home. Soon . . . only minutes perhaps.

A sudden lightning bolt split the sky, turning it as bright as a sunny day.

That was when they saw the mountain.

Twenty-four

NINETEEN HUNDRED AND SIXTY TWO turned out to be the biggest year in Patsy Cline's life. She recorded an amazing number of songs—twenty-one in all, including her third album, *Sentimentally Yours*, her next number-one hit, "She's Got You," and another song that made it into the top ten, "When I Get Through With You, You'll Love Me, Too." Music just flowed from her like a waterfall.

Patsy was on top, hot and cooking; she could do no wrong. Everybody wanted a piece of her; she did a guest spot on the Tennessee Ernie Ford television show, and appeared on Dick Clark's program, one of the most popular on TV.

In June, she played the Hollywood Bowl, in a country program with other headliners—Johnny Cash, the Carter Family, George Jones, and other big bluegrass stars. Charlie didn't go with Patsy to Los Angeles; Randy Hughes did. And Hilda, thrilled to pieces, went along and was introduced to the vast and enthusiastic Bowl audience by Patsy as "my mother and my very best friend."

1962 was also the year that Patsy Cline walked away with ten honors, the big female winner in the Eleventh Annual WSM Country Music Festival. She managed to grab up just about every award they had; she got "Female Vocalist of the Year" for "Crazy" and "She's Got You"; she won the *Billboard* award for "Favorite Female Artist"; she won awards for being the most programmed artist, having the most programmed song, the most programmed album, and other categories as well.

Most important of all, for the second year in a row, Patsy knocked Kitty Wells right out of the box, winning both titles—"Music Vocalist of the Year" and "Star of the Year."

The new official "queen of country music" was indisputably Patsy Cline.

The irony was that she was dead broke. Absolutely flat busted, even with all that money pouring in.

First of all, there was the monstrous hospital bill resulting from her accident; that ran into many thousands of dollars. The private room, the night nurses, the surgeon, the operating room, the anesthesiologist, the recuperative therapy, the drugs and meals and phone bills—Patsy could have bought a small country in Europe with what she'd had to shell out for her thirty-five-day hospital stay and its long, painful aftermath.

There were John's hospital bills, too; they weren't as monumental as Patsy's, but they were big enough. When she added them to her own, Patsy had the equivalent of the national debt.

Also, once she was on the road to recovery, Patsy had taken a great deal of money from Decca Records as advances against her royalties—to pay for her house, for the furnishings, her Cadillacs, her mother's house and Cadillac, her silver-fox fur, and to hand out cash left and right to anyone she knew had a need for it. Although her records were literally coining money, Patsy Cline was in the red with the company.

Nobody ever left Patsy Cline's house empty-handed. Her purse, even when nearly empty, was open to all.

The house on Nella Drive had become her obsession. Everything in it had to be the best, and it had to be right. She threw her energies into making it a showplace, and it ate and drank up money like a starving hyena.

But this house was Patsy's dream, and she *had* to make it come true. Always with her, haunting her, was the fear that she wouldn't live long enough to see it completed. The furniture and draperies were custom-made to Patsy's own design and exact specifications. There was real gold dust not only in the marble sink top but also scattered throughout the bathroom wallpaper and embedded in the huge marble bathtub downstairs. The house boasted a formal dining room, as well as a breakfast room and an eat-in kitchen, a western-theme music room with a built-in bar, a flagstone patio, and a vast master bedroom. There were crystal chandeliers and imported mirrors and fireplaces and lawn furniture, and every damn thing had to be absolutely perfect. And it all kept Patsy broke.

Partly because she didn't have the time to stop running long enough to take care of herself, partly because she was always short of money, and partly because she had already been through so much pain that she wasn't up to facing any more, Patsy never did have the plastic surgery.

Instead, she took to wearing wigs to cover that ugly gash in her forehead. They were big, hideous wigs in ugly colors—yellows and reds that didn't go with her own soft complexion tones. Randy Hughes quietly deplored them; here he was, toning her image down, and the wigs kept getting in the way of the new Patsy. But he didn't argue with her; he cared too much for her.

Irony piled on irony. The home that was so precious to her, the fulfillment of all her dreams, cost her so much that she was almost never able to spend any time in it.

"I'm always out bustin' my butt," she'd complain. "But I'm doing it for the kids."

The kids. She had a girl in to take care of them, because Patsy was always on the road these days—one-nighters, club dates, multicity tours, personal appearances, TV guest spots, anything that would bring in the money that her new life was costing her. Randy raised her price: if you wanted Patsy Cline to sing, you had to pay her a thousand a night. But even a thousand dollars a night, when you deducted manager's fees and travel expenses, didn't amount to a whole hell of a lot unless you put in a hell of a lot of nights.

Like Alice in Wonderland, Patsy Cline had to keep on running fast just to stay in the same place.

The house that was supposed to bring Charlie and Patsy closer together only succeeded in driving them farther and farther apart.

Oh, Charlie had gotten used to the luxury of it pretty quickly, but he never did get used to not having Patsy around. And it wasn't really a place he could bring his own friends to. Not the guys from down at the paper, not the girls they hung out with, who came on to Charlie Dick because he was "Mr. Patsy Cline."

How he hated that, being "Mr. Patsy Cline." It brought out the nastiest and most resentful side of him, the side that picked fights and called names and was given to fits of the "mean reds."

Whenever he did see Patsy, she was different. Distant, distracted. She dressed differently and she even talked differently, more subdued, more ladylike. It was that Randy Hughes who had changed her; he was the only one besides Owen Bradley who appeared to have any real influence on Patsy. Charlie was certain the two of them were sleeping together, although he had no concrete evidence to go on.

It was more the way that Randy Hughes looked at Patsy than anything else. Love was plain on his face, and it ate at Charlie's guts. The thought of losing Patsy was unbearable. But he didn't know how to hold on to her. She seemed to be changing, growing, and he was still Good Time Charlie.

Yet, Charlie was wrong. Patsy Cline and Randy Hughes weren't sleeping together. At least, not yet.

"You love Charlie?" Randy asked her once.

The question took her by surprise and unnerved her. *"What?"*

"You love him?" asked Randy again. Patsy searched his face; it was deadly serious.

She turned her eyes away. "I couldn't get along without

old Charlie." She kept her voice light. "What's the old song that says, 'He may have been a headache, but he never was a bore'? That's Charlie."

"Is that an answer?"

She owed him some kind of answer, but Patsy was damned if she could find the right words for it. "Charlie and I are stuck with each other," she said at last.

"But you're not sure you love him."

She couldn't answer that; she didn't *know* the answer. Once she had been more certain of that love than of anything in life. Now . . .

Randy looked keenly into her face. "If you ever *get* sure, let me know," he told her.

Patsy remembered those words; every now and again she would take them out of her treasure box of memories and play them over again. For some reason she couldn't explain to herself, Randy Hughes's words gave her comfort.

The tension between Charlie and Patsy increased as they spent less and less time in each other's company. The only chance they had of a good time together seemed to be when they went out partying, and too much booze would make both of them truculent.

One warm night in early June, Charlie and Patsy met Bill and Dottie West at Tootsie's, and it started out with laughter and joking banter tossed back and forth across the table. The drinks were followed by a benefit concert, where both Patsy and Dottie had promised to appear. There was a party after the concert, but it had hardly gotten under way when Patsy tugged Charlie by the sleeve.

"Hon, we've got to go. I'm beat. I'm standin' on my stumps."

"Damn, Patsy, this party's just startin' to get good! I sure as hell don't want to go home now."

He turned and walked away from her, looking for the bar to find himself another drink.

After a few minutes, Patsy went in search of him. She

found him grinning in the middle of a group of strangers, the life of the party, Good Time Charlie.

"I've got the keys to the car," she said shortly. "And I'm going home. Now!"

Grousing, he followed her out to the car, but he was pissed as hell at being dragged away from what promised to be a good party. Who the hell did she think she was, calling all the shots all the time?

Patsy had no eyes for fighting; as a way of life it was the most exhausting one she could possibly imagine. If fighting was all the two of them had in common after six years and two children together, then maybe it was time to call the whole thing off. Life was filled with wonderful things to experience and enjoy, but all Charlie seemed to want to do these days was get loaded and get laid. And fight. Every living moment they were together there was enough negative energy flowing between them to run a generator backward.

Fighting used to mean something so different. It meant that each of them could stand up to the other and give as good as they got. It meant making up, with kisses, with loving, with good warm sex and waking up together in the morning all lovy-dovy and happy again.

These days, fighting meant just that—fighting—and Patsy was heartily sick of it. From Randy she had learned that there were other ways for men and women to spend time together than starting World War Three.

So, when he bitched and moaned about going home early, Patsy answered Charlie as quietly as she could.

"Look, Charlie, I'm busting my butt ever' damn night, and I'm tired to the bone. I want to get up with the kids in the morning."

"Hell, I get up with them more than you do. You ain't been around that much. Or haven't you noticed?"

Slipping behind the wheel, Patsy put the key in the ignition. "Well, I'm the one earnin' the damn money, so I'm the one has to go out and work," she retorted.

"Looks to me like you're enjoyin' the road quite a bit."

"Now what the hell's that supposed to mean?" demanded Patsy, but a pang of guilt told her that she knew exactly what he was driving at. Randy Hughes. She was too damn bushed to get into *that* argument now.

They had reached the house on Nella Drive and were pulling into the carport. She reached down to switch off the engine, but Charlie was too fast for her; he already had his hand on the keys.

"What's your goddamn hurry?" he snarled.

Patsy pulled away from him, tired and irritated. "Screw you!"

A sudden stinging slap caught her across the face, followed by another blow, even harder. Patsy cried out in pain and fear; her face still had not healed fully from the operation; the scars were tender and sometimes quite painful.

Now she was screaming at him, calling him names, using every dirty word she knew, but he went after her more, shaking her and slapping her wherever he could reach, lashing out at her in the confined space of the front seat.

All at once, he pushed her backward into the steering wheel. Patsy felt the wheel jab painfully into her ribs, and, suddenly, the accident was before her again, to be relived with all its horrors. Patsy screamed in terror.

Instantly, Charlie let her go, remorse written on his features.

"Did I hurt you, darlin'? I didn't mean to hurt you. I got carried away."

Saying nothing, Patsy shrank away from her husband. But her mind was clear and cold, like a machine.

That's the last time you'll ever raise your hand to me, Charlie Dick, and get away with it. My hand to God, you are never going to beat me again!

But there was to be one more time.

One night, Patsy was so tired when she got home that she could barely stand up. She was astonished to find the house ablaze with lights; they were on in every room. Cars of all description, none of them new or elegant, stood parked almost on top of one another in the driveway, and even on her beautifully cared for and expensive lawn. It looked like Charlie was having himself a party. And had forgotten to invite Patsy.

Patsy stopped in the doorway, a grim look on her face. She didn't know most of these people except by sight, although one or two of them worked down at the printing plant with Charlie. But they were making themselves right at home.

The ashtrays were overflowing onto the cocktail table, and somebody had dropped or thrown a beer bottle onto the floor; beer was spilled in a messy puddle on the expensive wall-to-wall carpeting. A couple of chairs were overturned, and several couples were dancing; there were at least half-a-dozen cheap-looking girls in tight capri pants and low-cut sleeveless tops; their lipstick was imprinted on the rims of the good glasses.

One of them was dancing with Charlie; they were cheek-to-cheek, and everything else was pressed close together as well. Obviously nobody was expecting Patsy Cline to come home from work this early.

As soon as he saw Patsy, Charlie broke away from the girl's hold, and she ran wide-eyed back to her boyfriend.

Patsy said nothing, but looked hard at her husband, who decided to brazen it out.

"We're havin' a party. We went out jukin' and I bought me an old clunker for seventy-five bucks, to drive in the demolition derby tomorrow."

He waited for her to say something, but she was silent.

"I think you know most ever'body," continued Charlie. "This here's Skip Cartmill. He sold me the car."

Being civil, Patsy nodded, but she didn't trust herself to say even "howdy" to this houseful of strangers. For years, the Patsy Cline trademark, her signature tune, had been a hospitality song called "Come On In." It seemed these strangers had taken her literally, and she didn't like it one damn bit.

"Want a beer, Patsy?" one of the men offered.

She shook her head. "I'm so tired I feel real faintyfied. I think I'll just go on up to bed."

She turned to go upstairs, and Charlie followed her.

"That girl I was dancin' with?" he began nervously. "She goes with one of the guys from the derby. Cleo? The guy in the white shirt?"

Patsy moved icily away. "Obviously you've got me mixed up with somebody who gives a shit. Now let me get some rest."

By the morning, the air between them had cleared enough for them to be civil to each other. After all, they had planned this day together for a long time.

The annual county fair was a pretty big deal. Patsy had been engaged to entertain from the bandstand, and Charlie had been looking forward for weeks to driving in the demolition derby on the fairgrounds.

He didn't win, of course; he was too crazy wild and reckless. With ferocious energy, Charlie just gunned his motor and rammed those old junk heaps left and right, yelling his rebel yell. Of the eight cars that started in the derby, his was the third to be eliminated. His clunker was totalled, a junk pile of nuts and bolts, rusted fenders, and broken glass. But Charlie emerged unscathed and grinning like a pig in shit. He'd had a *wonderful* time.

An hour or two after the demo was over and the musicians were taking a break, Patsy came looking for Charlie. She found him sitting at a table that had been set up by the outdoor dance floor, but he wasn't alone. He was drinking with Annie, the little girl he'd been dancing with the night before, and both of them were pretty high and cosy.

"Wanna dance?" asked Patsy pleasantly.

"Why don't you take yourself a little walk?" retorted

Charlie, showing off for his little floozy. "Go sing another song."

Without a word, Patsy turned coldly on her heel and marched off.

Inside of twenty minutes, she was back, and not alone. No fewer than three men were dancing attendance on her, lighting her cigarettes, paying her compliments. She took a seat across the dance floor, making sure that she was well within Charlie Dick's line of sight, and continued her flirtation, "accidentally" letting her skirt hike up high enough to expose her legs to mid-thigh.

Knowing all Charlie's buttons so well, Patsy pressed each and every one of them. When at last she rose from her break and started back to the bandstand, Charlie stood up from his table and intercepted her. He grabbed at her arm, but she shook him off.

"Bitch!" he threw at her.

"Bastard!" she flung back.

"What the hell do you think you're doing?"

"Same question back to you!"

"I'm just *talkin'* to her," Charlie tried to explain, but his words came out slurred.

"Me, too, buster. I'm just '*talking*' to them. How old *is* she, anyway?"

"She said she was twenty-four."

Patsy snorted scornfully. "Ask her how old she is counting the years she went barefoot on the farm."

"God, you got a mean mouth," answered Charlie angrily. "I'd like to pull that tongue of yours out with a pair of pliers."

"Yeah, well, that's real interesting. Try it sometime."

"I'm warning you," snarled Charlie. "You just put your ass down at *my* table, you hear me?"

Instantly, the old Patsy flared. "Don't you warn me! You spend the whole goddamn evening rubbing up against some tramp with a boil on her neck! I'll do what I please. I'll walk out with the first guy I lay my eyes on!"

Charlie gave her a cocky grin. "Sure you will," he told her, confident that she wouldn't.

"Charlie." Her voice warned him not to go a quarter inch farther. Above everything else, she didn't want to be dared.

"I dare you," said Charlie recklessly.

Patsy didn't deign to reply. Instead, she spun around and walked toward the table she'd just left. She whistled once loudly, through her teeth. A guy with a slick pompadour looked up eagerly, and she motioned to him, just the merest gesture of her hand. At once, the young man came riding toward her.

Before Charlie Dick could think of anything to say or do, Patsy, her arms locked tightly around the young man's waist, left.

It was hours before Patsy returned home. Charlie was sitting in their oversize living room, a drink in his hand. He was quiet, dangerously quiet.

"Well. The slut's home," he said when he saw Patsy.

"Yeah. She came home to see the pig."

"Where is that guy?"

"I had him let me off a block away. We just '*talked*,'" she taunted him.

"You bitch." His voice was cold and expressionless.

Suddenly, Patsy was weary of the entire business. What a farce. Here she'd been doing nothing but riding around on that goddamn bike for hours, just to make Charlie jealous, and the whole thing struck her as meaningless and stupid.

"Oh, Charlie, let's not do any name-calling," she pleaded, her head throbbing. "It don't do any good. We still have to wake up tomorrow morning and look at each other."

But Charlie was not so easily placated. "Well, I'm not having any more nights where my wife goes off with another man—"

The explosion was as unexpected as it was ferocious. One moment Patsy was holding her tired hand to the aching scar on her forehead and the next she was standing over Charlie like an avenging angel, eyes blazing.

"Don't tell me what you will and will not have!" Her voice seared his ear in its fury. "I looked at you tonight and thought, 'God help you, Patsy. No matter how hard you try, you're never gonna make your life come out right. Old Good Time Charlie's gonna keep draggin' you back down.'"

"Don't you whine about me!" Charlie shouted back, as indignant as she. "Where the hell are *you* when the kids want their oatmeal in the mornings? *Where are you* when Julie pukes in her bed from the flu? You sure ain't *here*!"

Turning away from him in disgust, Patsy retorted, "Oh, you just *lie*. You never changed a shitty diaper in your life, between Mama, the baby-sitter, and me." Her anger was fierce as the unfairness of it all struck her afresh.

"And *no*, I'm not here all the time! I'm out singin' in ever' shithouse between here and Kansas City, so you can wear thirty-dollar silk shirts!"

Instantly, Charlie ripped the shirt off his body, the buttons flying in all directions, crumpled it up into a ball, and hurled it like a missile straight at Patsy.

"Take the goddamn thing!" he yelled.

That was it; she'd had enough. Patsy wasn't going to escalate this fight another inch. She was sick to death of squabbling, arguing, disagreeing, fighting—all of it, whatever name you put on it. She threw her hands up and turned away, bending to pick up some of the children's toys that were scattered on the floor.

"Did you lay down for that guy tonight?" asked Charlie in his mean-red voice.

This wasn't even worth talking about. "Oh, don't ask," she replied wearily.

"I'm asking, slut," hissed Charlie.

Patsy whirled on him, eyes blazing, going for the jugular.

"Yes," she lied. "Yes. Yes. *Yes!* And it was wonderful. Better than it ever was with you. We're in love, me and the big motorcycle man. We're gonna move in together!" She threw the words in his face as though they were knives to cut him. But she never expected that he would believe her.

What Patsy underestimated was exactly how much Charlie had already had to drink, how long he'd been sitting there waiting for her to come home, and what dirty pictures had been unreeling in his mind as he waited.

The full import of all of it was brought home to Patsy in that first slap, an open-handed blow so powerful it knocked her down. Blood poured from her lip. In panic, Patsy scrambled hastily to her feet.

"Jesus, Charlie, don't! I was only kidding!"

But it was too late to get through to him, for he had traveled that long, dark desperate road from anger to rage to fury to reach, at last, temporary insanity.

Stalking her like an animal, Charlie cornered her, slapping and punching Patsy again and again, beating her brutally. It wasn't that he didn't pay attention to her cries and pleas; he simply didn't hear them. Charlie Dick was no longer in control of his actions. He'd crossed over the line.

Patsy threw her arms up over her head to protect her face the best way she could, but Charlie's blows forced her to her knees, where she cowered, sobbing, begging him to stop, the blood streaming from her nose and lips. It was never, never going to end. He would beat her to death; she was certain of it.

But it did end, at last. At last he was out of breath, and satisfied to see her groveling on the floor, bleeding. At last he thought she'd had enough, and he left the room to pour himself another drink.

Slowly, painfully, inch by excruciating inch, Patsy crawled across the floor, unable to stand. There was only one thing in her mind—a firm resolve.

She had never been able to do this before; pride had kept her from it. But her pride had been battered out of her; it lay broken on the floor, mingled with blood.

Patsy Cline inched her way to the telephone and called the police, whispering hoarsely into the receiver so that

Charlie wouldn't overhear her from the next room. In broken syllables, she gave them her name and address and begged them, pleaded with them, for Jesus' sweet sake, to hurry.

It took three officers to subdue Charlie Dick and wrestle him into the patrol car. He had no idea who the cops were or what they wanted or where they were taking him. He was too damn drunk. So he fought, as it was his instinct to do.

As the police car pulled away, Charlie seemed to come to life a little. He turned around in the back seat, his eyes peering through the glass to find Patsy, a mute plea in their depths.

Exhausted, aching in every bone, her face swollen beyond recognition, Patsy looked away, refusing to meet Charlie's gaze of desperation. She felt in her heart that she'd done the right thing, the *only* thing.

This was the lowest point in her life. On this night, she had turned the man she had married over to the police. On this night, Charlie Dick was going to jail, and it was Patsy Cline who sent him.

Long after the police car had disappeared from sight, she stood there on the grass, shivering.

Twenty-five

FOR THREE SOLID HOURS Charlie Dick slept like a stone on one of the benches in the communal holding cell of the local jail. Then, unbidden, a dream came darting into his mind, and he woke up startled, sitting bolt upright, suddenly cold sober and shaking with chilly sweat. Even his hands were clammy.

He'd dreamed that Patsy was a bird falling out of the sky. Knowing that if she hit the ground she'd die, Charlie had tried to catch her, but she slipped through his fingers, leaving him holding only a handful of dark, glossy feathers. She was lost, lost forever, and in his dream he began to weep.

He looked around, and the whole scene came back to him. Charlie remembered everything. He'd beaten Patsy up again, terribly this time. She'd called the cops on him, and here he was in jail.

Now, for the first time, he realized that she'd been only taunting him. He knew for a fact that she hadn't been with that motorcycle bum, that she was innocent of any wrongdoing. The knowledge cut him to the heart like a long, sharp, serrated knife.

Jesus God, what am I gonna do? This is the worst it's ever been. Let her forgive me, Lord, and I'll never lift a finger against Patsy again.

All around him, men were sleeping on benches, or just

sitting around loose-handed, in attitudes of despair. Losers. *Like me*.

Close by Charlie was an elderly man with thinning white hair and trembling hands, obviously an alcoholic. The old guy fished around in his pocket, pulling out a crumpled pack of Camel cigarettes. His aged hands were shaking so badly he could barely get one lit. When he spotted Charlie eyeballing the pack hungrily, he held it out, mutely offering one.

Charlie managed a weak smile. "I was just thinking I'd trade an eye for one of 'em." He nodded his thanks.

The old man put the package down between them.

"Take one when you want," he told Charlie hospitably. "So how come you're in here?"

'Cause I beat up the queen of country music just one time too many. Out loud, Charlie merely said, "Argument with the wife."

"Me, I was asleep in a doorway," shrugged the old-timer. He looked sharply over at Charlie, inspecting him.

"You look like you got the weight of the world on your shoulders," he observed with a rheumy cough.

Immediately, Charlie's defenses came up and the wall came down.

"Look," he said stiffly, "you gave me a cigarette. If all these questions go with it, you can have the damn thing back."

"No, no, sorry. Just thought we could pass the time."

Time in jail passes very slowly indeed, but a man does get a chance to think. It's not always a pleasurable or even a profitable pastime, thinking. There's often a heap of pain involved, and much regretting, much fruitless wishing that the hands of time could be turned back and certain episodes erased as though they'd never occurred.

The old-timer was asleep, but Charlie Dick was convinced that he himself would never shut an eye again. His entire body was one big mass of sorry, and he'd have sold his soul to the lowest bidder for one more cigarette. Right now, he valued that smoke more than he valued his so-called immortal soul.

The package was still there between them, but it looked just about empty. And everybody knows that, no matter what, you don't take a man's last cigarette. Nevertheless, Charlie found his hand reaching slowly and carefully, stealthily, toward that enticing pack.

"Help yourself," said the old guy, his eyes still closed.

Charlie pulled his hand back as though it had been burned, and his cheeks flushed red with guilt.

"Naw, I mean it," the old-timer insisted. "I smoke too much, anyhow."

He sat up, rubbing his eyes, and as though to prove the truth of his admission, bent over double from a hacking smoker's cough.

Eagerly and gratefully, Charlie helped himself to the last cigarette and crumpled up the package. He drew in a long, deep drag, and offered it to his cellmate, who shook his white head.

"You sleep light, don't you?" asked Charlie. "Just like my old man." He stared at the smoke curling up from the Camel.

"He smoked Camels, too, my old man," he continued softly, reminiscently. "He started 'em when he was nine years old. There he was, he used to tell me, nine years old and in the fourth grade, still wearing knickers. You know those short pants that stop right there?"

Charlie pointed to just below his kneecap and the old man nodded. He remembered.

"Well, he'd get up ever' morning and have a cup of coffee and a cigarette right at the breakfast table, big as you please." A small, proud smile touched the corners of Charlie's lips. "He was a pisscutter, my daddy. Always could make me laugh."

"I never knew who my daddy was," the old-timer put in. "Don't think my mama knew either."

But Charlie wasn't listening; his mind was turned inward, deep into his memory. He wasn't even aware he had talking out loud. For twenty years he was buried these memories, never even sharing them with Patsy. Now, for some unfathomable reason, he was spilling his guts to a total stranger.

"He was six feet tall when six feet tall was *big*, and he could walk halfway around the block on his hands, and he had a real high tenor voice. Beautiful voice."

There was a look on Charlie's face that nobody—not even Patsy—had ever seen, faraway yet very fragile, vulnerable, and young. But his tone was matter-of-fact, with no special emphasis.

"One day, when I was gettin' ready for school, Daddy stayed home from work, and was sittin' at the kitchen table smokin' Camels one right after the other one, just about eatin' 'em. I went to get myself some cornflakes and I heard this noise. Thought the goddamn house was fallin' down. I turned around and he's shot hisself in the head."

"Sweet Jesus," whispered the old man.

"I knew he was dead," went on Charlie conversationally, "but I didn't know much else. I put down them cornflakes and went in and set down for five days—wouldn't talk to nobody, wouldn't go to the funeral." He sat silent for a few seconds. "On the fifth day, I got up and went out the door. Since that day, I never looked back. I just . . ." He moved his hand along, like a wave flowing. "I just keep on movin'. Know what I mean? Just . . . keep on movin'."

"Sweet Jesus," the old man said again.

Charlie smiled wryly. "You wanna pass the time some more?"

When Randy Hughes saw Patsy Cline's swollen, discolored, and beaten face, his big hands balled into fists, and he had an urge to drag Charlie Dick out of that jail where he was sitting so safe and comfortable and do to him what Charlie had done to Patsy, turn a human face into hamburger.

"Oh, *horse*shit you ran into a cupboard door!" Randy yelled, when Patsy tried to make one of her lame excuses. "The last time you said you slipped and hit your face on the kitchen sink. *Horse*shit!"

Patsy squirmed uneasily on the edge of the sofa. She was feeling terrible now about Charlie rotting in that awful jail. Terrible and guilty.

"Well, hell, it's probably half my fault. Nobody can argue and fight all by hisself. Besides, I think I was *supposed* to meet Charlie. It was fated." She tried a jaunty little smile, but her face was too swollen and stiff to pull it off. "I had my palm read once, and this woman told me that when I grew up, I'd marry..."

Her voice trailed off miserably, and her lips began to quiver. Jaunty was not how she was feeling.

Randy was all efficiency now.

"I tell you what," he informed Patsy in a tone of voice that allowed no argument. "I'm getting you out of this. You've got to get a divorce." At Patsy's startled look, Randy amended it somewhat.

"A separation, anyway. He's been in there two days now, he ought to be ready to listen to reason by tomorrow morning. I'll just tell him: a separation, or you'll press charges."

Divorce. If she'd thought the word before this, she'd never dared speak it out loud. Rising, Patsy walked over to the tall French window that led out onto the lawn; she looked out, seeing nothing but Charlie's miserable, remorseful, handsome face in front of her. Yet she felt no affection for the image.

"I can't find anything to hold on to," she said slowly. "My whole goddamn life is falling apart."

But Randy Hughes had no sympathy with this train of thought. Her whole goddamn life would be put together much more easily without Charlie Dick as the glue.

"I'll have my lawyer call Judge Burgard in the morning," he informed her, and then waited, delicately, indicating by his silence that his statement was more of a question, that he needed Patsy's permission to act.

She stood at the window, not turning to him, but she nodded her head. A silent agreement—go ahead with the preliminaries.

When she turned to Randy, he saw a look in Patsy's eyes he'd never seen before. It was sorrow, mourning for a love which had been killed, a dead marriage that had once been the most important thing in her life. She looked at him plaintively, questioningly, as though he could tell her the answer. Why was all this happening?

"I keep saying to myself that I don't have to live the trashy dog's life my daddy led my mama. I can make it different. I can make it *right*. But here I am with a busted-up face and callin' the police in the middle of the night, just like Mama."

Her voice rose to a wail of anger and indignation. "Where the hell is the difference?" Then, more quietly, Patsy added bitterly, "Nothin' ever changes in this goddamn world!"

A single tear welled up in her eye and rolled down her aching cheek. Her entire body was one hurting lump of sorrow. Sorrow for herself, sorrow for Charlie.

But it was Randy who was stepping forward to put his arms around her tenderly, Randy holding her close but not tightly, careful of her bruises. Randy who was looking with the greatest love into Patsy's face and telling her, "Yes, they do. Some things change."

She looked up at him, searching deeply into his dark eyes, seeking something . . . something very precious, but something she couldn't put a name to. Yet.

They kissed, gently at first, then with passion. And, although the kiss was painful to her cut and bruised lips, Patsy welcomed the pain. It made her feel alive again.

Twenty-six

E ARLY IN FEBRUARY 1963, Patsy Cline called Loretta Lynn on the phone, and her voice was trembling with excitement.

"Honey, I'm so danged happy I could bust!" she told her best friend.

"What is it?" asked Loretta. "Did you and Charlie get back together?"

There was a moment of uncomfortable silence on the phone, and then Patsy answered briskly. "It's a song, Loretta. It's the prettiest song I've ever been given to record. I can't wait for you to hear it. Don Gibson wrote it for me, and it's called 'Sweet Dreams.' I'm goin' into the studio with it at the end of the week, and, hoss, I'll bet my old white cowboy boots that it's a sure-fire number one."

"I got my fingers crossed for you, Patsy, darlin'. You can do it if anybody can. Now, as soon as you get the first advance copy of the record, you better call me and Doo and invite us over to listen to it, hear?"

"Honey, don't I always?"

"'Course ya do. And I'm gonna miss ya. Won't be seein' you for weeks?"

"Loretta, what in the ever-lovin' world are you talkin' about? Ain't you going to Kansas City for the benefit for Cactus Jack's widow?"

"Patsy, I wish I could, but me and Mooney have a singing

296

engagement that night, and I can't break it. I can't afford to. It pays twenty-five dollars, and we need the money. And you're goin' off in a week or so, ain't you?"

"Soon's we finish cutting the new album and some singles and get out of the studio. I'm goin' on the road, and God alone knows when I'll be settlin' down home again. We're goin' to Lima, Ohio, and probably back to Vegas, and then I have to fly to Birmingham for an appearance, and from there Randy and me are goin' directly to Kansas City. But we should be back in Nashville to stay for a while, on the sixth or seventh of March."

"Hell, that's a lifetime away," observed Loretta.

"Sure is," agreed Patsy. "Tell you what, honey. I'll be back home for a couple of days before Birmingham, and we ought to have the 'Sweet Dreams' tapes by then. Let's make us a date. How about Thursday evening, March second? You free then?"

"Lemme check. Yeah, that's good."

"Okay, you and Mooney come over for supper, and I'll play you 'Sweet Dreams,' and I guarantee that it's the prettiest song you ever heard in your life."

"If you sing it, it's bound to be."

The recording sessions went more smoothly than any that Patsy had done so far. In four days, they laid down twelve good tracks, an average of three a day. Patsy's professionalism was remarkable, and her voice had never been so piercingly sweet. There were notes she could reach that made you want to cry.

Not all the songs were love songs. She did a rip-roaring rouser of an old favorite of hers, "Bill Bailey, Won't You Please Come Home." But it was "Sweet Dreams" that knocked everybody for a loop, just as Patsy had predicted. Anybody would have to be stone deaf not to know the song had "number one" written all over it.

On the last day of the tapings, Charlie Dick turned up

at the studio. He looked like somebody who'd looked down into hell, hollow in the face, haunted in the eyes. A changed man.

Patsy was standing at the microphone and had just begun singing "I'll Sail My Ship Alone" when the music cut off suddenly at a signal from Owen Bradley.

Surprised, she sang on for a bar without accompaniment, and then her voice trailed off. She looked over at Owen and Randy, a question mark in her dark eyes, and then she saw Charlie.

For a moment, she thought she was going to faint, but it was only a passing dizziness; then she was in command again, and started over to Charlie.

As she moved toward her husband, Randy Hughes took a step forward, but with a shake of her head, Patsy waved him off. She wanted to see Charlie alone; she hadn't seen him since he'd gotten out of jail over a week ago.

He'd tried to call her on the phone. The phone rang again and again, thirty times a day and more. It was more than irritating, it was torture, but Patsy steeled herself not to answer it, knowing that Charlie was on the other end of the line.

She was finding happiness with Randy now, but that was not the only reason she didn't want to talk to Charlie. She was afraid of what she might say to him; too much or perhaps too little. But now, with him here in the studio face to face with her, she had to come to terms with it.

Leading him around a corner for more privacy from the others, Patsy waited for the first word from him. It wasn't up to her to speak it.

But, without a word, Charlie took Patsy's face into his hands. His eyes searched out every cut and bruise; the bruises were fading now, and the swelling was almost gone. But slowly, with infinite care, he kissed her bruises one by one.

"I did wrong," Charlie said earnestly. "I can be better. I'll never raise my hand to you again." He looked deeply, lovingly, into her eyes.

She said nothing, regarding him steadily. Whatever she was thinking, Patsy kept it to herself.

"I can tell you're thinkin' about leavin' me, and I swear to God, Patsy, I don't think I could stand it!" His voice broke. "Let's make it right again."

Patsy bit her lip hard; she was determined not to cry. Just seeing the tenderness on Charlie's face unleashed so many memories that she had to fight them back with all her strength. When she'd mastered some control, she spoke, but it was one of the hardest things she had ever done in her life.

"I don't know, Charlie. That's not a very good answer, but it's all I can come up with." She hesitated a beat, then went on. "If you want a definite answer right now, it's 'no.'"

Patsy's eyes dropped as she saw Charlie flinch, but there was no turning back now. She owed him this honesty.

"Aside from that, the best I can do is sit here and say I just simply do not know whether I want to live with you anymore."

That was all she could tell him; he would have to accept it and deal with it the best way he could. As for Patsy Cline, she had to get on with her own life. What else could she do? With Charlie or without him, life would go on.

It was always hard for Patsy to part with Julie and little Randy; she had to kiss them twenty times apiece and then twenty times more. God, how she hated to let them go!

"What do you want me to bring you from Kansas City?" she asked her daughter,

"A doll with red hair!" answered the little girl promptly.

"You got it!" grinned Patsy.

"A *big* one!"

"I'll get you one you can't lift!" promised her mother.

Turning to Hilda, Patsy made an unhappy little face. "I don't want to *go!*"

"Sooner started, sooner home," replied Patsy's mother with her country wisdom.

Patsy nodded and sighed, but before she could step out on the runway, Julie held her arms out.

"Dance me, Mama!" she begged.

Although Randy was waiting for her, she had to give more time to her children. She knew how proud Randy was of his new pilot's license and especially of his spanking-new Comanche twin-engine. She wasn't keen on small air-craft, and she had those crazy superstitions about dying. She talked about dying a lot; it was a morbid habit that she knew she should break...one of these days. Right now, though, she was keeping Randy waiting. Stooping, she gathered both of her babies up in her arms and waltzed around and around with them, humming a happy snatch of tune. If only she could do this forever, she wouldn't ask God for anything more ever again.

Until the next time.

The concert hall in the Kansas City Memorial Building was packed; all three shows were completely sold out. It would be safe to say that most of the people in the audience had come mainly to hear Patsy Cline.

She looked marvelous. She was dressed in a simple, flattering floor-length gown, almost unheard of in a country singer in 1963, and certainly undreamed of by a round-faced Ginny Hensley in her fringed-skirts-and-cowboy-boots days. Her hair was simply coiffed; the wigs had been left behind. Patsy Cline looked like lady.

It was a large auditorium, with a huge, distant balcony. Holding one hand up to shield her eyes from the lights, Patsy peered up into the balcony and called out to them.

"I can see these folks down here, but how're y'all way up there in the back? You guys okay?"

A deafening roar of laughter and applause greeted her.

"Good. 'Cause I feel fine, too. It's a pretty night, and I had a good dinner, and I got on a new dress my mama made for me. You like it?"

"YES!" came from every quarter of the house, and when

the yell died down, some wiseass called out, "Oh, honey, yeah!" and everybody had another good laugh.

"Anyway, this next song is one I really like. It's not for all of you, maybe. It's for those of you who save souvenirs from ever' place you ever been. It's for those of you who keep lookin' back over your shoulder, wondering if you missed the good place or the right person. It's for those of you that like to just sit and look out the window when it rains."

She turned to the band. "Let's do it pretty for 'em," she said softly.

And then she sang them "Sweet Dreams" in the fullest, most melodious voice of her life, a voice that broke you up and pasted you back together again, a voice that carried you out and brought you back home, a voice that would melt a rock into lava.

Tell us, Patsy, when you sang about forgetting the past and starting life anew, who were you singing to besides the audience? Was it Randy? Or was it Charlie?

Or was it yourself?

Or, maybe, all three?

March 5, 1963

IT WAS THERE, suddenly, terrifyingly and fatally there, looming before them a mere seventy-five yards away. A Tennessee mountain, pine-covered, deadly.

Randy had been flying low, hoping to find some flat place to put down. But with visibility zero, he had been flying too low. And with no instruments. Neither he nor Hawk had seen anything ahead of them until it was too late; the mountain had been totally shrouded in mist.

They had prepared for death before, the four of them, as the Comanche had plummeted earthward. They'd been granted a minute or two for prayer, for regret, for terror. And they'd come out of it, into joy, into gratitude, into the sweet, sweet knowledge of life regained.

Now there was nothing, a split second merely, as the realization of death took chill, instant hold. A split second in which to right all wrongs, make all farewells, leave behind all blessings, surrender all grudges, forgive all sins.

In that split second, a lifetime gained, a lifetime lost.

And, in that split second before the monstrous impact and the fireball engulfed them all, Patsy Cline cried out one word. Randy turned to stare at her, hearing it with disbelief, registering only with unutterable sadness that he had lost, not merely in this life, but throughout eternity.

For Patsy, clutching her babies' toys to her breast, had cried out a name. His name. The name that defined her life.

"Charlie!"

And After...

THE FLIGHT HAD BEEN expected home around six-thirty or seven in the evening, according to Randy's last telephone call from Dyersburg. By seven-thirty, the family and friends of Hawk, Cowboy, Randy, and Patsy had begun to wonder a little; and by nine o'clock the wonder had turned to worry and the worry was very real. Phone calls criss-crossed Nashville, creating busy signals that drove callers frantic.

"Did you hear from them?"

"No, did you?"

"Has anybody called you yet? Hawk? Anybody?"

"No, you?"

After nine o'clock, the Civil Aeronautics Board got in touch with Randy's wife; the Comanche had taken off from Dyersburg hours before and there had been no radio contact with the little plane for too long a time now. The CAB was considering a radio search.

Of course, there was always the possibility that they had turned back. Randy Hughes had said they might. But, if they had, where were they? Why no attempt at contact with any of the nearby control towers or weather stations? Still, everyone held his breath, clinging to the possibility that somewhere the four of them were sitting safely on the ground, just waiting it out.

The runway lights had been turned on at Cornelia Field hours before, as Randy had requested. They still burned brightly, their beacons like giant prayer votives, sending a message of hope into the darkness.

WSM, the Nashville country-and-western radio station, mounted an all-night vigil, with frequent bulletins that urged listeners not to give up hope. By now, Randy's plane had been officially reported missing, and prayers went up all over the nation for the four beloved passengers.

The search party, made up of federal and civilian aviation officials, state police, and volunteers who knew and loved them, like country stars Roger Miller and Carl Perkins, were combing the area around Camden, Tennessee, where farmers had reported hearing the sound of an airplane engine sputtering and faltering, and the explosion of a crash.

At nine the following morning, the WSM announcer broke the news that the wreckage of a downed plane had been located near Camden.

"Let's all pray to God that they are alive," he said, near tears himself.

But it was only a few minutes later that the announcement came over the air, and this time there *were* tears.

"No survivors."

Debris, pitiful and grisly, was scattered around in a quarter-mile radius. They found Patsy's fringed cowboy shirt, and a tooled leather belt with her name on it, and her favorite cigarette lighter, with the Confederate flag of Dixie enameled on it. Charlie had given it to her. And one of her little gold slippers, torn and stained with mud.

Four maroon-colored hearses carried the four coffins back home to Nashville, to the Phillips-Robinson Funeral Home in Madison. The escort for the sorrowful procession was provided by the Tennessee Highway Patrol.

When they reached the funeral home, the coffins were set up in the same large room. They were, of course, closed, and each bore on its lid a photograph of the deceased. Four of the Opry's own, of Nashville's own, snuffed out at once. It was inconceivable.

A special prayer service for Patsy Cline was set for Thursday afternoon at five. Her body, at the request of her mother, was then to be flown home to Winchester for the funeral service and the burial. Hilda wanted her baby near her.

But, before he let her go, Charlie brought his wife home. He intended for her to spend one more night in the dream house she had worked so hard to achieve, which she had loved so much and was so proud of. On Wednesday, the day before the prayer service, Patsy Cline's coffin was driven to her home on Nella Drive.

Everyone was there to receive it. Everyone who had ever loved Patsy and been loved by her in return. Her husband, her children, her mother. Loretta and Mooney. Dottie and Bill. Jan and Harlan. Minnie Pearl. Owen Bradley. Roger Miller. Hank Cochran and his wife. Skeeter Davis. Roy Acuff. Ferlin Husky. June Carter and her sisters. Faron Young—and so many others. They had all assembled, in a daze, to grieve and say good-bye to Patsy. Patsy, so vital, so earthy and boisterous, with that mischievous smile, those jokes, that loud, happy laugh, those bouncing curls. Patsy, all curves, all voice, all heart. Patsy gone? Impossible! Who would mother-hen them, cuss them out when they were wrong, help them through bad times, pour them a drink or fry them a chicken or bake them a biscuit or call them "hoss"?

Maybe Loretta Lynn had unintentionally put it into the best words. When she had been told that Patsy Cline had been killed, she exclaimed with a gasp, "Baloney! Her and me is going shopping!"

It wasn't yet to be believed. This death could not be accepted. It would take time; the mourning would go on for a very, very long time, during which she would be missed more and more, in ways they'd never anticipated.

It was the sight of the coffin set up in her beautiful living room, so grim and so final, the intrusive, looming box containing "remains," which brought the realization into focus. This box held all of Patsy Cline that would ever be coming home.

"Daddy, where's Mama?" asked little Julie, running to Charlie. All he could do was hold her tightly and mingle his tears with her own.

Later, weeping, he asked his friends to leave, so that he could be alone with "his girl." They left reluctantly, afraid that Charlie Dick would do himself some injury, he was that sorrowful. But they went, and the door closed behind them, leaving only Charlie, Hilda, the two children, and the coffin of Patsy Cline. She had been their friend, and had claimed a part of their hearts forever.

The day of Patsy's prayer service over a thousand people showed up. The police had to close off part of Gallatin Street to traffic, and the funeral home was forced to set up extra broadcast speakers so that the vast crowd milling outside, who couldn't fit into the funeral home, could hear the service.

As though four weren't enough to die, another grim loss marked the day. Country star Jack Anglin, on his way to Patsy's prayer service, had been killed in an automobile accident. Not four, but five! When would the tragedies end?

There were so many floral tributes that they overwhelmed the funeral home, and many of them had to be sent on directly to Forest Lawn Cemetery. Because Patsy was not being buried with the others, Charlie requested that the flowers sent to her be sent on later to the others' funerals, to be set up there with Hawk's and Randy's and Cowboy's.

More than six hundred cars rode in each of the funeral processions, and telegrams poured in from all over the world. It was the largest funeral Nashville had ever seen.

That Saturday night, the Grand Old Opry paid tribute to its own. There had been some talk that perhaps there wouldn't *be* a Grand Old Opry broadcast that Saturday night, but the final decision was that the deceased would have wanted the show to go on. The audience stood for a minute of silent prayer to remember the dead, and the silence was broken by the sound of weeping from all over the Ryman Auditorium, including the stage. Later in the broadcast, when the Jordanaires sang the lovely old hymn, "How Great Art Thou," weeping broke out afresh.

Patsy was buried in the Shenandoah Memorial Park, Winchester, Virginia, on Sunday, March 10, 1963. Twenty-five thousand people lined the funeral route. Thousands of fans jammed the Jones Funeral Home, and traffic was so completely tied up that cars couldn't move for hours. Even Gerald Cline attended, and, afterward, clasped Charles Dick by the hand.

It was the funeral of a star; Patsy would have loved it.

ABOUT THE AUTHORS

George Vecsey and Leonore Fleischer bring an extraordinary blend of talent and experience to *Sweet Dreams*. Vecsey wrote *The New York Times* bestseller *Coal Miner's Daughter*, the biography of country singer Loretta Lynn, and the critically acclaimed biography of tennis star Martina Navratilova, *Martina*. Leonore Fleischer is a regular columnist for *Publishers Weekly* and has written over fifty books, including *The Rose*, *A Star Is Born*, and *Ice Castles*.

At the time of her death, Patsy Cline had two singles in the top ten—"Faded Love" and "Leavin' On Your Mind." After her death, Decca released "Sweet Dreams." It, too, made it into the top ten.

Ten years after her death, on October 15, 1973, Patsy Cline was elected to the Country Music Hall of Fame.